Also by Alexander Theroux

NOVELS

Three Wogs

Darconville's Cat

FABLES

The Schinocephalic Waif

The Great Wheadle Tragedy

Master Snickup's Cloak

*Julia De Chateauroux; or, The Girl
with Blue Hair and Other Fables*

POETRY

The Lollipop Trollops

ESSAYS

The Primary Colors

The Secondary Colors

AN
ADULTERY

AN ADULTERY

A Novel

Alexander Theroux

AN OWL BOOK

Henry Holt and Company · New York

Henry Holt and Company, Inc.
Publishers since 1866
115 West 18th Street
New York, New York 10011

Henry Holt ® is a registered
trademark of Henry Holt and Company, Inc.

Published in Canada by Fitzhenry & Whiteside Ltd.,
195 Allstate Parkway, Markham, Ontario L3R 4T8.

Library of Congress Cataloging-in-Publication Data
Theroux, Alexander.
An adultery /
Alexander Theroux.—1st Owl book ed.
p.   cm.
"An Owl book."
I. Title.
[PS3570.H38A67   1997]   96-47183
813'.54—dc21   CIP

ISBN 0-8050-4460-4

Henry Holt books are available for special promotions and
premiums. For details contact: Director, Special Markets.

First published in hardcover in 1987 by
Simon and Schuster.

First Owl Book Edition—1997

Designed by Stan Drate/Folio Graphics

Printed in the United States of America
All first editions are printed on acid-free paper.∞

1   3   5   7   9   10   8   6   4   2

The author gratefully acknowledges permission to reprint from the following:

"Two Songs from a Play" in *The Collected Poems of W. B. Yeats.* Copyright 1928 Macmillan Publishing Company, renewed 1956 by Georgie Yeats. Permission also granted by A. P. Watt Ltd. on behalf of Michael B. Yeats and Macmillan London Ltd.

The Autobiography of Alice B. Toklas by Gertrude Stein. Copyright 1933 and renewed 1961 by Alice B. Toklas. Reprinted by permission of Random House, Ltd.

"The painter's brush consumes his dream."

—W. B. YEATS, "Two Songs from a Play"

"They exchanged pictures as was the habit in those days. Each painter chose the one of the other one that presumably interested him most. Matisse and Picasso chose the picture that was undoubtedly the least interesting either of them had done. Later each one used it as an example, the picture he had chosen, of the weakness of the other one."

—GERTRUDE STEIN, *The Autobiography of Alice B. Toklas*

"One boy's a boy. Two boys are half a boy. Three boys are no boy at all."

—ALEXANDER THEROUX

Part
ONE

1

All women are mortal. I wonder if I believed it that autumn day I walked into the art gallery in St. Ives, New Hampshire—I paint—and saw her for the first time. She was a tall, striking woman about thirty or so who worked with her head down as if she'd have to work that way, framing, until the day she died. She was wearing trousers and a maroon turtleneck jersey under a light quilted vest and had the stamp, I thought, of someone often photographed. And yet she seemed sad. Was it perhaps because she was new to the place and had yet made no friends? I didn't know. My only thought was: *lovely*.

There was something lankly tomboyish in her movements. Her shoulders, though shapely, were almost too sturdy in comparison with her smallish head and slight bosom. Her hair was ash blond, like flax, and cut in the dutch-boy fashion, her athletic body showing the kind of beauty that is often indistinguishable from good health.

She looked up at me. She seemed to know immediately what I felt as unreservedly her eyes met mine. But it was a look of silent detachment as much, it seemed, from the two other women working at tables near her, moons to her sun, as from anything whatsoever intrusive, including such customers (I imagined there couldn't be few) so instantly captured as I by the mixture of vulnerability and strength composing her beauty. I felt in that look an invitation to know her further, although she said nothing. I had a girlfriend in Boston at the time to whom I was attached, not so much, however, that I wasn't taken with and in fact slightly oppressed by the memory of this woman much of the following week. I thought of her. I kept thinking of her. And then I didn't think of her again.

Her name was Farol Colorado.

The surname, her husband's—it took some time to learn both—almost served itself as a dark and desperate coloration to those first unsettling, now solved questions, and the next few weeks I spent my free afternoons either working on canvases or walking around to take in the beautiful foliage that held all that month. It was the beginning of my second year living in St. Ives, where to meet expenses I'd been teaching at the prep school there, a distinguished one, which a few hundred years ago had given the town its name.

I'd been moderately successful as a painter and sold things, watercolors mostly, landscapes, oil on wood panels, and lately primitives had begun to attract me. One of my "yellow" paintings, *Marina Among Giant Cowslips and Tulips,* hangs along with my small reputation in the Museum of Fine Arts in Boston. My palette is chromatic. I find monochrome severe and negative shape gloomy. I've always avoided reflections in the rain. My wants were few. In a way, I was too busy to make money. I was thirty-six, and still hadn't married. I wanted to, but nothing yet had come of it. I was nevertheless happy, silly word I suppose. But things had been falling together for me.

This seemed confirmed in a wonderful way sometime around mid-October when I stopped by the gallery to have a picture framed, and Farol smiled at me. We talked briefly. She told me with some self-deprecation—she had an elusive and regionless accent—that she'd always been the unapproachable type. I approached, however, and the next day I returned with a painting of mine I wanted her to have, small compensation, I felt, for the generosity of self she had begun to reveal.

"You're new around here?"

"Not really. This is my second year in St. Ives. Academic year," I added. "I teach up on the hill." I paused. "But you're new."

"Oh, I'm new everywhere," she said with level green eyes.

"New in the sense of recent," I asked playfully, "or unused?"

She laughed.

I wrote down my address for her—with some misgivings, I might add, less for the fact, oddly enough, that she was married than for the lack of privacy there in the inner part of the shop where invariably we stood surrounded by those gooishly attentive middle-aged colleagues of hers whose gongster-loud voices always diminished upon anyone's entrance and whose ears somehow always grew in proportion to their sudden interest in the proximate conversation. Some time passed. I didn't hear from her, and soon I began to be busy.

And then one night, late and unannounced, Farol Colorado appeared at my door, pushing the bell and standing hesitantly back in the shadows. I was surprised to see her. I never quite believed she'd come. Something in me also wondered if I really wanted her to. My passion, strangely enough, often took that form of love which avoided dealing with what was near, refusing the immediate and inventing distance in order to realize, I don't know, perhaps even exalt, someone more completely. I've often felt that way. Don't participate, happiness lies in the imagination, not the act, that sort of thing.

It's hard to explain, but I've always found something terrible in what we have that also can be lost—a melancholy thought, but one that's come to make me work a certain way. By working quickly I've always tried to reduce to nothing the margin for reflection between the canvas and myself. It's kept me from giving a formula to any of the thoughts overflowing in my mind. They changed ceaselessly, like painting. Truth can at any moment become its opposite: to halt an image you have to go further than movement. At any rate, I invited Farol in. She paused, jangling her car keys, and asked if she'd come at a bad time. I knew what she meant: *are you with someone?*

There was something drawn-in about her. She didn't look young so much as she came near to looking fit. She was determined, not graceful, and swung her arms and shoulders when she walked. Once we were upstairs I found in my own lack of composure maddeningly little to say to her of value as she explained over a glass of wine, and in a kind of disconnected way, what she'd been going through—she mentioned her husband—these last few years. They'd recently moved to New Hampshire, bought a house, and weren't very happy. I realized it wasn't tightness I saw in her. She wasn't nervous. She was dry and matter-of-fact, almost phlegmatic.

I listened to her somewhat sadly, for if beauty was her first accomplishment, a troubled spirit was the next, and the distinction, I'd soon come to see, her name first produced the mention of. She seemed practical, almost aggressively so, and very conscious of her rights; she was also intimidated by reflection and, I thought, doubtful. But then what did I know? We were strangers to each other.

I watched her as I listened. She had a lovely balanced mouth, though somewhat impersonal and noncommittal, with lips everted and a bit too full. Her pert and upturned nose resembled a short pretty thumb. The perfection of her soft green eyes gave a magnificence to every inclination of her head, yet when she glanced away her profile somehow belonged to someone different. She seemed uniquely able to convey an almost disembodied spirituality, a kind of untouchable remoteness, and a real physicality both at the same time. But she bore her body uncomfortably, and it robbed her of character. "My head's too small," she said when I complimented her looks.

Or was it the hair style? Tall women with their hair cut short tend to look pinheaded. She was also a bit wedge-bottomed, too long in the waist, and had, I saw, a blond person's myopia—eyeglasses, she said, didn't look right on her—as she peered around my rooms looking at my work. She seemed interested. And it gave me an opening.

I told her something of my own life. I talked at some length. I figured if nothing else I was at least a change from the women she worked with at the gallery. I said they'd always struck me as rather pathetic, she quickly agreed, and her smile put me at ease. I motioned to some of my work beyond the mess of solvents and thinners, varnish mediums, bottles of glue water, half-sized canvases, and row upon row of dry pigments in glass jars.

"I'll summon up the mighty effort it takes," I said, "not to discuss my paintings and just say I hope you like them. I'll bet you collect antiques—it's okay, I used to—and please tell me you don't jog." She didn't jog. She rode a bicycle. And swam. Or said she wanted to. She said because of work she had no time for anything. I could understand. I mentioned teaching. I said jobs cost money to keep.

Farol smiled and said she loved the way I talked. I have a tendency to speak with the spasmodic cadences of a person who wants words out of the way in a hurry and along with something of a regional accent have a way of extending my vowels so that I seem to be racing through lists of possible meanings of statements in mid-word, almost stuttering to get on with an idea. She noted humorously I had a lot of opinions. "Oh, and theories," I said. "Tons. Staring's rest. Conversation pets cats. Children from the same family always have different parents. There should be blue tulips." I saw she was amused, and touching the scarf I always wore, added, "A muffler's a hug."

"Nothing else?" laughed Farol.

"Only the observation that in zoos people have the most direct emotional connection to penguins," I laughed. "And there should be a law prohibiting anyone under age twenty-six from marrying."

"Why?" She looked suddenly embarrassed.

"The divorce rate's too high." A crimson blush rose high in her cheeks as she turned away. She sighed, sucking in her cheeks, and lowered her head. It was awkward. I felt her inconfidence immediately, a side of her (at complete loggerheads with what is expected in beauty of self-assurance) she ascribed, when I mentioned it, not to what I'd presumed was an unhappy marriage, though this entered into it, but oddly enough to her father, an artist, she from childhood loved far more, she felt, than he her—I thought I heard a therapist's echo—a matter of import apparently in that she admitted to an interest in the arts herself, drawing, sculpting, whatever.

"I guess I've always wanted his approval," she said, adding that his small capacity for praise, indeed recognition, had in consequence left her all her life, she said, with feelings of little adequacy and less worth.

As she spoke she used words lightly, glancingly, and not always correctly. There were only hints of things, no declarations. I noticed she visibly squirmed at the possibility of verbal accident and when doing so a flushing jump to change the subject quickly followed.

It was a brief story: painful trial, apologetic error. Mistakes. The real-life version of herself now looked up. For an instant she seemed close to her father again, or so I thought, for then she turned away murmuring in a tone nonetheless penetrating for being low, "I feel very much alone."

I reached sympathetically for her arm. She looked at me. She asked me if I was involved with anyone. I told her halfheartedly I was. I was, halfheartedly. Direct questions didn't seem to bother her—or offend me, why should they?—but she seemed to be contemplating a future at once so dreary and insecure with an indifference, or maybe an objectivity, in which she felt a kind of determinism that it didn't seem to matter what the answer was. "I have fears," she tried to explain. I discovered myself wanting to get at everything my visitor represented, to enter into her consciousness, to be, as it were, on her side. But I didn't know how to respond. What does one say under such circumstances?

"But you're beautiful," I said. "You're—"

It was immediately clear that wasn't what she wanted to hear, she seemed to cringe, and I realized she had heard that much too often.

"I don't feel beautiful. I feel useless," she said. "I've always defined myself by what I'm not." It was almost as if making a gloss on that thought that she suddenly looked at her watch with some alarm, and standing up to finish her drink said she had to leave. "I'm sorry. Don't mind me. I should just go off somewhere and make some decisions is what I should do."

I found a sort of hard-won courage in it all. She struck me as a symbol of all sorts of beautiful lost things. But the lost dialogue taking place between the bravest part of her and the rest left nothing to know. It was clear at least to her—though I felt it—she appeared better than she was. I couldn't have said what I felt about her except that she seemed undefended. I became aware that protection was wholly absent from her life. I truly couldn't fathom her being lost on someone. My imagination couldn't reach that far, at least not without my heart dissolving in front of her. And I felt ashamed for being powerless, not so much in changing her sad life, but frankly in failing to feel more about it.

We were walking downstairs. She stopped on the lower landing, and grew somewhat meditative. She said I'd accomplished a lot. "Nothing worth mentioning," I said. "I've led mostly a furtive, reclusive life, preaching loudly from the sidelines and avoiding danger." I smiled. "A love of creation stimulates a wish to create. And I guess I do what I love. But painting is only another way of looking at painting—the pictures we paint we are also being shown." Her silence made me continue. "It's not magic, only necessity. I've often wondered if the secret at the core of all creativity hasn't something to do with—"

"Go ahead."

"Well, I was going to say hasn't something to do with a desire beyond that need." I shrugged. "You know?"

I shrugged.

"Human desire."

Looking strangely troubled by those words, Farol turned away and peered through a dark window by the door. I thought she was going to cry. "I know," she said in a trembling voice. "I know that." As we stood there I felt the sorrow of her heart enter mine. I was busy struggling to understand why she'd come, bewildered in a way who she was, yet out of some music in her heart, or perhaps an ache for it in mine, one note sounded the same, and immediately I felt the same sorrow, shared the same heart. And I touched her.

She turned quickly, and this time she was in my arms. She whispered, "I love to be hugged," her pelvis lifting against me. And we met in an imploring inexplicable kiss. Her tongue parted my lips, and while I remember its warmth left a pull on my soul equal to nothing less than the same plaintive cry within it, the full magnitude of that moment, its extent and consecutive intoxication, no prodding of memory has ever allowed me to recall.

I only know when I looked up she was gone.

2

An affair began.

I had a small bed in my house and little furniture. I can't bear eye distractions when I work. I lived at the dead end of a long winding lane in the last house, no one ever bothered us, and the privacy it left us always made Farol sexually vibrant. I often saw her around noon during her lunch break when she'd stop by and ask if she could come by after work. "I'll make it worth your while," she'd say roguishly, laughing in her eyes. Sometimes her husband was away. And when it was convenient she stayed all night. Her ritual of going to bed never varied: she'd set out the glass of water, take out her contacts, unhook her earrings, and slipping into bed wriggle up close to me with a suction kiss to my shoulder.

She had eyelash kisses, cowpecks, pushsoft kisses, lizard kisses, bitesucks, flicks, and of course deep soulful kisses with the tongue. We even had a special kiss of our own devising where one tightly pressed one's lips together and noiselessly bonked the other's. Silliness, initially, lessened our inhibitions. We smoked pot sometimes. It often made her flush. And babble. She was somewhat proud of her fair skin and described herself as a "pink person," me a "yellow" one, an oversimplified distinction, amusing her, by which she used to theorize body humors and, as I recall, temperaments.

At first it was simple sex. Her lovemaking was less passionate than technically proficient, the bourgeois solidity of marriage fighting the craving to be wild. She wasn't sure how much skill to show in bed, which made her both detached and desperate at the same time. She clearly felt lust but in a manner both half-shrewd and half-innocent didn't want to confess to having had too much experience. But she had strong sexual urges, and after a while no longer tried to hide them. She loved oral sex. And the sensation of roughness, even domination. "Make me suck you," she'd whisper, "force me to. I love that. I like everything. I'll do anything you want." She had shuddering orgasms making love, arching forward whenever I climaxed and deeply pressing my back and buttocks into her to feel the rush in a hot, heaving abandon. I'd gasp gold, and she'd roll up flushed and happy, kissing my eyes, sitting astride me sometimes to give me a rubdown.

Her hands, while large, were tender and gentle and narrow-palmed. And afterwards she would curve her body into the soft reception of my arms and say, "I feel comfortable with you." She would kiss me. "I do, I do. You make me feel like myself." And then we would go to sleep.

I began to notice, however, even in the middle of the night that she was always alert. I knew she was a light sleeper, but this was uncanny. I would merely stir, never mind get up and in that very instant—this could be two or three in the morning—she'd be immediately awake doubtful and asking, "What's the matter?" or "Are you all right?" It always happened, and I was astonished each time. What seemed strangely inconsistent with this was that she also had nightmares—terrible ones—in which she'd cry out in her sleep, and then sit up gasping, sweat gleaming on her small tallowy breasts, and claiming the room was too hot. She spoke later of hearing knocking. I was confused by it all until I suddenly realized they were of course related. I shouldn't have been surprised. Alertness and anxiety. Wasn't it a case of one merely calling to the other?

The following morning it was as though she were someone else. Farol would kiss me, maybe listen a moment for a whistling bird, and then slowly inch closer into my body with the special way she had, like a cat, stretching sensuously and twisting her soft but supple body in a reach of awakening love to greet the day. It was always one of her most beautiful moments. She might pause a minute, taking a sip of water, to narrate some dream or other in a matter-of-fact way, then get up, hook in her earrings, pull on her shirt and trousers, and carefully picking up those contact lenses the color of Pernod—always licking them with her tongue before she put them in—run downstairs, jump in her car, and drive off to the gallery.

She was simple and unadorned and full of helpful ideas, freely offered, as to how we could continue seeing more of each other without complication. "I can come over tonight," she'd say, or "Want to have lunch?" My interest in her was mainly sexual; she represented nothing to me that I wanted beyond that. I thought it was best that way. What sex adds to friendship is possessiveness, and we were in this for entirely different reasons. We spent most of our time laughing, making love, sometimes even talking—the sort of easy affable remarks a man and woman make when seeking to readjust themselves and quell the after-effects of intimate physical relations.

I learned more about her. She enjoyed gardening. She liked wicker-work. And of course biking and swimming. ("I have six-liter lungs," she boasted.) She sewed. She said she had several old egg beaters and wanted to start a collection. And she loved to eat, among her favorite things being brownies, tapioca, chocolate malts. Eggs Benedict. Oh, and strawberry rhubarb pie! "Yummo!" she exclaimed. She played volley-ball and enjoyed mime. She said she liked music and mentioned *Bolero* and the *New World Symphony*. She once owned an MG, she told me, and loved cars. She spoke a great deal about cars.

"Do you like to travel?" I asked.

"I've seen a lot of the United States. But I had a grandfather who was a sea captain in Nova Scotia and sailed around the world lots of times. He had three missing fingers! And look." She pointed to an al-most imperceptible scar she had over one eye. "From a tobogganing ac-cident when I was twelve. I should have girded my loins," she laughed. "Instead I went flying!"

I came to see certain favorite words and expressions she liked to repeat, with a flourish of self-consciousness and a pronunciation usu-ally as flat as a duck's instep like *maple surple* and *roast beef au jus* and *gird your loins*. And I also couldn't help but notice she never used the word *marriage,* only relationship.

And she loved nature. She said she was an amateur bird-watcher (I'd noted the Audubon sticker on her car window) and could do with amazing accuracy a whole array of animal sounds, ducks, pigs, croaking frogs, a lapping dog, but far and away the best of all was the jungle sound of a whooping gorilla, which, with my encouragement, she per-formed several times—loudly, I must say—and with radiant embarrass-ment! "Would you like to eat?" I'd asked. She'd play along with it. "What do you have?" "Coconuts." *"Wooh-wooh-wooh, ya-ya-ya!"* came her wild reverberant shrieks, echoing through my rooms as if they were the rain forests of Gombe. One of her early nicknames, Farol said laugh-ing, was "Yodel."

Above all, she liked being in the woods and climbing mountains and near open lakes and said of all the many things in life she might have been she wished she'd been born a sea otter. "And not a penguin?" I asked.

She laughed. "How about you?"

"A jumbo shrimp," I said. "That way I could be both large and small at the same time."

We arranged our moods as best we could to prevent the seriousness we each thought would spook the other, leaving me bewildered as to her mysterious selves. Her career of ups and downs had rubbed most of the hallmarks off her, so that it was not easy to discern her intelligence or guess her age or know the social background to which she properly belonged. Her select conversation, in fact, not only failed to explain her background, it indicated she preferred it that way. I didn't care. I wanted it that way myself. She seemed nevertheless to show a lineage in direct contradiction to her lot.

I saw her at strange, irregular intervals, the headlights of her blue Honda Accord always turning up the winding side street where I lived as if searching a way out of a maze far darker and more nameless than those particular but unpredictable nights when she could get away. She had more time than she cared to admit. Wasting it she connected to a lack of accomplishment. Her lack of accomplishment she linked to lack of money. Money was a favorite subject with her. And flight. I didn't blame her because I understood. As to her husband, we agreed it was something we would not discuss. But her super-simple notions and pardonable if unsubtle fictions about solving everything by making one key move truly amazed me.

I saw on nearer view that Farol's elegance was intermittent, that her parts didn't always match. It came to me slowly, sometimes dimly, but there was something of an indication now of what I might be getting in for. She often looked when she appeared as if she had been crying. It was the face, more than anything, of someone undergoing martyrdom not by fire but by freezing. She was often tense and pulled-in. I could tell, despite her interest in me, that she was angry at her husband and yet terrified at the estimable image of her I insisted on holding to keep her at some sort of breathing distance but which somehow made her responsible, as time passed, for all she wasn't. And didn't mean. And couldn't be. And shouldn't have.

I felt her chronic uncertainty, and shared it. But wondering of myself whether I needed someone to be independent of or to be dependent on me before I could care seemed at the time irrelevant. I was merely trying to determine whether in all of it I *liked* her or not. She took getting used to, as I'm sure I myself did for finding that a problem. She was mercurial and on first acquaintance glinting with inconsequent confusion. And though occasionally she'd try to explain various things, her explanations only deepened darkness.

She'd spoken only vaguely of her husband. Her comments seemed to ask for no reply. I thought she despised him in an unspoken way but didn't have the vocabulary for the fierce emotions she felt. Their news conveyed nothing whatever to me. Only the rational surface of my intelligence was engaged. And rationality with her I could already tell was the exception to the rule. Whereas at first she spoke constantly of her fears—increasingly she tended toward the abstract—now she hadn't the words to express them or found them in spite of the deep moans reverberating through her too unbearable to utter. The closer we got, the more secrets there were to guard. She'd become a good friend. She was also a stranger.

Initially, neither of us had any individual experience that seemed to fit us for an altogether conscientious estimate of all we could together become, and whenever our thoughts did wander to some tale or circumstance that threatened to present a parallel—for we were persuaded at times we did think alike—we somehow always ended up by deciding our situation was not to be measured by any other, an attempt, I think, to protect whatever it was that by chance allowed us to meet in the first place. Or was it rather our fear of repeating by habit all we were afraid we might lose?

It was, in short, that period of procedural confusion in which two people trying to please one another act out their own interpretation of what each thinks the other wants. Both wear masks, of course, trying feverishly not to be caught without them. Imitation of emotions, always sad, sometimes dangerous, follow in response. And you soon begin to resent what you cannot be—yourself.

Farol was alone. Not caring was being alone. I understood much of her by what she reminded me of in myself. But there was always that place where one had to begin again. Where is happiness unless you give happiness away? The irony was that it was easier for me to share it with a relative stranger than for her to share it with a husband she claimed was indifferent to it, for now she began to mention conflicts with him (conflicts, I noticed, that never left her in the wrong). I listened, and I tried to sympathize. I certainly didn't want to put the boot in. I told her I cared. I did, to a great degree. I sometimes felt guilty in sharing her guilt, sometimes not. I think at the time I told myself I wanted to be courageous enough, which was a lie, to risk losing innocence, which was a lie, to see if I might come to love her, which was the biggest lie of all.

I didn't care. I doubted she could ever understand me, for one thing. It wasn't that I was so deep, she simply didn't seem the type of person who'd bother to find out. Secondly, I've always been suspicious of conclusions that reinforce uncritical hope, and I could already see I

puzzled her. I was strange, a bit uncivilized, too intense, used to solitude, up at all hours of the night, and in many ways too eccentric for
her. But the unavoidable truth of the matter was, I didn't want to get
involved.

Surely she suspected that. I thought she felt the same way herself.
I was taking advantage of her, but where was the difference if she was
using me to abuse her husband? I wanted her body, not her complicity,
and I wanted to keep it that way. The way I understood her fatigued
me, but it also told me how little I cared, and I was challenged more
than entertained by the pointless conversation that was always the result
of both. We went to bed, we seemed to remember each other only when
next we met, and then went to bed again.

Whenever we finished having sex, I was often silent and usually
thinking to myself: *thank you for having allowed me, without interruption, my special thoughts.* What showed on her face was doubt—a
woman sparring with two men in the process of selecting one for the
night's finale, and wondering if she'd chosen right.

We were not combined. We were adulterated. I was available,
nonchalant, and to tell the truth most of the time bored. One night,
when we went out for dinner together, she became upset by droning
on and on about the fundamentalist disapproval her husband's parents
had for alcohol. She was pompous in her disapproval, and I tried to
ignore it. But she kept it up. "Look," I said, "I don't know what to
say. I don't know them. I wish I could help. But does going on about
them to such lengths make it help?" I also felt immune. I honestly
didn't care one way or the other the way things turned out between us.
Whether she came or whether she didn't amounted to the same thing.
And it made me bold. I often conveyed in a strained and unfair way
what was wrong without being at all direct about what was right. But
whatever was right was lost in the chill of a misadventure in which we
were betraying two other people. She gave herself, as I say, less out of
affection for me than anger at her husband, and I took from her out of
that surety. There were times, nevertheless, when because of this her
ordinary tones had the penetrating quality of two people quarreling,
which implicated me in all she felt of him.

I often found her a decided burden instead of a fairy of delight.
Her main fault derived mainly from a fundamental seriousness about
herself that often led to a deadening blandness. She was extremely lit-
eral. And unimaginative. I began to pine for friends of years gone by,
the understanding of experiences shared, or even a sign of wit. She

asked nothing of my work, only of my situation. It seemed alone sufficient for her that I was unattached. And I resented that.

I also resented her constant questions about my life, which somehow gave me a certain personality, or, to put it another way, made one for her she presumed to understand. She could also be puzzlingly sarcastic. "Where's your furniture? You know, like chairs?" "Why don't you have a telephone?" "And why are you always shutting off lights?" She didn't like my car—a battered twelve-year-old Triumph TR4-A without shocks—though her own was unpaid for! And all the while she showed this tendency to feel she deserved to be taken care of. I noticed, for example, she preferred only upscale restaurants, ones with bowing waiters and leather-bound menus. She wouldn't expressly tell me that, it wasn't the form her delicacy took, but she would convey it in an arch way whenever that opportunity wasn't met by quiet disapproval or various oblique remarks. What didn't make her happy made her depressed. She often betrayed a forbidding listlessness and lack of enthusiasm for no reason, to the degree that I began seriously to wonder if she was well.

Farol was beautiful but, I thought, self-impaired. She was at times extremely unresponsive. It was an arrogance I thought an extreme form of shyness. I was wrong. I kept reminding myself, however, people aren't perfect; the only unfailing rule is, if they seem so, they can't be. She seemed tired and thirsty a lot and had an ill person's crankiness and need for attention. I began to wonder about diabetes. Always, there was that fixed and certain way with her, the earrings, the contact lenses, the glass of water within arm's reach on the bed table. We didn't make love. We called it that, but it was the kind of sex that in its unspoken division turned me into one broken half of a couple, her into the other.

Soon, the frequency of our questions dropped off. I did not wish to know her secrets. I was convinced she was in for a solitary life no matter where she went or what she did. As she had it, the world had used her ill. She had suffered. I saw she also suspected herself. She often repeated—I had no idea what she meant—"I seem to do everything wrong." But it seemed to me as she searched the bottom of her grief looking for some way to express it that she overemphasized her defects in order to feel sorry for herself, not so much to invite my sympathy as to avoid the feelings of guilt she sustained for sleeping with me. At least that's what I thought. But it turned out I was wrong, it wasn't guilt, it was only loss of face.

"I wouldn't be doing this," she often repeated, "if things were right with me and John." It was always her remark sitting up after making love, wrists crossed, catching her breath with that quaver in her voice, a tremor touched with a small vibration of frailty and muffled anguish. She'd get up, pull on the mannish trousers she always wore—I came to see why, for she was markedly saber-shinned, her calves as fleshless as the joint of a cane—and then go to the bathroom to bathe from her face the incriminating traces of my after-shave lotion.

"Do you know that?" she'd ask. "You know that, don't you?" I would nod, anything for agreement. And then she'd be gone, driving off into the darkness that always exacerbated for the two of us, whenever we dared think of it, more of penalty than peace.

And eventually Farol was driven to justify her actions. I listened to what one night she divulged of her husband and found it traitorous. She said he was overbearing and pompous and often didn't speak to her for weeks. I wasn't surprised when she told me he had already been married and divorced once before. She told me his first wife had ignored him. She complained he ignored her. Good old-fashioned unshapely resentment surfaced everywhere. All the clichés were there. I thought it was almost funny. "John hates sex," she said. This wasn't only tactless, or merely disloyal and vulgar—I didn't believe it. I took it as a matter of course that the only sufficient real reason for a woman saying her husband hated sex was to seduce the man to whom she was telling it, a fact swiftly corroborated in this instance when in the very next breath Farol, immune to paradox, told me he was also clumsy and awkward. She meant, of course, *in making love.*

"He used to keep a watch by the side of the bed," she added scornfully—"I swear—and actually time himself when he did it." And whereas before she'd once or twice mentioned divorce, she now did so more frequently.

But as I was not in love with her I asked little of what I preferred not to know. Upon strict reflection I felt I would not have willingly had it otherwise. Her world was eye-level and down. And as she was troubled there would be no answer to any question I might have asked that wouldn't lead back, I knew, to the thousand depressing irrelevancies by which she rationalized her visits and upon which our random acquaintance was so tenuously based. There were no rules. Not a rule. I had none to go by, and neither had she.

It wasn't a romance. It was a relationship. Sleeping together—it's blackly comic, I suppose—creates entanglements. It leads to obligations by not talking and often perversely fosters an alliance that should be the result of clarification, not the cause of it. But because we could hardly imagine a future, time stood still, giving us over to an unreality which because of the stark consequences neither of us ever spoke of, and so always did, left us a legacy wherein magic was displaced by method and fantasy by fact.

Strangeness we accepted; familiarity we refused. It was as if mortality itself, a feeble mimicry aspiring to what it shouldn't, could only be known by what it couldn't have of the immortal, leaving us both in a dreadful stasis that had to ignore in terms of hope deferred what could only be accepted as despair. And that was something I didn't need.

I'd been there before.

3
_____

I had moved up to New Hampshire several years before. There was never any real reason to stay there. I had no ties nor those inner family relations which are hardly possible between those other than parents and children, husbands and wives. I've often discussed with myself the necessity of such bonds for a person's happiness, and although I'd once generally satisfied myself with the answer that there wasn't a need, I found I was wrong.

I was brought up in Boston. I never knew my parents. My mother died when I was born. The Fords, if they were finally without luck, were not without talent. Many of them had been prominent writers. My great-grandfather's younger brother, my great-uncle, discovered the magnetic monopole at M.I.T. in 1902. Neither were they without public spirit. My father, a polar explorer, was descended from prominent members of society who inherited, and in due course bequeathed, substantial amounts of capital to various academies and institutes, one among them, ironically enough, the very orphanage to which we ourselves soon had to be sent, for although he'd married again—I have a half brother and a half sister—he went down in a plane crash over Antarctica three years later, or so I was told.

A child at the time, I was dimly and undefinably witness to this dark beginning. The crisis of being suddenly uprooted proved neither broad nor slow for me. A fatal suspicion already existed in my mind that nothing really lasted.

There are memories both sad and dear of those early years. The institution in which I found myself—and whose name rather quaintly referred to a century gone by—was called the Home for Little Wanderers. We walked in file. There was chapel. We were the victims of strict ordinance and were punished for leaving lights on and wasting water and not making our beds. And along with schoolwork, various jobs were assigned us: buffing floors, washing dishes, shaking down ashes in the coal room. The rest of our leisure went unchallenged. I remember on Sundays, all of us being herded together and wearing name tags on coats of uniform manufacture, being taken on supervised trips to the Arboretum and the Forsyth Dental Clinic and the Children's Museum and other places of historical interest.

But my loneliness was extreme. That I always kept to myself still further checked my acquaintances; in fact, it took some time before I actually learned that Tarquin was my brother. (My sister, Daisy, I came to know only later, by letters.) I often wanted to confide in them, to share my distress, but I couldn't. It wasn't that they were younger, merely that I was apprehensive. I feared the very nature of coming close to them meant they'd be taken away.

If I had been clever, I should doubtless have attracted the jealousy of my fellows, but I was spared this by the mediocrity of my performance in classes as in everything else. These young fellows, many of whom ought long before to have left the place—we were usually sent to learn a trade at a nearby linotype school if no one adopted us—did nothing overtly unkind to me. I was conscious only of a sharp and instinctive disappointment with myself. And shame. I began to wet the bed. It was my humiliation. My first feelings were temporary frenzy, despair followed, then it condemned me to silence.

My deepest anxiety in growing up there was the fear of being deserted. I coped with it, out of a confused throng no doubt of immature impressions, in the only way I could and sought just so much as would bring me into communion with an inner world which by some miracle of availing tenderness always managed to lessen the pain of the outer. The artist is beyond anything else one of those who tries to get a second chance in life. I asked for no more than to be left alone with my reflections and my reveries. I took refuge in dreams.

Several things tended even then to alienate my conscience from the line which the home had so rigidly traced for it. I wasn't intractable.

But I felt different from the other boys, as much for my evasive and wayward dreams as for those bouts of nightly incontinence that continued and for which it was now required I see a doctor. I was powerless against this man whose terrible ghost, pronouncing upon so many memories, still haunts that home for me, my relationship to it renewed at long intervals and never without pain until the day he died. Dr. Trinity—I confused his name with that of his college diploma on the wall—was a stern hemorrhoidal functionary with a long nose and yellow neck and glasses tinted dark. He claimed rather jealously to have known my family, by which I'm sure he meant he was important himself and well-connected.

He had a heavy vein of irrationality in his makeup and used a rubber cushion wherever he sat, one of his front teeth was edged all the way around with gold, and his hair was slicked down with so much hair cream, it glistened like butter. He was a bully and, taking special initiative in belittling me, made it known to me in so many words that involuntary and protracted bed-wetting was nothing more than disguised tantrums.

One dark afternoon I was sitting in his office, and he was sorting through some papers, when a terrible thunderstorm, blowing up outside, brought down flashes of lightning and loud insistent booming that terrified me.

"Are you superstitious?" he asked, looking up.

I waited a moment, and shook my head.

He smiled confidently.

"Thank God," he said. "The last time lightning flashed like that your father was found hanging."

There were rumors, I found out later, that he'd been ill. Some said he'd had a falling-out with the Navy and that an expedition had been taken away from him. But I shall never forget that that was the way I had to learn how the poor man who gave me life, met with its indifference, left the world.

I should perhaps mention at this point a certain trait in my personality that for better or worse has so long informed it: I can't forget anything. Meek as I may have seemed way back then, and gently respondent, this particular then as now—itself a reminder of all it hints at—has always been mine. I don't forget a thing. In the matter of forgiveness, I can't say. I'm not sure. But I forget nothing.

I have the memory of a pale little boy with dark eyes, uncombed hair, and rough corduroy trousers seated in that office answering hundreds of pointless questions and doing drawings—my very first—I then had to interpret. I could barely speak. I was afraid of what he'd do to me. I tried to oblige him, but couldn't, and he began sending letters upstairs about me. Doctors create sickness. It's a curious prejudice of mine, but I believe it. I ate little and slept badly. I tried for a period, in fact, to avoid sleeping, and it worked for a while. He asked me what I did to occupy my time at night. I told him, quoting a remark I once heard my father make: "I lie awake and think about the past." My silences invariably angered him, and he called me a sissy and said if I ever married I'd pee on my wife and gave out prophecies wrapped around dark sayings about my future.

Once searching my face he exasperatedly told me, "You're always trying to get out of the world"—which was true but, in that he'd become a metonym for it, something I thought obvious—finally suggesting that if I so desired he could easily gratify my wish and send me away, which frightened me, until I thought: *away where?*

About this time—I was thirteen—something wonderful happened. I kept to myself as usual, somewhat a misfit, often leaving the school yard to wander around the common rooms or poke about the attics or linger in the library. It was there I discovered on a bookshelf one day an old illustrated Vasari. I can't account for the flame it awakened in me, romantic fervor no doubt, but I shall never forget how for days at every available hour I sat perched in a window seat poring over stories of those artists whose lives like their paintings, born of endless struggle, somehow reflected, or so it seemed to me, my own. I chose somewhat mystically to believe that if their origins were similar to mine, like talent would logically follow. From then on I slept with that book next to me. And soon I began to draw in secret.

And then one day I volunteered, prompted somewhat by the teacher, to do a frieze in history class of a prehistoric scene. Excused from lessons—"Christian," said kindly old Mr. Madwed, pinching his glasses, "you're our artist"—I drew with pastel chalks on a long strip of craft paper a multicolored array of mammoths and fierce saber-toothed tigers that surprised even me. I never felt so happy or so proud. And that became a turning point for me. From that time forth I lay no longer under the stigma of invisibility. I had produced my material shape and if only for a fleeting moment found something in the world of actual aim that matched my sleeping visions.

A small trust fund, set up for us, couldn't be claimed until we reached our majority. (I was later to be given one of my parents' houses on Cape Cod.) I lived alone immediately upon leaving the home, work-ing as a linotypist and living in a dim single room over Uncle Ned's Loan Co. under the Northampton Street train station in the South End of Boston. It is impossible to define the exact outline of a period so lonely and fugitive, except to say that it seemed that time itself ceased to move. My practical isolation was no less than it had been before, but in spite of the almost incommunicable dreariness of the job I made nimble escape whenever possible to what most preyed on my fascination. I turned to art. I virtually lived in museums. I rarely went anywhere without my pads of Whatman and D'Arches in hand, my back pocket filled with pencils and various brushes I bought and treasured, long flats, shorter brights, filberts, and rounds.

My work became less frigid and mechanical—sheets of sketches, abandoned variants, vestigial beginnings—and I drew on everything. I never saw a flat surface, wall, or board I didn't want to fill with some-thing of booming, undaunted apocalypse. More important, I grew inde-pendent of mind, reading with unchecked voracity in several directions and laboring to gain those elements of knowledge which up to that point had been singularly lacking. And soon I was ready for college.

At Yale I studied with Belestat, La Vallière, and Trublet. I began to acquire some conception of English watercolor painting, which inter-ested me at the time, and to learn the intricacies of composition and technique, which sharpened my own executions. I was something over six feet now and from twenty self-portraits knew my face well, finding shadows others often did not recognize in that solemn and ghostly pale-ness always startled by a bandit's dark eyes and darker hair. I won the Sterling Prize. The work I entered didn't deserve it, but I did. And I went to France a year later.

I came to see that it was not education that made me a painter, but rather its opposite—my own sense of incompleteness, of being power-less, unshaped, and outside the currents of society. Duress only helped me. No schmoozing at openings, or cafes or late-night parties. I had that kind of drama going on in my own mind. I worked toward a style of my own, one both fanciful and unexpected. My vocabulary of images, painted in stark colors often underscored with Jacobean black, included pilgrims, lost faces, cats, running men, people with goose heads, cruci-fixes, eggs, mosques, and waterfalls, all recurring visual themes that have stuck in my head for years.

I attended the Petite Ecole on the rue d'Ulm, where Montrésor himself—to whose face at that time age had brought the likeness of

Veronese—asked me to draw a woman who happened to be standing there, and when I did he accepted me. She was a half-black dancer from the Seychelles whose delicate depravity needed the freedom that made her at once both passionate and remote. I stayed abroad for five years, working feverishly, when not pursuing her, on guises in charcoal, figure and landscape painting, graphic work in etching and lithography, and red chalk drawings, many of which I still have in a portfolio somewhere: heads rotated in passion, torsos twisted, arms forcibly flexed, arranged hands, figures kneeling in adoration. I was single-minded, unkempt, prolific, but too canonical and still making nonlucrative quixotic imperfections. My poverty-stricken appearance did little to inspire enough confidence in cafes to allow me credit, but I was helped out by this woman who was sufficiently satisfied, before finally leaving Paris on a lark, to see a small exhibition of mine go up one spring in the Jardin des Plantes.

I moved to the country outside the village of Thérouanne to be near her. I lived there for a time painting its blue-green perspectives under a sky always accentuated at twilight by those mysterious rays that slant to this day still into the rich brown gloom of my remembrance. In Europe I'd been once in love, three or four times almost in love, and five or six additional times not quite almost in love, with no end of one-night stands. But with her it had been more than a seasonal idyll. She meant a lot to me, and I was miserable. I came back to America because of that broken love affair.

I took a teaching job in Cambridge, Massachusetts—the loveliness of New England was something I had missed—which offered very little money but allowed me a small studio and brought me in contact again with Tarquin, who'd married and become a lawyer, and Daisy, herself now the mother of three. But I saw little of them, I'm afraid, for almost coincident with my return I met someone for whom even the exercise of my own rushing fancy hadn't prepared me. I first saw her in a studio—she was only eighteen years old—and I fell deeply in love with her. Her name was Marina Falieri and she was easily the most beautiful girl I have ever seen. I have always had a conscious dread of my own intoxicated spells whose approach I feel as a kind of awful duty required, like epilepsy, by my demon half.

Artists are never complete people. But if it's art that completes them, then what is taken away?

I'd never known anyone like Marina. She was completely unassuming and imbued with all the complications of goodness and the introspective nature that went with it. Our contentment was complete and unfeigned. She lived with her parents, and I loved being with her whenever I could. I never had a single thought in the six continuous years we were together of a future that excluded her. She was everything to me. And then I was offered a position—along with a bit more money and free housing—as artist-in-residence at St. Ives. Once I got there it was almost as if by some half-dealt but sinister decree for all that had been given us that we began to see less of each other. It happened slowly, however, and shapelessly.

It wasn't that expecting to see a glorious summit I suddenly found a miserable declivity steal into view preventing its reach. I felt only a strange untenable melancholy settle over my heart that yet ceased to be distinct. And yet it was an indistinctness I'd never felt before.

At one point in my life I discovered the paradox that being completely open about oneself is one way of protecting your privacy—nobody can say anything worse about you than what you have already said about yourself. And explaining something, in a sense, makes it go away. There had been other girls before Marina. I had told her about them. Now that had changed. For the first time, I willfully disregarded that principle. I couldn't conceive of losing her. And yet I knew it was happening.

We were not only separated now. It was worse than that. We were divided.

4

Christmas passed with vague promises—the Colorados went to the Adirondacks—but the new year found those promises unfulfilled. I'd given Farol a pair of round gold earrings before she left. I remember upon receiving them she didn't know what to say, which is exactly what she said. A thank-you would have done fine. But sharing was foreign to her. And I let it go at that.

It snowed some, the weeks following Farol's return a succession of empty days with the weather gull-gray and smokerise in the damp. I wanted to get out of St. Ives. I had gone to Boston for part of the holidays, but Marina's sick father and a mother whose awfulness, expressing itself in this instance as one continuous high-maintenance effort to come between me and her daughter, ruined any chance we had together. I was quiet and surely trying, which Marina didn't deserve. I was preoccupied, of two minds. I have no idea what she thought. No, she felt neglected. And so did I. But by whom? That was my question. By whom?

I spent a few days alone afterwards at Squam Lake, leaving in my sketchbook some muddled half-finishes in diluted ink with pen and brush, and then returned to St. Ives. My thoughts were of Farol. I had formalized and internalized an image of her I was sure was unhealthy, for everybody. I had been thinking in but not with the discourse implanted in me amplified only by my physical attraction for her. And it seemed a slim and unrewarding indulgence for all it involved. One afternoon I saw her shopping in Galloupi's, a local grocery store. She didn't see me, and so I kept going. She left several notes in my door hinting of further trouble at home. "John's been horrible—I can't see you tonight." "We're having two sessions with Dr. Varion this week." "You're always in my heart and in my mind. Know that."

I felt bad for her but half the time didn't know what to do to help. And yet for some reason I felt constantly bound to try.

I went down to the gallery after my classes one Friday. I had come to loathe the place. The women who worked with her were unbearable. I'd never met three such cynical or hypocritical creatures—three women, six faces—but under the circumstances there was no avoiding them. I tried for a while, briefly and unsuccessfully, suffering for Farol the minor abasement of exchanging hollow pleasantries with them, but it soon became impossible. It was as if their moral repulsiveness found a perfect correlative in each of them, for they were almost willfully ugly, their conversation a flood of commonplaces, malice, and stupidity. But the worst part of it was they exercised a dreadful influence over Farol, giving her advice, prying into her life, and too often inviting her to their point of view essentially by ignoring hers. I came to see them as nothing less than highly skilled manipulators of each other's emotions who spent hours together in an endless loop of exchange, dawdling away in sort of mumbling combat and making each other cry.

It was an awful situation for her there. I often walked in and found Farol in her corner, zero self-image, adaptable, leaking light like a badly cut diamond. She had told me more than once she knew no one in town. So why did she pick these women? Why did she oblige *them?* Was she that hard up for friends?

She spoke of a miserable Christmas—and she couldn't see me that weekend. She and John were going to Vermont with a group of other people to a cabin in which they had part interest. She lowered her voice to a whisper and asked me to understand. She was trying to work things out. I looked around. I had begun to notice that she was made by these women to feel awkward whenever I stopped by; they disapproved of this weakness of hers, needing someone, especially men. They hated her husband, they knew about us, and they made grudging efforts to interfere.

My own cruelty was as excessive in response as it was misdirected. I wasn't betrayed into malice. I was perversely seeking the kind of justice that satisfied my own need for healing—though I've never been able to find the full source of my anger—and as my aggression for these women was transformed into moral superiority, I wrote them off without mercy. "You're too intense," Farol often repeated. "They don't matter! Those women don't matter!"

So it was unnerving to see Farol change colors so fast, so obligingly, her greeting to me under their predatory surveillance invariably giving way to a kind of flippancy, and at times even insolence. I was blind to her participation in this during that period and at the time merely wanted to save her from their clutches and their bitchery.

I thought of them as Lear's spaniels: Trey, Blanche, and Sweetheart. There was, first of all, Ruth Gumplowitz, a near dwarf with an endocrine defect and a nose of such length and mobility she could bring its tip and underlip into ghoulish contact. Then there was tall homely Charlotte Tweeze. And finally there was Maxine Scrulock—whom I'm afraid I shall be accused of having invented—a woman of almost fabled viciousness with a moon face permanently fire-flushed and a shape that bore a striking resemblance to a hydrant or a warped viola da gamba. The Three Graces. It's true. Names are behavior. We become the dog we buy. The worst of them was also the fattest and ugliest. Shallow as a pie pan. Scum. I called her Mother Scrulock.

"I like your scarf," she said to me. "Is it part of your uniform?"

I turned away from her, following Farol into the lobby as she saw me out.

"It's a funny little shop," she said apologetically.

"There are many funny little things," I replied, "aren't there? One of them was sitting across from you. Or was she standing?"

Farol laughed.

"Tiny Maxine," she said.

And I went home, packed, and spent the weekend in a drizzle on Cape Cod.

When I returned I discovered a letter from Farol on my desk upstairs. It was written on stationery of the pale-blue matching variety, which she usually reserved for matters of consequence. Her handwriting always plainly attested to the state of mind informing it. She had a draftsman's calligraphy—of the blocky cuboidal kind usually found on blueprints—except when she was unstrung or out of control, as now she was, and then it was the hysteric's, her sentences galloping without period into one another in a spate of crossed-out words, smudges, broken syntax, ungrammatical howlers, and misspellings.

It was the kind of grim report I'd come to know; the story, as she told it, was brief: a tire went suddenly flat just as they were setting off on their trip, a crisis Farol's husband apparently met after fixing it by turning around, folding his arms, and sitting out the weekend in a long spiteful silence. They never went to Vermont.

I read it over with difficulty. Her anger made her seem even more illiterate. Farol was only a high school graduate—no sacrifice, as she told it, had been made by her parents to give her an education—although she had attended, briefly and without success, two or three community colleges I'd never heard of somewhere in Pennsylvania or upstate New York or wherever. What was I supposed to do? I thought she should either settle things with him or cease seeing me. But I wanted resolution now. Something. Anything. Any one thing. I began to think it could come, however, in the only form I'd ever known it, these notes, this vacillation.

Within the week Farol came by again, stamping off the snow and pacing back and forth in a distraught manner in front of me crying, "I don't care! I'm going to leave him! I don't care!" She was a tall woman, as I say—about five feet ten inches—and just pigeon-toed enough of one foot, I came to see, to make her appear when walking to go slightly sideways and seem to tack. I came to make a connection between this peculiarity of hers and the pathetic voice in which, lowering her head in tearful confusion, she always vented her anger. I heard no preface to any conclusion this time, only her refrain as she kept repeating, "I'm going to leave him! I'm going to leave him!"

There was one resolution: they weren't simply drifting apart—they were under full sail. They were not merely fighting each other; they'd become each other in their fights. They knew each other so well that truth was no longer sought to support but rather singled out to sever, the words she spoke so quickly and angrily in echo of his shouted out like some profane but competing exequy over what together they'd become, spitting and proximate, as if crucified face-to-face they were watching each other die.

I questioned her this time. The facts I had of her husband were scant. He was in his early thirties, worked in advanced communications management—come again?—and had few friends. He was also very tall, cooked Mexican food, cultivated a garden, and was authentically menacing if half the things she said of him were true. He owned a boat. He always did the shopping himself from a written list. As I got it, he ran the household. And then there was the sex business. *He times it.* Everything else was lost in the blur of a harrowing personality she cobbled together by way of a portrait that for me remained only an empty oval. I waited to hear more, but she became evasive and soon spoke quite beside the question. It didn't matter. "I remember last year we went to a party. A young guy was there, in his late teens maybe, and the two of them got into a disagreement about something, I don't remember what, but John wouldn't drop it and began browbeating him with facts and figures and just humiliated him!" She exhaled frustration. "That's just a small part of what I have to live with."

They were—horrible expression—together alone. She repeated only that he wouldn't speak to her, his particular mode of anger, a cold and studied indifference that often became so unendurable, she said, that it sent her at times screaming out of the house and into her car, which she'd drive about for hours revolving in her mind all sorts of schemes for her own welfare, her head throbbing with the echo of what she said were always his final words: *"And you needn't come back, okay?"*

She began to cry. Tears fit every limitation of hers, though there was something prematurely captious in the sudden flow. Whenever she cried, it made her face look fat and swollen, her eyelids red.

"Why don't you leave him now?" I asked.

"I am! I am going to leave him!" A meditative movement in one hand seemed to belie the fact, but she kept walking up and down the room with the palms of her hands pressed tightly together. And then turning, almost coiling, she exclaimed, "I will not die a weak and beaten creature!"

A mournful look came into her eyes as she wiped them. They seemed to be asking a perpetual question. But what was it? The sorrow that comes from the thought that when one begins again one always has to begin from the beginning? The thought that because she had no resources she'd be left deserted? The terror at the sudden loss of security?

I wondered about that particularly.

Farol was a woman who held to certain high tastes but, I thought, hadn't the money to gratify them—there were hints of a low purse—and though I could sympathize with that it puzzled me: did her husband refuse to provide for her? Was she working to support herself? She was poorly read, had never been out of the country, and as I say had no education. She nevertheless dressed neatly, and while she professed to have a real aversion for fashion, indeed for shopping in general, she was also a fabric snob and often told me when she did buy clothes they were always the very best. She liked subdued colors, soft greens, blues, maroons, and nothing flashy.

Although she assured me it didn't matter I often felt slovenly in her presence, wearing old jackets and sweaters and rarely seeing a barber. I've been told more than once I have the vaguely dilapidated look of a stage ruffian or a character out of Chekhov. But she dressed down herself, hip-length jackets, jeans, serviceable shoes. She looked in fact, at times, as though she'd renounced gender. Her stride, neither smooth nor willowy like a woman's, was in a way very masculine. She never once wore a skirt. I honestly don't believe she owned one, a rather amazing thing for a woman, at least to me.

She also avoided wearing makeup. But as her complexion was good it never made a difference, or whatever difference there was only enhanced her natural look. Her face was lovely. She was clean. She had such little luck. And her sorrowful smile broke my heart.

We talked late that night, I remember. I found out that she'd been at one time or other on various drugs for depression and that she and her husband had been seeing a psychiatrist for a number of years, and still did—"group," she called it. It was a marriage group, she explained, and was held in Boston every Tuesday night.

"What do you do there?" I asked.

"Talk. We discuss things."

"With?"

"Each other."

"About?"

"Ourselves."

"Yourselves? Or each other?"

"Both."

"Both talk?"

"No, I mean we talk both about ourselves and each other, in order to face our problems."

She paused.

"Anyway, we sit in a circle."

The very idea sounded ridiculous. It was one of those tag-you're-it expeditions, I imagined, where as a kind of verbal equivalent of wandering in the desert the lonely and disaffiliated cultivated each other's weaknesses instead of imparting any strengths.

Tuesday was the night I usually saw her. Now I understood why. I realized Farol always stopped by my house on the way home—she and her husband drove both to and from Boston in separate cars—and she was almost always in low spirits. Again and again she'd either speak bitterly of her father—I'd begun to think in light of her androgynous name that maybe her father hadn't even *wanted* a daughter—or deliver long discombobulated soliloquies about her husband and his faults. But by now there was need of no embellishment to suggest the ominous coexistence of these two entirely different people locked in what I'd come to see as the tortuous last movements of some weird ritualistic or fugal dance preliminary to a beheading.

And soon Farol was asking me point-blank about my feelings for her, and then about my feelings for Marina. Although I had known Marina for a long time, and certainly in contrast to my interrogator, the very questions she asked often served to discount, at times even destroy, that perspective. Farol was at once too obvious and too obscure. And the incredible thing, I think, was that she didn't want to get away with being either, which sent her recklessness in several directions. Sometimes I thought I loved her, sometimes I was only touched by the degree to which I thought she might love me. Sometimes my sense of self was enhanced, sometimes diminished by it.

Anyway, I distrusted her most of the time and thought of her as lawless. I had the feeling moreover that to risk not losing me she concealed, no, she did not insist that I see, certain important facets of her real nature, pretending with that nervous energy and effort she could show that she was more content than she was.

She was never morally at ease. She had no spiritual resources. And she had a husband in only the broadest sense of the term. I had no understanding of what their intentions were. I had known couples before who took pride in one another's tawdry behavior, each pursuing the other's folly, the other's vanity, the other's weaknesses. Was that after all what they wanted? Something that lay beyond what they appeared to seek? Some final confirmation perhaps that mankind itself was in-eradicably corrupt, that life was nothing more than a nightmare taking place inside the head of an imbecile?

I didn't know. I was nevertheless getting involved. But I was get-ting involved not only with Farol Colorado. I was getting involved, I saw, in a situation where there actually might be no end to the conse-quences of wholehearted *agreement!*

"If you'd like," she said, "you can come with me next Tuesday and meet Dr. Varion."

"Who?"

"My therapist."

She explained she and her husband were now seeing him sepa-rately.

"Want to?"

"No," I said. "Definitely not."

5
___

John Colorado's job periodically required that he travel. Farol and I of course went nowhere ourselves—couldn't—and whenever we ven-tured to do so it was usually a short drive in my unremarkable but un-marked car to no place in particular, during which times she always seemed afraid of who'd appear and see us, ask us questions, or, I don't know, shoot us. And sometimes she drove.

We selected whose car we'd use according to convenience, some-times by time of day, occasionally by whim, but never without strict con-sideration to her husband's work hours. I remember a drive to Kingston we took in her car one Monday, her day off, when she was so silent, so melancholy, so depressing, so maddeningly unaware, as it were, that reality had any inherent nature which we might hope to identify as some sort of truth or value between us that I actually became nauseous and got physically ill. She had to turn back at my request and let me out.

Anxiety became the unspoken expression of her fears. She hinted vaguely at illnesses, the suggestion of which was limited but in no way confined to the array of sniffs and sniffles I heard whenever I asked what they were. She seemed self-defeating to me. I mistrusted her when she mentioned things she wanted in the same breath with what she saw as being prevented from having. I listened sympathetically, but my thoughts were: *who has many wishes has often but little will. Who has energy of will has few diverging wishes. Whose will is bent with energy on one must renounce the wishes for many things.*

A person, I've always thought, should be intelligent if not more honest enough to wish she were more so. But talking often seemed to frighten her. A lack of courage somehow collapsed all she had to tell. Was it that she wanted to talk but hadn't the words? Her pressures at the time were carried out more in silence than in speech. She had no conversation, and when she attempted it it was all tributaries and no streams. My sense of definition, anyway, needed to be spoken. There were odd moments when she responded, but frankly most of the time she had the personality of the back wall of a handball court.

Sometimes when darkness fell we'd park up by the school on a hidden overlook and effortfully but evasively discuss various things, sitting in her car, which in a state of chaos as if she lived out of it—as I gather often she did—was a jumble of magazines, wood planks, spools of thread, clothes, ski poles, tools, hats, parking tickets, and assortments of paper, a disorganization to me that remained as much a symptom of her lack of love as part of the cause of it. Carelessness was her past belief. She was an outcast literally. She would sit in her car, set her legs over my knees, cross her putty-colored ankle boots, and lean her fluffily fair head against the closed icy window, submerged in all the unidentification and lost in thought that somehow unnerving her will without tempering her passion rarely got spoken.

She seemed determined only to escape.

"Will you—leave?"

"That depends," she said.

"On?"

She paused.

"Me. And him." She looked away. "You, if you want."

Me? It took no genius to see that her readiness on my behalf was a measure of her unhappy marriage and not her feelings for me. It was rash. It was also bold and dramatic and gave her a sense of mystery. What I understood by it all was that she seemed to be trying out various thoughts and attitudes in order to see how it felt not only to hear herself say such things but to discover how I might respond without it being assumed she was committed to what she said.

There was so much mystery between us. I knew it. In trying to explain obscure matters—Occam's Razor—imaginary things should never be postulated as existing, right? The artist's failure is, he tries. When it's not his glory it's almost always his mistake. Where the cause doesn't delight in the consequence, the suggestion of menace supplants the suggestion of relief. We prove what's missing by what we want. Our dreams are always our temptations.

Farol's husband's absence, anyway, became the occasion one week in February—he had to go to California—of my being secretly invited to the Colorado house. I deliberated it beforehand for weeks. I saw the harm in it, I didn't see the harm, I never knew which. But of course I went, one freezing night following her car in my own to a dimly lit side street on the outskirts of St. Ives where a mock couple, a mimic marriage, we had dinner and listened to music—she played soft jazz over and over—and talked in an anxiety-ridden preappointed mood as doubly indistinct as the faint gradations of tone perceptible in the sky outside the large winter window of the living room that brought a constant chill into rooms as sterile and white as the snow outside, a dampness which Farol, constantly feeding logs into the wood stove, sought to buffer in spite of the general caveat there, her husband's upon leaving, that she not waste wood. Several times, almost fearful of the enterprise, she dared put up the thermostat.

I was secretly saddened to hear of such niggardliness—it somehow reflected on me, for I myself, if I gave, only gave to get, the simulacrum of generosity faithless lovers use only to appease the self and so make, in a charade of mutual need, what is only a parody of reciprocation. I'm certain I wanted to prove my prowess where another man had bungled. And yet there was something sincerely intended between us. She wanted now to tell me what she really felt, I thought, and I wanted to hear it to believe I was allowed to tell her the same. There were words on our lips that in our loneliness alone wanted utterance, and the need by itself virtually created the feeling.

Farol couldn't cook. She had tried but failed, and whatever she failed at didn't much interest her. Our first night together there however she took as some sort of exam, a small experiment in living, to show all she was capable of. It was a genuine attempt to put paid, I think, to the dolefulness of that shrugging adultery characterized for months by imposing silences, unspoken fears, and that kind of sadness in which for too long no gesture of affection, no moment of closeness, no attempt at spontaneity had any real meaning. Nothing was ever referred to any kind of future in which either of us, as I say, had any faith, and, I must admit, part of me despised her for asking me over, but I was there, wasn't I, she wanted me there, and, no matter what, stupid or foolish or whatever, there was comfort and at least an approximation of love in finding ourselves there together.

I can say I wanted her even way back then to know the happiness she was capable of giving. But I couldn't feel happy myself, not really. I couldn't bear the thought that she was the unfaithful woman I was nevertheless making her. It was vulgar and confusing. Strangely enough, I found I wanted to be in the presence of the very sort of decency I was preventing, and when I thought of pity that night I'm afraid I thought it applied more to me than anyone else.

Nevertheless, I felt a change in us take place at that time. Something happened, but I couldn't then, and can't even now, put my finger on what it was, whether positive or simply less negative I can't say. In any case, Farol prepared—nervously, in an attempt to please me—a meal of t-bone steaks, potatoes, and asparagus. She had bought a pie. I could see she was ill at ease in the kitchen. She had a fit with the hollandaise sauce, the meat, which she burned, was dry as a handclap, and the asparagus was soggy. And yet she seemed for being in her house fairly unflappable, at least less nervous, and soon began to talk. I detected more and more traces of a provincial accent. I smiled every time she asked for butter—"*bud-dear*"—to put on a vegetable she pronounced with three lumpy bumps: badayders. She tried to unsay it by mimicking herself whenever she said it, but the self-mockery I hadn't seen before became only endearing. "It's nice to be able to talk to you. I feel I can," she said. "My mother didn't know my father disliked salads until thirty years after they were married. I don't want to end up like that."

"And how would you like to end up?"

Farol gave me a long kiss.

"Like that," she said.

And smiling she took my hand, and she led me into the living room.

The house was an undistinguished mustard-colored garrison in North St. Ives. It bore in its every feature the characteristics of tentativeness, as if everything, furniture, rugs, the lot, could have been moved out to no consequence upon the instant. The mood of deploration there had no more immediate a source than in the terrible echoes I felt of the deep and incriminating accusations, recently shouted there, calling out of every wall. I heard arguments, screams, slamming doors, revved-up motors, and disappearing cars. Indistinguishable, at first remote, the sounds came to me with a quality of awakening resurgence, as though the house itself, though once asleep, now roused itself in the red animistic outrage of some kind of fury and interruption. There seemed to linger the spent ghosts of strange tension and dead lusts. Hollow pipes carried noises through the rooms. The hoarse flinty rumbling had something of the ring and register—the grumbling resonance—of her husband's voice as I imagined it. I couldn't stop thinking of him. And I knew Farol knew it. A creak of wood settling somewhere made me turn.

"It feels eerie," I said.

She stroked her cat. "Don't worry."

"He seems to be here."

"He's in Palo Alto," she said.

We continued sipping our wine. There was one large print on the wall: a scene of white empty chairs on a summer porch—it was almost sinister, despite the cool yellows and greens. There were no figures in the picture, which somehow stood for the idea of us, the chairs for the act. The rooms in the house were uncannily spare, of a one-eyed aspect, except for several potted shrubs, a stereo, and a large gumwood hutch behind the sofa. I noticed the shelves were filled with what were essentially superficial books, many of the self-help genre but predominantly those of the outdoor sort, camping, boating, that kind of thing. I haven't mentioned this, but Farol and her husband were—or had been, in happier times—hikers, serious ones, I thought, if the huge boots on the stairwell or the trapper's shoes in the back hallway meant anything. All the camping, hiking, and outdoor gear didn't suggest adventure to me so much as flight, and I suddenly thought: *travelers have bad marriages.*

She showed me the porch where cords of wood were stacked. I saw a sailboat outside. It was his sailboat, she said. Beyond were the bent poles of a garden plot. She said it was his garden. And she repeated, as if determined to make a distinction between them I should know, that she was interested in art. She led me into the cellar, pulled on the light, and said, "This is where I plan to do my sculpting."

I saw only a man's lumber jacket, waterproofs, boat equipment.

I remember the vague felonious thoughts troubling my mind that seemed to follow my footsteps through the house as we moved to other rooms. My vision became internal with growing remorse, and the shadows of memory still tell—even as they told me then—of someone else being there. My impression was that of a specter.

But there was a remarkable calmness about Farol. The inclination of her head indicated contentment, even complacency. And their cat, named Neko—she affectionately called him "tiny guy"—she continued to pat with the kind of effusive attention certain people always use as a displacement activity for what elsewhere remains the focus of their thought. I mean me, of course. And I mean her husband as well.

I was both, so was he. It was interesting. We had interchanged, unelaborately.

6

We talked quietly. It was one of those times when for two people loneliness is exchanged in the flush of hope, in the chance at last for new belief, for a version of one's life to be heard in that private and select arrangement by which so seen it must be told.

Farol was born in Nutley, New Jersey, the second of four children—with an older brother and two sisters, twins—of an uncommunicative family named Sprat ("We never shared words, questions, anything!") which in her early years constantly had to relocate. Her father's job necessitated such shifts. Then he took a job in New York City designing silver for Bulgari, work so expensive, she said, he himself couldn't afford it. She told me she once had a country accent for which when they moved to the city she was mocked at school.

"You lost it," I said.

"Yes."

"When you moved."

She nodded.

"And you live—"

"In Mamaroneck, New York. My parents do," she said, correcting me. She gestured vaguely. "I guess you could say I've lived all over. Lived." She sighed. "I mean *adapted,* I guess." She stepped into the kitchen, mixing dry and wet cat food together, and set out a bowl for the cat. She looked back. "I want to share, I have a lot to share, but I've never—never met a person who accepted me for what I am." She paused. "I don't know if I can even accept myself."

"Yes, you told me that once. But doesn't one often make the other happen?" She didn't answer. "You're isolated here." I waited. "You must feel that."

"I've always felt isolated," she said.

A sensation of dreary and abject humiliation overcame her on this subject and tears started to her eyes. "I've made such a mess of things. I sometimes feel I can't do anything *deep*. I've so often given in to my fears." Fears: the word, I'd come to see, would virtually become her signature. "I remember one night calling my parents when things were going really wrong with John and me, only another disaster, and my mother literally had nothing to say," she sobbed, "and my father told me, 'You're no gem yourself.' " There was a look Farol had—I'd seen it once or twice—that showed a potential not for mere intensity but for very unsettling sharpness. "My own father!"

She confessed he never complimented her, never told her he loved her, couldn't get the words out. She told me he'd been orphaned when a boy in Pugwash, Nova Scotia, and had been shown little love himself by his stepparents. His indifference had seared the forming concept of young Farol and, once formed, left a scar that remained in that small head like a root across a path to trip every last thought that came its way. Years passing had only tightened its fiber. She seemed not to have been brought up, rather made up, and left in solitude from childhood, where she lurked in secret, voiceless and displaced, moving in a hush as if down some inescapable corridor from one closed door to the next.

I kissed her fine hair and hugged her. I had the impression she'd been born of man alone—stillborn—a mother fluttered in the offing somewhere but merely as a spectator. To her parents, as I understood it, she was hopeless and by that judgment ignored, dismissed without thought, let off the hook in some grim armistice like someone retarded or whistling mad who was free to come and go, marry or not, simply because nothing else was expected of her. I comprehended the strange hammerlock of her being in chronic opposition to a father she loved only because he didn't and the dreadful reaction she feared of reproducing in herself the anger he caused if only to tell him why. I've often felt the source of my own harshness was the buried hurt of being abandoned. I pitied her. It wasn't only that she felt unacceptable. She felt betrayed.

I wanted to change the subject.

"What about your brother?" I asked.

"Bart," she said. "I don't know where to begin. We fought all the time growing up. He's insecure, and has a violent streak, one of those people you care about which in a way I do, but secretly resent for all the hurt he's inflicted upon you. Even now he's a know-it-all. Oh, he's got to be right." She hadn't much to say about him. She vaguely described him. She told me a few things about him, his marriage and so forth. He sounded about as interesting as a change of shirts. "I remember he would force me onto the ground when we were kids, how many times I can't tell you, demanding I plead for mercy, but no matter how much I cried I refused to give in." She looked at me with cold deliberation. "I wouldn't give him the satisfaction." She crossed her wrists. "I've talked about him in group. He teaches in Connecticut. He has a beard."

"And your sisters?"

Farol kicked off her shoes and got up and took a cardboard box from a shelf. She carefully edited what she farmed through. I was then shown a tiny photo on old Velox of three girls—the little sunny towhead in a cap-with-flaps of about four years old smiling into the camera I recognized. "And that's 'La La' and 'Babycakes,'" she said, pointing to her younger sisters, two plump-cheeked girls with vacant expressions and large rabbity teeth. I said they were cute.

"Cute," said Farol, dryly.

I looked at her. Her voice was flat and unfocused, almost belittling. Didn't she believe me?

"I've always thought Lenore and Lucy were prettier than me"—unlikely, I thought—"even boys in high school, the few who ever dropped by, seemed to like them better. Lenore's a great athlete." She showed me a more recent picture of them, now tidy elongated brunettes rather horse-faced and unremarkably plain. "They're very straight and proper. You know, organized and all? Not like me," she laughed. "Anyway, that's it. Them's us." It was good to see her laugh—only because it was different than crying.

And she seemed to grow more relaxed. She spoke, smiling inwardly, of some happy childhood memories—of a red truck she once had and a blue hat and her old tin train set and of eating raspberries on a farm one summer in a place called Big Flats. Oh, she had Tonka Toys and Lincoln Logs and the best little beach shovel on earth. She wondered where they were now. "Maybe I ate them!" she exclaimed, doing her gorilla call and falling backwards in laughter. "I have perfect occlusion," she said with a straight face, then rolling up began to nuzzle my neck. "And I've always liked to bite things!"

She said she didn't talk until she was four or learn to read until the age of seven and told me a funny story—her first failure of character!—of how in the first grade she'd once put cotton in her ears, which gave her an infection, so she wouldn't have to listen to the teacher. She confessed she'd also been a bed wetter.

As she talked she seemed to be a woman who had not yet become accustomed to the discovery that she was no longer a child. I personally found that touching, and mentioned it. I said I thought it was nice.

"Nice," she repeated.

I said nothing but fancied I heard in these echoes a certain tone of custom, a sarcasm lazily habituated to her. Somehow I felt disapproval in it, an attitude of the worn-out, the critical, the deeply cynical. It was as if she were trying to contain not so much her expressions but her enthusiasm, never large but oblique and on the point of going off in peculiar directions. With Farol you never quite knew what her amusement was.

Moods shifted abruptly. She was frank, boldly inquisitive at times. Intimate conversation nevertheless came hard to her. She had only small talk and no natural or easy passage from one subject to another. She could be rendered speechless by agitation, a shivering reflection of, well, of distances I couldn't see. I sensed a husband's dominance in her reactions, for her tendentious explanations were never without hesitation, as if something were always waiting to arrest her in inner rehearsal of what she should or shouldn't omit, of what she knew or didn't know, her facts coming, for instance, like figures of dissimilar size in scale painting, seeking to establish a depth, yes, but on chosen and distinct planes in order to lead the eye into the picture by illusions where it seems she always stood undisguised and desperate for love.

At one point she took a pill. I'd noticed that before. There were in the medicine chest a countless number of bottles. "What's that?" I asked.

"Sulfisoxazole."

"For what?"

"A bladder infection."

She got up to stoke the wood stove. She said she thought stress made her susceptible to illness. She said she spent a lot of time alone. She mentioned a few friends, but pointed out they were all dispersed around the country, people named Sue and Penny and Janet and Bill and Gustave and Patty and Allen. I was given a melancholy reflection or two about each but only shadowy first names.

"Wait," I said. "Don't forget your friends at the gallery."

She couldn't help laughing and said, "Mother Scrulock."

I winked. "Sugar Shorts."

"The Creepy Feature Creature."

Farol hadn't read much—a few books by Farley Mowat—and wasn't a student. She spoke of her years in high school without enthusiasm. She said she rarely dated. I love details. Details are never small. I prodded her. The first boy she kissed was Fred Mockery. She smiled and told me how an early crush on an older boy named Leo Helmkamp went unrequited. She mentioned back in those days she was too tall and homely. It was hard to believe. I begged to see her yearbook, which grudgingly she showed me, laughing but fighting my hand in a vain attempt to flash by certain photos—she'd been a high jumper—that she kept trying to prevent me from seeing.

A description a girl gives of her own photograph, especially if it's unfavorable, is never to be trusted over her photograph. But when I looked at the photograph I saw she *wasn't* pretty. I saw a towering teenage girl with wide bridgeworker's shoulders and ham-sized thighs. "I was taller than the boys!" she exclaimed, slamming the book shut. "I was homely. I told you, I always felt I had a small head. And look"— she comically exaggerated a rubber face—"fat lips!"

I laughed. It was the joke the beautiful woman can afford, pretending one of her best features was her worst. She knew she was pretty— or at least had become so—it was only too obvious she did, and yet as the evening passed I realized nothing else seemed to please her much. She had apparently done nothing for any length of time—gone to school or held a job or sustained a marriage. She never had the chances others had in college of going to parties, football games, meeting people in class. She felt left out. She gave me the impression of a woman with a sense of purpose but of a person whose life was lived at three- or four-year intervals at which point, unhappy, she'd turn away impulsively and steer in another direction.

She'd lived at times, isolated, all over the country: Syracuse, Big Flats, Lisle, Chicago, Concord, Massachusetts, Dexter, Michigan, a spell in Pennsylvania, first in King of Prussia and then Philadelphia—"Phoophadoophia," she called it, derisively—North Andover, Goshen, New Hampshire, and now St. Ives. She had been to Wyoming—*why?*—and had worked at one time or other, always at entry-level and semiskilled jobs, with a publisher, in a bank, at a hospital, and behind the counter of a dime store. I began to think that much of her life was a quest-in-reverse: an attempt to shed its meaning rather than find it. She changed addresses, took rooms, shifted jobs, donned different uniforms, met acquaintances, lost friends, and then moved on, only to have to discover the same kind of situation somewhere else. It had been one dodge after another involving gray questions of career guidance, insurance, and finding jobs. I didn't know how or why or when. I only felt a longing now more than ever to minister to her necessities.

Rooms, rooms, loneliness, loneliness. She was afraid to fail, she said, and so failed at everything. She recognized herself this way. An induced appetite failed to grow what it fed on. Still she drove on and on. I had the impression, as she recounted one trial after another, of a stubborn woman in whom a little girl was always trying to get something of her own back that was long, long ago stolen. And so she did what little girls do. She was trying to bluff, to counterfeit even as she spoke all she was and how she described herself by the very act of what in simultaneously condemning might make her appear better in my eyes. She tried to "make-believe." But she also knew what older women couldn't avoid knowing—that you can't. I wanted to tell her that you couldn't fail unless you fail yourself and wanted to shout it with all my heart's strength.

There were now real rips in the fabric through which I saw her life. She shook her head in despair and looked at me with those lambent green eyes whose indeflectable beauty, blinding with tears, only made me hug her in the protracted shock of a forsakenness I now saw with absolute clarity I couldn't help but share. I remember feeling at the time I'd never met anyone in all my life who seemed so vulnerable. I told her I wanted to be with her, to somehow bring some joy in her life. She looked squarely at me.

"Would you like to play squash sometime?"

"I don't know how to play," I said.

"I'll teach you."

"That will be fun."

"Fun," she repeated, sarcastically.

7

Darkness that evening had long since fallen. An immunity from the seriousness, the marching dread over the many miles still left to travel, was diverted by the music we together sat back to listen to, something primitive adulterating the tension and exacting nothing of either of us that had to be transmitted. Farol wanted to forget as a woman what she didn't want to remember as a wife. And night after night it was always the same. The boss was out of town, and she gave away the store. "Would you like to stay over?" she'd ask with her usual diffidence, sometimes desperately needing me to, sometimes, I think, hoping not, and sometimes wondering whether it mattered. But it did matter—now, to me, these nights. They did.

I told Farol from the first I'd always wanted to be in love with someone who really loved me, someone whose courage allowed for the wholehearted daring love requires. I'd never once in my life been hugged to paralysis by someone totally committed to me without imponderables or conciliating doubt or lies. I've already mentioned as regards the emotion of desire having felt only the desire to purge it. I remember the charges of various classmates in my adolescent years of my being indifferent to girls, but it wasn't true. My imagination, so fixedly intent on them, actually became the more authentic intimacy and somehow rendered the reality of secondary importance.

I have often been very bad for myself. I've always felt dangerous when I was alone. Loneliness is an empty quarter. Its outposts are fiercesome.

And so I always stayed. The worst moment in adultery is when you are climbing the stairs. I'd go up to the top bedroom, undress in the cold dark, and then suddenly she'd be there in bed beside me where both of us sought to rescue, as each rolled toward the other with primordial hunger, what together in a desperate act of sinister dexterity we separately were yet convinced we neither of us could save. It was prohibited to care. You held on, a ghostly give-off into the delirium of descendingly darkened circles where lying under the blankets and listening to the tortuous wind in the chimney you firmly held your eyes shut to a wrong only the mystery of uninquisitive sleep allowed to make unmistakably right. It seemed hopeless. What attracted me to her didn't make me feel close to her. What linked us, also severed. If there was no sanctuary in another man's bed from the memory of his being there, there was even less forgiveness for the woman who in the exchange made it a refuge with no memory at all.

There in that marriage bed, the very thing it was formulated to prohibit and exclude, was bound the unbound, making any vows spoken in one place retracted in another. But it wasn't only her meandering pursuit of truth. I wanted her to hate what we were doing, I think, so I could love her for what she was and not for what she seemed, a dissatisfaction surely hers as well, for above and beyond the deceived principals in our lives were two other people involved in this affair: the people we ultimately each wanted the other to be.

Late one night her husband actually telephoned—the instrument shrieking beside the bed—and with my heart bulging as if a bolt of terror had leapt across the lip of one life into another to become death I quickly got up and groped my way through the darkness to another room, leaning one arm against the wall with my eyes closed. I awoke and was blind and couldn't find myself in a blackness so complete and so thick that I felt myself virtually being dyed by it. I could only hear a puppet speaking somewhere, a wooden jojo transformed out of sleep and impersonating someone calm in muffled tones ("No, only fixed a sandwich and watched TV" "When will you be leaving?" "I'm missing you too") until suddenly I heard nothing anymore. I've never heard of a long-distance phone call that didn't cause trouble for someone, so I was surprised she took it so casually. But it was only later that I realized, the rubrics of adultery taking some time to learn, her lack of concern that night only confirmed the fact, her husband was far, far away.

It was during one such night, her eyes showing something of that green light, just momentarily lurid, from which almost spontaneously I often felt I must turn, but rarely could, that Farol told me—she was hugging a pillow, staring into the middle distance—that she and her husband had met four years before at a party. She described him, without being specific, as very good-looking ("People always looked at him," she said, "not me") and frankly mentioned that walking across a crowded room that first time it was she who approached him. They began dating, found they had common interests, lived together for a year, and then got married.

After locating haphazardly in city after city, they finally settled in

St. Ives, hastily buying a house over a weekend ("I hate it," she said) within driving distance of her husband's new job, one, she pointed out, he disliked from the start. Or was it his previous job he disliked?

I don't remember. I don't think she herself did. It was all a confused calendar of dates and designations to me—a fact foreshortened, a detail lengthened—and yet as she continued speaking I remember I almost couldn't cope with the overwhelming burden of never before having found two people quite so strategically ill suited. They'd lost their love, yet somehow creating fixed boundaries between themselves beyond which neither could pass held to them at first. Their social life improved in the hideous way it often does when both members of a married couple suddenly need other people in their lives to keep from meeting each other. They rarely did anything together, so managed to do everything apart. When one set off, the other stayed home. No sooner did one go in than the other went out. And day after day their horrid unromantic war ground on along its muddy course. It was the classic quandary, one irrationally refusing to admit the existence of the other, yet both conspiring toward the same end. And what that end was seemed inevitable.

Farol tried further to explain him, almost as much to herself as to me. He was bright, he was oafish. He was a master of argument, he was wild and irrational. He could be tender but then took her on interminable camping trips when she had to follow carrying sixty-pound backpacks in the rain. Again, as if to convince herself, she described him as oddly arresting. The features, one by one, were right, she said, yet taken altogether they were somehow improbable, and his height gave him—she paused—an awkwardness. This plus his glacial manner added up to something that repelled her. He was vain, she said. And obsessive, I thought. The unforeseen, the unorganized, the unpredictable apparently confused more than maddened him and much of the time made him impossible to live with. He had a tropism for order.

"He has to put on special work clothes for each specific project," said Farol. "He always has to follow a system whenever we go shopping at the market. He picks up groceries in the order that they're written on his list," she added. "If the milk and the cheese are next to each other in the same aisle but not one after the other on his list, he'll walk past the milk and then go back for it later when he reaches it on his list. And he draws up precise plans of approach whenever we go on a trip. And if anything unexpected happens—forget it. He goes into a wicked snit."

He was a Midwesterner. She said he showed in many ways the naiveté of that region. He was big for the outdoors. He was thrifty. He liked Big Ten football. A moral man, she said, he also had something of a compulsion to watch strippers. No, he didn't go out with other women. "I wish he would," muttered Farol, looking away. "It would make things easier." He was spoiled growing up, she said. She admitted that she preferred the company of a more pleasant younger brother of his, a person of whom he was somewhat jealous. Probably because of that, I thought.

She said, "He has a hard time relating to women. It's because of the way he was raised. His parents are Plymouth Brethren." As I heard it, they'd welcomed her as a daughter-in-law, but she disliked them. "They're strict and narrow. They don't drink—they disapprove of drinking. We have to hide our bottles of wine when they visit. But why should we? Who are they? Just because people out there live that way, we have to act like hypocrites? I'm sick of it," she puffed angrily. "So is John. But now you see why he's like he is."

I saw, needless to say, on whatever frequency, an unsatisfied man. (I seriously began to wonder now whether half the drugs and prescriptions in the bathroom cabinet weren't his.) And yet he specialized in iniquity and was truly reptilian if she was not dissembling in the even blacker appraisal of him that followed. He nightly returned from work in "moods," drank too much, and once threatened to kill the cat. Advanced communications management! He excluded her from most of his activities, left her alone at parties they attended together, and refused to socialize with any new friends she'd made at the gallery, a job she took, she said, to make ends meet. Food. Car payments. Her share of the mortgage. She explained that they had separate bank accounts against which of course they wrote separate checks. I thought she was glad in spite of some self-disgust to have proof of her husband's *not* wanting her. She even exclaimed against his car, a station wagon she disdainfully called "The Bourgeoismobile." And she repeated—illogically—he hated sex.

I asked for some reason, "Did he ever hit you?"

"He once pushed me up against the wall and threatened me."

"Why?"

She closed her eyes.

"I wouldn't—"

"Tell me."

"I could no longer—please him. If you know what I mean." I

asked, "In bed?" She nodded, guardedly. "Even if I did want to reach over and touch him, I swear, my hand would freeze and fall off." I suspected, at least in this matter, that she was ascribing to him her own problems and through some kind of bizarre transferral or subconscious identification making her fears his own.

"And children? Had he any by his first wife?"

"He never wanted children," she said directly.

"Do you?"

I found her reply incredible. "I don't know any," she said. And then she put her head down and added in a whisper, "I've never been given the chance."

I took her side, inevitably, in the light of his having failed to. It was interesting. I could easily accept this dark demoralizing account of him and by a kind of algebra previously unavailable to me, by a sort of pythagorean transferral all my own, find this secret misalliance of ours not only less pernicious but now in the light of this report suddenly excused, even forgiven. And worse. I was even able to rationalize by dint of the soul-destroying monotony which had cocooned the two of them in a world where, ironically, she had spent her days more single than otherwise—the paradox of the unhappily married woman who, for whatever reason, often knows less of passion and sharing and affection than the single—that ours was therefore the truer exchange.

I figured by logic we could gain nothing of lovely plunder unless we dared to lose all. I entered with joy the priesthood of seizing lovers, and felt absolved. It gave me the courage to ask a question, which she answered forthwith.

No, she said, she didn't love him. She didn't. She did not.

A silence held. "But now you have an idea of the mess I've made of my life," she said. "It's like death. It *is* death. It's like being buried alive," said Farol, voice uncertain—that quaver in her throat always so close to a sob—and, shaking her beautiful head almost as if to free it of the complexities that tortured her, she leaned back upon the pillow. And then I become her advocate.

"It's surely not your doing," I said, kissing her forehead. "You mustn't be so hard on yourself. Many marriages—I don't know, fail." I paused. "Don't they?" There followed a long pause. The minute was reigned over by a startling and inexplicable silence, a certain stillness I immediately found strangely foreboding and eerie. "Don't they?"

Farol Colorado slipped out of bed wearing only pink panties and hugging herself from the chill crossed to the far end of the bedroom, turned, and waited. She remained silent, waiting out those crucial moments with her head lowered, as if about to utter some revelation or launch into that kind of announcement it was never safe to make. And then she spoke, chopping off her words as if to make the most economical use of sound. It was brief.

"Two of them?"

I sat up, astonished. I tried to look at her through twenty feet of darkness.

"Now you see," she said. "Now you understand."

8

There was something of an almost physical visitation in that confession. I slept by her side fitfully that night, if at all. The bedroom seemed a box-set in hell. I woke before dawn the following morning, furtively perhaps, and maybe touching her in a perfunctory way. I remember seeing her face bewildered but recall badly wanting to get out of there. I knew it was my moment of exodus. I crept downstairs, scraped the ice from my car window, and quickly drove away.

I couldn't believe it. She was notorious. And yet for all she confessed it was her having deceived me—her lying about it—that mattered most.

But *two* failed marriages! They were mistakes of fondness, perhaps. I didn't know. Maybe she wasn't the kind of person who could live with someone. I felt a staleness of sensibility in connection with them in any case which blocked out every aspect of that relationship for me but that of its being finished and done with. I suppose she had been decent in the end: it was a plea for acceptance, charity perhaps, understanding. But I'm afraid I was sick of the mere doing anymore. There was nevertheless in the general strain of my effort to avoid the danger of repetition a fatal puncture.

I have no deep-seated preference for comprehensive presentation, but in this I found what, once presented, had to be dismissed. What had become increasingly more forbidding now became forbidden. There was wreckage all around. I recall feeling with relief I'd come to the end of an insidious and overingenious labor in trying to discern a figure who came to me only in shadowy multiplication. She had lied, then shared this confidence. I recalled the first time she had been sarcastic and complained and ordered what she didn't eat; it didn't matter. It is only repetition and history that makes people hateful. No one is awful without having first been better.

It was all I could do to understand one of her, but this was impossible. She was a franchise. Turnaround property. A revolving door. I couldn't conceive of getting further involved wtih someone who'd have to spend the better part of a week photocopying anniversary cards. She once told me she was afraid she'd end up in life a bag lady or a poorhouse crone, alone and friendless. At times, I began to believe it.

I am not alone, I'm sure, in the impulse of being susceptible to mythologizing someone and then having to face instead a sudden and spirit-sagging demystification. But it didn't matter. No contract, no criticism. No complaint, no crime. It wasn't anger I felt; it was just nothing. I wanted to start painting again. I had already wasted too much time. There was no problem getting back to work, let me add, for nothing else in the provincial town where I lived ever beckoned to tempt me otherwise. Cow Hampshire. The Granite State. The few years I already spent there seemed an eternity.

St. Ives was a little prep-school town. Old, gentrified, quaint—having managed somehow to avoid the run-down look seen elsewhere in much of the state—it was incredibly pretentious and had the silly belatedness to it that is typical of such places. Prerevolutionary cannons on the common. The town pump nodding over its trough. May apples elfing up near the old cistern. Something like Ye Olde Porter's Tavern on the corner, famous in story and song, and though still green in the memory of the town fathers now a commercial restaurant with huge folding menus with tassels printed in pseudo-eighteenth-century ligature featuring the "compleate fare." It was, so much of it, the fraudulence of nostalgia without history.

There was a patrician air to the few venerable mansions, white-steepled churches, and milk-painted colonial houses which, cuter than they ought to be, seemed huddled as if in mobilized defense against the encroachment of the many modern storefronts that had sprouted up along the main streets where somehow could always be found two matrons, side by side, tugging the leashes of their sharpei dogs and waiting for the lights to change. There was the usual brick box: banks, city hall, schools, a hospital. A tearoom or two. An art gallery. And various candle-and-heather shops. An effort of anxious gentility had been made, along with recent developments built on exquisite lines—Jacobethan and Early American Tudor and Shuttered Sheraton—to keep the predominant New England look of white cupolas, coach lanterns, and a proliferation of brass eagles which pleased those people so easily identified as natives by their knowing tweeds and lockjawed speech and excessive self-possession. I'd never seen such intensive single-minded pains-in-the-ass.

And I've never known such snobs. Their aspirations to elegance, grounded in defense of rural embarrassment, turned them into cartoons of civility. It was a boomist, self-promoting, idea-distrusting constituency of upwardly mobile members of the middle class, a town full of big overfed Republican ladies in golf shoes; guys named Wellesley and Needham who wore red slacks and white belts; peppy doctors' wives with leathery faces and pastel-tinted bandannas for whom a day's work consisted of an hour of aerobic dancing and a few tennis lessons; pipe-smoking ministers who believed in nothing, and group after group of wolfish couples from the country club, fat blustering men and their silly talkative wives, slag-fadges in their late sixties with the withered faces of monkeys, wealthy, hair bleached pink, and that five-martini affability at parties I dread more than anything else on earth.

They had no manners, only etiquette, and yet to emphasize correctness made every attempt whenever possible to drink port, play racquetball, sail boats, see art films, flambé food, affect ascots, collect paintings, cross their sevens, wear legible clothing, subscribe to concerts, hire help, and in general follow no fashion by which first hadn't been established a precise—and identifiable—semiotic function.

There was no end to their social get-togethers, open houses, wine-and-cheese functions, craft bazaars, or those wonderful tailgating parties that little groups held in private before every St. Ives football game when you heard things like "Trish! Trish Carlisle! Over here! It's Mopsy and Tom Grottlesex. Remember, Princeton '68? Have some munchies. Lance? Oh no, Lance graduated and is starting Wharton come Fall. Jed's our littlest. Grey and Bingo are of course here at Exeter. Grey, come over here and say hello. And Skimper—you remember last summer in pigtails? At Squirrel Island? She's into her third year at Sarah Lawrence, how do you do! Lime daiquiris with nutmeg, try it. The tuna's the cellophane. There's more deviled ham in the hamper. And Triscuits. Have you seen Skye and Pony Deerfield or are they still in Marbelle? Grey, have I or have I not asked you to come over here. No, Carter *was* in Antibes, but is now working in Larchmont and dating a doctor, don't you know. (Young lady, I do *not* like that tone of voice!) And let's see, for us, Bermuda's coming up and Ritchy and Mum want Boca Raton for Easter. I'm not saying a *word!* Oh, and do come to Wolf Trap to hear Tiggy—that's her in the rust cardigan and forearms, can you believe it?—where she'll be playing the hammer dulcimer. I just adore your pendant. Is it Peru?"

At St. Ives teachers treated the students as their betters. It was an admission not only of their own insecurity but their way of confessing to a merciless snobbery, for usually the richer the student, the better he was treated. A teaching colleague once told me, "Wealthy kids tend to be very good-looking." Teachers tended to measure one another's worth not by his effectiveness or ability in the classroom but by how favored he was among the students, by how many *liked* him. It was only a variation of a vice peculiar to the modern American family where married couples, ignoring each other, choose instead to focus exclusively on their children. Teachers "collected" students in the same way Boy Scouts compiled merit badges, seeking the same kind of recognition. This woeful imbalance in the school community, virtually reversing roles, turned teachers into crouching sycophants and students into smug and often hopeless egotists. And while many students were thoughtful and well-bred, too many of them, firm, vigorous, and golden-skinned, were like the pears and peaches of a dishonest fruit vendor, resplendent without and rotten within.

What was even more shameless was that the teachers allowed themselves to be co-opted by the school. St. Ives paid for everything. It fostered in the working faculty a terrible dependence. The academy paid for their houses, lent them cars, cashed their checks, tendered them grants, and gave them all their meals for nothing. It provided doctors, paid for their insurance, and educated their children at no cost. The teachers lived on school ground, saw school movies, attended free lectures, and had free run of libraries, computers, and playing fields. The school even hired their wives and children for various jobs. They never had to do dishes or pay water bills or mow lawns or fix broken machinery or notify the oil company. They even took trips—once to the Soviet Union—at school expense. It was like the company store.

The sad result was not only that it reflected a single unified perspective but that it made for mediocrities who stayed on for years there (salaries were determined by longevity, not degrees) gathered together in a scrum, as it were, and got rid of any real talents who threatened them by doing nothing more than questioning the value of a system

that so quickly undermined the imagination and turned educated people into pensioners and pets.

There was, in fact, something about the bully, running-about-the-
fields, hockey-sticks aspect of the school bordering the town that in-
stilled a kind of permanent adolescence in not only teachers but townsfolk, making most of them conspicuous failures as adults. It drew in
the old school ties. It dressed them in sporty windbreakers with lots of
drawstrings and turned them into hearty hoopoes in floppy white tennis
hats and colored trousers with little frogs embroidered all over them.
Or signal flags. Or bell buoys. And always it set a tone based upon principles of enshrining precedent, evoking a vanished eden of grace and
asset that forced every one of them to look back with longing on the
class distinctions they knew when young and now not only imitated but
elaborated and intensified in the ludicrous and obsessive need for a
tradition by which in pursuing all lost their identity and which in perpetuating none ever failed to reproduce of its moldering repose.

It was a spitefully incloistered world, laughable in its fundamental
pretense, but built upon such a system of extrusion and scaffolded round
so dangerously by the inflexible and uniform that I often wondered if
that school, and the young mortals within, were not part of some last
twisted scheme devised by the townsfolk in compendious illustration of
their social genius to satisfy their own dubious distinction.

And so it was a period during which I never felt a greater need
to get away from teaching, from Farol, from the confines of the whole
damned place. And I was lucky enough to be able to do it. I dropped
out and soon met myself again, with the too lagging, loitering amend-
ments of my past condition mercifully outdistanced by an impatient and
now thankfully insistent drive once again to paint.

9

I went on vacation in early March to Vermont and took Marina. It
was a delight to be with her again. She was as different from the people of St. Ives as their public face was from their private. She was
younger and actually prettier than Farol, a pale blonde with full breasts

and a refined and beautiful face. There was a mellow beauty about her in which her radiance had the quality of an emotion. You could almost read by the light of her smile. The pinafores she wore, revealing the most voluptuous figure I'd ever seen, were as simple as the gold locket she always wore around her neck. But the whole mystery of her beauty lay in her wide-set delphinium-blue eyes, which were positively breathtaking. She was passionate, though also shy in social situations, and had none of the sterility of always having to be right. I felt no moral backsliding with her, never for a moment, and she was utterly and completely unassuming.

She hadn't an ounce of humbug. She had no airs at all. A warm Christmassy person, filled with sympathy and light, she had infinite, unfluctuating kindness. And while it soothed me, it also let me take advantage. She was a perfect lover for a narcissist like me who could easily see her in the light of my own egotism. Her deep feelings were invisible because her manner was so quiet. Nothing was expected of me. I could put a drop cloth over her, as I could a painting, which of course in my vanity was just what I had done.

Marina lived at home. She had been doing all right there for a while, taking care of her father. But her mother demanded she work, and as she was a person with one of those special natures which unnaturally focused on what she couldn't do, it was a catastrophe. She began working at a supermarket where because of her looks she was constantly harassed. Apparently one night the manager tried something with her in a freezer and by the time she came home she was hysterical. Her mother soon enrolled her in typing school, hoping that she would learn to be a stenographer, but that didn't turn out well either—she could sustain neither the pressure nor the group contact—and she was very quickly dismissed. This was followed by the job she took at the studio, infuriating her mother. She was forced to drop that. And she became more and more reclusive, suffering from what was eventually diagnosed as chronic nonspecific anxiety. The situation became so alarming that she was told by several doctors she wouldn't recover unless she got out and took a job. And so she became a darkroom technician at the Boston City Hospital.

She had a secret smile. She was unathletic, Catholic, and not much interested in marriage—we'd discussed it, inconclusively, years before. I think she feared the changes it wrought in people. I know she was scandalized by her parents, who fought all the time, and yet she felt obligations to her family. The Falieris had no money. Her father, who worked in the shipyards down on the Boston waterfront, wasn't well. Her mother was a great fat self-indulgent Italian baba who slept till noon and never did a lick of work. She was a perfect savage and came between us over the years with such monstrous and inspired regularity that it came to constitute for me in its jealous abruption a kind of adultery all its own. I soon came to see she hated her daughter, who was everything she wasn't. She made threats and bullied her and tried to humiliate her in front of me. Marina was virtually a prisoner at home. It broke my heart.

There were little things about Marina I loved. She wore her hair in a Gainsborough braid at the back, which gave her a melting prettiness. She loved music, had an almost oriental love of hearing stories, and kept scraps of paper listing Mass schedules in her handbag. She lived somewhat in a fantasy world. She sewed beanbags and painted clothespin figures and made doilies from photographs of snowflakes. She was a collector of stray animals, and in her menagerie, along with two finches, were a cat with a lobotomy and a small dog with stunted legs. She mispronounced words and said "volumtuous" and "typerope" and "turpentime," always giggling through her hand when she recognized her mistake. She loved poetry, especially Shakespeare, and when quoting a line from some poem she liked would turn pale, her eyes filling with tears. I often heard her recite Poe's "A Dream Within a Dream," her favorite, and almost wept myself.

> *Take this kiss upon the brow!*
> *And, in parting from you now,*
> *Thus much let me avow—*
> *You are not wrong, who deem*
> *That my days have been a dream.*

She was not intellectual. She never spoke much, only when she had something to say. When I first met her she told me about her doctors and what they'd said of her apprehensions—it was the first and last time she mentioned it in all the time I knew her—and I often worried about that. She was also a city girl, and in many ways realistic, a sweet phenomenon with a perfect fullness of appreciation simply because she had no preconceptions of happiness at all. It was amazing. She asked nothing of the gods above, nothing of men below, not even their company. Her rich dark pessimism, oddly enough, allowed her to accept things the way they came without dismay, and this often became the occasion of her serendipitous delight. She kept mostly to herself in a lone and detached way from the competition others of her age and sex pursued—I mean security, social advancement, men.

It was a fault sometimes, or so it seemed to me. She could be too docile. Strangely passive. She had that curious amenability of the victim, simply accepting as fate the way things were. (I remember only one exception, when once in a restaurant she opened a fortune cookie that was empty and suddenly began to cry.) I personally thought she victimized herself in fact by converting hope to fate, whereby all tissue of consequence for her simply fell outside any measure or sense. It exceeded my comprehension much of the time. I was often sad, frequently disappointed, because I wasn't pessimistic. Disappointment left no unfavoring argument with Marina, however, nor did fluctuation lead to dismay. She hadn't the rage of reflection. She simply shrugged at finding no design to living, took life at whatever pitch it came, and asked for nothing.

I painted her whenever I could, almost as often as Cézanne painted his wife. A box of colors, sunlight, and Marina made me a gypsying dreamer. She was the soul of my best work. My "marinascapes" I called them: Marina at the beach, Marina in a trilby hat, Marina in the Harvard Yard, Marina in a black schoolgirl jumper, Marina dancing with a blue ribbon, Marina holding a dog, etc. Simple color schemes, features refined, nothing overmannered or elusive. My brush always knew just what to do with her.

We hadn't grown apart, too much had merely happened to us separately. The passion we once felt for each other hadn't dwindled—I found her even more beautiful now than before—yet something had come between us. I began to feel after I met Farol that Marina was gradually losing all corporeality and physicality in my mind and turning into a kind of legend or myth inscribed on parchment. She had a driver's license but didn't drive and didn't care to. She never once came to St. Ives. The legacy of habit and long absences had for a while now begun to leave us whenever we met to that kind of tentative silence that creates in its unease a canon of form. I sensed that, and yet we'd known each other so well I felt I could presume to deal in a graceful or at least tactful fashion with the areas of smashed correspondence—my infidelity—I wanted to patch up, and on our trip, which was in a good way a renewal of our old times together, I did, I think, a wonderful painting of her, a gouache, a slightly heavier impasto this time, one reinforced by a couple of sittings on a cold sunlit balcony in Brattleboro which I transformed to summer in the canvas and that very week finished.

Marina is weaving a chain of crowflowers, nettles, daisies, and long purples, textures I teased out with various scumbles and individual brush-shaped marks of whitened viridian, blue, and orange. The simple smock she's wearing is subdued by earth colors, an iron-oxide red giving it the warmth of Millet. I always had the right direction of light with her and never failed to catch the liquid delicate quality of her skin tone, Sargent's alabaster, white and blue like milk in shadow. I gave her the painting. She asked, "What are you going to call it?" I kissed her and asked what she thought.

"Isn't that a Shakespeare dress?" she asked innocently, biting her lip in doubt and shyly looking at me.

"Yes," I said.

"Ophelia. Call it Ophelia."

Before I met her my choice of subjects—landscapes, interiors, still lifes—were chosen from the familiar and close at hand. I'd often played with views through windows and doors, using room verticals and horizontals to organize my schemes. But this earlier work, in which there can be felt a sort of starkly northeastern touch, soon went and I began stronger, brighter, broader things, more complicated, stressing paint and color rather than contour and shading. I became more primitive and wilder, and this particular painting showed it. I always saw her in sunshine bright as the sunsets of Baghdad and its gold minarets and the yellow winds of the Asian plain. We grew into renewed feelings for each other, finding appreciation and a requisite loveliness even for the short time we had together that March when the beautiful mountains and hills and meadows were throwing off their winter wear.

To me she was the dearest person in the world. She was part of me. Love *makes* people profound. I loved her even when I wasn't sure how much in love with her I was.

My classes again became enjoyable. The teaching took a large bite out of the day but reinforced without exception an idea I thought I'd lost, that the give-and-take of words actually works. It left me in a state of health of a kind altogether better than recently I'd known, and it fixed my confidence on the precious simplifications of available truth. I love to talk. It came late to me as a habit, but emphatically. The classroom—a print of Vermeer's *Officer and Laughing Girl* hung on the wall—was a bright mess of paint-filled jam jars, brushes, stretchers, muddied paper, rumpled tubes, bulldog clips, bottles of turpentine, and small birds and animals that had been stuffed and placed on shelves. My classroom manner was usually one of informality and alert nonchalance.

We avoided textbooks. I relied on their interest in the various questions we raised. Why do pebbles look brighter when wet? Is there a right order in which to arrange a set of crayons? How is the mouth the key to a portrait? What about feet? And hands? Do the hands show vanity or trouble? And what about the protective curve to the way people stand? Does he show fear? She hide her breasts? How tall is a person when he sits down? Why do certain clothes change color when ironed? What are the colors you see when you press your eyes? I told them stories about the cave art of Altamira, Les Eyzies, and Lascaux, explaining how all writing arose out of pictograms, and spoke of style: why was Gericault so interested in painting the faces of the insane? Goya his nightmares? Caravaggio those shadows? Crivelli his delicate details? I urged them to work with their own eyes and encouraged them to do a lot of drawing in their notebooks where because of the low commitment there a lot of surprising things came out.

I loved my students, and their energy, their willingness led me up and down and around desks and telescopic easels commending something or in feverish and excited dashes seizing a quick hand to shape it to a finer line. Sometimes students were difficult or arrogant. But docile students never challenged me, the dreamy less organized ones did. I avoided marching them along the inexorable route through Impressionism and Cubism to the more abstract and just let them paint. Much of the work was inoffensively untransportable—skies, typically, covering fully half the picture, a few circumflexes called sea gulls, and the usual vast expanse of water below showing reflections—but even when I saw scraps where there should have been presences I still found in a kind of poor, scratchy, inky way something contributing at least to the saving human sum of joy and self-delight. It was basic stuff I taught, priming canvases to color key to simple brush marking.

It didn't matter. We had energy and drive. They liked figure drawing and landscapes and, a magnificent beckoning looseness for me, arranging in bowls and vases the crocuses, branches of foliage, and wildflowers they now brought in to paint. A sudden buoyancy that filled my heart surprised me. I felt a sense of renewal. And when I opened the window and looked out, I smelled April in the air.

10

Spring had come, and I felt lonelier for it. I felt a mean economy of spirit which with me rarely depended on weather or season to make it rise or fall but usually whether or not I was in love. I wasn't in love. I sympathized with Marina, who got nothing in desiring so little, and pitied Farol, who found so little in desiring so much. I was placed between them, feeling not so much the need to choose one or the other as to determine what was missing in myself that I needed to fulfill. There was an absurd and disheartening symmetry in the fact that I could comfortably call neither of them at home or work. And I suppose part of the void within me was the awful feeling I had in finding myself in two situations which for all their differences were so much the same.

I was fairly resigned then to waiting for whatever appeal awaited me elsewhere when one afternoon I found a note left on the windshield of my car:

> *Would you like to play squash with me tonight at 7?*
> *Love, Fat Lips*

There exists a kind of sentiment of rationality, and the satisfaction of that sentiment in a certain situation may be as important as logic. I don't know, it was always a great curse to me not to be densely indifferent to impossible things. Most things are impossible for me, but, foolish to say, I could rarely brazen it out that they were no loss. Brazening it out—I never understood things any other way.

I drove down to the gallery. I couldn't remember the last time I'd been there, not that it bothered me. It was a damp little cellar no bigger than a bun shop off the main street in town and smelled of must. On a second floor was a showroom with arsenical-green walls where on occasion "openings" were held, but the framing was done downstairs behind a small lobby in the bad woodpeckerish light of a factory-like cellar strewn around with mats and glass, corner samples, racks of molding, unsorted frames, and piles of particleboard.

Customers coming into the gallery were made to feel like intruders by the help there. The women doing the framing in the back room made it clear they did not like to be bothered. There was a cold indifference felt upon entering that virtually challenged every person waiting there to prove that he or she was worthy enough to receive attention. I walked in, looked through the inner door, and saw Farol wasn't there.

"You have a picture to be framed?" asked Mother Scrulock, her cigarette wagging in a rictus of lipstick stoplight-red. She had a mouth like a disk drive. "Or do you just want to mount something?"

Whereupon I said, "I only wanted to know whether this building is fireproof or not."

"We can assure you of that," she replied with a mocking scrawl in her eyes.

"What a pity," I said.

And I waited in the lobby.

I was used to this by now. The women who worked there, divorcées in their late forties and all negotiating difficult passages in their domestic and sexual lives, were like witches who'd lost the power to cast spells: fat, hairy, big-bummed, and mean-spirited. Divorce had left them drudges. It was something they couldn't forgive. They would have had more freedom as wives, but all had tried and failed. Now they were only public pratts, housewives to the world, semicripples in the land of the work ethic. They pathetically communicated the insecurity of having to live with people who had more advantages than they in a society in which to be inferior in economic standing is to be inferior in being. The menial work they did, jobs mortgaged to necessity, humiliated them, which made them defensive and forced them to posture and boast and put on airs in an irony of self-contempt. It made them avaricious, as women of that age and temperament are commonly found to be. And it made them almost as nasty as I became cruel in hating them for it.

They were viperish and havering and claw-footed, creatures with secondary personalities who taken singly would have been nothing so made it a point as if by marching order to join forces in the daily things they faced as a kind of protection. Juxtaposition had married them, not love.

It was a freemasonry of sorts. They had little affection and less contentment. They professed no faith, gave no quarter, ruled out sharing, and insisted in that flat dismissive slang which always characterized the way they spoke that nobody got nothing free and you took what you could get. But as they'd long ago cut their losses in the way of romance, they were all of them forced to find in each other's relentless iterations and actions what mutually they had both to approve and to overlook in order to persuade themselves that they all thought alike, a sort of grotesque social compact where each depended on the other's inferiority to reinforce the friendships they had to make to keep from becoming enemies. They were a group, not a team. There was no real backing; behind, each was wired and screwed, and they actually framed each other.

The place was suffocating, the women all bite and cavity and showing that strategy of outspoken opinion that in its moral sluttishness always signifies militant self-promotion on the move. Most of their ideas and thoughts came from television shows and self-help books which told them how to survive by taking risks and filling personal needs and discovering themselves. They were always taking their own temperature. They wanted careers, not jobs, and spoke constantly of coping and the cost of living and the virtue of "single-parenting," surely the most hideous expression on earth. You heard things like "I'm just beginning to feel good about myself" and "I have to start learning to say no" and "For the first time in my life I've decided to do something just for me!" and "You know what turns me off? Rudeness. You know what really turns me off? Rude men."

There was the chief problem. The particular source of frustration of women observing their own self-study and measuring their worth as women by the distance they kept from men necessitated that a distance be kept, and so what vindicated them also poured fuel on the furnace of their rage. One delight preassumed another dissatisfaction, but their hatefulness confessed to their own lack of power to please. They hated men because they needed husbands, and they loathed the men they chased away for going.

They blamed men for everything—marriage, children, divorce. They had the sneaking (and rather original) suspicion that men and women never got married in exactly the same numbers. And all the while they mistook the flexibility of men as a sign of female strength, which was interesting because they not only had men's feet, men's bodies, and men's voices, but actually *looked* like men.

They were among the most facially unfavored women I'd ever seen, as I've said. In a very real way, no one's homely except in the way rage befits a face, fist-puppeting it into a particular mode where the nasty becomes the ugly. I've never found it difficult to understand why most women who abuse men are almost always those whom men have found unattractive. What I've never been able to figure out was why the female cause never seemed to be embodied by women who were healthy and strong, why it was always represented by those who were so bent and bitter—so close to the brink of breakdown and rage—that they actually helped perfect the defenses of their own prey.

None of the gallery women looked alike, but while their ugliness was stultifyingly dissimilar, something in their faces actually matched, as if they had a common purpose and like business and were acting under orders, thrice to mine, thrice to thine, and all that.

As I've mentioned, Ruth Gumplowitz was small and blear, a little thing with a mustache whose sex was not easy at first to determine. She wore bottle-thick eyeglasses—goggles, I thought—which magnified her gerbil's eyes, bringing them too close together, and her hair snarled out like a fright wig. It was the bewildered face of a dress-extra, mostly nose, full of pleats and tucks. She had a lot of the magpie about her and haunting outlet stores to save money wore clothing she bought at tag sales that hung limp about her and stank like merry hell. I could have whittled a better-looking woman.

Charlotte Tweeze was, without doubt, the gooniest. She looked as though she'd just wandered in from a goose fair. A tall woman with lead-colored lips and a cowcatcher chin, she blamed her ugliness on her height rather than on her face. Her hair was lank black. She was an irreconcilable illiterate, but claimed to know everything about modern art. She always wore flat shoes and stooped on her fiddle-splat feet, the sort like skis that allowed her to lean forward and hover over you with things like "You're wrong!" or "Total bullshit!" or "Degas had *no* sensuality!"

And Maxine Scrulock was built like a jukebox, a squat marauder in polyester bulletproof pants which fit her too tightly and left horrible bulges that made the obvious only more so. She was short and pie-faced with puffy smoker's eyes and along with a kind of sunburnt ugliness had the sort of pebbled skin that when you looked close resembled in texture lawn furniture webbing or the pseudo-cloth of high school yearbooks. The pearls screwed tight in her ears only made her look fatter, "so fat," one of the gallery wits, Neil Ringspotz, once told me, "that if she fell down she'd actually rock herself to sleep trying to get up."

Whereas classical proportion has long held that the head ideally goes seven and a half times into the length of the entire human being, some on-the-spot calculations with my pen once revealed Scrulock's unfortunate head—hairdo excluded—to go five or five and a half times into her total extension. Her total self-absorption left her more ignorant of than indifferent to the impatience of those annoyed by her crafty reticence and facial games. She had long fished in the overfished waters of women's experience and with smug conviction always told Farol she deserved more than she was getting, advice given not out of any kindness, she merely wanted her to be as dissatisfied as she was.

I once did a painting of them, one I hesitated to show Farol. Three hairy bumchums squatting around a kettle, its steam death-red and a a lot of backshadows in the witchy trees. Hysterical morts with ice-cold vulvas and twats like empty wallets, their faced stopped out with rubber cement and made leprous white. A cat's howling. Midnight. Drisk. Mauve cloudfists. I called it *The Mares of Glaucous.*

Farol, needless to say, was their star turn for looks. Their ugliness actually needed her beauty. The problems she faced with men because of it I think secretly excited them and gave them a kind of priapic envy and anger, all at the same time. It also won for Farol a sort of grudging tolerance, a crude regard born of her power to dazzle which they allowed—she conceded wisdom for it—as long as she knew enough to keep their counsel. Their clever knack in taking the offensive while pleading persecution proved effective. She began to show them an unexpected compliance which she often tried justifying to me, and for a while I tried accepting it. I wanted her to know I understood all the implications of her stupid job and its pointlessness.

But then I made small headway, for it turned out that every time I began to gain trust with Farol, somehow like a serpent Scrulock would slip out of the surrounding shadows to murmur something that putting iron in her gave her doubts all over again.

I often thought with dismay that Farol more highly esteemed those who thought alike, in preference not so much to those who thought differently as much as to those who thought at all. Silence cannot be exploited. And so she became a listener in their presence and showed to them in the face of their matronage the requisite doubt and deferral. They didn't understand their enemies were her friends only because she wouldn't reveal it. As long as they had her fealty, she had their friendship, attending on them, acting in their cause, obliging their whims. She did much of their work for them and repeated their words and in the worst instances gave me the impression of a sturdy yard dog frantic and slavering with the pleasure of performing and reperforming its feats of guardian service. It was desperate to have to watch. And yet I honestly believed she longed for family, some kind of shared vocabulary, a sense of inclusiveness. But *there?* And with *them?*

It frankly surprised me they were concerned with her at all. They disapproved of just about everything outside the grasp of their own dexterous trafficking, but their concern with her was mostly in relation to men, specifically to her husband, whom they advised she leave, and to me, whom they exhorted she drop. Under their threefold scrutiny we had no privacy at all. They came between us all the time, unsubtly, subtly, in every way. There was no winning them over to the way of things. They were just there, loud and insusceptible and relentless. And it wasn't only us. It was everybody. I never heard such gossip.

Gossip was history there—they helped shape it in language bold to coarseness whenever they lacked the occasion to be obscene which while fastidiously pretending never to be they always were. They went into furious monopologues, criticizing behind their backs everyone they knew, getting hold of the larger doings of perhaps ten or twelve people in St. Ives and making them out to be national tendencies. Jumping to conclusions was the only exercise they ever got. They got offended when others talked while they were interrupting. They were certain about everything in spite of their limited and skewed experience and became like others I'd known who worked in locked and departmental-ized environments the self-appointed guardians of morals and manners, civics and culture.

At times it became almost laughable. I remember how often they would ridicule and vilify the quality of the artwork that came into the shop, derisively holding up various pieces, as if their *framing* were art! I couldn't believe it. While others went on with their lives even if hap-lessly trying to put paint to paper, these mean and inefficient stooges clapping together ready-made sticks for that work actually tried to rep-resent themselves as being able to criticize it!

I began pacing through the lobby, I couldn't bear thinking how someone so dear to me could be left to the malice of these swart crows who seemed perpetually working in primitive exchange only for another victim to be brought down and, like themselves, buried among the very graves they sought to violate. To see such a person offered to fools amounted to sacrilege. My thoughts wandered as I waited.

And eventually Farol came whistling in. She brightened when she saw me, then quickly recollecting where we were looked immediately uneasy, peering nervously over my shoulder in the premonition of us being observed. She suggested we go outside and talk. I shut the inner door and kissed her.

At that very moment Mother Scrulock suddenly appeared, standing there shaking with rage and looking like one of Goya's frog caricatures in the *Visión Burlesca,* the creature with the nuts and bolts. She became almost apoplectic. *"Nobody closes a door"*—her voice was like a mangle eating shirts—*"in* this *shop!"*

But my foot was already off the floor. I never saw it closed again after I kicked it off its hinges.

Outside, in spite of herself, Farol gave me her tallest whitest smile.

11

And that night we met at the school gym. Farol seemed different. She'd gotten a haircut. She was prettier when her hair was left longer and brushed down—when it was too short it brought out the long and square aspects of her face, and I mention it only because I thought her failure to see this indicated a deeper artistic one. She was wearing a new green Northface jacket. She told me it was a gift from her husband, which gave me an indication of how things were, that is until she added she accepted it only to please him. Pulling close to me, she nuzzled into my neck and whispered, "I'd rather be wearing you around me It's been so long. I've missed you terribly."

We walked downstairs, talking happily but inconsequentially, and entering the squash courts through a door in the back wall, threw onto an upper ledge our coats and car keys. Farol asked nothing of what I'd been doing lately nor did I question her. She taught me how to play squash. We established a routine we always followed thereafter. There was usually a few minutes knock-up, then the best of a set of six, though we often played more, and finally the trek downtown where the loser had to spring for chocolate malts—but never, before we left, without her doing that ear-splitting gorilla call through the high empty courts which pierced the ceiling and came echoing back, *"Wooh-wooh-wooh-ya-ya-ya!"*

She seemed happier. I saw an antic side to her I came to love. She walked purposely dink-toed. She made faces with a sidelong glance from her sparkling eyes. She always went comically cross-eyed after a lob below the service line or a resonant shot to the telltale. I once inad-

vertently hit her above the eye with my racquet, and she clumsily
bounced balls off my head. We never argued—mostly conceded, in fact.
I was a smoker. Whenever I groaned, she'd tease me with a parody of
a childish taunt, "Baby, baby, baby." Then I would make a good shot
and always with that understated sarcasm of hers she would say in lilting mockery, "My hero."

St. Ives students before curfew occasionally stopped to watch us
from the overhead gallery, usually falling half in love with her before
the game was finished. She was fascinating to watch and admire. Farol
had a gorgeous swagger, a lithe athletic body—strong, even large thighs
and back—that only in bed looked better than when perspiring in those
blue sweatpants and feathery-yellow T-shirt she bounded all over the
court in a bright blur.

Farol was curiously competitive. Much of the time she was casual
enough. But she was always her brother's sister in sports. And her sense
of competition left a spot of the metallic in her charm. I always lost
our matches at first and out of necessity had a relaxed detachment. But
she often got down on herself for her awkwardness, running with boyish determination into the hard white walls, her red-and-cream racquet
swung at a scold, only to miss and muff. She played wildly and with a
kind of reckless anarchy, scrambling, going for backhand overheads,
reaching to spank shadows where once the ball flew by. She was always
falling. It was as if in a sort of strange lopsided way she were not built
to move easily.

She had weak, poorly turned ankles and small feet for her size.
Her legs, wide to narrow, had the shape of crutches. They had little
twisted faces on the kneecaps. And I was always reminded again and
again whenever she wore shorts that her calves were oddly shanked,
sloping narrowly down without form from the comparatively large
thighs that embarrassed her. I thought she might have had rickets as a
child.

We played a lot. And she was always game for more. But I felt
a fatigue in her blood. She grew tired easily. During these games her
face often grew very red, her lips white, and she'd become strangely
spent—which I found odd because she didn't smoke and looked otherwise in superb condition. She always needed to drink a lot of water, so
much so that when playing squash it often broke up our games, intervals during which at mid-play we often just sat on the floor and talked.
I noticed this particular time she'd grown quiet. I asked her if anything
was wrong. I was always asking her that. She said her maroon face

embarrassed her. I laughed and kissed her, looking of course for the glow on her face that this often brought. But her mood changes could be abrupt. And this time I saw only sobriety.

"I think you should know something," she said.

My heart froze.

"Two years ago, when John and I were going through a bad time, our marriage looked like it was over—he hadn't spoken to me for weeks—and I had a scare. I've mentioned something to you about this, but I didn't tell you all." She plucked the gut of the racquet she stared at. "I got up one morning and noticed something was wrong. My hands and feet were useless. The tips of my fingers were without feeling, like they were asleep. I found I had trouble walking. I was dizzy. My vision wasn't blurred, but I remember panicking. We immediately drove to the hospital, and I was given an examination. The diagnosis"—my throat was literally stuck shut—"well, it wasn't clear at first. It was uncertain. First the doctors thought they knew what it was, then they didn't." Tell me, I pleaded silently, tell me. "When we found out, I remember, we came home and both sat down and cried. There was this paralysis. It lasted for three months." But there were no blundering words. She wasn't baffled. It was a cold factual report. "I guess I've been meaning to tell you this for some time." She looked away, then closed her eyes. "They diagnosed it as multiple sclerosis."

It can hardly be imagined the effect on me this last portentous sentence had. The processes that engender tragedy are often said to be inevitable. But my breath was taken away.

What beastly frustration she had! It seemed iniquitous. Beauty plus pity! Where there is beauty, I thought, there is pity for the simple reason beauty must die. Beauty always dies. I felt only stupor. This intervening secret, I imagined, affected everything for her, an unspoken agony from the beginning. And I had wondered why she was tired! She apologized for having to tell me. She mentioned the feelings she first had of anger and bitterness and of the therapy that followed. She said she willed herself not to have the disease. She spoke of risks. I didn't know what to feel or think or say. I wanted to save her. I wanted to take her dear sweet self and bundle her in the warmest blankets and hold her in my arms and kiss her face until she melted. I ached for her and hugged her desperately, miscalculating in my confusion all I tried to make of the roaring and rushing injustice I suddenly saw everywhere. I knew there was nothing, ever, I wouldn't forgive her for.

"I'll take care of you," I said softly. She stiffened, almost superstitiously, and lowered her head. "I never want to have to be taken care of," she replied.

There was a long silence.

And then she said, "But I need you." She paused. "Can you see that now?"

It was late and the empty location made it seem even later. I got up slowly and shut off the lights, the last in the gym, hating the macabre and ghastly unimaginable blue it cast. We sat on beside each other, faceless in the pitch darkness, way past the hour, but how long we stayed there in the silence for a final saving sense of all that had been disclosed I can't remember. I recall only an awareness of something vividly never happening as it did and of being left touched by the vibration in a resolution beside me, however battered, not to be beaten. I touched her face and kissed lacerations. We kissed and kissed again, deeply, and in the solitude of that lonely place, deliberating no longer the torments of the obscure and fatal program that had brought us together but simply struck and inflamed by the suffering need that is at the heart of that love which acting otherwise only abandons it, quickly fumbled off our clothes and right there on the floor passionately made love.

The Wicked Monarch waited at home, but in another kingdom two lonely but crippled stepchildren overwhelmed in the intimate night that left no community any longer other than themselves had fallen into each other's arms to kiss away and hug away and love away all the sadness and pain waiting for them in the terrible world outside.

"I love you," I said to her.

"Oh, Kit," said Farol. "I love you. I love you too."

12

Our lives became intertwined now in ways I wondered about. We were together so much that I was now suddenly facing, and uneasily, pretty much the same situation she was, with the added twist that while I really knew neither John or Farol Colorado well I was seriously becoming involved in making a decision about both, one—it was becoming clear—that might affect my entire life. The dangers we flouted, the risks we took in being seen, sometimes left me breathless. "When you go home late at night," I asked, "what does he say? Where does he think you go? Is he ever suspicious?"

Farol would only shrug.

I wanted to ask, but didn't, if her husband knew about me. I thought he must have known. But what about her? "Do you ever worry that he'll find someone else?" I asked. She murmured, "That's what he should do. He'd better let someone love him before it's too late."

I noticed about this time she stopped wearing her wedding ring. And I mentioned it. She said she didn't love her husband anymore. And there it stood. Within such an arranged situation, expressing commitment but fearing in the conviction of giving all the heart all the soul, we continued to see each other. Among other things, I was concerned for her health. Sometimes I took her to lunch and sometimes I took her a sandwich at work. ("Where's ours?" Mother Scrulock always snapped. "What did you bring for us?") We left notes for each other every day and were now carefully determining when we could be together. She had Mondays off, and most weekends her husband went his own way, boating or bicycling, and left her alone.

Was he a king or a cup of custard? I didn't know. He was grim, self-inverted, isolated, methodical, nonreligious, nervous, and, I suspect, fighting with a sub-self that was quite unattractive and even possibly neurotic.

Whenever he went on a business trip, we went to her house and made love. Where before I had hesitated, now always I went back. We were like robbers in the dead of night, but worse, taking what we wanted but having the gall to return. At first I pretended not to see, because I couldn't face the man I was cuckolding, but with each consecutive visit my guilt began to compress the victim of my cruelty into an apparition I couldn't ignore. Again and again, he loomed up everywhere, in his books, his clothes, his computer equipment, closets, in the very boots that seemed to move at my approach. He was terribly there. I felt him in my fear like a phantom.

There is a facelessness to the cuckold. Is it because he is always the same or only because one simply refuses in one's mind to see him? He is a creature of holes and gaps and negatives, starkly finite, a ghost unable to cry out. I felt brutish, shabby, desolate. Surely even here the ordinary man begins to catch a fleeting glimpse of himself in the mirror of his own deliberate treachery—the source of dark plotting energy, molestation, and disruption—and to seize in the painful irony all around him what the convex has of the concave. The language of one's own deceit yet calls up that poor man whose cries of black and obscurantist rage can't fail to be heard from the pithead of all he's being cheated of whether he knows it or not. He doesn't have to know any level of category to convey what you can't avoid. Lust is among the saddest emotions. It has no object, only poles and holes. And I began to sense there more than faintly that secrecy is the keystone of all tyranny.

And I felt a sob in my heart, unable to costume the tragedy my fake and compensating sightlessness sought to decorate by duplicity and deter by deed. It was blasphemous. I was captured in a despised allegiance to him, a hostage, both guest and enemy: the stranger in the house. I can still remember no more of him, a great deal, than was ever needed to give proper expression to his features, which I never saw. I felt, while being with both of them, she was the closer presence but a lesser power, a stone that achieved weightlessness while its shadow condensed into mass. He seemed close to lacking existence altogether, yet he bulked up, and does, in such a spate of reverberating and illicit recollections so concretely painful to me that I can still identify in detail all of him that even though missing proceeded to blot me out. I felt hell in the percussive blankness I made of him, and the gun I had to murder him instead shot me dead for all I stole of all he loved, and shot me, and shot me again.

What Farol felt I don't know. I was disturbed at the ease with which she spoke of him and at how casually I was accommodated with what seemed such offhand and unaffected reflection. We sat there on the pale white sofa and drank more wine, but I remember thinking: Lucianus merely by killing Gonzago immediately wins his wife. And it crossed my mind more than once that I might simply be an object of deliberate use for those two cohabitating solitudes to invoke a crisis, set something in motion, begin with calculated art to precipitate for them the comprehension on some plane or other of his neglect and her need. I once mentioned this in passing by way of wondering if she thought they'd ever resolve anything. She circumvented my question for the minute with a thinness of words—phrases—lost to all warmth and flowing out of that certain and select contemplation, I saw, to which I had no access but which like an arrow to its target touched to the center of her archfoe.

She felt a certain power, a justice, I think, in hurting the man whom she felt so often had hurt her. But it was her hurting him that ironically made me distrust her. Our salvation always manufactured to our sin, for I felt in her arms a grotesque contrapositive: if a implies b, then not-b implies not-a. I thought her hating him may have been a way of hating herself, or perhaps a way of refuting her own infidelity. By the way she gave herself to me from the beginning I knew she held her husband in contempt, and yet what she shared with me on those quick and timid trips, attempting to transubstantiate acrimony into ardor, was also and at the same time her way of *keeping it* from someone else. It was at once a theft as well as a gift. She gave away only what she stole.

I was a full partner in all this, of course, in every way. But I was not certain whether to be pleased at our natural appetite or appalled by the rush of unnatural opportunity we took for whatever reason to that advantage. It created silences equal to a great commotion in my ears, for I feared that sooner or later with her I myself might be facing not so much a life I did not want as much as facing another man, another visitor to another interior which I might in my own blindness think mine. If the past was irretrievable, it still controlled much of the present, and I distinctly remember thinking at the time I wanted to remember what maybe one day I might have had to.

We went for drives. We stopped at yard sales. I bought a bird house at one and she an old broken sewing machine. And we visited antique shops. She gave me tours of her husband's garden, which though it was only April had already been staked out and marked in orderly fashion. Squash. Jerusalem artichokes. Corn. Farol explained to me the difference between Golden Bantam and Silver Queen. And onions. These were Ebenezers, not white onions. And then beans. "Pole beans," she said. "They're better than bush beans, which really don't give you your money's worth." I often had to look over to see if she was joking—and always realized she was not. What pronouncements! It sounded as though she were speaking through bamboo.

Unfortunately, she forgot half the time what she'd already told me he'd said on fully four fifths of the subjects she spoke about and was simply repeating her husband's words like a parrot. The trouble was, she tried to make them her own. I never knew anyone so earnest.

I remember many of those long drives. I'm afraid they often purchased more of my time than my enthusiasm. I saw more of that damn state than I ever thought there was of it. New Hampshire has always been cheap, mean, rural, small-minded, and reactionary. It's one of the few states in the nation with neither a sales tax nor an income tax. Social services are totally inadequate there, it ranks at the bottom in state aid to education—the state is literally *shaped* like a dunce cap—and its medical assistance program is virtually nonexistent. Expecting aid for the poor there is like looking for an egg under a basilisk. It places lowest nationally in what it spends on anything. The state encourages skinflints, cheapskates, shutwallets, and pinched little joykillers who move there as a tax refuge to save money. There isn't a significant cultural center anywhere. There are part-time police forces, all-volunteer fire departments, and no municipal water or sewage or disposal facilities. People climb it, and ski down it, and skate across it, but they don't live there in any way that matters.

There is no bottle bill for recycling in New Hampshire, rural-delivery mail is always late, and mammoth diesel skidders and eighteen-wheel logging trucks are being driven everywhere. Deer-hunting season lasts about a quarter of the year. A hunter may legally shoot a dog in the state that threatens a deer. (New Hampshire has an agency whose job it is every day or two to salvage "road kills"—animals run over on the highways—so that the pelts can be sold on the fur market.) It's a state that ranks forty-fourth in the nation for punishing drunk drivers.

"I live in New Hampshire," said Maxfield Parrish once, "so I can get a better view of Vermont." There is snow cover four months of the year. Its mountains, unlike Vermont's, are jagged and bleak and scarred in the north, the soil sparse and acidic. Mud season is long, frost heaves are everywhere, and blackflies should be denominated the state bird. New Hampshire also has had some of the highest winds ever recorded since Enoch hung out his anemometer. You can smell its mill towns before you see them, and half the time you can't tell if it's night or raining or you're just lost in the woods. The lower part of the state is a lumpy, overzoned, hard-to-define diner culture—an illegal dumper's dream. Four fifths of its people live in the southern third of the state which is the grimmest part. Pompous little pockets like St. Ives fool nobody. There are almost interminable road miles where one can see nothing but ugly strings of gas stations, fast-food places, motels, billboards, ramshackle malls, garish signs, outlets and crowded trailer parks. Of the twenty-three or so states having coastline, New Hampshire's is the shortest at seventeen miles, and that is adorned with a nuclear power plant which sits like a wheal in the middle of everything. Its newspapers are among the most right-wing on earth. It has the dumbest bumper sticker on earth—"This car climbed Mt. Washington." And though there's plenty of religion, principle can always be bent, and it's one of the easiest places on earth to get divorced.

I found that depressing, for obvious reasons, and tried to choose a more promising place. This time I drove. Farol was no more easy to please than before; inexplicably moody, she was quite willing to show when she was bored. I once mentioned going to the circus and found no response. I mentioned the Museum of Fine Arts. "I've already been to the MFA," she said, with the same kind of flat and dismissive assertion that one might use in claiming she'd loaded a stapler or learned the alphabet or had her appendix removed. "I don't like zoos," she said another time, at another suggestion, forcing me, I remember, to stifle a remark about the gallery. She seemed dull. At first I thought her dullness was only sadness, and kept on trying. We saw several films at the Orson Welles Cinema in Cambridge. And we often went to the elegant Towne Lyne House on beautiful Lake Suntaug for dinner and to the North End for Italian food.

Anxious to show her something of Boston, I remember asking if she wanted to see the Sargent mural at the BPL, or go to the Athenaeum, or visit King's Chapel. But ignorant of things she tried to make a *virtue* of being indifferent to, she scorned my suggestions as lessons to be learned and remained unimpressed.

It was as if along the lines of some Tartarean punishment the very things presented for her enjoyment took something away from her. When a person nods before you've finished talking, they're almost always telling you to shut up, and I could see Farol felt somehow oddly diminished by what she was shown, even threatened by it, and seemed constantly to have to assure me with just a little too much push that she herself had good taste. I found it sad, and tiresome. And, at times, hard to believe.

Her curious snobbery about eating only in good restaurants—always a convention, in my opinion, of bad cooks—was almost always the occasion, for example, of her ordering a large meal and then leaving half of it on the plate. She was abrupt with waitresses, I noticed, and rarely said please or thank you. I remember we were once joined at dinner by one of her sisters—Lenore, I think—a sour rigid-looking wally with whipthin hands and a disapproving stare. The photograph I'd once seen of her did her an injustice: it looked like her. Long neck, hydra curls, and ceramic-cold eyes. I asked her several questions, which she chose not to answer. When she did say anything it was with a tart tongue and convoluted snippiness of speech. I disliked her on sight. And Farol disapproved of my disliking her, which at the time, I suppose, set a bad precedent.

But there was always this contesting need for Farol to prove herself as good as anyone else and usually by whatever means she found at hand for leverage. I didn't trace it to her father or her husbands or her brother. To me the trouble seemed deeper. I thought in a very real way she was the child she never had and she indulged it.

We had once passed a field of pumpkins the previous fall, and I'd told her that Yankee farmers sometimes fed their pumpkins milk intravenously, getting them to grow hundreds of pounds. She didn't believe me. Once I mentioned a science prize—on electricity—which I'd won in my last year at school. "My hero," she said. Someone else's knowledge meant boasting to her: she had to compensate, by contrast, and compete. Another time we saw a pup tent at a yard sale. As I say, Farol was big for the outdoors. Assuming all kinds of knowledge on the subject, she immediately proceeded to distinguish for me the difference between ridge poles and canopy poles, brace poles and eave poles. These were French seams. That was a grommet. Those were stake loops. I never saw anyone make a meal of something so little. And now the words and phrasing were so familiar that I swear I was able by the process of simple transitivity to tell the timbre of her husband's voice! I kept wondering why she just couldn't be who she was. Ignorance is homely. I began to realize with some surprise that when she tried to hide her ignorance by claiming to know what she didn't it wasn't so much the more stupid she seemed as less attractive.

A huge maple tree that spring had fallen in my yard, and one day Farol accompanied me to the Cape to cut it up. It was typical of her to take up the ax without waiting and wade into the work. I watched her flailing away for ten minutes, the ax head bouncing and bonking off the logs with the promise of cutting her feet off.

"Split logs on the edges, not on the center," I advised. "It's easier."

"The wood's not old enough," she said, bent over double and puffing. "It's too fresh."

"But the opposite's true," I said. "Green wood is easier to split."

She stood up, and her face took on a blunt aggressive breadth. "No way."

And she handed me the ax.

"You do it."

Although Farol generally used me as a foil, almost rhythmically, to belittle her husband, she'd often do the same thing to me in order to lessen her infidelity, or so I concluded, and maybe even convince herself she hadn't made a mistake in marrying that man. I remember incidents.

It was a rainy Sunday, and we were not in love. We went to a bookstore. She was dissatisfied about something, I don't recall what. I remember only that I bought a secondhand copy of Whitehead's *Process and Reality* (1929), a complete and systematic exposition of his philosophy of the organism, one of the most difficult philosophical books, vying with the works of Plotinus and Hegel, that can be found anywhere. Later I told her I couldn't make much of it. "John would understand it," she quickly interposed. So, shrugging, I gave it to her for him. A week later she said rather blithely that he'd read and understood it. I knew at least one of them was a bullshitter. I only wondered which.

And it was the same with her husband's boat. She once unsnapped the canvas for me, unfurling it with a proprietary sweep, determined to show off all she knew of what she assumed I couldn't discern he'd obviously told her. *Strake* was a word she loved. And *clew*. The caviler is always a pedant. But she mistakenly called thwarts seats, charts maps, and lines ropes. (I hadn't the heart to tell her I'd spent half a dozen summers with Tarquin sailing in his dory around Nantucket Sound.)

I came to see over the months now the dreadful irony of how in having to promote herself as a woman with wide interests she had to depend for this identity not on anything she said but, rather ruinously, on what she quoted of her husband. Sadly, the more she cited him, the more she hated him, for of course every truth of his she confessed to somehow made *her* the more false. It was an awful siuation to be in. I wondered if she ever talked about it in "group." She certainly never did with me.

She was so earnest. There was an endearing human resource I realized I'd always taken for granted until coming to St. Ives I suddenly found a place that had none, and that was irony. I can honestly say I often thought that quality missing in Farol sometimes harder to take than her being so relentlessly superficial.

We seldom broached serious subjects on those drives. She talked by way of remarks and in isolated phrases. I was amazed that her speech effectively allowed her to appear seemingly present while in fact she was totally absent. Since she depended on others for a voice, I thought her inability to do more than this was an indirect confession of her own failure. It was as if her mind had narrowed, congealed, to a hard ten or fifteen or so facts she lived by to get what she could. She was not often lighthearted, but that didn't stop her from telling jokes. Not jokes. Her way of trying to be funny—it is often the humor of the non-reader—was becoming fixated with and constantly repeating certain words and phrases she found odd. *Mung beans. Aqua wawa. Maple surple. Yummo.*

Secondhand phrases. Conned mottos. Received wisdom in pellet form. She never seemed to affect any of her thoughts by speech—it was as if her tongue never taught her anything new. She tended to speak of trivial things usually, like the best route to New Rochelle and how her cat was able to fetch and what "gorp" was.

Earnest people are like this: a bit predictable, tiring on the long haul, but helpful and full of information about things like how to detect termites and the many uses of Mylar and the best time to see the northern lights. I heard a lot about bike paths and ditty bags and trail signs and blazes. Backpacks had to have toggle locks, sleeping bags the right loft. Facts seemed not so much to enter her head as lodge there or get stranded. And every time we passed a certain kind of house she would always nod and say, "Greek Revival." I soon realized it was the only type of architecture she knew.

It was as if, almost superstitiously now, she avoided anything personal, leaving to the dark shadows the things she could no longer face, and in this regard I felt no different than I imagined her husband did. It was safer to talk about other things. Boats. Backpacks. Cars.

She loved to talk about cars.

13

As I've already mentioned, my own car was old. Farol rarely missed the occasion to suggest I buy a new one. And so one afternoon we decided to look at some. I have a low tolerance for *vehicles*—I can't stand the subject—and merely discussing them makes me want to chew gum and cry. But let me tell you, she was in her glory that day. I hadn't the slightest idea of what I was looking for. But that didn't matter. She had no problem taking charge.

"I don't like sunroofs," said Farol to no one. "Who needs alloy wheels?" She leaned low into one car—her head disappeared—and spoke to the salesman behind her. "And power door locks are unnecessary."

She talked to dealers like a pro, kicking tires and inquiring about power trains and banging hoods. "Are these all you have?" she asked, slamming the car door. "Because these are overpriced. And so is that one. And that. What kind of financing do you have here, anyway? What percentage minimum down payment?" I couldn't believe it. She was not only competitive, but actually combative. Harvester became scythe. Her directness was a scold, all done on my behalf perhaps, but in her approach there was something disagreeable, even manic. The little she knew always left her views peculiarly amorphous and, because her almost lethal self-absorption usually deflected her mind from anything else, considerably inadequate. But that didn't stop her, not that day, not buying cars.

Farol rose to the occasion with the self-conscious aggression and familiarity of the person, so often denied it, finally given the chance to convey that particular bit of knowledge of which she feels so robustly constituted. It was knowledge of the tactical, practical, factual sort. She loved to show an iron chin in such matters. And although all her questions struck me as rather trivial, where could one find a better place for such a thing? I'd never seen anything like it. What was the MPG? Were these close-ratio five-speeds? Where was the hazard warning? And how about rustproofing, emission control, book values, service warranties? Bam, bam, bam.

I never bought a car, although we drove around everywhere, Epping, Portsmouth, Dover, over to Manchester, looking at every make and model. I didn't mind. But there was something yet, something in visiting those dealerships and showrooms, of her strained and oddly unremitting efforts that left a cadence of real discomfort in me. Couldn't she see she didn't have to prove anything to me, merely accept the simple truth that love manifested itself not by knowledge but by loyalty?

The subject had been on my mind, you see. Several times Farol had invited me to parties in town. They were unspeakably dull, mixed gatherings of painters with local reputations, phony photographers, various craft-and-hobbyists, and loud dizzy women with plucking fingers and snatching elongated hands who made things at home like mobiles and wind chimes and baskets to sell at neighborhood fairs.

Is there anything on earth worse than a provincial celebrity?

We'd arrive at these parties—I'd noticed it before, her theatrical pause upon entering a room—and Farol would suddenly adopt a mood of not wanting to be interfered with. Was I wrong in thinking here was a woman whose sense of privation at home made her fully adept at socializing? She combined an impenetrable personal reserve—actuated, I

thought, by her failed marriages, which she took as a personal humiliation—with a distinct public gregariousness. Ill at ease on a one-to-one
basis, she shone in groups. I was taken by surprise, at first.

Farol was well aware of her good looks and always made a quick
survey upon entrances to see if there were any women present as attractive as herself. She moved in the gallery circle with confidence. She was
tolerated here, she felt, as nowhere else, and it gave a certain cock to her
hat. One moved with her among phenomena mismatched and unrelated.
Nothing in her talk ever matched anything outside of it, but it didn't
seem to bother her, or anybody else. Except me. It caused my curiosity.
I saw her there like a rumor long accepted, maybe ignored, but successful, frankly, by some art that the enumeration of her merits didn't explain and that the mention of her lapses didn't affect.

It was under such circumstances that St. Ives, because of these people, seemed more than ever a wilderness of know-nothings—but where
Farol, whom I'd for some time now taken to be intellectually self-conscious (at times even slenderly furnished), showed another side of herself. Her discomfitingly overpronounced need to secure the goodwill
and agreement of all with whom she came in contact seemed to go un-
noticed. I could only conclude that most of the people there were either
aware of her situation at home or themselves shared the same ardent
desire she showed to annul or reconcile such differences and prove herself of the same cut and quality as everyone else.

I was struck by the fact that she could represent anything, including the gentility she lacked. When she put on airs I thought her doing so
was nothing more than a device for coping with the various frustrations
she was facing both at home and at work. "You swim?" someone asked
her. "I have six-liter lungs," said Farol, laughing but full of herself.
"But I prefer mountain climbing and would rather be in the Adirondacks." She sipped some white wine. "The region's rich in magnetic
ores." As she spoke it was obvious her turns of speech were not only
threadbare but on most subjects acquired thirdhand and punched out
for consumption like filler information in newspapers. Repetition very
quickly becomes insincerity. And I began to find myself listening for
one in order to hear the other.

The most disconcerting thing, however, was that on these occasions
she rarely stayed in the same room with me, leaving me prey to perfect
strangers when I wanted to be with her. Her surprised but nearsighted
reply whenever afterwards I asked for an explanation was that it was a
habit carried over from her husband, who'd always done it to her. But

I thought it bad manners and told her so, asking her why she'd go and do to someone else the very thing she hated having done to her. Was it done to prove her independence to the gallery people who were always there?

They were everywhere—and were never more visible than at their "openings." I attended more than a few with Farol. She had social needs of this kind. Wine. Cheese. Reception sandwiches. It wasn't that she particularly liked social events (she claimed she hated them)—or fit in—she merely found assurances here she needed and took a sort of philistine delight in being part of a select circle who knew her. Why did it bother me so much? I suppose I saw framed somewhere on something like the bile-green walls all around the two of us in some picture, in such an awful place, and became unhappy at seeing in what pleased her only what I found so unbearable. The pretentious people. The twee remarks. The scribble and shirk they called art.

All the while her silence made me more critical, her disapproval of me, more disgusted. My lack of mercy brought no art to my observations, let me add, only contempt, and filled me with derision for what she seemed so willing to ignore.

I should explain that St. Ives was full of what were called "creative people." I love that expression. Most of them were imposters who in their squadrons of cutouts and convulsive oils and pop icons used primary forms (cones, spirals, etc.) and materials (stone, earth, etc.) as an expression of some kind of horrid environmentalism where lack of talent took refuge in feckless attempts at self-improvement. And because an artist there was usually someone who made art mean the thing he or she *did,* a person became an artist by nature of his very own definition, whether knitting nose cones or thumbfumbling margarine or dipping his nose into alum and wiping it around on a linen canvas. I thought much of the work frankly psychotic. It was all washline clothing and String Art and Dude Ranch Dada. Gumballs. Abstradjectives and hooplesticks. What cobblers!

And that was the serious work! There was literally no end to the other stuff—the sort of things usually eliciting the response "What a fun *idea!*"—predominantly the creations of hysterical middle-aged divorcées who made things like cornhusk bags and clay antics and mystery arbors and personalized mugs and shaggy sheep vests and scented candles and nonfunctional ceramics and dried-flower arrangements and stone jewelry and wool hats and pull toys and titanium brooches and facade appliqués and bead belts and burnt-wood art and crocheted tea

cozies and laminated rolling pins and floral embedments and porcelain
cats and woven dinner bags and soft-sculpture dolls and handpressed
Christmas cards and pot holders and nesting boxes and place mats and
driftwood lamps and clowns on black velvet. I never saw so much hand-
wrought, hand-woven, hand-rubbed, hand-fired, hand-forged, toss-it-up-
in-the-air-and-see-what-comes-down horseshit in all my life.

Farol's face was always quick to narrow in anger—a tightness to
her forehead and a stubborn set to her jaw—whenever I made a quip
about such things. At first I thought her merely grave. The earnest person, often a self-improver, stands at the shoreline of art casting a net
that does not extend very far in the direction of irony or irreverence or
humor. And I always had to remember she had ambitions along this line
herself and thought of herself as an artist. Which was fine, I suppose.
The only trouble was, the closest she'd ever came to art was saying she
had no time to do it.

The gallery was locally thought of as a center of culture, and these
openings drew the same people from the same town who went to the
same parties for the same reason—it made a nice change. I had the pleasure of meeting them all. The wimp wonderment group. The mineral-
water purists. And all the other locals. A fat man named Mr. Menager-
anian who sold rugs. Harvey Frakes, a dean at St. Ives and a photog-
rapher of local repute whose skin was so transparent and white it
looked like a coating of food glaze. Jerry ("Jolly") Jumfries who had a
crush on Farol. Two poofters, Gary Woodvile and Cory Wallpoodle,
wore each other's bracelets and were into Found Art. A manic depres-
sive, Paul Jawcelf, had his own loom. The Yawnwinders, David and
Cornelia—I called them "Snowcone" and "Frisette"—sculpted things
out of shrapnel that looked like cannon snouts and wharf bumpers and
pig-creep feeders. And of course there was Neil Ringspotz, who worked
in gold jewelry. I remember him one night laughing out loud—he
didn't know me—over something I'd said in admiration of Farol.

"You find her *pretty?* Come on! Give me a break! Hasn't she been
married to half the male population of southern New Hampshire? I'll
bet she has more diseases than you could stuff into the cunt of a cow."

Then he covered his mouth. "Oh dear," he said, "do you mind my
saying that?"

And of course there were a lot of preppie women full of refine-
ments and angles who came to these things. They all used three names,
like Sarah Munster Townshend and Phyllis Grisley Colmore and Marge
Jackson Mixter, but were usually called "Cokey" or "Poky" or "Mopsy"

and were horribly energetic and ran boutiques and wore wraparound dresses and sunglasses on top of their heads. They were the kind of people who cultivated tans in January and listened to public radio and left ski tickets on their parkas until late July. The expensive earrings they wore did nothing to soften their overtanned faces, which were cracked and leathery like catcher's mitts, and all spoke with that basic preppie honk that had ripened over the years into a hoarse crowsquawk.

Most of them were heavy smokers, drank bourbon, shopped by catalog, carried Bermuda bags, and drove station wagons whose interiors smelled of dog, and all had spoiled teenage daughters with names like Tracy and Cybele and Kimberly. They liked to think of themselves as political and had completely exaggerated ideas about their capacities to function as women. Except with men. All those not divorced had what they called "creative marriages," which always got them into serious discussions about alternate ways of living like founding fruit farms or running off to transpersonal communities where they could wear dirndls and play zithers and get into self-expression and find themselves. "I'm into Relaxation Techniques," said one. "Oh, Polarity Therapy and Total Person Facilitation Training is the hot button now." "Well," said another, "I'm fascinated by nutripathy and macrobiotics." And yet another: "I first opted for a clothing-optional life-style, then thought why not go the whole nine yards and become a nudist?"

They always talked a lot about money. Some had inherited it, others had married into it, but most had gotten it from divorce settlements. It actually depressed me more that Farol took them seriously than that she liked them and tried to ingratiate herself with them.

And of course it was always great ramping fun at these get-togethers to meet Tweeze, Scrulock, and Gumplowitz again socially.

I remember leaving such an opening one night when Farol happened to repeat something Scrulock had said—it had to do with alimony—that echoed with a kind of metropolitan knowingness everything I loathed and despised in that woman, in all the worthless opportunists who hung around there, and, most of all, in myself for what all along I'd been doing to her husband.

I asked if she approved.

"Why not?" said Farol. "She's a survivor."

"And that's a flattering term?"

She stopped.

"Why?" I asked angrily. I had spent too much time alone that evening. "Go on, tell me! I think it's unforgivable, don't you, a person's

willingness to take advantage of another as a thing to be used? To survive? To live on top? Stepping over people? Choosing survival before
honor for the sake of saving your own skin? Rifling the world for what
according to its lights it feels it deserves but which almost by definition
isn't enough?" I was almost shouting. "But it's never satisfied, is it?
I'm all right, jack!"

It was me that was speaking but it was Farol who lost her breath.
My words hung in the air. I suddenly stopped under a streetlight.

"I hate that word—*survivor!* It never dreams," I cried. "It only
aspires, acquires, appropriates! It stinks. Doesn't it? You don't think
so? Cheating? Grabbing? Shoving people out of the way? Scheming to
own what owned by someone else it nevertheless sees as stolen from
them?"

I hated myself for yelling. And I hated the word. But what saddened me was something else.

For a minute, I almost hated her.

14

There was a lot of sadness that first year. I didn't know what Farol
really wanted, and she feared the tentativeness I showed because of it.
Conviction makes for consideration. As proof of any confidence, or
some sort of prospect for our free association in the future, any words of
love for each other seemed dim. I was no longer convinced she wanted
to disclose anything to me that grew out of her thought. Thought
seemed to delay her. Between thought and action there was no discernible gap.

I thought she entertained a strong impulse to say something personal, something violent and deep and important—at least important to
her, but she was too often engaged in a sort of "rope reasoning," a
vague chain of partial resemblances between components, where nothing was clear. The words on her lips were rarely spoken, but when
spoken—and only on those subjects she had appropriated as hers—they
were mechanical and secondhand and adapted from other people's
views, and I had the sense not that she didn't know me well enough as

much as she didn't know herself well enough to dare sound her own heart.

And yet even when she did make the attempt to confide in me it sounded insincere. She often seemed not to be telling me something but arguing moot points that never led anywhere, anywhere, that is, to deeper understanding. When I thought that I knew what she was asserting and what she was alleging as the ground for it, I often failed to see how the latter proved or made probable the former. I don't even know myself what I wanted from her. I only know what I didn't want—and on many of those days together found it.

One afternoon Farol had to feed the cat and taking me by their house made it the occasion of giving me some vegetables from her husband's garden. The construction of it was amazing. His garden looked like the Shevárdino Redoubt. It was neat, elaborate, and professionally intercropped, with each square foot of ground utilized and every plant meticulously mulched and staked and tied. I recognized him in the precision. But I felt uneasy and was anxious only to leave. I remember telling her it was the last time, that I would never go back to that house again. And so we only went on more drives—shops, museums, an afternoon by the ocean—returning always before dark to part sadly and silently, no closer in truth to each other really for what we said or planned than the gnarled elms at distant intervals lining the street down which we passed, always I feared for the last time, the mute self-chastisement in the car being levied against all four of us, Marina and John included, and whatever might have made us striking together or at least significant apart was lost utterly in palpable guilt. It made for striking ironies.

"I'd like someday," Farol once exclaimed, "just to walk openly down the street in the sunshine with someone who loved me."

And whom you loved?

But I said nothing. I couldn't. I merely let it suffice that I shared the feeling.

I certainly understand her frustration at having to spend the rest of her life shrink-wrapping prints and snipping mats out of paper, but she seemed only to want what she couldn't do. It was always the way with her. She seemed to find solace, not so much in the memory of deeds, but in the memory of past anticipations. She tried to engage me in contests. Several times she ran next to me around a track and got winded and couldn't keep up. Once she challenged me to a swimming-pool race and lost. I also remember her weeping at her incompetence on the golf course. We had been lugging heavy leather bags and racking up twelves and thirteens until on one of the holes of the back nine she flubbed her drive four times. She had to play well, of course, and immediately. A slice on the next try went bonking off several trees like a pinball and plopped into the rough. I called her, lagging, after I found it. "Go ahead," I said. "Head down. Eyes on the ball."

She swung and missed.

And again. The harder she tried the worse she got.

"Try?"

Again she swung. Divot.

She stood still, staring toward Canada.

Gritting her teeth, she tightened her grip and sucked air.

Whooom, again. She riffled the air.

"Fuck."

This time she swung so angrily and so hard the club head sank into the ground like a hatchet. Barely able to conceal her fury, she stood there, her eyes misting over, and asked, "Can we go?"

We visited my house on Cape Cod several times—increasingly I wanted her to know me—and I remember that first occasion well. I'd forgotten my house key. And when we arrived I had to crawl through a tiny cellar window to fetch a long heavy ladder, dragging it through the bulkhead to reach a high window out front. Farol directly grabbed one end of the ladder to help. I was pleased by that, her putting a shoulder in, and though a small act it told me largely of what it was our power to become. I remember she didn't seem to like my house much. She took little notice of the paintings, a MacKillop, a Cahoon, a Paul Noble James, some Eichenberg wood engravings, and merely walked around with her hands in her pockets in silent appraisal.

We had stopped by Tarquin's summer house earlier where I drew the same lack of response showing her, among some of the family's paintings, an extremely stylized Derain of an early period when he was at his best; a series of beautiful Hiroshiges; two Quelvée landscapes, and a fairly rare Utrillo, not one of the Paris series of streets he did demonstrating perspective, fine as they are, but a picture from the white period, about 1910, and painted in Brittany.

Afterwards, I showed her around my grounds, four acres of rolling land that gave way to a vista in back of the quiet salt marshes. She hadn't much to say, and I admit much of the tension was my fault. Her being there, and not Marina, was disquieting to me, and I know Farol sensed it.

I remember later that afternoon while I was showing her some old books and papers and things a packet of letters from Marina and some photographs fell out. I scooped them up with visible embarrassment. And it was then that Farol mentioned she could talk to Marina. Talk to her! I couldn't believe my ears. About what? Trail signs? Toggle locks? Our affair? *Me?* I have no idea what she intended by it because I never asked.

On a subsequent visit to the Cape, however, I decided to tell her all about Marina, whose name had long been preamble to the silent presence I knew she felt in the house as well as in my heart. It was either that or leave her to the more harmful conjectures I thought might only make her ill. And of course it was long in coming. Farol always found fault with her in anything reported, as I did with her husband, which is why we'd spoken only of our duties to them, our obligations, our frustrating ties.

Deceit is a cruel debt. I felt thick with guilt. It oppressed me. I decided to show Farol not only Marina's photograph but several paintings I'd done of her. Farol said equivocally, "She's pretty." I explained the situation in full, what I felt at the time for the girl in the room, love, and what I felt for the ghost in the room, less. And yet I knew Farol inevitably felt there in the cold loss of confidence the sleuthing heart assigns itself of insufficiency what I myself had felt at her house under similar circumstances that mournful winter week that seemed so long ago. I thought that momentum nevertheless bore some evidence of being broken when we went upstairs and made love, as now became our custom, but just as we set off in the falling dusk to head back to New Hampshire something happened. I locked the door to the house and was walking toward the car when I turned to point out the bats circling my chimney.

Farol said they weren't bats.

"They're swallows."

I said, "They're bats."

Nature was a point with her.

"Swallows."

"Farol," I said, "swallows resemble bats. It's in the wing shape. And they zigzag the same way. But I'm telling you, one of those once came into my bedroom."

A hard face shook negatively. She was tenacious. "You're wrong," she said.

She was smiling angrily at me.

I was astonished.

Then I understood what she was trying to say: *those may be bats, but, don't you see, I'm the one who's supposed to know about such things? Don't you see, that's all I know? Can't you let me know it? Can't you care?*

And it was then I knew that neither of us was going to be rushed into anything. If there was in all this an admixture of both cordiality and contempt, as to me upon recollection there seemed, other feelings had also boiled up. It was strange: two personalities coming together can create a third, with each being different, yet together making up one they are surprised at separately.

We both knew as we stood there, actually more disappointed in ourselves than with each other, that we weren't speaking of birds or bats. We were speaking about our fears, we were speaking in a way about not talking, we were speaking above all about the deep and desperate need for the benediction each of us wanted from the other, who met only stern disregard, who found no transfiguration, who no matter how hard we tried still remained unblessed. We might live. There was yet no ransom. We might want to reign together. But there was no resurrection.

15

Farol was both single and married all at once. We would possess her, as it were, in rotation—me physically, her husband psychically, or maybe both of us in both ways did both—but everything she gave to me reminded her precisely of what she took from her husband. In fact, being with one of us almost instantaneously created a sense of obligation in her for being with the other, and so pain informed pleasure, as pleasure did pain, of what in one mood was summoned by the other.

And frustratedly I began to feel the reflection in looking at Farol in relation to her husband of a similar moral dilemma with myself and poor Marina. It was almost unearthly, puzzling me, to find a back door on each of four sides of a building. We were going around in circles, untogether, as it were, where four equaled two, and two equaled zero.

Perversely, there wasn't room for love in those we no longer *could*—
only responsibility, custom, habit, and obligation. We couldn't forgive
ourselves for what we wanted to forget. Forgetting was unforgivable. I
remember, for example, telling Farol I had to go to New York for a
few days in May to be on hand for a small exhibit of mine being held
of some seascapes I'd done the previous summer. She wanted to join
me; she couldn't, of course, which hampered her in upward struggle,
making her incoherency of sadness much larger than the consolation of
love for her I assured her, in leaving, I'd feel. It didn't seem to obtain.
But then what did? "I have to make a decision, I have to," she kept saying. "I have to make a decision."

Our every embrace was also a separation, our sudden reunions, as
if by definition, only comments on our continual division. I told her to
leave her husband. I honestly thought she should. She told me she
couldn't, not yet. I continued to bring the subject up until, when I
didn't, she thought me too indifferent to bother. She found herself to be
in a contradictory system in which, weakly, she was interchangeable and
yet, willfully, without substitute. Arrogant, then abject. Having alternately two men and none left her personality eerily uneven, up one
minute, down the next. Abject, then arrogant. I couldn't bear the insouciance of her flexible recuperations, and yet I pitied her for them.

Our deepest feelings seemed to be built on nothing but their own
opposites, which left a semantic void—the accepted discourse becoming
only the spoken to the broken word—for we had regressed to a kind of
prelingual state, a strategy of indirection by which the unsayable and
unutterable and unmentionable revealed what most they concealed. And
I think for the first time since knowing Farol I understood why her husband might want to be free of her. It was as with adulteration. We
mixed her. We mingled her. But it was surely because of a changing
perspective she herself caused or in some way engendered by a deprivation of one thing that made her selfish for all. She changed moods daily:
one day cringing, another confident; one day determined, another diffident. She seemed to live a kind of reflected life that was not really her
own, but someone else's, who'd come from the long dark past.

She was coming by now every day even if it was only to tell me she
had to leave, and yet she was postholing at such wide and divergent intervals that there was no knowing what would come next. I wasn't
painting; it took all the powers of my imagination trying to disentangle
the motives of her behavior. She was an enigma, understanding and
compassionate on the one hand, heartless and posturing on the other.

An announcement on one visit was annulled on the next. There was something almost psychopathic in the way she met with inappropriate energy on a given morning the very problems that enervated her by afternoon. But by so hysterically imposing herself on me, she incurred the very rebuffs that increased those very same self-doubts that made her continue to force me into a détente I wasn't ready to make for precisely that reason. I soon came to look upon dreams of her as dire warnings of something about to happen.

I never knew from one hour to the next what I'd see. She had three prevailing moods: deep depression, brief excitement, and obvious boredom. She was supportive at one time, at another she mocked my enthusiasms. There was something in this—not only mocking my enthusiasms, but her need to mitigate kindness—that became too constant for me to think her well. Uncertainty pleased her just a shade too much for me to take her seriously whenever she sought assurance. She found something basically fraudulent in uncomplicated emotions, calling up, as perhaps they did, all that was missing in the way she lived. Every one of us has his or her adjective. Hers was *inconsistent*.

I began to be concerned about her almost neurotic irresponsibility. She had such pent-up rage. She expressed it in headaches, fatigue, ill health. I thought it possible she was unable to compete with her husband's irascibility and quick temper or even relate to the intensity of his tyrannical loudness and instruction and so became periodically ill as the only outlet. I wanted, both weakly and willfully myself, to avoid the evidence of it, but all the evidence suggesting that it was only in putting up the most violent opposition to the marriage she had that she was seeking to contract another bode ill. I loved her but couldn't tell how much I *cared* for her until she ceased suffocating me with feelings so irrational and impulsive and yet so insistent, while changeable, that I grew to be burdened by them, for I couldn't put paid to the fear that much of it was only compensation for the unpronounceable guilt she felt in cuckolding her husband.

In the oddest way I was interested less in what she told her husband than what she confided to herself. But no simple declaration of love could ever remain uncomplicated for her, for while a long computation in her mind, based upon a thousand reasons, was marshaled to disprove it—the refusal to accept with brutally limited self-tolerance what secretly she despised in herself coupled with the genuine fear of not daring to accede again, through vulnerability, to what again might only break her heart—she at the same time felt she deserved it.

The very thing she emotionally needed she intellectually felt obliged to try to prevent. It was intake and output all at once. And it made me wonder: did this woman want *everything?* But I was looking into a mirror! I swear, I needed her half the time to condemn what I thought of myself for finding those very insufficiencies in her I alone made. What emotionally I needed I loathed myself in the mind for doing as well, and in this I was her twin. Don't extremes meet? When all is said and done, isn't it really the glutton who exercises? The pornophile who always has a palate full of prayer?

I felt one incontrovertible fact. She needed men, more than even she cared to admit. One part of her never knew it—or refused to accept it—another part depended on it. And while I found no reason to assume she made a collection of such episodes, a mental album of declarations and refusals, I secretly felt at bottom she'd come to care for any fellow *not* likely to accept her, that she was ready—poised almost—to suffer her fate, not necessarily to know it, as if truth were so precious it could not only not be known but had to be guarded by a bodyguard of lies, which is to say that in the knowing of herself so well she could only be disappointed in having to model herself on someone's estimable image of her, so couldn't accept anybody so dim as to love her not only in spite of but for her imperfections. She had to be told she was loved, so to speak, to be able to tell herself of all she was unworthy of. Or was it only to feed a monstrous ego?

I couldn't believe that. Maybe I couldn't bear to believe it. My reflections on it even now are crooked and demented. Adulterated colors always get darker, grayer, muddier. And if Degas is correct in saying that a painter paints with the same passion that a criminal commits a crime, he only means that both reach to steal in an utterance a word for their own fabrications. Judge me only by what in blaming another for I have trouble admitting myself. Everything vertical wants to fall. I was Farol, twice over, even in being alone.

I came to the conclusion that she had to be loved to be told what she couldn't give, and yet wanted to be disliked for it, severely, that might be confirmed what was finally the truth she felt about herself, that loving me but made her a base betrayer—an adulteress.

Her coming to see me was a desertion, her going home a capitulation. These were irreconcilable opposites. I thought in knowing herself so well she couldn't accept anybody who would have her so readily. What she appropriated she had to give away as being undeserving of, but what she lost told her precisely what otherwise she felt she also deserved. There were alternatives. But there was no choice.

There was, however, Elavil.

No wonder she began taking it—a dosage of four tablets a night prescribed by yet another psychiatrist named Dr. Solomon to combat the fits of long-term depression she'd been having that were now becoming real black dogs.

16

I felt the infection. I was part of it. I feared her illness was behind much of it, something she faced every day with dawning anguish and intimate horror, a malaise so vivid in effect yet enigmatic in cause that it filled me with thoughts touching every misfortune, and yet I was facing a riddle for the penetration of which I hadn't a single password. I only found standing hugely above us, throwing its shadow, a Spouting Devil—some grim, equivocal, veiled, and faceless figure about to lower its dread and diseased hand.

Such a threat couldn't stand. I have always had a theory that one gets lost not by anything one does but by what one leaves undone. The way to keep from getting lost is to stay found. I wasted much of my early education failing to see this. We were often taught in school by insidious suggestion to smother the remarkable and inventive within us, to swallow the same fanciful drives by which we were personally notified of our own worth. That became the cause for the longest time in stifling within me a pressing need to communicate, something made paradoxically significant by Dr. Trinity, the very man whose questions were never asked to be answered. I remember at one point refusing to do so any longer. It has made me a person with a profound hostility toward authority, intense, rebellious, verbose, fantastically impatient, at times bold, and even gregarious, which has always made me suspicious of groups. I have a genius for friendship and also a genius for the reverse. I have the imagination of disaster, but I dream.

Truth is trouble. So what? I decided to follow one stream downhill—or, to put it another way, not to follow the old custom of leaving all the unexplored areas on maps intimidatingly white. "See with one eye, learn with another," said Old Mr. Madwed. And he was right. One didn't possess one's soul unless one squared oneself well, in fact very hard indeed, for the purpose; but in proportion as one succeeded, that meant preparation, and preparation had already been slow. I wanted to help and to help I had to know something.

And so I called an old friend of mine, Dr. Derek Schreiner, and told him I needed to talk. I rarely saw him more than several times a year, as he was very busy teaching at the Harvard Medical School. We had been friends since Yale. I drove to Boston that night in the rain, he lived in the North End, and we went to an old Irish pub in Jamaica Plain called Doyle's, had dinner, and talked. He who had seen me happy with Marina over the years was saddened to see me—uncharacteristically—without her. I told him about Farol, everything I knew, and then listened to what he had to say about MS, its mysteriousness, and how so little was known of the disease.

It was thought to be a viral infection, he said, as deep a symbol of mystery and dread as blindness, even more so. He spoke of focal disorders, impaired senses, bladder dysfunction, paraplegia, intention trauma, of relapses and remission. Women had a higher prevalence and incidence of it than men, striking in mean distribution, he pointed out, those generally between the ages of thirty and thirty-five. He mentioned that one of its features was alteration in emotional responses; sometimes patients developed in mutual change euphoria—a pathological cheerfulness or abstract lack of concern—and then became depressed, irritable, and short-tempered. I thought I had the textbook case and never felt more disheartened. And Derek could tell. But was I sure it was MS? Had it been properly diagnosed? Had I ever heard of Huntington's chorea? Or amyotrophic lateral sclerosis? Or hysterical paralysis?

I didn't know, I couldn't say, I wasn't sure. I only remember as he talked thinking over and over: *darkness in painting is necessary to show light. Darkness makes light.* And then: *light transforms darkness.* What else could I think? I felt so ignorant and sad. And I was completely powerless. I thought of Farol's strength and physique, how much I loved her, the future. I asked him if one has MS whether it could affect or be affected by pregnancy. He looked surprisingly put out with me and told me plainly, "You never had MS, you *have* MS!"

It seemed so much like Farol: so much she had I couldn't see.

"Has she ever been pregnant?"

"No," I said.

"Was she ever injured?"

I recalled the tobogganing incident, her brother's bullying abuse, a minor car crash in a MG in which she once told me she'd been involved. I also saw her in a vivid platinum flash before my eyes running, biking, swimming. Her laughter. Her glory.

"No."

"How long has she been in remission?"

"Years," I said. "Two or three, more maybe."

That puzzled him.

"Has she been, I don't know, thwarted in some way or other?"

"No," I said. "Well, she fancies herself an artist—"

"A painter?"

"Whatever."

"And she isn't."

I shook my head.

" 'The impulse to create,' " he quoted, " 'is more elemental and far-reaching than the sexual urge.' For Otto Rank anyway." He laughed. "Not me. Anyway, Kit, what about emotional trauma with . . . ?"

"Farol," I said.

"Has she had any?"

My heart sank.

I reviewed for Derek the dense crush of leaden correspondences she faced in the black relics of two failed marriages, a father's unforthcomingness, the resultant weariness of lost ideals and wasted effort, our own confused involvement, and the malevolent fingermarks she particularly felt in having accomplished nothing of personal success in college or through a career or by creativity. I mentioned everything I could think of, the gallery, group therapy, the prescription drugs. I told him she was so confused, ill equipped to erase in herself the long depressing days she at once felt she'd caused and yet for which, in having been traduced by, she remained so ill disposed to accept final responsibility.

As a girl, I explained, she'd lost comfort in the severities of the Dutch Reformed Church (she briefly attended, she told me, in high school), and that experience, another solace flown, compounded by a disappointed faith in a disappointing father—prefiguring, perhaps, what in her future husbands fate had arranged for future defeat—left her a woman not only with a terrible dependence on the need that assured love alone can provide but also with a deep suspicion of its ever being possible. Life and happiness, as she understood them, contradicted each other. "She seems selfish only for a misery she feels she deserves," I said, "the student subjected to the lesson by which, simultaneously, she becomes the teacher. Who wouldn't be ill? And isn't that her illness?"

We returned to Derek's house, still talking. He thought it possible her problem might have its origins elsewhere. He pointed out that we were having an affair. Had she had others? At the time of her illness, for instance? He wondered if her paralysis mightn't have been the symptom of some fear or scruple against sexual love on her part. I told him she had no problems with sexual love. He smiled. What about sexual excesses? I knew nothing about other affairs. I realized how little I did know. Variables were the only constants, and my thoughts running on only emptied the pockets of my mind.

I was exhausted driving back the fifty miles to St. Ives, I remember, and for some reason went straight to the Catholic church, I don't know why, where for an hour or so I sat staring at the altar. I saw paradise painted and hell where the damned broil and my high accessibility to impressions on either side made my misgivings complete. A custodian then came by and told me he had to lock up. And when I went outside it was raining harder than ever.

17

I left for New York two days later, pages unturned, *i*'s undotted in my mind about Farol's illness. She was constantly in my thoughts. Before I went she wrote down for me her father's business address and telephone number in Manhattan and told me if I had time to stop by and say hello. She seemed to want this, though she'd never said much good about him. Quite the contrary. And so while this seemed unusually generous, I had the impression there was something in it of the remorseful daughter determined to make last-minute amends for any false charges she might have made but felt in the end mightn't stick.

The opening in a gallery on East Tenth Street was the usual affair: wine, skimpy little wedges of winceyette, and a lot of sympathetic, refined, and inquiring nancies and noddies in a low tide of attenuated gabble revolving around the room with their thumbs hooked in their waistcoats and that settled gloom of countenance supposed to indicate comprehension and deep deliberation. If anyone noticed I wasn't there long, I wouldn't have noticed myself, because *I* wasn't.

I was over at the Frick Collection looking into space: I mean, the

planned expanses, creating depth and illusion, of some specific tradi-
tional work I had to see again and also certain abstract nonrepresenta-
tional aspects of other pictures that fascinated me for what, so to speak,
was missing or unconfined. I called Marina long-distance out of guilt,
which her innocence only exacerbated, and that night went alone to
hear *Tristan und Isolde* at the Met. I stopped by the museum again the
following morning and then spent that afternoon in the Bronx at the
Multiple Sclerosis Care Center buttonholing a few doctors with questions about the disease and reading whatever on the subject I could get
my hands on.

And the next few days I went shopping and bought a neck chain
for Farol and for myself some brushes, a roll of good linen canvas, and
a beautiful icon (one of my weaknesses) inscribed in Old Church
Slavonic.

Then I went to see Farol's father. It was characteristic of me, I'm
afraid, not to have telephoned first, and so when I landed cold at the
Bulgari offices on Fifth Avenue in late afternoon and asked for him I
suddenly got that fatal-to-everything feeling in my stomach of being
exactly somewhere I shouldn't be. I wasn't wrong. Mr. Sprat appeared
suddenly in a doorway with a scowl of doubt on his face registering
interruption. His ungainly way of dodging in with a furtive glance of
precaution, his lips and eyes wide open but unreceptive, gave him a
blundering effect. He looked like a man expecting to be robbed.

"Who are you?" he grumped. "What do you want?" I noticed his
lips were curious in being the exact shade of swarthiness as his face,
which showed itself to be a tight fit. I think he feared an endless and
atrocious visitation. But from whom? I gave my name and said, "I'm a
friend of Farol."

He acknowledged me, nodded, and sucked his teeth. His hand-
shake was thick and seemed to have a touch of malice in it. He never
smiled. *Orphaned,* I thought.

Strange to me, he was most unlike her. He had an iron pumper's
head and was bullish and stoutly short with a sumo wrestler's face and
eyes—almost as if he had undergone some degree of racial alteration—
and big shaven cheeks, certain leading features that led me immediately
to accentuate and fill in, as to stony ugliness, what I'd known of his disaffiliation and detachment, and with heavy lips that remained gridlocked
he took me upstairs through nooks of lusterless light to a tiny office that
smelled of oil where, sullenly at first, and then with some softening, he
showed me a bit of his work.

"You don't have to pretend to like it," he said darkly. "Say it's good. Say it's crap. Same thing."

"It's good," I said.

"Same thing," he muttered.

He finished eating a chipped-beef sandwich while I looked around peering at some sconces, epergnes, and silver bowls with elaborate circling filigree he'd helped design and at some other unfinished work, little metal animals he was in the process of hammering out, filing, and twisting into whimsies of gemmed metal. This last was undistinguished stuff but predominantly his line of work at the company. It was clever enough—I said so—though silly. He waved at it all and shrugged. He looked liverish. His ears looked like the rooster hammers of a shotgun. He sucked his teeth loudly. He asked me, "Ever worked in metal?" I said I hadn't. "Don't matter." He gave me a sketchy idea of what he did. He spoke of thrumming and swaging. This was paillon, that was tang. "Don't consider it art," he said picking up one of the animal figures. "Never did. Never claimed I did, either."

He was cooperative but brusque and reserved and spare with words. He had a noisy bigness of head, so big it had the effect of being magnified—its baldness had a shine that seemed bountiful—but he said little. He gave nothing away.

I felt a graceless rigor in him and an impenetrable self-absorption, of the kind, however, that didn't produce ideas but rather ruminated on the ones already there. I could sense a sterile force, authority, humorlessness. I tried to look through him for a second to a child's small world, but in vain; there was nothing discernible beyond. We were both discreetly aware all the while, needless to say, of a third person there in our midst. And of her there were a hundred things I wanted to ask, fifty I wanted to tell, but of course I said nothing. I brought up his daughter's name several times in the general exchange, but he asked nothing of her and only smacked his bluish lips. Not once did he mention her name. I thought instead of a heart he had a lump of fat. I remember once thinking of Farol's lot being in direct contradiction to her lineage. I was wrong. Pugwash, Nova Scotia, fit. Perfectly.

They were up against entirely different things was all I knew and, if related, related in some fierce disagreement, some deep and incalculable estrangement I knew I'd never understand or fully fathom. I was sure of one thing. She was in competition with her father—not to outdo him, but to win him over. I thought of the long campaign that all this involved, her drive toward art to have his approval, and took warning within to be careful. It had to do with something I've always believed. The person unable to *make* is dangerous. A criminal is a creator gone wrong. Those who cannot create will always destroy.

I remember, for some reason, telling him as I left that Farol loved him. Maybe because I loved her. "Good-bye," he said abruptly, turning away without a smile. *Unloved himself,* I thought. Mr. Sprat obviously disapproved of the men she associated with—not without reason, I thought. And who was I to tell him he was wrong? I left with a secretary the book I'd brought as a gift and was gone. I flew back to Boston the following morning, returning a few days early.

Reaching St. Ives around noon I stopped by the school and immediately called Farol at work who drove over to my house, I remember, in what I thought was record time. She was wearing jeans and an old blue and gold University of Michigan sweatshirt with the sleeves rolled up. She was perspiring. I gave her the neck chain. She kissed me and, laughing, gave me a coffee cup with a multitude of copulating bunnies all over it. She seemed excited and undulating with news. She said she had a surprise.

I asked what was up.

"I've moved out," she said.

18

We drove to a small white colonial house with peach-colored doors across from the prep school and something less than a quarter of a mile from where I lived. I remember the feeling of being happy for her but also of being drawn into what was suddenly a rather extraordinary circle of incidents—spring term was ending at school and I'd soon be leaving for the Cape. She unlocked the door and led me into a musty hall and up a stairway of frayed red carpeting to the second-floor apartment, a narrow passageway leading to a single large room with one closet and small walk-in kitchen. She was exhausted, she said, having driven over one carload after another the previous evening. She kicked aside a drop cloth and said it needed curtains.

"What do you think?" she asked.

"You're painting it?"

"White."

There were boxes scattered everywhere, cartons of books, clothes, and kitchen utensils. An old red tin bread box, a sewing machine, an oak chest. Dishes. I saw leaning against the wall the print with the empty chairs. I found the few items depressing. This was all she had after two marriages. On a low round wooden table was a majolica sculpture of a kneeling woman, and some plants, and flat on the floor a plain unadorned mattress with a single rumpled sheet. She said she needed to buy a sofa bed. Another room, another shift, another divorce. And no bed!

I thought it perversely symbolic. I didn't have the heart to ask how she could be left this way. I wanted to inquire, with some acrimony, why her *first* husband wasn't helping her out financially, and how even after deserting her he felt no responsibility, but the impertinence of the question was pulled from my mouth before I could speak. And then it struck me, I didn't even know who he was. He didn't have a name, a face, an occupation, a discernible past, or even an identifiable native tongue. And I didn't want to think of her second husband, for all the blame I felt. Who deserved his reproaches more than we?

Theirs was not a legal separation. She said she needed time, and perspective. The whole thing had been discussed at "group." Goes without saying, I thought. I feared a hasty misjudgment on her part, and fought an image in my mind of lowered shades, pulled curtains, and isolation. I was trying to pay attention to where all this led simply because it made for all kinds of possible alterations in the formation of our plans, ironically enough, by clarifying them! I realized Farol would be living near me now. I knew she'd have a good deal of time on her hands, and I wondered if I wanted that. And yet I could not, how could I, turn away. I felt anxious because she had become for me something of an absorbing passion, a woman indulged in to the neglect of other obligations, and yet one so unindulged and neglected herself, it seemed to me, as I looked at the mess she now had to face in terms of another adjustment.

I stepped over some dismantled shelves, moved a box of toiletries, and made a general survey. It was such a closed-in place with everything jammed in and much to do. We shifted and rearranged some things. But placing one thing here only seemed to challenge something else over there. There were long silences which I intermittently sought to fill first by plugging in a radio to get some music (she mentioned her husband refused to let her take the stereo) and then giving her a cursory report, with tactful omissions I might add, of my visit with her father. I told her he sent his love. She listened with interest, and seemed heartened, but there was a trace of inexplicable sadness about her as we lifted this, moved that, and tried to put the place in order. Then she set a box down, hard.

"Please," she suddenly cried, "this was not a decision I made easily."

I hadn't said a word!

It was suddenly brought home to me that my sense of finding her content was merely a projection of my own wishes.

"Did—he agree to your leaving?"

"Who?"

I looked at her.

"We agreed," she gloomed.

"I only want everything to be right for you. I wonder, will you be able to afford it?" I could feel her attention lift from her weary limbs to a need for understanding. "Can you—get along?"

"We talked about that at 'group,' " she said. The very word struck me as nonsense and made me want to scream. "I'll continue framing."

That expression.

She looked at me for a moment, as if listening, and then leaning against the window closed her eyes. An eerie presence looming suddenly in the room seemed to affect her. She shook her head slowly and in a low voice that had less of shame in it than wounded pride finally admitted, *"He's* paying for it." She sighed. "John's paying the rent."

I should have known. I suddenly felt his forgiveness. He loved her and wanted her back. What was wrong he hoped would be made right, something, he felt, better achieved by absence than by argument. I let pass over my mind what I didn't care to welcome, that maybe soon she might come to oblige him. So, he was not what she said he was after all. Strangely, his generosity had the effect on me of diminishing her. Nevertheless, I saw I was her husband now who wasn't, and converted in consequence he now wasn't who was. I also saw she'd been sundered from a faith, no matter how weak, in which she had been schooled and felt in the sudden freedom she faced the terrible burden of it. Love, even much of the uncurtained portion of it, is strangely built upon secrets, and feeds on them. In a way, love itself is a secret. When it's lost or disappears you can never tell anyone what it's meant to you—and sometimes can't even remember yourself.

"I once read that the best revenge is success," said Farol. "You know?" I thought: *revenge?* "I'll sew curtains. And paint the walls. If only I had a draftsman's table, I'd draw. I'll be working. And I want to take a course at Bradford in sculpting." She turned and looked at me. She'd grown suddenly tired with enthusiasm. Something never left this mood profligate in her. There was now no intoxication at all. "There's lots to do," she said.

"That'll keep you busy."

"Busy," she repeated.

I tried not to hear that. I sat down on the mattress and tried to assure her everything would be all right. I remember trying to convince her, even when I couldn't convince myself, of acting in favor of what she thought was right—even when in that spasmodic way of hers she attempted to regulate the very thoughts that shredded the moment she tried to put them together.

I doubted her interest in art. I was convinced she actually loathed the creative world and all it asked of her as only another thing of the many there were that reminded her of what she wasn't. The various artists coming into the gallery not only generated an interest in her for what she couldn't do but at the same time made her suffer by comparison for her own indirection, incapacity, and lack of production. She claimed to have artistic sensibilities—perhaps she meant appreciation— but I'd never seen a sign of it. Talent is work, more than anything else, getting an idea from one place to another as important as getting an idea. A hobby's actually a way of getting *away* from work. I'd never seen a thing she'd done, her understanding of painting was nonexistent, and yet there were these continuing aspirations. Her father's aspirations, I thought. Her father's *approval* of her aspirations, for hers were half-hearted and certainly unformed if indeed they were there at all.

At the same time, my disregard for Farol's lack of talent was worse than the fact of it, and because of that I felt unworthy of my own. Why did I refuse to share with her any of my techniques, even the fundamentals of contour drawing? Of the shading of an apple? Of a face?

No one is finally talentless, and the closest thing to such a person is the one who begins saying otherwise.

We were sitting on the mattress next to each other. I felt an uneasy silence. We'd arrived at the flat only an hour earlier when her excitement over her solution to contract out showed at least part of a slanting revelation, a sort of euphoria felt on the brink of this huge, daring, and desired readjustment to the world. Now something had gone missing. She seemed to feel her power disappear in the emptiness. It was a waiting room. Summary with sadness, too swift to joy, with long protracting and detaining intervals—that was Farol. She seemed like a lost little girl. And yet sometimes I wondered if she had ever been a girl. She suddenly got up. A song called "Desperado" was playing on the radio, which she quickly snapped off, and shoving her hands into her pockets she lowered her head and started to cry.

"Are you—undecided?" I asked.

"No, but you think I am," she sobbed. And I did. "That's why you're sorry for me, isn't it?" And it was.

"We're both sort of locked up."

"Not you." She was clasping her arms as if she were freezing. If there were times when she looked young and vulnerable, there were moments when she looked old and used, and the transition took place sometimes in a matter of a minute. "Not you. You're free. You can do what you want."

"All I do, which isn't much, is all I could ever do," I said. "All I could ever do was read and draw, paint little pictures on paper and dissolve myself into situations where I've been little more than invisible."

"You're free. You don't know what it's like for me. You don't appreciate it. That's what I think sometimes. You don't appreciate it. Suppose *you*—"

"I don't think we ought to quarrel."

"Who's quarreling? I'm just telling you how it is—that it's me that's locked up."

"Please, Farol."

"Locked up. And I can't get away. Not really. Get away to see people that don't think of women like me—" She paused and looked rueful and had a hunted expression in her eyes.

"You're being unfair."

"No, I'm not," she said.

"To yourself."

"I am not."

There was in Farol something I couldn't close my eyes to any longer. She was hopelessly self-referential. I mean, once she had made up her mind—in the illogical, leaping, overconfident, and often self-defeating way that she did—no argument whether from a lover or a husband could ever make the slightest bit of headway. There was just no debate or distraction, only the intensity she brought to bear with startling and incredible swiftness upon the focus of whatever deed she found necessary to perform. What she was ready to start, however, she immediately began to fear she could never finish. I tell you, this was a woman who started things she couldn't even begin!

She sought simplicity, and immediately mistrusted it. If she was always beforehand with rapture, regret soon followed. What exhilarated her also provoked her. Action untaken taught her fear. Fear unaddressed prevented action. Furiously, she often couldn't proceed in time with her desire to act but dwarfed in the discomfiture stood in the pause frenetically planning where she should be from where she was supposed to begin, hideously neglecting both. Farol actually looked decisive in the same way foolhardiness looks like bravery. Humiliated by her inability to take deliberate action, she acted impulsively all the time. She may have lived with her husband all along in theory, for example, but at one point she never again did in fact. It wasn't that she wasn't concerned about him, or that some of that concern didn't linger, but it was over and she knew it was over and she had to find some worth in herself as an alternative to not caring in order to exorcise herself of that fault for whatever it was she suddenly and stubbornly decided to *do*.

I began to think she wanted us both only in the sense that she felt she deserved all she could have. It wasn't only an impossible situation; she thwarted its ever being solved by keeping it that way, for she always had a dozen plans ready for consideration which in the conspiratorial disconnectedness created by two contrasting selves always amounted to the same thing—nothing. She couldn't define the nature of distinctions, distinct though she'd have them, and what was formerly clear to her often became clouded. Why was she surprised she failed so often? Why did this so amaze her? It was ridiculous. How could someone ever succeed who in the realm of the imaginary sought to identify with what immediately became opposition when looked at through fact.

She balanced by check, forging and uttering at the same time. All misdemeanors are initially the same. It's the degree of punishment levied that makes one a felony. And she punished herself, in effect, for the crime she saw she caused in the aimless aspiration of finally doing nothing with her life. I found, for instance, that when often she had completed a miserable picture of her thoughts, she was actually thinking specifically about nothing at all. I discovered that when she tried to imagine things about herself, there was never any success taken from it that she used, only a sense of fearful obscurity, a kind of quaking tangle not to be understood but filled with desperate wishes that quarreled with one another. Even in brighter moods, elevated by some arbitrary whim or wishet or other, she'd be suddenly and impossibly thinking about everything. She constantly used these words: *nothing, everything*. But where everything is open to question, nothing is. I had the strange impression in all of this that she was deliberating how to feel when she heard the ultimate call. But were there ultimate calls?

Hadn't she once said to me that she'd always defined herself by what she wasn't? Accepted. Understood. But what was she? And who? I wanted to know. If I persisted patiently in pursuit of that employment, however, she herself wouldn't. It agitated her and caused her inexpressible distress, and despite her toing and froing was in fact the last thing she wanted to learn. She wouldn't discuss it, only hide and bury her face under a coverlid from which nevertheless I always heard a little girl's voice come up, muffled, begging to be preserved from the evil spirits that walked in the darkness and to be saved from the bottomless deep ready to swallow her up.

She once told me she adapted. I began to doubt it. I began to think, no, I began to feel that of the many things about her that might be said, that was precisely and exactly the one thing she couldn't do. Adapt.

"I've made such a mess of things," she said. I hugged her, tightly, and kissed her swollen face. I tasted her tears on my lips; they burned and stung. Her shoulders were collapsing as I held her, and I could feel her breathing hot upon my neck. She looked down into the street, almost pleading for a word that would tell her at least one of her dreams might go on unfolding as reality. I wasn't sure even then which one of her dreams it was. I knew only her wishes for a real world, just like mine, could often be frightened stiff by an answer.

Farol leaned her chin on my shoulder and continued staring out of the window. She was quiet for the longest time and then—much to my astonishment—said, "I'm tired of always being on the outside looking in." I wiped her tears, and repeated that everything would be all right.

"Oh, can we go somewhere tomorrow?" she asked suddenly. "Just the two of us?"

"I'd love to," I said. "Where?"

"I know just the place."

19

We went to Plum Island.

It was a quiet drive. But our drives were always quiet, with Farol's hand on my knee and mine on hers, a simple communion I loved but with little exchanged of what in substance I didn't want to exhort and I imagined she was disinclined to interpret. We made remarks, casual observations. We didn't want to disappoint each other, I think. Her silence often made her seem shallow to me. I thought she remained shallow out of the fear of experiencing deep emotions, that intimacy, closeness was seen by her as something dangerous, something that might expose her to the pain of rejection and disappointment and potentially disturbing self-discoveries she feared might get out of control.

We crossed a bridge, passing a remote stretch of flat low-lying marshes and malodorous tidal pools and were soon bouncing over a section of rut stretches—I could smell the sea—into a little dorp of un-inhabited summer shacks and boarded-up shanties hugging the sandy shore. There was an odor of rotted wood with a salty blend of other waterside smells. I saw rusty discarded oil drums. Seawalls everywhere were crumbling. The stroller who didn't belong was forced to recognize it in so much exclusion. A few signs said: *Private Keep Out.*

It was a deserted and lonely place, with no people about and some-thing haunting in the air on that gray day of the forsaken and van-dalized which I've always associated with empty vacation resorts. Farol slowed her car down to a creep, negotiating the rough sand strip be-tween the clammy conglomerate of huts and faded beach shacks on which wood, wire, and sheet tin overlapped at impulsive angles. She seemed to know where we were and along the way pointed out gulls and rock basins fringed by fronds of seaweed and misshapen terraces of beach that could only be glimpsed through broken palings and slanting old maroon snow fences yet to be taken down. A few battered boats sat corroded and mouth-down in the sand. I smelled the damp seasmoke and distantly heard the thudding waves.

We drove to one end of the promontory, turned around, and head-ing back she slowed down again. She said nothing. She pulled over at one spot, got out, and pausing briefly to inspect some weeds in a pool silently walked ahead of me with her hands in her pockets all the way down to the beach and out along the desolate stretch of shore. I followed her. I saw wet split boards and bights of bleached hemp. She stared out, breathing the air, and then turned as if introspectively to survey from memory to moment what seemed all familiar and yet bittersweet to her.

I asked what she was thinking. She hesitated and then nodded to an abandoned little house beyond and told me that for a year she once lived there.

I felt suddenly cold.

"Alone?"

She nodded.

"When?"

"After my divorce."

I felt my throat close. "I thought you lived in Concord."

"I did."

"And worked in a hospital."

Again she nodded.

"Which you left."

"Yes."

"Why?"

"Hospital politics."

"And you came here?"

"No," she said, kicking a stone. "No."

She seemed nettled and cross with me.

"After my first marriage," she said, "after. When I left Syracuse. That's when I came here, and that's where I lived. *There.*"

I wanted to talk. But I fell quiet. I resigned myself to the weird cavalcade of entailments and entanglements, omissions and truncations our intimacy only contributed somehow to deepening and making the more confused. But I felt nettled and cross myself. No relation with her, I realized, could ever be so short or so superficial that it couldn't hurt you. She didn't want to talk or confide anything. But she needed to call attention to herself. Not for anything she'd done, she'd done nothing. It was interesting. Her need for attention was more a measure of her failure than her success. She walked to the car with a certain preoccupation, and I joined her, unnerved and fully wishing I weren't there. *There.*

Morbidity, I realized, can make a person selfish and gloom unreceptive to solution. I once thought it was because she wouldn't share that we got nowhere, I was wrong, it was because she wouldn't think! It was as if she imagined that by not thinking she could alter the unwelcome patterns of her life when quite literally the reverse was true. I began to feel her idea of reality was only to escape it. I thought: *the most interesting part of a movie is the audience's faces.*

She headed in complete silence to the other side of the island and followed a marked trail into the bird sanctuary. She began to depress me. I'd truly come to loathe this extracorporeal detachment of hers. I found it hard to keep a grip on my sense of humor and my affection for her at the same time. I asked questions; she answered axioms—or not at all. "The first bird guides were written by painters, you know?" "Who?" she asked, eyeing me doubtfully. "Alexander Wilson, the Scot. And Audubon," I said. "You have his sticker on your car." She said nothing in reply. There was only the white air of her nonutterance. It wasn't her conditional and circumstantial life. The only mind is a reflecting one, a mind curious and anxious to learn. I was tired of her received notions, her pugnacious and idiosyncratic prejudices put in phrase. Her verbal formulas demoralized me, for in repudiating talk and what it touched of real thought she repudiated trust. Her tenuous moods prevented talk, and when she did talk her tone always created the impression, as in abstract painting, of space advancing and receding at the same time. *Homage to the Square: Departing in Yellow.* Josef Albers. That sort of thing. But, good god, this was a circle!

Farol was at home in the stillness of this forest preserve—thankfully, I saw she'd undergone a mood change—and taking out the binoculars she'd brought began to peer about. She suddenly pointed to a snowy egret, which she said was rare. One would have thought she had more pressing things to worry about. But, no, her eyes were only for the whimbrel and the grebe and the tufted titmouse. I thought she might change into a heron. Oh, it was serious business, I saw. She was painfully conscientious in the enterprise of searching trees and bushes and horizons for certain birds she knew, all information on the subject being equally welcome, to pass on the news she always proudly held on physical nature. Frankly, being natural is one of the most irritating poses I know in people. Still, I suppose it lifted her burdens.

As her eyes roamed the glint of green between her lashes might have been borrowed from the setting or simply belonged to it. Farol said, "Damn people, over on the footbridge."

I watched her.

What *was* it about campers and bird-watchers and hikers? I had often noticed before that affection for nature in certain people is seldom untinged by a touch of superiority and contempt for things human. I slowly pondered that, sitting there watching her. "They come here, walking around, and think they own the place." And then it came to me all of a sudden as she sat there with her bombadier glasses peeking into the trees that nature freaks—some of the most artificial people I know—are fantastically misanthropic!

I realized this was her dominion, her garden, a wilderness, imparting its importance and dignity, whose mystic fancy forgave her faults and blessed her for all she knew of it. Here was a chaos that dispensed without valuation. It leveled matters, in fact. You can be alone with a person, you can't be alone with a tree. The violent but always victorious expanse of forest and field diminishes one's errors and lets one play the deluded game of being above or beyond consequence, lost in the headiness of a wisdom disclosed to the chosen but incommunicable of course to those of less spiritual provision. And yet while it improvised a kind of space not socially available to her, a communion of utter simplicity, it was obvious that Farol was looking in nature for the things missing in her soul and with an aggressiveness that undermined the sweetness of her life. And the pretense was that while it appeared to be a strategy to cope with, it actually *avoided* the problematical. That I thought was the travesty.

And that I thought was the fraud. The spirit that claims to be in awe of nature's marvels is often a spirit that tries to usurp them. I thought she showed not so much *more* feeling for birds and plants and trees than for humans as much as a deeper, more desperate need to manipulate them to her ends. Nothing obtained here she had to defend which let her assert or deny anything at will. It was just the kind of place with its peace and unimposing quiet that allowed her the rich opportunity not so much to expend any sanctified feelings as much as *assume* them, and in the process, let me add, display some of the worst examples of pedantry I'd ever seen.

She would beckon me silently to see a bird or duck I somehow never could. It was all rudimentary to me, though I struggled as best I could to enjoy this solitary specialty in which she seemed so correctly versed. There was a sniffing sense of authority when she spoke, something more academic than genuine in her delivery—the repeated rote of the tour guide—and I'm sure I was hearing the voice of her husband once again. She introduced me to various birds we never saw with her wonderful imitations. She did a wood thrush (a liquid *quirt* and low tut-tut), a field sparrow (a gentle *tsip*), a whippoorwill (a low grunting, something like *dack dack*), and, what I thought was her best one, a brown thrasher (a loud smack, a plaintive whistle *ti-you-oo* or *wheurr* and a sharp click).

"How do these birds survive in winter?"

This struck her as very funny for some reason, and she laughed in the charming way she often did of clasping her hands while falling backwards and holding them against her breast.

"They go into the evergreens and puff up!" she said.

She hugged me.

Appreciation made her happy—I don't know what I'd said that had affected her so—but happiness made her trustful, and trustfulness made her talk, which of course made her serious.

And it was then that she told me about Lloyd.

20

Lloyd was her first husband.

I was not allowed to know his full name. It had been a hasty marriage, lasted less than two years, and was apparently doomed from the start. He was short, Slavic, and had a beard. She was brash, stubborn, and unthinkably young—twenty-one years old. They'd met through her brother, who was one of his friends, which wasn't odd, she added, because everything that was drab about her brother was also drab about Lloyd. (The very name, sluggish, and dull, itself seemed to bear a load.) She heaped scorn on the whole experience. "It was a proper little wedding, all white satin, baskets of roses, rice, old shoes, and bows tied upon the baggage. Syracuse, New York." She shook her head glumly. "Almost ten years ago." She said it seemed like another lifetime, a century ago, which I thought very long ago indeed.

She always spoke in a knowing, exhausted way about men. When it came to accounting for this one she had a choice as to the length and elaboration of her history.

She told me he married again soon after their divorce. (She added with a settled sense of pleasure that his second wife looked exactly like her.) I was given enough of the history of their courtship to conclude nothing could have been more forced and passionless, that is not until I was subsequently told something of their married life. And the years following. She seemed to become vaguer, however, as the story got darker, and it was soon obvious she wished she'd not brought the matter up. I got facts, versions of things, in strips and shreds as usual. She was defensive and stiff as she spoke. It was all truth, no doubt, but not all the truth, I was sure of it. Much was missing. There were errors of addition. Turning points she avoided, transitions she skipped by. Scorpions slept in unsatisfactory sequence. Whole years I heard nothing about.

It was an unavoidable fact that Farol hated the past. To me the past never seemed what it was, but only a continuation of the voyage. It was clear as she continued speaking of the years after her divorce that she pretended she didn't remember places she did or lovers she had. There are certain spasms of shame in faces. No words on her part, however, always disjointed, frequently disguised, attempted to solve what only words could, whether of the past or present. I was frankly much less startled by what she said than by the temporizing way she said it. Even as she spoke her speech gave evidence against her own understanding.

The painful ordeal for her in having to speak, never mind explain, led to the continual risk she felt of having what she said make fun of the very person saying it, which is why I detected fabrications in her words of both utterance and repression *at the same time!*

Farol was determined, as I saw it, to say nothing that might discourage me in what of her past I might conclude. I found it, oddly enough, discouraging. And yet she was always calling for someone in a sort of muted scream to help her, to answer her, to love her. It wasn't only her unpredictability that made her lonely. In the secrecy and shame by which she sought to put something in a better light she also forced herself into a cruel condition of interiority. I knew what I meant by exactly what measured to me, for what was missing in me I was at the same time trying to give to Marina, and it was impossible. Love is not only a talkative passion. Language itself can lose chastity and in its ambiguity become also depraved, as when on the adulterous tongue two meanings that should remain separate become suddenly coupled. A parody of communication begins to take place. And soon all distinctions are lost.

Still more, how could contradictions correspond? And if this first fellow she married, or the second, was a metaphor for what she thought of herself, what then was I? Wasn't I more or less simply a restatement of rather than a solution to her problem? Hadn't a pattern been set? Wouldn't all her marriages be failures? Wouldn't ours?

"What did your first husband do?"

"He made me miserable," said Farol.

She strove to flatten out as she sat and folded her arms grumpily.

"He was an engineer," she sighed. "His parents dominated him. We had to drive hundreds of miles every weekend, every weekend, to visit them. They expected it! We were ungrateful, see, if we didn't. And oh you had to be grateful for everything. Letters? Thank-you notes?" She grew disgusted. "They gave us a refrigerator, I remember. I wanted to tell them, 'Tuck it!' And his father. Oh, his precious father. Whenever his father took one of his famous naps, everyone had to walk around on tiptoe so as not to wake him up." Her eyes was focused on an outdoor gloom. "I was a jerk."

"Didn't you complain?"

"They wouldn't allow it! Anyway I wanted to please them in the beginning, show them something. I was your good little Farol-doll"— she sarcastically worked her head and arms with wooden marionette-like jerks—"and at first, well, I guess I wanted things to work out."

"I mean complain to—"

"Lloyd? I would! I would complain! But what good would it do? He'd fall asleep. That was his solution to everything. He'd just put his feet out and fall asleep. Let me ask you, would you call that a marriage?" His falling asleep—I suppose I could picture that. Her ambition to discuss, to communicate, to probe? That took a bit more imagination. She was squirming through to a destination in her own way, that was clear, but as she spoke I couldn't help but hear a vigorous, angry, and pursuing sound within her, a sort of drumming incantatory oath repeating *I survived, I am surviving, I will survive.* "Seriously, you wouldn't call that a marriage, would you?"

"Were your parents against your going ahead with it?"

That struck a nerve.

She looked at me from the corner of her eye, brooding, waiting in a long dark pout.

"Yes."

"Why did you marry so young?"

"I felt mediocre!" she cried. "I was flattered someone wanted me—

anyone! I had no sense of self-worth!" There was that tremolo in her voice I always heard of rehearsed psychotherapeutic anguish, the whimper from under the blanket of darkness crying, "Hold, hold." It may have been vague terror. She was furious. She began to weep and reached for a handkerchief from the straw tote bag she always carried. "My father never encouraged us to think otherwise! Wouldn't you find that a little distressing?" I nodded unhappily. "Don't you understand? We never measured up. I think my father was ashamed of us. He never said otherwise. He never said anything. He never once said 'I'm proud of you' or 'I love you' or 'You're as good as anybody else.' Never!"

Quotation does but scant justice to her rage in this regard. The fund of contortions and objurgations, tensions and collapses on this subject were literally bottomless. I thought hers was not a whole mind. It was cut neatly in half right down the middle, a division between adult and the permanent child. I also saw she was an injustice collector.

She glared angrily at me—or was it at *him?* Her husband resembled her father as he slept. I saw Farol but I heard Lady Macbeth. If her father weren't her father, I felt, he would have been one of the men she most hated. She did hate him, I think, so tried to outface by love all she couldn't bear to face otherwise. I couldn't fail to feel her great unspoken anger toward him and wondered if hers wasn't the case of a child in some immutable nursery ritual having exalted the father she'd now come to loathe for his having disappointed her as an adult. In every point twice done and then done double. It's a paradoxical madness to hate someone you love, and I thought it gave her phobias.

As I say, Farol seemed unable to accept somehow that she was no longer a child, and yet she left you with the distinct feeling that nothing in her life had ever been done *for the first time!* All we did, spoke of, everywhere we went, our very existence together seemed as if acted out in some kind of secondary environment she'd seen or known before. She seemed in spite of the facts to have done everything and been everywhere several times. In fact, marriage was her only adventure. It alone gave any definition she had—much, she liked to imply—but there seemed no breadth at all. It wasn't that she had a lot of experience, she merely had one experience a lot of times, and her wantonness was only her ignorance.

The tragic aspect was that part of her wanted to be identified as experienced and part of her did not. She wanted to convey a kind of kinetic sense of independence. But she was also terribly dependent on men, which left her appropriated and static. In other words, while she went about giving the impression of being proud, for which she hadn't the slightest reason, she was also incapable of being humble, for which she had infinite reason, and it made her behavior erratic. But it wasn't only that her self-knowledge was nonexistent, she had an almost dyslexic incapacity to distinguish between men in general and those whom, having loved, she now hated and the order in which they came because of it. I came to realize hers was the type of mind that could take up a relationship to a fact only after her own queer fancy had worked to transform that fact, not to understanding, but to her own stubborn way of seeing the world. The measurement of her understanding against her experience was not only narrow but nonexistent. I was less surprised now by the trouble she had with men than in finding her willing to admit it.

I smelled in the air the heavy marrow of pine trees and listened to the doleful tale as ugly in its funds of pessimism as the nightmarish crow I watched brooding on a faraway branch.

There was nothing original to that first marriage in the sketchy story I heard. Cruelty bred cruelty, a cold bed became a grave, and then there was flight. Luck in love never seemed proportionate to Farol's taste in men. He was either a simpleton, I gathered, or unfeeling. But she wasn't gullible. I figured as a punished and self-hating person herself, she'd been drawn to punished men. The recalcitrant fact was she'd been passed on, or passed herself on, from one piece of bad news to the next like a twenty-five-cent bag of candy, a cycle in eternal recurrence of rebellion, pigheadedness, and false pride. There had been a serious falling out. Her parents were clearly disappointed with her, and perhaps even unforgiving.

But something else bothered me, and I wondered about it: the move from being someone's daughter, unsuccessfully, to someone's wife, successfully, had become, I thought, impossible for her. Who is a more self-canceled figure than an unloved daughter, who a more disobedient one, who more disposed to become in everything she's once faced of paternal interdiction and refusal the unfaithful wife, whore, and mistress all in one unassimilable category?

"You don't think as you look back"—I hesitated—"that there was anything in the marriage left to save?"

"No. Nothing. Not at all," she said. "No way."

She looked at me.

"The next time I'm with someone"—again, the word *marriage* stuck in her throat—"it will be final. You'll never get rid of me," she said, hugging my arm. There was a long pause. "I can't afford to make a third mistake."

"I know the feeling," I said. "When someone leaves you, it's often worse than physical pain. Much worse."

She drew back, looking suddenly indignant.

"What are you saying?"

I looked at her.

"I left *him*," exclaimed Farol.

Of course, I thought. I shouldn't have been surprised. Why had the second husband left her accursed? None wed the second but who killed the first. "I walked right out," she said. "I couldn't bear another minute of it. I dropped everything right there, right on the spot. I never even returned to pick up anything." She waved a hand. "I bothered with nothing."

Nothing. Everything. Something. Anything.

I listened, and although I thought at last I understood her version of the world, it was a strain having versions. I'd never come up against such a thing before: Farol seemed always to have been doing what she did for a long time, but in fact if long in emotional excursions these were often periods short as months, brief as minutes! And the periods were places, places only, places from which she always drove away. She drove, and she drove. More was explained than revealed, but I had the impression she had concentrated literally all her adult years on men, on finding a husband, which after more than a decade horribly left her without one! It had also left her ignorant, for in having fixed on such a thing exclusively she had focused on absolutely nothing else. It had been a noiseless search, not only embarrassing but the very kind she'd find impossible to defend. Maybe that's why talking came so hard to her. Questions *were* enemies. But answers were only worse.

Accumulated stupidities, as she told it, appeared to carry along with them a certain kind of patience—or, I don't know, a power of endurance—which seemed almost infinite to me, but no explanation could ever make clear to me how she could have managed to affect so dramatic a blunder *twice!* There was no tracing the twists of it. I knew one thing, however. Every picture filled her mind with possibilities and potential participation. She could simply never make them come true. She would climb mountains only to fall and perish in the lowermost snows. She was always running toward the point to be gained, for somewhere way beyond for her, always, floated huge alluring dreams of sheer excitement, action, accomplishment, and significant men. Perhaps she understood daring by her rashness. I don't know. Her visions were as vague as vapor, and yet they drew her on all the more imperatively. Where she lived, the close remained the worst. The farthest music, the outlying bird, that one missing man—that's the music she heard, the bird she missed, the man she wanted.

A confession of failure couldn't have been more complete. It was a relief for her, I suppose, that this missing man had at last become mentionable. As she spoke the need to dismiss him again seemed required. I thought it was maybe here at Plum Island that she was seeking to conquer loss by going to the place that summoned it and replaying it from some measure of advantage.

But I was mistaken. It wasn't a personal loss, it was a loss of advantage, a setback that wasted her time and frightened her. She had to face living by herself for the first time, she said, and couldn't bear it. I saw there was a sense of protection she felt in not having to stand alone anymore with all of this unsaid.

"I remember living alone," she said, "the two years after my divorce. It was like looking over the edge of the world. I never felt such panic. What would I do? How would I get by?" Yes, I thought. That would have been the worst for her, being alone. She was terrified at the prospect and had often told me so. I saw affairs—"situations"—during those years. And others of an even more obscure relationship hovered beyond. Many affairs. Or one. No, many. One she wanted and didn't have.

"I don't think you'd have liked me very much then. You wouldn't want to have known me," she said. She took my hand. "I was so cynical."

I thought perhaps it was true, that the weak and the defeated have no sins, only follies. We sat there in the smallness of the car; she looked too big. It was pitiful, it seemed to me, that sins so often get their label from the outward consequence. The crushed have no benefit of the doubt. And yet while her sedulous cultivation of stubbornness as a gesture of defiance disgusted and repelled me, I pitied her, aware as I was at the same time that once you start pitying people, it is often easy to end up hating them.

I folded her hands in mine.

"And yet," said Farol, "how often I've wished I'd met you then."

"But that was when you met—"

"I met no one," she said, coldly.

"I mean—"

She frowned. "John, yes."

She exasperatedly blew air in being reminded of him. Was this unfair of me? To ask?

"I joined the AMC," she said in an insulted voice. "The Appalachian Mountain Club. It was at one of their parties we met."

I paused for this one. "Have you ever come here with him?"

Her jaw shifted. She nodded.

"Often?"

She turned away, which was sufficient enough answer for me. And then she abruptly started the engine, spraying up a flock of bewildered birds from the trees, backed up, and drove away.

"I've told you the rest," she said.

And so I knew why I was there. It was why under the same colors she was with me on other occasions, at my house on the Cape, for instance, or in particular restaurants. Without divulging it, we often took each other to specific places previously visited in the company of the people we were now betraying that some sense—elimination, perhaps—might teach us something of what, by contrast or comparison or both, we were giving up and whether in fact we should.

We stopped on the way home for clam chowder at a small restaurant in Newburyport called the Grog, another town, another place, with which to my surprise she seemed familiar. There were so many things she seemed familiar with, routes and roads, houses and hamlets, states and cities and islands. Islands. They were really the only places familiar to her, banished from the outside world, secluded by ghostly necessity from any measure of consolation, stranded from home. It was in the familiar that she felt isolation and in the isolation the terrible familiarity with all she was—and wasn't.

My thought was only in wondering how she would feel with the *unfamiliar*, the tender and the trusting and the true.

And would she ever be happy?

21

We had a decision to make. It was almost June. And so I proposed—let me clarify, I proposed that we remain apart for the summer to examine the precise nature of our feelings. It seemed the only way, and Farol agreed, showing a tender tacit assent which both surprised and touched me deeply. She had her job, she said, and now with her apartment she could sculpt in her free hours. I prayed she remain healthy. The room was pleasant enough: she'd fixed it up with a certain eye-to-the-teacher style of furnishing, the outward effects of print and plant and periodical lying faceup expressing a sort of wish to be seen. She said she wanted to read more. In the meantime, she bought a television set.

Farol added that she still had obligations to her husband—*not* sexual, she assured me. She explained that for his trust she wanted to show him a requisite amount of loyalty before she left for good. I wonder when I heard that if my expression was as strained as hers upon saying it, or my heart as ambitious to find it right.

The last thing we discussed was whether we should write to each other. We decided against it. We slept together on her floor mattress that last night and the next morning in a hush marking the emptiness that had a kind of color I found her trying unsuccessfully to smile, her face sad and pulled like a Hans Memling. I smoothed back her hair with a quick gesture. "Please," she pleaded, "don't forget me?" I kissed her and promised, "I will never forget you." I told her I loved her and wanted to be with her. And then I left for Cape Cod.

I found, as usual, no end of work to take my attention, both in the house and on the extensive grounds. It was an old white Victorian house with black shutters which, near the sea and open to the harsh elements of wind and water, stood constantly in need of repair at the end of every winter. There were acres of grass to mow. I kept a small garden, usually planted a few trees, and hacked away in the orchard, usually reserving the quiet of the early morning hours to work in my studio.

The weather stayed warm and sunny. I seemed to step into an enchanted atmosphere, a turning in the path of joy, lasting joy, made rich by the wilderness I loved of woods, meadow flowers, and marshes of sunlit green. Aloneness had a dimension. I made no effort to get a telephone. I rarely checked my mail, although one day a letter came offering me a teaching job in Iowa. I did several paintings, a whimsical thing with paint sticks entitled *Chickens Biting Light,* another one—oil on Masonite—a brisk brutal commination in red and black called *Man Sucking Teeth,* the enigmatic *Tiverton,* and a watercolor of a dark lonely house in desolate fog called *Riverwood Road.* But there was another larger project, one month in the devising, that was kindling in me to be painted.

Tarquin and Daisy with their kids—five now altogether—spent some of the summer nearby when time permitted, and Marina, as for years she had, visited as well. Farol and I had decided upon it: she would periodically see her husband and I would see Marina in external consideration of simple courtesy. The prior always gave us less problems than the possible. There was no need to discuss celibacy. That promise was certain. I well remember how Farol and I debated everything before I'd left, often less with statement, I suppose, than sensibility. We'd gone over plan after plan, each failureproof, each unworkable, one for this reason, one for that. And over the weeks whether sketching outlines for an idea still awaiting objective coherence or seeing to various tasks, indoors and out, I never failed in whatever temperament on whatever toil to reflect on all those visions and revisions.

Farol told me—without wanting to pressure me, she said—of her anxiety about other women in my life but laughably dismissed my own fears of her meeting someone else, repeating her phrase that she was unapproachable. I wondered as I thought of her at work and the baneful influences to which she was susceptible of the gallery gorgons, Trey, Blanche, and Sweetheart. I was due back to teach at St. Ives in September, a job I kept now frankly only with a view of being with her, and, as I say, we'd planned plans famous with deliberation and projected projects with doubts for that faraway month. I remember feeling as I left what I'm certain she felt in seeing me go, both relief and regret, and yet in a hopfrogging sort of coincidence my leaving her seemed with a kind of stammering and obstinate insistence to recapitulate, because it so quickly followed, her leaving her husband. Our sympathies had been overwrought, I concluded anyway, and so foreground duty prevailed.

And then there were the ghosts—who'd never met, or been met, as befits the nature of ghosts. I'd long of course felt the strain of her husband's spectral presence, just as she had the presence of her rival in my life, and these, like afterthoughts, were transmogrified by apprehension into almost operatic apparitions, the worse in our not loving them for being there, of subtle but teeming doubt. Doubt is a form of contradiction. It's ironic: one often becomes the premature victim, perversely, of what in fact the other initially seeks to vitiate. We'd communicated only our hopes, doubt's double. We were two independent people with great dependence on each other—or was it the reverse?—who feared most of all perhaps the responsibility our interdependence created in leaving behind two others.

I thought perhaps I'd met in Farol my perfect double, for the artist, while he's obliged to immerse himself in the world, constantly leaves it to make his own—to be in the world, not of it. Ours was no different than making dreamscapes in the apprehension of that spring. It was as if we'd been afraid less of asking questions than of hearing answers all too readily provided in our minds, for each of us having been so long confirmed in the weary reality that in expecting love one must be prepared to accept what often inevitably arrives in its stead, loss. But if accident made a difference, I figured, our relationship was only an accident. We needed continuing proof of—what? I don't know, maybe discontinuity. But that was all back in St. Ives. And I left it at that.

The summer proceeded in a rather recitative-like way, flat and unadvancing, no arias. I kept my faith while enduring long periods of disbelief. I had my doubts and yet my faith grew as well. I would never forget one beautiful day when walking along the Provincetown docks Marina and I had been talking about love and how she astonished me by making a crucial distinction—she often had shattering insights—between belief and faith. "I believe in faith," she said, laughing at the paradox. "Faith is above belief," she said, "isn't it?" And of course she was right. Belief is funded on reason, which frankly isn't quite the faculty I'd cite as to logical explanation over the year, ever, of where I was or what I was thinking or how I got there, never mind what I could justify. I couldn't explain it to myself, much less to her. I took comfort in telling myself that my vision of the world was essentially beyond or, I don't know, beneath or below language anyway, which I suppose is why I paint.

And this I did. The passing days had sharpened an approach for me and confidently I started my picture with the prototypical presences I had in mind, working upstairs, alone, listening to Pachelbel and often working late at night in a room scented with the sweet smell of bitumen, Japan drier, and oil. It was large, seven-by-nine feet on board, onto each side of which I brushed shellac, and the eagerness I felt in the rapid discharge of paint made it true. I often never finished until morning when the low-angled dawn sun struck what looked like frost covering the fields, but it was a blanket of dew, sparkling and misty.

I should mention here I'd undergone a strong experience, a vivid and almost verifiable hallucination involving Farol and myself the first night I'd spent in New York the previous spring. I'd had a dream. My dream went something like this: we are trying to reach each other by means of a rope over a wide distance, and because below us yawns a monstrous black chasm I'm terrified of her being sucked into a vacuum of sensation and letting go. "The rope is going to break," I cry, "and I can't keep my grip!" She's caught in the middle, as on one end, in an attempt to save her, I am also in the tension on the verge of falling myself. She sees this. If one of us lets go of the rope he—or she—can save him or herself only by killing the other. It was this idea that had been germinating in my mind during those private little consultations I had with myself and a few masterpieces on the second floor of the Frick.

I preferred oils this time. Acrylics can give an ugly surface, which, along with being airless, tends to have a raincoat quality to it. I laid the canvas on the floor so that I could blend a higher ratio of varnish into my pigment, which gives it an enamelled shiny quality. But the large amount of varnish meant the painting was so liquid that it would drip down the whole work if it were placed upright.

The canvas came alive with brushy passion, duns, cad red, violent ochres, and a hue I ingeniously ground with secret pride into a mid-tone between kettlesteam and blue soot, but space was aggressive, endangering but nicely, while avoiding the attentive angles of art school—no mother necessity here, thank you—the wide-open surface spare as suspense on the upper right, which like the negative virtue of keeping quiet can be also made loud, the rope coming out like a flash of lightning from below and two tiny torn and tormented victims being warned in the face of the horror of loss! There is no timbering or uprights, only a fall like a disrupted narrative that drops into eternity. A painting can take weight only on the left side. I often spent a morning making a minimal movement in it the monotony of a month wouldn't reveal. I knifed tension out of the muscles and used for surprise in two places straight ivory black, a paint timid painters won't even keep on the palette. I sat cold wind in it. I beveled by beauty and lit by fracture. And when I stepped back one morning and looked at it, a voice inside me said, that's it, that's it!

I called the painting *An Adultery*. I had a strange feeling finishing it: in having done something so well I was reminded how little work I'd done in all my time with Farol. Not a jot, not a dot. And yet what had been missing then that was now present, and which somehow reminding me of her, seemed to call up in me as if in gratitude a lovely current of feeling that ran deeper than I thought. Where's a joy unless it's shared? I felt monkish and windowblinded and lonely. And temptation resisted seemed pleasure lost. I didn't like, then, however, still don't, and never will, the whole mode of *assessment*. You never get the real world as solid as that. And it was only a survivor's game, anyway, tempering extremities with deliberation. It fell trick to the light.

Whatever reasoning followed came from what all along I wanted of her. I thought: *if you mean to be loved, give more than what is asked, but not more than what is wanted, and ask for less than what is expected.* We had made a pact. I resisted the temptation to write. And I lost the pleasure.

It was almost July, I recall, when all of that became irrelevant anyway. I heard from Farol. I remember the confusion I faced (I who felt, perhaps absurdly, destiny to be always in the hands of the destined) watching the distant sunsets stain the sky, dusk after dusk, with the lingering watercolors of rose, email, and purple as I wondered how to respond. I must have looked at that blue envelope with its engineering lettering and its content of two pages a hundred times. It had been characteristically brief: she asked to come down on my birthday in August. It seemed odd for her to make such a request a month early, but I quickly realized she saw the invitation as symbolic of how I felt.

I wasn't sure what to do. I began to think her too conclusively and too entirely tender not to feel the sacrifices that had been asked of her. And I missed her. I was in love with her, I was sure of it. A dilemma of another kind was forming, however. And it had been a long time coming.

Farol followed with a longer letter, and while scarcely an hour passed when I didn't take them out to reread the frankly passionate and in places even desperate feelings she expressed, and now in print— it was somehow as with numbers, the more difficult to comprehend when written out—I felt oppressively, but truthfully, the pull of another need as well.

I sat down before the week was out to answer her with a definite but desperate devotion I couldn't quite explain, letters, as I read them back, arranged almost as if asking myself whether, if in telling her at present more than she cared or dared to know, I wasn't just making up for my hitherto having told her less of what now seemed overwhelmingly a fact I could no longer ignore. But now neither could she.

There was, after all, still someone else in my life.

22

Marina made people happy. There was little to match the ease of her sweet disposition. She expected nothing. It had the effect in her of being always generous. In expecting anything from life, she felt she was breaking a bargain with it. I often wondered if it was because her mother was so tyrannical that, rather than deplore, she simply enjoyed what she could with the special transforming joy of an artist. She found nothing diminished by repetition and never tried to second-guess the confusion in living she'd long accepted as natural.

Her beautiful eyes kept only to their own reflections. No one knew what they were. She always seemed peculiarly and secretly both saddened and elated about something deep within, something of which one had only glimpses but in which one fancied difficulties she herself refused to recognize, or, I don't know, maybe recognized but wouldn't let reality ruin. She was trusting. She was so sure that the truth about the world was kind that she could look upon honor without fear. Unlike Farol, she never complained and her unstrategic loveliness—I'd often seen perfect strangers stop her in shops or on the street to exclaim on her beauty—always left her modest and retiring nature astonished at the welcome surprises of day-to-day life in which she considered herself a lucky but irrelevant guest. I'd never known anyone so undesigning or so quiet. There was in her that special art of making herself disappear into her own inner melody, which was as gentle as the music of a Gabrieli Mass. She was soft blue. I cared for her so much. And that's why she was with me on my birthday.

I made a point of inviting Farol down the following day but, as fate would have it, she couldn't come—she and her husband had planned to have dinner out that night. I had the not fully unfounded suspicion it was because of Marina. There are certain truths in life of an absolute sort. Everything is flux. All things can be reduced to moisture, whence they came. And I had to add another: nothing ever went right for us. Reverse the changes, change the verses.

I felt traitorous to Marina. I went about quietly, I remember, pulsing with disaffiliation in my heart for the grudge I harbored in not loving someone I cared for, but had invited, and in loving someone I was coming to think I didn't care for at all, but couldn't invite, and nothing, not bats, nor swallows, could relieve my mood those three or four days she stayed, a matter that must have bewildered the poor girl, whose custom year after year had always been to feel happily at home there. It had been for six years as much her home as mine. Everywhere the house showed her personal touches: vases of flowers, handsome curtains, prisms hung on the shade pulls, keepsakes all over she'd given me. But I refused to appreciate her, took exception to trifles, intentionally misinterpreted her, and remorselessly wished her away.

Can I have meant myself when I spoke of Farol's needing the tender, the trusting, and the true?

What is it about love that once having it we so suddenly lose? To like someone I didn't love, perhaps because of it? And at the same time to dislike someone I loved, possibly in spite of it? It was impossible!

Where's the virtue in adding I despised myself for all this? Or that into Marina's eyes, whenever I dared look, there seemed to steal half of the mournfulness of Farol's without diminishing hers? I was too cowardly to be cruel. I remained immune only to her goodness, choosing to believe her innocence incompetence and showing an inexplicable ugliness which her already half-disqualified self in its love and simple ruth only made the more emphatic. We all betray our ideals. But why? By attaching myself to Farol was I trying to bring myself hardship and misfortune, thereby cloaking over my immature need to rebel and subsequently suffer? I don't know what I wanted. I hated my secrets. I hated the deceit and bootlegging lies. I remember especially hating myself that day driving Marina back to Boston—one possibility suggested for the last time—when she sweetly kissed me in the sad reluctance of leaving as thanks for having such a good time. And of course in having the whole time thought of her I felt traitorous to Farol as well.

It was an impasse. I was in a flood of two confusions—the middle of a riddle—where differences left no distinctions. Whatever decision I made seemed to leave somebody's needs out. But if you felt the same way about both, how could you feel one way about either? I felt the need to keep Farol from being gloomy, at least prevent her from pretending to be cheerful, and to act honestly and judiciously without driving her weeping into the arms of yet another psychiatrist, never mind another man. I didn't want to fail her. I deliberated for months about being able to strengthen and support someone living her life out in a wheelchair. And yet I couldn't bear hurting Marina any longer. I've always felt the worst thing a person can do in life is come close to someone and then turn around and betray them.

I was nevertheless placed between these two women to choose one or the other. The very resolution that promised love to Farol involved the tranquility of Marina and threatened the happiness of the very person who was being bound for ransom for Farol's salvation. I was aware all the while in deceiving Marina of an insidious self-interest informing the heartless but unavoidable trade-off I faced in the subterfuge that was also a *duty*. It poisoned a spot previously unprovided with any sovereign antidote of sense. Souls were at stake. I detested it! I carried the principle to the point of torture—overabundance and insufficiency all at once—but all the prosing consultations I had with myself only repulsed me, and the daily assault of sensation besetting me wherever I turned for an answer became too insistent for deliberate report.

My final decision became clear. I knew I had to say good-bye to Farol. It was something that couldn't be avoided; if I continued to be with her there would be no end to her suffering and no end to my own. I didn't feel her commitment, first of all, not her full commitment. And of course she wasn't in a position to show it. But more than anything I realized if I stayed with her I'd be abandoning the one human being who relied upon me and needed me most.

I thought I had solved the problem. I was mistaken. Supreme beauty suddenly revealed is apt to strike us as a possible illusion, playing with our desire—and I thought it fantasy mocking fact. But I looked up the very next morning and found Farol, unannounced, standing at my door. She had driven all the way down from St. Ives. I was amazed to see her again so suddenly after so long, and while I only half-believed her there—luminous and lovely in tight blue shorts and a maroon designer jersey I'd given her across the front of which was written the name "Rembrandt"—there she stood, smiling and charged with the morning freshness.

Summer had touched her with a radiance I saw as a revelation. Her hair was chopped short and sun-streaked, and her face was tanned. Her delight in having surprised me my surprised joy matched as, hugging and kissing her, I went to pull her in. But she paused.

She stepped back and reached down to pick up a carton holding something she said she'd made. I saw she was excited. She carefully unboxed a shape. It was a sculpture, she said, made from a block of salt. I saw a lump, a sort of abstract pretzel of fat interlocking ovals sanded and buffed to a high white. Was this her summer's accomplishment? She asked what I thought of it, which put me in an awkward position. I didn't like it, to overdo understatement. It wasn't only bad, it was as banal as a blue puddle in March. I don't think in all my experience an active desire for beauty was ever accompanied by so little technical ability and even less talent.

I heard the void of her father's missing praise in the echo of my exaggerated claims of its worth—slight, I'm afraid, which was sad, for she clearly revealed a desperate underlying need less for an affectionate eye to observe than a nourishing faith to embrace all she wanted to be as an artist. I hadn't known what to say. I tried to be positive—but made the fatal error of complimenting her. I would never know until later how big a mistake it was.

We had breakfast together, pancakes and what she called "maple surple." And afterwards I showed her my painting. Farol never exclaimed. She looked at it a moment and said it was good. But nothing impressed her; she couldn't allow it; it stole too much from her. Her awed reaction may have even made her despise it. I'd noticed it before. Whenever I showed her anything I'd done, her lips drawing out in a long sarcastic curve gave to her face a look of what I can only describe as *disgusted admiration.* She would approve it, commend it, respond, but never without stepping back after a moment with a whimsical, almost laughing back-glance at me to see how I took the faint praise. It was as if, deeper than memory but acting with the force of a remembered crime, she recalled with galling indignation all her parents wouldn't give for what she couldn't be and so held back from others all she felt was due her—and I thought she needed this secret as much as she needed me.

I didn't care. I wanted to share my work with her only because I loved her. I wanted her to feel the same way in relation to me. I didn't want criticism. Criticism is never the equivalent of a work of art. And she hadn't the words anyway.

Within minutes Tarquin with his kids stopped by to ask me if I wanted to go to the beach. I took the moment to introduce them to Farol. There were the usual exchanges and polite questions and small talk. It was a bit awkward. My nephews didn't quite know what to make of her. They could never remember seeing anyone there but Marina—it was all too obvious Farol felt that herself. I suspected, in fact, it was the reason she'd come down in the first place. I also thought she envied me the freedom she for some reason still didn't have. I asked if she'd like to go swimming. She said she'd love to but could only stay the morning. I asked her why. But I knew by her look it was the same old story and made no more inquiries.

We were awkward and nervous ourselves. There was too much ceremony. Partners without full definition often become for each other victims of a kind of infuriating restraint, victims largely unaware that they are the servitors, not of a language, but a formula used to avoid the painful ordeal in having to speak, and so confess, of having their speech mock them by insufficiency. There is a terrible blindness in the love that wants only to accommodate. It's not only to do with omissions and half-truths. It implants a lack of being in the speaker and robs the self of an identity without which it is impossible for one to grow close to another.

Some time had passed since we'd seen each other. It became weighty. We feared returning to that point where safety in form prevailed over joy in substance. We needed assurance. We needed forgiveness, for too often the sorrow we should have shared we doubled, the pain we should have sought to stop we only quickened to anguish. But we needed more than forgiveness, something deeper, of elemental force, that had the nature of infinity. We needed each other to hold, and to touch.

And that assurance was always there. We had our bodies to absolve each other, our passion to apologize.

23

We made love.

And the next weekend was the same. And so also the following Monday, her day off. Whatever oaths we made that summer now meant nothing.

Farol began to visit me whenever she could. It wasn't that, tempting fate, we failed to consider the consequences. No one was around. We were always alone. The very idea of being together left moods that teased. There was nothing to interfere. My house was portentously quiet. There was something of the intimacy of proposal in that locked door that suddenly left us in secret, our voices growing low, altering in the apprehension of possible fantasy, and a sauciness gleamed in her eyes. I felt such unutterable desire for her, such intensity, that most of the time it seemed almost painful.

And we always found each other in those wordless moments we most craved. Farol was like the trumpet flower in Italy that freezing in winter returns to life in summer. She was breathing with ardor. She would touch me lightly under the ear and draw her fingertips along my arm, kissing my face, my eyes, gently biting my neck with her warm lips and exploring mouth. I felt her all over, pulling her toward me with a deepening ache. Once upstairs, I'd draw the shades against the hot sense-drenching sun and in the stifled darkness there which seemed a kind of lust itself suddenly become all throat as I undressed her, jersey, jeans, knee socks, her bras that unsnapped from the front with a sound like a light kiss. I would sit on the bed with her before me naked but for the wisp of panties she teased me to remove—often impishly pulling away to test my urgency—which, pinning her arms to her side, I thrilled in doing with my teeth. She'd shiver under kisses to her stomach, her groin, my tongue lapping at the sweet musky wetness between her spreading legs. And then quickly she'd run her hands under my shirt, unbuttoning it, unhooking my belt and trousers, and wildly freeing me.

I always felt the gods rising like an inundation when with luminous eyes and a breathlessness that almost robbed her of pronunciation she'd whisper in my ear with her nose rubbing in the words, "Make me suck you, please make me suck all of you." She loved the force of being taken this way, pushed to it in the helpless lust she felt under my commanding hands that drove her down to kneel and hungrily feed on me. I'd push her, and she'd struggle forward. I'd pull back, tempting her. But she had no shame and would writhe onto me again, moaning, almost incoherent, begging to drink me.

And then I'd back up slowly, insinuating her onto the bed, and roll her backwards, kissing her everywhere, biting her lightly on those moving thighs, scissoring and bucking the blankets. She loved to have her breasts sucked and quivered under my tongue as her passion grew. She loved the violence, the tenderness together, and the soft spankings she began to crave opened to that need with a frantic rhythmic smacking against me. I struck her buttocks, pale as platinum, as she squirmed with pleasure and rebounded and twisted with spread legs, her limbs straining and thrashing to invite more and more, and it was not only my hand but her heart drawing it in upon herself so that I felt I was beating with love upon the swell of her heart itself. Quickly, she'd turn rolling up in real urgency, her face flushed, her body glistening with perspiration, and greedily lapping kisses pull me into her warmth, her effortless body now rising and falling in a beat of steady participation.

I felt each time I floated on the brink of my own extinction, so long and so deeply did I hold my breath and my heart within it; indeed, so high did I rise on the very roar of the sounds within myself that I could have been above a cataract washing me out of myself forever into her. Her eyes would roll back, a moist glow dawning in the hollow of her throat and breasts, as we'd become one eye, one breath, one throwing movement. I'd hold her fast at moments, ordering her not to move, but she'd cry out sobbing with delight she couldn't stop, couldn't, wouldn't, moving, moving, her low voice whispering huskily and with alarm "I'm coming, I'm coming!"—her breath catching in a gasp as she'd go rigid, her head jerking up, as if suddenly shot, and then flow into my arms like melting gold and lie still.

We'd lie there dazed. There were times, lying with her through those hours, when I thought in the protracted joy of half-sleep, the sun hot on the shades, that I watched her from a distance with such a revisiting attention that I felt no wonder couldn't be realized and that nothing whatever should be neglected again preventing us from a supreme pledge with each other. I dreamt in my bed, waking usually to a dewy nose and soft feet and a cry of "Woof!"

Opening my eyes, I'd usually find her face comically on mine—Farol was one of those people who boasted she never blinked first—her eyes filled with impish lights. Her ash-blond hair fell around her lowered head. She'd outstare me until I burst into laughter, and then biting my lip she'd begin laughing, too, blowing on my face to cool my brow and kissing my shoulder as always she'd snuggle up to sleep. I tried not to think of anyone else. I swam through so many layers of so many dreams, trying not to think of anyone else. I cloaked my eyes with prayer like blinders to avoid thinking of anyone else, and there in the darkness that I made I slept.

Farol would be suddenly awake. She'd take a drink of water. I'd wait as she put in her contact lenses and slip on her earrings—always she had to hurry back to St. Ives—and then watch her dress. I felt a softness in my heart looking at those thin shins, that listing walk, the way she went about everything looking away that had something of the waif in it. I worried. I wondered about more than her health. I wondered if she needed me as much as I loved her, wondered that I needed her as much as she loved me, for I confess I wasn't yet certain either of us had the bravery and willingness to risk all in the game—that is, not until that day in Newport.

24

Farol stood below my window, calling up at me. I looked out. She'd crossed the bridge before the morning sun and arrived at my house with a spirit overflowing, I thought, with a marked sense of adventure. She looked beautiful, wearing white shorts and a powder-blue shirt, and seemed happier than I'd seen her for some time. We had breakfast together and decided to go to Newport.

It was a day filled with bright sunshine. The drive was enjoyable. We parked the car once we got there, and walked along the docks. We had lunch by a sparkling sea the color of mist, teaberry, and neptune blue, and later visited many of the shops on Thames Street. I did some quick pencil sketches of a stone house in which Henry James once lived, and then we cut up along Bellevue Avenue where Farol, swinging her sandals in her hand, took strides in a mood so light she somehow irradiated all she looked upon, matching in the bright effluence of her fancy the splendor of the fountains and gardens and generous views everywhere.

The mansions were all noble and charming and sympathetic on their great scale and extent. I might easily have found distasteful, never mind unconscionable, all the lavishness and excesses of wealth we were asked to admire, but nothing could have been wrong that day. It was magic, and wherein lies magic there is also beauty. We were somehow in a place with each other where we could be free. We toured several of the estates, Marble House and Belcourt Castle, where in spite of the crowds of tourists we could never get close enough to one another. The great beauty that flowed about us reached sharp contact in the lovely softness of her fingers squeezing mine, pulling me back to be near her.

There was in the context of that poetic afternoon miraculously nothing of doubt, or hesitation, or disbelief. It wasn't her old precautionary self. Nor was anything shown of its impulsive opposite. A strange new beauty was in her, born of what it both had and hadn't. Her hair grew more golden even as I looked and in the strong sunlight positively made me blink. We spoke quietly of ourselves, lingering behind to do so, as others passed, on paths, under gateways, and in the massive rooms. We talked and talked, and, as our talk became confession, confession became truth. She threw sweet remembrances over all we'd shared together up to that time, enkindling such a fire in my heart that all the corners of conviction were as suddenly lighted up. I felt impatient of any other light, staring amazed upon waking to feel a kind of power in her I'd never taken into account before and by sweet shock on shock received deep and intimating forestastes of what our life together could be.

We visited the largest mansion last, The Breakers, and walked out across the lawns onto the cliff walk overlooking the sea into a sunlight so brilliant that exposing my mind it must have made my thoughts clear to her. The sun was flaming in hues too positively overwhelming for genteel reproduction. There was nothing but color—no line, no abhorrency of distinction. Everything belonged. Her golden hair, her pale-blue shirt, her white shorts, were all one moment with the world. I could not hold all the fullness I felt. It had to be shared.

A softness in the sky carried a wishing warmth, and I hugged Farol for the longest time, pressing her to myself and thanking the human summer and the joyful human sun in the sky. I looked into her eyes.

She smiled. Oh, it was a permanent smile, though not a soul was there to see it but me, to have it but me, to know it but me. It was as if she were there by the operation of my feeling, alone. The nameless and inexpressible tenderness of her smile traceable to, and blending with, that of another sweet and gentle soul far away I refused any longer to link, the strange transfer always previously beckoning me to such reflections I decided no longer to make. I wanted only Farol now. I didn't have to tell her. She knew it. I had an unavoidable feeling I'd always been hers, the long doubts I'd had over the year relative only to how far away she'd kept me from her.

Farol looked at me. She took my hands. She told me she could never live with her husband again. I held her face. And I wondered.

Was it possible? Did the same return not, save to bring the different? There was something so august in the trustful renunciation of her eyes, something in them that seemed to say that she'd long been ready to wait for me. I knew at last I had been given the full value of a woman's heart, which can only be the highest happiness.

We met in a long warm kiss. And in the light of that sun, in that expanse of fable, she was just then to my vision the most definite, the most beautiful, the most incomparable gift in the entire world. She kissed me again and her kiss seemed to go down my throat and spread into my shoulders, running like light through all the veins of my body. She leaned into me passionately, breathing out to speak upon the beauty all around us which, transformed, somehow lived as I upon her words as she said, "My love is entirely yours."

It was later driving back to my house with Farol's head upon my shoulder that the mystery of that wonderful night settled down around us, though neither of us spoke. Not a word was uttered. But this time we knew full well what was being said, for deep within that silence like proof of its enchantment came a truth telling us all that was real was now possible and that at last we were quietly, finally, very much in love.

Absence is a kind of presence. The pain of missing her took on a richness I now took as a resolve. I knew I couldn't live without her again. I wanted to marry her. Her life away from me flooded me with a desire to see her, feel her, be with her. I missed her and the quixotic life she led. She was busy now, but she wrote and said she missed me and my sense of outrage and opinions. We missed each other's faults! It was the best of signs, the surest of signals. She was straight as string and wrote almost every day, letters that fell off only toward the end of summer in the midst of a visit she made to see her parents. I was in a rush, meanwhile, working on two more canvases and gathering myself up to return to St. Ives.

I knew she had had to fight hard to make her decision. But I felt I knew her, she was high-principled, and I believed she was doing the right thing. Our separation that summer seemed years, a lifetime. I comprehended the beauty of her spirit at the very moment I could not reach its use. I desperately wanted her to know the happiness, in spite of her absence, she was capable of giving, for I felt and knew and loved the happiness she gave. I was that happiness.

When was the last time you were happy? How far back can you remember? Can you recall the last time you were gloriously happy, happy even about nothing? That mysterious urge within that in an outpouring and drenching of the spirit upon the self made you want to sing and never stop singing? You could only jump up and down. You couldn't keep still. You were too happy, bursting with happiness. You ran as if you were flying, without feeling your feet. You felt the wind, the wind within you, the wind without, flying over the world. And all the time you ran you thought over and over with a bright, tight feeling high up in your throat: *I'm happy!—I'm happy!—I'm happy!*

Part

TWO

1

Farol Colorado was a woman.

There was about her the mysterious loveliness of a woman, with something yet deeper, something of such baffling uncertainty that I felt no matter how fixed my resolution to know her, some part would remain forever unfathomable. She was changeable. I'd long come to accept her abrupt reversals as the result of physical and mental injuries. I'd always taken her, provisionally, as a semi-invalid but never knew quite how badly the mixture of finding impossible to lose what was yet impossible to render made up her personality. If we tend to believe improvement comes with change, acknowledging of it the power to alter one's nature, we somehow fail to consider the fact that change itself often changes, bringing one back to where one always was. In a very real way, Farol was always the same. And that only compounded the mystery.

I'll never forget driving up to St. Ives that early fall day to see her again. The sky was blue as eternity, the September sun filling my heart with expectations even brighter than the radiance I felt all around. I headed straight for the gallery and ran in breathlessly to see her. It turned out I had to wait. I paced back and forth as some time passed. And then she appeared silently in the inner doorway. I had to look twice before I could believe it. I met only a dismal stranger.

Farol seemed morbidly changed. She looked tight and white and unhappy. She stood there, hands in pockets, and said nothing. At first I was shaken with fear: her health. But that wasn't it. There was something missing in her face. I saw once again, in what seemed a hideous reversal of fate, someone who longed for something in herself that she hadn't been able to find, or didn't have, or couldn't share. I'd seen smaller variations of this mood before, a silence one might have called the exhaustion of uncertainty. But this was the very contagion of indifference. I felt in her maimed nature the alteration called change that is only the growth of self-distrust and self-disgust which ruins all resolve.

She often thought where she wasn't and therefore lived where she didn't think. She had spent the best part of her life doing the wrong thing, changing jobs, towns, attitudes, names, and husbands. And now I sensed with nervous dread something more to come. I felt my heart begin to sink, for she seemed clearly resolved on some decision she'd made necessary to cope with the thought she refused which, making choice irrelevant, left her no alternative.

"I've been fearing this moment for a long time," said Farol, her voice low and hardly loud enough to reach me. She sighed. "It's not easy for me to tell you this."

Waiting, I held my breath.

"I've given in to my fears," she said. She lowered her head. "John and I have started seeing Dr. Varion again—together."

But what did that mean? Nothing registered. I couldn't reconcile the two remarks or understand either separately. I couldn't understand what I was hearing. I asked what she meant. I remember only the pale and determined figure standing there turn away, then half turn back. Delicate pauses gathered like webs between us. She almost began to explain but suddenly stopped, as if calculating consideration, exhausting all the relations and possible consequences of words, crippled the power of resolution.

I went to touch her. "No," she said, backing away. "I don't think you understand." She shook her head, raising one hand to shadow an eye, figuring the facts, the futility, the failures, and then shifting her guilt by suddenly confessing it she burst out, "I can't make it, this way, not any longer. I have to end our relationship."

I remember being in a lobby.

My immediate reaction was desperate. I pulled at her arm in panic—I couldn't speak—but Farol wasn't there. She had forgotten or refused to remember who I was or what we'd promised each other, substituting for the love of love the hatred of it, and what meaning both had was coextensive with the reach of her imagination, which, stretched to its limits, had settled on a scheme I wasn't certain solved or rewarded or betrayed. Her only freedom, paradoxically, was the deliverance from it, the choice, chosen, never to choose again. Holding herself off from conclusions had actually formed one. She'd given up.

I squeezed her arm, squeezed it. It was not only odd, suddenly sad, it was impossible. The love she promised couldn't have been false. I tried unsuccessfully to look into her face, which was moving, changing.

It was fading. I couldn't believe it. I heard words, but they separated and resembled nothing I knew. A voice from somewhere said, "I'll never forget you." It was a voice I couldn't recognize. "All you've meant to me."

What suddenly else was wrong? And where? And then I knew. It was the sun, the sunlight streaming into the lobby, the incongruous sun reversing black and white and leaving only afterimages that confused. It didn't belong, it became horrible, merciless, and yet so madly insistent it actually hurt me in the eyes. I fell back against the banister and waited a moment.

And then my hearing began to return.

"Have you—gone back?"

"Gone back?" she asked.

I swallowed.

"Home."

Farol looked older. Her eyes, worn with cynicism—the lines around them overwise—gave her face a stingy beauty. She took the line of saying she loved me, but could no longer see me. She had fallen in love, I realized, as she might have broken an ankle and merely had the certainty of having found someone she was convinced she was only going to lose anyway. It seemed guaranteed by her mistrust. She alleged she was hurt in not having been invited down in August for my birthday and told me so. But she said that wasn't it, not any longer. "I'm not ready to go anywhere, or be with anyone, or do anything," she said. I heard prefaces that made no introduction, saw method that embarrassed rather than explained, and found her calling upon me at the same time she questioned me out of a self-indulgence that implied if blame must be coupled with the cause of someone suffering it somehow didn't attach to the person who caused it.

She blamed love, habit, duty, responsibility, impossibility of real romance with anybody. And what was the point of anything? And didn't everything only come to nothing? And wasn't life just a muddle anyway?

I was torn between compassion and anxiety but her arrogant despair left one thing certain, and I knew with conviction what having known I still knew—she was not in love with her husband.

What had happened then? Was it that she took herself to be a defective? Was it that in loving me she wanted to save me from herself, that in knowing herself so well she couldn't accept anyone who'd have her so readily? "Do you feel so much guilt for what we've done? Total despair? Is it a moral decision you're making or a practical one?" She didn't reply. "Why would anyone under such circumstances return to the sleep-death of a futile and loveless marriage?" Still she·said nothing.

"What about what we said to each other?" The way we feel about someone often makes the way they feel about us less magical, and what corroborates an emotion often drains it. "You said you loved me. 'My love is entirely yours,' you told me. Why?"

But she wouldn't discuss it. Her passion seemed to combine itself with the indefinite alone. She had lost the power of action in the energy of resolve. She took in her marked mortality nothing as given; in having tested all she'd seen in the sum of things, what she saw of stubborn reality alone constituted its force. She suspected success but refused to interrogate failure, which was what she knew best. In the front door, out the back. Run, don't walk. Off with the future, return to the past. There are two kinds of weakness, that which breaks and that which bends. Was she bent? Or was it that she'd been broken so often she simply didn't care anymore? Wasn't it that in having been married twice she couldn't trust herself—parody herself—in chancing the third failure she'd convinced herself was inevitable?

I questioned her, but she wouldn't respond. I saw only a woman who in some intricate but unintelligible way had thrown over everything but the right to destroy and the right to enjoy life and who with vexing limitation now merely stood there with stricken eyes to tell me in a prevision of her own fate, my own.

As I looked at that secret defiant face—the inscrutable face, I thought, of someone to whom either nothing had happened or perhaps so much that each event merely wiped out what had happened previously—I knew it was useless to try to represent to her what she'd promised of love and faith, for she kept returning with greater emphasis on and objection to pressure from every side. I tried to find hope. But it was completely hopeless.

"It has to be like this," she said, closing her eyes as if provoked by unreasonable interruption. "Please, let it alone."

"Why?" I asked. *"Why?"*

"I don't know, I don't know! I need time. I need breathing space. I don't want to see anybody."

I looked at her and thought: *confused passion makes people indistinguishable.* I couldn't tell in the persistence of her silence whether she was too emotional, too scrupulous, too sensitive or—happier in the love she inspired than in that which she felt—merely incapable of representing the feelings she aroused in others. She was unstable, I knew that, but nothing could explain this sudden turnabout, this about-face, this fatal dismissal. It wasn't even a change, only an imperceptible and banal mutation like a person forgetting a fact or losing a tan or becoming slowly evil. Then it dawned on me she might be acting out her parlous relationship with her parents. And I wondered: *if you can't create— was it true—you can only destroy?*

Something terrible, long ago, I thought, must have happened to her, something snatched from her by one of the wicked forces she always felt afflicting her. I couldn't imagine her walking down the street, for instance, looking into strange faces here and there without her somehow reflecting on what they had done to her. What she never confessed to became all the more horrible—and dangerous—for never coming into the open, never to be touched by sympathetic argument or exploded by logic or reasoned away by love. It lay dormant like a tumor, and like a tumor it grew.

Weirdly, her father's face, not her husband's, loomed up before me, and I thought for an instant that I saw in what she wore on her face of his disappointment with her what shaped the mask her own hollow life epitomized. She could respond to guilt more easily than she could to love. I loved her, I did, but aware of her own bad fortune, she was immune to it—maybe even passive to caring.

Farol didn't cry or break down, not this time. She was not of an age to be sentimental. She had paid romance its due respects, given herself a shake, and would now concentrate on the elements in her life that were controllable. Wasn't that it? Utility maximization? What's the payoff? Survival? Her husband wanted her back. She didn't love him. But she had his name. She'd had another's. Could she have had yet one more stamped on her devastatingly to obscure in further adulteration her already precarious sense of identity? Divorce is a public admission of failure. What would the people at "group" say? Her friends? The gallery women?

No, what was awkward, elaborate, or fantastic—love, for example—had to go, for far back in her mind lay certain permanent conceptions to which she always reverted when left alone. Anybody could see that. And I was the anybody she had decided no longer to see. She looked suddenly nervous.

I turned only to see Gumplowitz and Scrulock in fake conversation by the inner door. As usual whenever we spoke their ears suddenly expanded into vast hoppers for sound between which even their narrow heads were crowded. I think they were proud of their protégée.

"I'll give you time. I've come back here to be with you." It was necessary to wet my lips to crease them into a smile. I said softly, "I love you, Farol."

She shook her head.

"That's over, I'm afraid."

"No, please. No."

"Yes," she said flatly.

I closed my eyes.

She stood stonily silent, ending on that note. As a consequence of refusing to face herself—like all weak people she thought every deed easy—there was no other place she could come out. I took her arms, trying to hug her good-bye. There was no answering warmth, only concern. "Given the situation," she said, "I think you should make it a point not to come to the apartment anymore. It might be awkward, for everybody."

My mouth went completely dry. I couldn't stammer out even the most faltering words. I felt tears mount in my throat. I nodded, more to hide the revealing pain in my eyes than to express agreement, for in my appalled state I knew I was only the more appalling to her. Her resistance seemed to grow by the very sight of me. I felt the chill of her icy aloofness. She wanted only to be at a distance from the catastrophe in which she moved, from the thought she refused, from the deed she performed.

"It's a beautiful day," she said, opening the front door of the gallery. She suddenly gave me her most accomplished smile. The smile did not leave her face. "Why don't you take a walk? Or a drive? Go to Plum Island."

Plum Island? *Plum Island?*

I stumbled out the door into a sunshot hell—not the Newport sun, not even a sunshine of light, no, only a white unendurable glare that was a recommendation to darkness for sharpening the shadow I threw, which seemed deserted without me. She said good-bye and turned away. I called to her.

"Will you do me one favor?"

She hesitated.

"Just say you're sorry?"

She lowered her head.

"I'm sorry."

"That's all right," I said.

And I left.

2

I never felt so alone.

I do not know how long or how far—or, indeed, in just what direction—I drove that day, or even why in the ensuing vacancy I ever returned for whatever it was I was now forced to face. I don't remember the next few days passing at all. I closed my eyes on her name and slept tightly with her in my mind, feeling that with the least word or movement I would break into pieces. Days became questions, nights fears.

My rooms became lonely as a trance. An absence was in the air, something missing that dwelt within something gone. It was always at the preluding hour of night when Farol finished work that I always expected her to come by. I ached to see her, if only for a word. But she never came by. There was only the lonely and exhausting repetition day after day of her never appearing. I never saw her. She was not in my life anymore.

As the weeks passed I tried to let go of the pain as it charred in my heart, but whatever I did seemed meaningless and the very act of trying to forget her only summoned memories reminding me of what I'd lost. Badly missing someone depopulates a world. I couldn't work. I tried, but hadn't enough strength and felt my very self a subtracted irrelevancy from the fields of vision I tried to contemplate. It became a just tolerable occupation to try to sleep, for no sooner did I go to bed than I had an immediate impulse to get up. I tried to be resigned. The shadow love of monks. All you have to do is make a desert of your heart and call it peace. It didn't work. I looked for her through the windows on long afternoons and listened bodingly in the dark for the sound of her car, often waiting through the night in a vigil of obscure memory only to see the haggard hours return cloaked in that not quite brown color in which dusk and dawn somehow always find each other. There was only silence, and the silence seemed to make me disappear. I began to feel invisible.

I soon felt with terror, desolate and growing further and further from forgiveness, that I'd lost the power of intelligence to get better. It wasn't only mental. My mind was cast down, but my body had taken a blow as well. I felt like the little boy back in that home once again, abandoned to fend for myself, specializing in quiet desperation, hiding false starts, mistakes, and failures. I realized Farol had let me come close enough to her only to reestablish her own self-assurance. I should have accepted that and let hang the dogs of war. But art is the artifice of recollection, and my memories haunted me. I stayed away as I was told, but couldn't put her out of my mind. I was constantly pleading to her in my mind: write and tell me you miss me. The night is long. The linoleum snaps. The lights of the faraway buildings flicker out.

Rueful thoughts came to me of a kind I hadn't had since, when I was a boy without parents, I looked through the glass of my own lop-sided observations and, thinking *nobody ever loves another enough,* began to feel no bond was so strong it couldn't at a given time and with any excuse be broken, dissolved, or forgotten. I remembered old Mr. Madwed once telling me sometime before he died, "One must be really brave to choose love or painting as one's guides," he said, "because they may lead one to the space in which the meaning of our life is hidden—and who can say that this space may not be the land of death?"

I found everything an effort. The weather turned bad, and I spent days watching the demented rain bead on my windows or staring out at nothing at all. I began struggling against this inertness as the most treacherous and deadly of symptoms and resumed teaching, though it became repulsive and incompatible with my loneliness. I did some drawing, but it was second-string stuff, and so I went out, inventing errands, looking for any diversion. The lowering skies seemed to conspire in my madness, coming down in shrouds of dreary mist over the dripping trees and on the wet roads. Davy's gray, middle values, drisk and fog. Many, many times I drove by the gallery and looked at it but kept on going.

At the post office one afternoon I had a sudden glimpse of a nut-cracker nose and chin. It was Ruth Gumplowitz, who was carrying a bag of rumpled old clothes that smelled like bread crumbs. She peered at me through her bottle-thick glasses. The shawl she wore looked like a tea leaf after long infusion. I walked over to her and said, "Will you tell Farol I love her?" She wiped a dewdrop from the end of her nose and walked away.

I drove aimlessly around the outlying reaches of St. Ives on many afternoons—to Rye or out by the Kingston fairgrounds or along the river—but only saw my reflection in the countryside, where instead of fulfilling their bright autumn promise, the fields were nipped and soggy, the trees cold and colorless. I felt as if all my thoughts had changed into leaves that had fallen. Dull dun dead leaves. I ached for Farol. I found myself several times for what seemed hours, it didn't matter when, though mostly evenings, standing on a walkway near the school gym and gazing over at her apartment, watching from a distance when it was late the gray light of her television set flickering far away in her room.

And I drove by her apartment all the time, often rising in the middle of the night to do so, sometimes way past midnight, and when I discovered her car missing from the driveway, I'd drive miles to try to find her, sick with apprehension, rushing through the deserted streets to see if she was with her husband. She never was. But then where was she? With friends? But who? And where? Whereas once I felt a tightening in my throat every time I saw a blue car, I now began to feel that way because I never saw it.

Days crawled by, the showery weather continued. It got to be terrifying, the intensity, this sort of brooding smoldering passion which couldn't be shrugged off, for finally I saw with a wave of fright that the action of my own will, having succumbed to hers, was now beyond me. Or so it seemed. I felt betrayed by what ended too quickly and so unnaturally; it was the kind of desertion that recalled my worst nightmares and deepest apprehensions. I couldn't get her out of my mind. She pounded about in my head, making no sense. I was so absorbed in her as to be surprised whenever I met people going about their affairs with calm or detected the routine of the daily world being still maintained. I was obsessed with her. It happens over the most unexceptional people. It happens over money. It happens over *things*.

I felt in my hybrid heart crushed and suspicious and jealous all at once. Jealousy. I'd always regarded it as a base and fundamentally stupid vice and all my life would rather have been caught dead than show it. But in this terrible situation my reason could give me no assistance. I couldn't accept that Farol had made up all she'd told me at Newport. I missed her in the lonely night. I missed her in the weeping of the rain. I didn't hate her, my misery was to love her, but half the time I wondered if I did. A man thinking himself in love, I thought, may only be trying to understand, ideally to complete himself, that which is most different from him; so different, opposed; opposed, then— who knew what.

And then I thought—or, I don't know, guessed—that she was looking for the mysterious right thing to do, whatever that was. I could see she was runing desperately round and round in circles in the only space

left her for circulation, and yet knew also the apparently certain knowledge she drew on was in fact a lethal ignorance, a passive refusal of
truth, in fact, that only mongered her unexamined half-knowledge in
support of what fully undermined any point of decision. Was it simply
the neurosis of having handed herself over so often to gaps that now
she was merely all holes—a cipher, utterly empty? Was that her despair? But then what was mine in fearing that? In needing that? My god,
in *loving* that?

Did she find in me my very own ignorance and incapacities? Was
that why she ended it? Had she somehow rediscovered in adultery all
the platitudes of marriage? Or was it merely that Farol, made lustrous
by adultery, now seemed more desirable to her husband who suddenly
wanted her back?

Each person in a couple does enough bad things in a relationship
to feel that when it breaks down he or she is alone responsible. I began
to feel that way. I thought I was surely part of the cause of what she
rejected. I hadn't given Marina the brush, for one thing. I was too intense, and eccentric. I also had too many words; silent people suspect
language, often finding it a source of trickery, falsehood, and deception.
It occurred to me she even blamed me for being single. There is also
such a thing as too much love. Overconsideration will do it. Over-
giving. She had grown to hate her dependency on me, I was sure of it.
Or was it that my life as an artist provoked her sharp elbows to equivalizing tendencies and forced her to face in me the faithless father who
foreordained that fact?

Why had she so suddenly decided to return to her husband? Was
it appeasement or affirmation? Did she think someone she didn't love
would overlook the faults and imperfections that someone she did love
wouldn't? Had she merely decided to reenter a game the rules of which
she'd learned even if she couldn't follow them? Or was it born of disavowal and denial? I'll return to marry you to show everyone what I
don't deserve to prove the injustice of everything everywhere. Hadn't
the definition she needed in living apart from her husband only proven
to show the lack of definition she felt in living with herself? Or was her
sense of insufficiency merely calling her back to test by perspective in
the incompatibility of all he couldn't give what, instead of her own lack
of self-worth, was in fact actually *his?*

I didn't know. I knew so little. I suppose at the time I was hoping
she felt guilt. At least I could respect that. I didn't hate her. I merely
felt a striving to forget her. I remember even trying to find something

high-principled in her decision to go back, though I'm convinced I harbored a rather deep-seated fear—and not without reason—that from the beginning she had the air of someone who without deliberation could easily hurry a parting, quickly pointing the way out and which door.

I was not ready, in any case, to make a judgment or utter a word until I knew all the matter to be judged. And while everything seemed so unimportant compared to being right with her I could no longer put myself to ponder the little I knew, except that in the pitiful discrepancy between what this love promised and what it delivered—the condition by which alone I understood it—another painful truth supervened. Each reflection of mine, every question, was a knifish reminder of how unconcerned I'd become about something else.

I was jealous of her husband! This was a married woman! She was another man's *wife!*

3

And late one afternoon I saw her buying cat food in Galloupi's. She was dressed in her dark blue gabardine jacket and jeans. I noticed for the first time in almost a year she wasn't wearing the gold earrings I'd given her. She had on small garnet earrings that seemed the color of the sad congested eyes she turned from me to hide, I thought, the grief besetting her in the renewed saturation of an experience too insistent, or too sad, for deliberate report.

Farol, pausing stealthily, muttered, "Nothing has changed."

"No," I agreed.

"John wants me to give up the apartment and to come home."

"He speaks of his feelings for you?"

She nodded soberly. I'd never seen her looking so dry and dead.

"And you haven't returned his—affection?"

We walked slowly to the back of the store. There were questions I was burning to ask. She met my look as she gathered her thoughts.

"We don't make love, if that's what you mean. He has a lot of resentment," she said resentfully. "He'd only turn away from me anyway if I tried."

I felt a snap within me hearing that.

"But all along he's been indifferent to you. Hasn't he? Wasn't he that way with his first wife? You told me that. That's what you told me."

Farol waited for a customer to pass out of sight. "I've never told you about something else," she said, head down. "I'm partially to blame in all this too. When we were living in Chicago, he hated his job. I mean *hated* it. We had a small apartment there and were new to the place. We felt locked in. He become depressed a lot, and I didn't give him the support he needed. He reached out, but I was silent, I just wasn't there." She looked away, bitterly. "I do nothing right, as you know." She paused. "I wanted to please him, I'd have done anything to please him"—I remembered her saying to me in bed: *I'll do anything you want*—"but I failed."

She stirred her big awkward shoulders.

"I feel responsible."

"Are you?" I asked.

"Yes. *Yes.*"

She looked inward at her aggravated mental state and perceiving unknown forces I couldn't see seemed only to find an intimacy beyond entangling, a complexity of premises in their own particular lives to which not being privy I could only have the conclusion.

"He's put up with a lot. He's been patient. He's been"—she shrugged exasperatedly—"fair." She hated the word for being the only one she had. Or perhaps the only one she'd use. I knew she was being elusive. It wasn't only vagueness. There was something else, something she was holding back, something still untold. I began to wonder if she'd been lying to me.

"And yet you knew all this before, didn't you?"

"I didn't know he'd started drinking. Yesterday I went over there to feed the cat—that's where I'm going now—and the house literally reeked of alcohol. Empty bottles. Glasses." She shook her head and said sententiously, "His prison is walking through the world all alone."

It sounded like something that had been stitched on a pillow.

"What about you?"

"I have the people at the gallery. And 'group,' " she said. "Friends." I wondered if she believed that. I asked her why they weren't his friends.

Farol assured me he couldn't get along with anybody. "There's no one he can turn to, no one around here he knows. He has no friends." She wrung her hands. "And besides . . ."

I waited.

"He depends on me," she said. "He needs me, he wants me, he . . ."

"Loves you," I said.

I knew that.

She looked at me.

"But you don't love him."

It was as if for the first time she heard the truth spoken, and the words seemed to perforate her. And then I knew something else: she loathed him precisely because she needed him. I wondered why she needed him and came right out and asked her. "And why do you lie to yourself?" She made no reply. There was a draggled look to her as she went to the front of the store, nothing combative or fractious now; she was only miserable. It was a wickerwork face. She paid for her purchases in silence.

I was determined now to try to find in her conduct some explanation other than the mere fact of its taking place. The guilt she felt in her weakness became, as her will atrophied, a matter of fact. She was never on the spot where her life was. She was knowing in retrospect but ignorant in foresight, but why did she have such anachronistic hope with a history of such chronic mistakes? And why did she think she was moving onwards and upwards when she was so obviously moving backwards and down?

One thing was certain. No report she gave again of her husband could ever be taken as gospel. She had versions only, forms or paraphrases corroborated by mood. I never saw such a tangle of thorns. If she made him look good, she was blameable in leaving him. On the other hand, too grim a picture of him always put her in a position she belied by her guilt. A fully positive review of him became an admission of her own failure, and yet she wanted to leave him. A totally negative picture was tantamount to a contradiction of her forbearance, and yet it was clear he loved her! What was truth? Did her husband love her? And did she really want to leave him? It was a gallery portrait turned to the wall, invisible and inscrutable. But, in point of fact, none of it really mattered. I had the key to the truth within my very own being. I knew him simply by what I knew of myself. The victim is always a partner. He was a man, like me, hurt by someone—was it rational?—whom he wanted back.

And in a way she was even more of a victim than we. She had sacrificed her capacity for a man, several men, and now compounding the interest of her errors began to look like a fool. How frustrated she must have been the first time she found out she couldn't do it the second time. But what of the even greater frustration the second time she couldn't do it the first?

Farol was afraid to fail, yes, but there was something deeper behind it. I heard the suppression of relevant facts in her sketchy confession. We walked outside. It crossed my mind she might be afraid of abandonment to the degree she might actually try to cause it, willingly complying with disaster before it came to her unexpectedly either by exaggerating too much the happiness she didn't have or by grizzling over the false ideas she remained stubbornly convinced were about to happen. Were present fears less than horrible imaginings? She was punctually impulsive about deciding whom she preferred, perhaps even wondering, nevertheless, how she could afford to commit her happiness to anyone's keeping, and yet cautious about assuring herself, by a prevention voluminously part of the same ego, that she must never be deserted. But deserted how? And in what way?

She spoke constantly of going away, beginning again, starting over. I felt uneasily she had more to admit.

"Wouldn't it help if—if you told your husband the truth?"

"The truth?"

"Yes."

"Which is what?"

Any evenness had now gone out of her voice.

"What you told me. That you're not ready to be with anyone."

"I told him!" she snapped. "I told them at 'group'! I told Dr. Varion! What good does it do?"

Wickerwork.

She looked in a virtual delirium of longing for the end of everything. "I should just pack my things and move back, even if it does mean spending the rest of my life going on bike rides! You know what I'd like? I'd like to go somewhere where no one even knows me, not a soul!" She gritted her teeth, facing away from the traffic on the main street. "I sometimes wish I could die."

I couldn't understand. She began walking to her car in the back parking lot, and I followed.

"You told me your husband was fair."

"He is," she said. "And he isn't."

What on earth was she saying?

"He has his pride," she exclaimed. "He told me not to call him or leave him notes, or letters. He won't discuss anything! He told me either to come back or forget it. He's difficult in ways you can't understand. He has a lot of anger and hostility and . . ."

She spoke in a quickening tempo.

"And?"

"Nothing, nothing."

Tears trembled in her voice.

"Tell me."

Seeing her face break up into planes of grief, I took her by the elbows and forced away the hands that had gone to her blinded eyes as she cried out, "I hate my life! I hate it! I do! I hate it!"

"Please, what is it? Tell me?"

Farol went slack, weakening at last into the full consciousness of the awful truth troubling her. There was a long evaluative pause as she looked at me. She pulled on her big uncertain fingers. And then she said, "John gave me an ultimatum. Either I go home or he threatened to cut me off from"—she actually seemed to shrink—"from help."

"Financial help?"

I thought: *money*.

She wiped her smeared eyes and glumly nodded.

"You wouldn't go back just for security," I said. "Would you?"

Fear made her angry.

"What else would I do? I have no medical insurance, his policy covers me." She blew air in exasperation. "There are car payments. I make practically nothing. I don't want to end up in the gutter." *Gud-dear.* She smiled condescendingly and tried to obviate any comment of mine. "I'm sorry there isn't more of me."

"There is more of you."

She arched an eyebrow. I let the equivocation stand.

I felt the sky above me a perilously sagging ceiling about to fall and crush me like tons of superincumbent masonry. She was never, never quite defined as being final. I took a breath.

"You're not easy to know."

"Probably not."

"Not probably," I said. "You're not."

She passed her tongue over her lips in great agitation.

"Then why do you try?" she asked defiantly.

"I love you," I said.

"I have to feed the cat."

And she was gone.

4

I took Farol's lunch to the gallery the next day. There was no welcome, only the adumbration I felt, once again, of having interrupted her there. I was not asked to leave. But I wanted more than that. I wanted not to be asked to stay away. It was awkward. Something she could feel in the intimidating silence behind her made her speaking eyes go suddenly cold and dark as a grate. The winter crows were perched all around. Scrulock, with her feet up on the table, was eating an orange like a macaque. Tweeze stopped hammering to glower at me. And Gumplowitz balancing a box of frames trudged past me with "Excuse, me, friend, I'm *wor*-king."

It was around this time that I think I began to frighten Farol. Fire is focus. The promiscuous may be less obsessive in their love than those whose passion is expended on one woman only. I say fire: perhaps obsession, which describes the insistence I felt, is closer to ice.

Alone in the lobby she met me, as now she always did, with her features adjusted to express sympathy. It was the sort of overpatient condescension one usually finds administered in a nurselike way, a mood I can only describe as monotonously considerate. She was seldom angry at me, her nature was too melancholy for that, but she was distant. She had only small talk again, and again I felt that her attempt to extract the simple solution she wanted from the midst of all this ambivalence would only prove once more with startling unoriginality the lunacy of trying to synthesize something that would only blow up in her face.

I called on her from the depth of what to her seemed a foregone act to look backward and by consent repeal what she insisted was ratified. I regarded with sad indulgence her utterly hungering wish to be quite through with thinking. But I couldn't give up. I asked her if there was any hope. She looked at me with gloomy kindness. I felt deep down she couldn't make up her mind. She thirsted for approbation yet could not forgive anyone's approval. Who approved her also accused her. "I need to feel what I am is okay," she said. "And who I am. I need some *me* time."

I almost stopped there. Her phrases were to English, so to speak, what Bowl-O-Rama Moderne was to interior decoration.

But it crossed my mind that tormented as she was by her own imperfections she might actually have been waiting for some glad proof of her husband's *not* wanting her back. On the other hand, living without her husband while he cajoled her to return was also a way for her of feeling needed.

And yet I knew that the love of even the most gifted man is esteemed as nothing so long as a woman remains conscious of having no love for him. "You're being hasty," I said. I said it was a mistake. "You're not giving us the time we need." But riddling confession found but riddling shrift. She came nearer, but if her grave face expressed a pity it yet declined a dread. Obsessions are puzzling to the unobsessed, and she was stubborn. Renunciation was in order lest all things around her got sucked into further explanation. She folded her arms and stood there. Then she shook her head and said, "I have to start learning to say no."

Oddly enough, it was during this period that I found her ringing my doorbell very late one night after returning from "group." She was outraged—it was her white-faced look—and told me that earlier that evening Dr. Varion in front of everyone had called her a "come-on." A mirror person with no reflections, without a secure sense of who she was, she tended to see herself as she was seen, adopting a persona that tried to live up to other people's expectations of what to them she implied she was capable of, and it was by that alone that she determined how she would behave. I wonder if she ever understood that most people had no expectations of her one way or the other. I tried to calm her down. "Why do you believe him?" "I don't," she raved. "I don't believe anybody anymore."

I saw Farol irregularly after that. I remember one afternoon talking to her in the St. Ives auditorium. She now needed to know everything in advance, asking where I'd be to schedule what she could and couldn't do—what day, what hour, what time. She told me one week what she'd be doing the next. Her indifference told me I was unwelcome. She was alive but never vital, responsive to a degree but never eager, alert but never intelligent.

She began to put up barriers and arrange distances between us. She was always either shopping or meeting her sisters for dinner or getting a tune-up on her car. Activity suggested a life filled with such purpose and so in a fury of bogus efficiency she put up vegetables and dilled beans. She lived in a system of tunnels. She and her husband went to a few concerts together, once a basketball game. She was always busy— busy at the gallery and busy taking a course in figure drawing and busy sewing curtains for a mountain cabin they shared with other couples somewhere up in Wonolancet or Winnebago or wherever.

But the art of her achievement was abdication. She assumed that being busy meant being active, not passive, but, again, because outside influences determined how she thought and felt, it was actually the reverse.

It didn't matter anyway. There was no longer any room for me in her life. I was a black thumb. I remember writing her a poem. I gave her all sorts of gifts—leg warmers, velvet knickers, books, jewelry, jars of sugared chestnuts, eggbeaters for her collection. I left a rose on her doorstep. I didn't have the words to leave her with, but nothing did any good. I once wrote out this passage and left it for her:

> *Whither thou goest, I will go; and where*
> *thou lodgest, I will lodge: thy people*
> *shall be my people, and thy God my God.*

The days passed. New Hampshire days—cold sun, steeples and the dying foliage that ironically took the color of human health. I bought some medium and made some acrylic pigments but rarely could work. The desire was there, but my imagination couldn't focus on anything— not so much because Farol was out of my life as because she was out having once been in. She had told me she loved me! Why had she? Why? I got up early in the dark to write letters to her I threw away. I continued teaching but it was awful. I had no close friends. I was alone all the time. I wanted to see her. I often drove by her apartment. The windows remained dark. She was never home.

There were escapes. Some were crude, some insidiously refined. She escaped her husband, he escaped her. They escaped me. Monday for her was devoted to laundry and errands and such; Tuesday night was "group"; Wednesday she went directly after work to Boston for anti-depressant drugs from Dr. Solomon and then drawing class; Thursday she played volleyball on a town team gotten up of local muttjacks and fat St. Ives businessmen; and Friday was saved either for shopping or bimonthly "openings" at the gallery—I wasn't invited anymore—where the same gray group she saw all week at work, including those fat-buttocked creatures of farce whose advice I thought behind much of this evasion, met to view some of the worst examples of shitshack art on the face of the earth. And Saturdays were never twice the same. Once or twice she went to Tweeze's house for a haircut. Sometimes she went to see Patty and Allen or Gustave and Sue. Or she went for walks, or took drives, or was off riding her bicycle, her flycycle, her goodbye-cycle.

I never saw her anymore. Whenever I pressed her, she said she was overtired and needed sleep as she didn't want to become ill again. What could I say? The spaces between leaves shape the leaves. I was beginning to get the picture.

I have to admit, nevertheless, I wasted all kinds of wonder on the subject. Was she going back? I didn't know. When? I didn't know. Was she lying? I didn't know that either. One had the feeling she was telling the truth, but not enough of it. I only knew she was suggestible. It led to the overreaching impulses she repeatedly showed in trying to realize possibilities through the sheer feat of physical decision: when she grabbed at an idea all her energy pushed at it in prolific concentration, and one could almost hear arriving from afar the servants of her slow but fearful intelligence to see it through. But she was also skeptical—it was the skepticism, not of reason, but of feeling, the root of which was the want of faith in herself. In her it was passive, a malady rather than a function of the mind, and yet by it, paradoxically, she sought to act.

It was an act, her decision to return to her husband, I first thought willful, then a weakness, but then I realized it was both, the will working against weakness in a sort of bellows movement expanding into false hope and then collapsing in true despair which all the while in its mad and hysterical precipitance lit no flame but only blew it out. It wasn't even action. And it wasn't merely wind. It was merely a show of doing something that she might escape the dreaded necessity of doing anything at all. Representing an act, it merely told her by indirection what in preventing by inaction she needn't be responsible for in her terrible aspiration to be more than she was while fearing to be nothing at all.

As her qualities were oppositely balanced, one set disabled the other. I remember her on one morning, for example, criticizing the shallowness of the gallery people, then that very evening at a party succumbing with them to the very kind of glib simplistic facility she pretended to scorn. It was cowardice. It was also greed, a way of having it all. She wanted everything.

One afternoon I saw Farol just pulling out of her driveway. She saw me and stopped her car, her face registering a slight strain at the sudden encounter. And I wondered: *are we nearer loving those who hate us than those who love us more than we wish?* To a degree her desire to avoid and perhaps displease me, oddly enough, had exactly the opposite effect. But I couldn't see her at her apartment, the gallery was impossible, and so I had to depend on pure luck. She was going to buy some shoes and said she was in a hurry because she was on her lunch hour. I asked if I could go with her. She pondered this a moment, sighed, and then relented.

We went to the Dexter Shoe Outlet.

She drove in silence. I asked a few questions, tried to converse. She gave short answers. I noticed the usual mess in her car: empty bags, broken frames, a parking ticket or two, pads of art paper. I inquired about her drawing course. She became evasive and grumbled something. The less she could abide her actions, I thought, the greater need she had for someone to approve them. There is a certain kind of wounded temperament that in its delinquency administers such irrational tests, going further and further astray solely to learn by means of trial whether this or that too will be condoned, the dispensable self fearfully asking another to prove her indispensability—one part of her running headlong faster and faster, the other keeping pace alongside, crying out in warning, pointing back.

Farol chose her shoes. I remember in an obsequious moment paying for them. I was trying too hard, I was indulgent, and it only irked her. Outside I remember her retrieving the cellophane from a pack of cigarettes I'd just unraveled and making a condescending and rather overelaborate remark about my littering. Littering! I thought of Lloyd and John and myself—and how many others?—but let the irony pass. It didn't matter anyway. I desperately wanted her back and told her so. She made no reply.

Whatever hopes I'd built up faded before the persistence of her silence. She wasn't so much sulking, she wasn't there. I remember I had to call on something.

"I've considered leaving St. Ives," I said, almost frightening myself at hearing the words. The chill of autumn was in the air. I was looking away, watching the fallen leaves, faded and crumpled. "I was offered a job teaching in Iowa."

A smile came into her eyes. She looked at the disappointment on my face in seeing the calmness with which she received the news. The Snow Queen. Cynicism feels superior; what it is indifferent to, it smiles at. She said, "I have several friends in Iowa, and they love it."

My wounded temperament diminished my pride. It was like swallowing stones to speak. "I'll wait for you. I'll promise Marina never to see her again."

She shrugged.

"We can have everything."

"No, we can't," she said.

"We can have the whole world."

"No, we can't."

"We can go anywhere."

"No, we can't."

"Please," I said, biting my lip, "what can we do about this?" My words sounded in a dry croak. "I'm hopelessly in love with you."

She looked through me. Her mouth was a straight noncommittal line.

I tried to gather her close until our faces were but a hand's width apart, but giving a fighting shake to her healthy head she pivoted and started to walk away without speaking. Something inside of me ran at her crying out in warning, pointing back. I felt crushed. I instantly felt the small boy's panic in me of being deserted, which made me think of my father, and what in reminding me of him—what was it?—he reminded me of.

There is a certain sagacity that constitutes the specific genius of the explorer; the great Amundsen proved his by guessing there was terra firma in the Bay of Whales as solid as on Ross Island. Then there is the quality of great leadership which is shown by daring to take a big chance. My father took a very big one indeed when he turned from the route to the Pole explored and ascertained by Scott and Shackleton and determined to find a second pass over the mountains from the Barrier to the plateau. He was the bravest, most farsighted of men. Yet for all of that he not only failed to provide a guardian for his children, he gave in to despair.

Suddenly I saw I resembled him in my own foolish design, looking far afield but missing crucial details right underneath my own nose. It made me feel heartsick and ridiculous. I thought: *two failed marriages*.

Farol got into her car and banged the door. I followed. She turned to look at me, very steadily, her face a cold white mask. The sheen in her eyes, enormously disturbing and cataleptic—almost cross-eyed in anger—seemed to ask, what do you want? And why do you want it from me?

High school education.

The futility of reaching her, of finding words reasonable or ruthless enough to convince her of anything at all had only minutes before filled me with despair. Slowly it began not to matter. I was quite positive now that nothing was worth this, nothing in heaven or on earth.

She had played with my vanity, my desire to possess her, and now didn't want it anymore.

Talentless, willful, bitter.

Her small head seemed to bristle as she turned away. She was a vulnerable, almost pathetic creature, injured only in that aware of her own bad fortune she was passive to caring about anyone else's, willing to let her behavior hurt whom it would. She'd spoken often of nurturing women. I looked at the Audubon sticker on her car with its suggestion that she was a fine person because she loved nature and spent a lot of time protecting it.

Under psychiatric care.

With her back half toward me she might have been addressing the world in the words she spoke. "Look," she said with a stern excommunicating air, "I'm just learning to feel better about myself. For once in my life I'm going to do exactly what I want to do. They told me this at 'group.' I have to learn to start saying no!"

Crippled.

There was a certain charity of cruelty for her at once to pronounce what was fated. She was feeling better about herself and I was dispensable.

"That's what you want?" I asked.

"Yes."

And indeed to me it meant no, at last.

5

I was determined to forget her. I threw away her letters. I took the few things she'd ever given me—a shirt, a wooden puzzle, two ceramic bowls, an oven thermometer, and a Wes Montgomery album—and dropped them into a box which I left in the doorway of a local thrift shop. If not to have is the beginning of desire, where's the possibility of remembering it? I wanted no reminders. I even took the jars of beans-in-brine she'd pickled for me, which tasted like wormwood, and pitched them out.

There was no longer complication, only a period of returning consciousness in which, beseeching all the angels above to help me prevail, I realized with a kind of exaltation I felt finally blessed.

I wanted no memories. I was tired of her tedious I-only-belong-to-the-night mood. I was fed up listening to one side of this boring and interminable domestic charade, the spiteful dialogues rehearsing inside her, and the mimicry of good judgment she was convinced settled, centralized, and confirmed her when, in fact, she only copycatted with preterimposterous stupidity what in her fancy she thought in federating she'd finalized. She was constitutionally incapable of being alone. It is often the way with impatient, aggrieved, expectant people. Temporizing for a while, they can't bear waiting—for no other reason most of the time than they find the presence of their own company intolerable.

Farol had reached no new solitude, I could tell, but for her any decision unleavened by distinction made the complicated simple. The vain person's ego tests nothing except upon its own ringing preconceptions and makes the mistake of identifying everything in terms of its own self-enlargement. She had the arrogance of the person not who felt fear but who lacked self-realization, but her lack of intellectual fiber, of mental muscle, was due not only to a lack of education, there was a deeper flaw in her makeup. She betrayed what she was in the way she changed direction: it was the way of a person swinging a sledgehammer, never bringing it down to stay but quickly reversing direction the better to come crashing back.

Yet the image gives her too much force. She seemed never convinced, never beguiled. For her nothing was symbolic, nothing allegorical or allusive in any way. It wasn't merely that in conversation she could relate only to what related to her, arguing why her errors were not errors and why mediocre work was excellent. It was more than that. There was want of a thinking heart. She was devoid of sympathetic imagination.

I found her pessimistic, secretive, ambitious, and totally lacking in the fostering principle which left nothing but a nonidentity that depended on separation, and even of that she was unaware. Was it all part of her illness? I didn't know, I didn't care. I'd come to see what I'd become in being with her—the kind of person making the sort of muttering judgments I did! When she was boring, I acted as if she were saying something important. When she was garrulous and talked to no consequence, I always nodded as if it mattered. When she was dull, I pretended she was interesting. When she was predictable, unimaginative, and routine, I listened as if to new and wonderful things, and I hated it! I swear, I didn't even want to be liked by her anymore. I didn't even want to be bothered.

And so I was just like her. I'd become as savage and intolerable myself, which is why the end of our affair, so long overdue, took the pressure off. I knew from the paradoxes of art the paradoxes of hope and expectation. The English sculptor John Deare caught a fatal cold by sleeping on a block of marble expecting to get inspiration in his dreams for carving it. I wanted to save myself the trouble. And before long I soon found release in the vow I made of resignation, where anguish fell away in the face of the right thing to unimagined peace and I could relax once more. And when I looked I couldn't believe what I saw. It was recognition, like the ringing of a bell somewhere. It was me. That relaxed person was *me!*

I began to paint again. I would have immediately left St. Ives if it hadn't been for the teaching commitment. I don't know, perhaps Bonnard perched on that hard bamboo chair of his was right, maybe comfort did mean the end of liberty. In any case, I began to work with a vengeance, and the greater the distance from Farol, I soon found the more perspective I got. I made a portraitlike collage of scourged and pasted papers based on my memory of her father—a refrigerator with a head—called *The Molybdenium Vault.* I did some flat and infinite landscapes, serigraphs called *Paler than Grass* (series one to five), all atmosphere, wordless moods affecting the heart without first consulting the mind. I did three watercolors, *Aunts at the Waldorf* and *Aga Babi.* And with *Sandy Neck Beach* I gave blue to the shore—following Vermeer—and brown to the sea.

What sense of release I felt was also linked to the painting fingers of November, the wind and color of which always called me to catechism and gave mile-high musings to my soul. To this period I can trace my rather successful *Death in Crimmitschau.* The large *Pilgrims at the al-Kadhemayn Mosque,* initially sketched in Baghdad, with its blue Persian tiles and gold central dome and minarets. A portrait of a beautiful student of mine, called *Catharine Weeks. Osric's Hat*—one Miró-red feather, the rest all gray and flat. And finally *The Wickerwork Woman,* a ghostly white nude in mid-scream with a crimped and crosshatched body, her hands gone up to her blinded eyes.

I entered not so much a new life as a life I had forgotten, finding out what I was before I'd lost myself and redeeming the time by completing my perspective on it. It should have told me what I didn't need.

As I put space between myself and my past misery I began to open up
emotionally in a constructive way. Whole areas of my heart were lib-
erated. And it wasn't only through work.

I called upon Marina again. Her mood like the light surf severed
from the billow which a breath disperses made humanity seem less hateful. I met her one evening in Boston after work. She was wearing a
yellow frock, a schoolgirlish tam on her head, and ran to hug me. She'd
lost weight, her body seemed as slight and as self-aware as a girl's before puberty, and I thought she might be ill. I found out she'd been
working very long hours. "I'm so happy to see you!" she exclaimed.
"We're still us, aren't we, happily and friendlily—can you say *friendlily*," she giggled. "I had a dream you and I were dancing together in
the sun!"

I couldn't help but compare her to the women at the gallery—their
selfishness, their imbecility!—squeezed together, disappointed at their
tables, stultified by each other's base concessions to the working schemes
tested day in and day out for all they could get.

Marina and I met whenever possible the following two weeks. She
was working, of course, and often had to be home evenings to do various jobs her mother refused to do herself so left waiting for her. But
we found the time. I remember we went on a picnic—apple cider and
gingersnaps—to Walden Pond and while I was sketching she found
an empty copper cartridge in the nearby woods, and we scribbled a
message on a slip of paper ("Christian Ford loves Marina Falieri")
which we rolled up into the cartridge and hammered flat and forced
into the crevice of a tree for all of eternity! We spent whole afternoons
together watching horror movies, buried in an avalanche of buttered
popcorn, at the old double-feature movie houses in Boston a few blocks
from the studio. We even attended the ballet, and taking a cue from
Bartok's *The Miraculous Mandarin* I later painted my own mandarin
at the very moment when, embraced by the girl he loves, wounded, he
bleeds to death.

And one time driving back from a day in the White Mountains
we passed through St. Ives, where out walking alone Farol actually saw
us—we came within a biscuit-toss of her—turning a corner on Route
51E. I caught a glimpse in my mirror of her quickly turning to look in
confusion only to fade behind like mist.

And I remember we went to the zoo, where Marina was the picture
of contentment looking at every bird and animal. I watched her laughing eyes following the flight of various birds, and caught the sunlit mo-

ment as one of them settled on her finger. I was struck by the lovely visitation and quickly sketched her in surprised delight. The Virgin of Beltraffio! Marina's face, unlike Farol's with its often unsettling dearth of expression, was not only full of character but also the stream of her attention, where it was drawn, what it lost or fled from, what tiny bursts of amazement and delight passed beneath its gaze. It was generosity itself. Her refined gaze reminded me in its soulfulness of Botticelli's women, and I thought: *their elegance like yours lies not so much in their clothes as in their bodies, and their bodies have received it, and continue unceasingly to receive it, from their souls, which are just like yours, lovely Simonetta.*

Several times we went to Cape Cod. It was wonderful to be with her again, looking at the sea through her eyes, walking through the woods, kicking through piles of leaves colored red and purple and deep vermilion. I used to tell her long stories at night, while I plied my brush, and she listened with charmed avidity. We were coming close to each other again, often talking into the wee hours of the morning. One always confides in what has no concealed creator. The quality of the way we were together told me how dull and painful it had been with Farol and that I didn't have to feel at fault. I remember once doing a pantomime—Marina was doubled up with laughter—to Mel Tormé's rendition of "The Brooklyn Bridge." And then we danced together in the dark to old 45's, Timi Yuro's "Hurt" and "Don't Say He's Gone" by the Short Cuts and John Lennon's "#9 Dream" and "Soul-Coaxing" by Raymond Lefevre and His Orchestra, and I began to wonder if magic wasn't the only thing that's real.

One afternoon we picked a bushel of Pound Sweets in my orchard, and she baked several pies. I mention this because, later, when the shushing trees held night in their branches and we were all alone in the falling moonlight of the yard, I said to Marina, "I don't want to leave you anymore." I hugged her and felt her thinness. I stepped back and took her face and looked into her eyes. Her lily-like paleness was suppressed in the beautiful rose that came blushing up when I asked, "Will you marry me—now, right now, tonight?"

She leaned fully into me, staying there for the longest time. Then she shook her head and said, "My mother."

Almost from the very moment we'd met she had become almost abnormally concerned with her family, the situation at home, and the harmony for living there that required she keep me at bay. I knew her mother opposed our ever being together, her selfish feelings toward her daughter becoming less the cause of keeping her from marriage than demonstrating by example how bad it could become by being what she was. And so what could I say?

Rather than deplore, however, Marina simply accepted and met life with the special transforming joy of the artist. I think it was her faintly disengaged way of loving things that made her so lovable. She even helped me in that direction. Before I met Marina I had virtually banished everything suggestive of impulse, pleasure, and freedom from my work, which for a while was a binge-and-purge cycle of bare doodles, stripe painting, and soulless nonfigural, planar, and geometric intricacies straitjacketing animated shapes for razor-sharp contours and abstractions. Deeply trivial, seriously overweight stuff. Bad. But I discovered in her what came out in my drawings. I thought how small unobtrusive objects, the reticent unself-dramatizing figures of Vuillard or Vermeer, are sometimes heroic and monumental almost in direct proportion to how "insignificant" they at first seem.

I've mentioned her goodness. Goodness is ungraspable, a quality beyond even being given a name. Marina had for a long time now been alive to some profound but untraceable displacing agency in our relationship, and yet all the while her almost preternatural calmness seemed able to cover whatever struggle was in her heart. It not only made the secrets I kept from her all the more foul to me, I'm certain it soon began to infect the way I saw her. I thought she was conscious of a premonition that her destiny was to prove unhappy—and that with a kind of scrupulosity for the ways of fate she showed no desire to escape it. She never told me this. She wasn't the kind of person who would. She never speculated, never mind complained. But I felt it somewhere within me.

We were driving back from the Cape after one of those trips, I remember, a lavender glow paling in the west, when speaking of our affections for one another she told me in so many words that the most important thing about love was not expecting it. That way, when it occurred, it was like a present. At that moment she struck me as immediately—and, in a way, breathtakingly—alone. I distinctly remember wanting to shout that it was thanks to her belief in such nonsense that she had allowed me to meet Farol. My attitude was insensitive enough to force her to the wall in the hurtful questions I didn't intend but had to pose about what she wanted or didn't want.

She was at first silent. I saw her eyes rimming with tears. I desperately wanted her to include me in her life, now more than ever. Then she said, "I've been trying to earn more money. It has nothing to do with my mother. It's my father. He can't work anymore," said Marina. I didn't understand.

"What do you mean?"

She paused a long time.

"He's dying of cancer."

I realized in her attempt that afternoon to spare me knowing this that it was Marina who showed me it was only when a person puts off his or her egotistical self, and with it the needs he demands, that one can become open to the truths not specially *determined* by those needs.

I found it ironic that Farol herself helped me see the same thing but in an indirect and opposite way, for in showing me all she *didn't* do of what she should I was told in all I observed what I finally couldn't ignore. We choose what we shouldn't. The things we crave aren't the things we need. We cannot shed our symptoms because we cannot shed ourselves. I was like her myself, often seeing the imaginary world too clearly to play a part in the real, and always selfishly trying to make a virtue of my vice. It's with ambition as it is with adultery. Her dangers were always mine.

Farol and Marina: it was as if, almost geometrically designed for it, each threw the other into sharp relief. And yet while both shared the same range, the same beauty, the same sort of background, the same lack of education, they nevertheless might have been from different species. Farol wanted things; Marina couldn't will. I sympathized with Marina.

But I pitied Farol. I thought her projection into the future a totally regressive urge. She was trying to pound up the crows by shutting the park gate. Strangely, when reality reaches a certain level of repulsiveness, when the human psyche is outraged by external circumstances it feels powerless to avoid, the remedy for survival among certain people is often a blindly developed attempt to try to make it seem actually desirable. Failures can virtually seem like success, bad memories assume a fairer form. I think she believed with overriding assessment that it was easier than not to stave off utter bankruptcy of conscience by taking up one unpaid promise with only yet another at larger, heavier interest until such self-swindling became habitual and by degrees almost painless.

But would it be painless?

I doubted it. She was a girl with a grudge. I saw her obstinacy, an obstinacy, an automatic opposition to the bullying—and nullifying—enforcement of both her husband and father. It was, in fact, the opposition *of* obstinacy. She wasn't a producing but a produced creature. She'd been ignored, she felt undefined, I'm certain she found her promises to me to be traitorous to another. But she wanted something else. She wanted money—more than she needed it, she felt she deserved it. Wasn't that the quickest way to succeed? To marry a successful man? I came to look upon her as no different than some sort of buzzer-show contestant in a bunny suit spinning wheels of fortune on a stage and lunging after baskets of cash.

Actually, Farol had less working credentials than a menial. The trouble was, she had even less faith in herself. The little education and small skills she had were a constant and derisive reminder of possible misfortune. It was unthinkable! Without someone to support her, she knew she could easily end up a carhop or cleaning lady or chain-store daisy. It has always annoyed me that people who rise above their station by marrying out of it not only make the loudest claims for independence but are usually the least patient with those who remaining below remind them of what once they were. But it was positively astonishing to think that the solution to all her problems was simply to give up and become a dim-witted parasitic luxury item at the beck and call of yet another authority.

Her husband had summoned her. She was called upon to submit. Middle-brows believe in authority. Her father, her husband, her therapist. She had to return. She found life alone hard, and uncertain, even frightening. There were bills. Expenses. She missed a certain standard of living, social prestige. Her husband could provide this. And that was her anchor to windward. She was realistic. And so I saw confirmed what all along she knew with the poet, that the instances that move a second marriage are base respects of thrift, but not of love. If people with money basically distrust people with power, people without money tend to give it a power all its own. The only trouble was, the financial advantages her husband gave her not only bestowed his authority but prevented her independence, the power of his incumbency robbing more than it rewarded.

He put up with her, he paid for things. But as women have long known, chivalry often masks dismissal, if not utter contempt. It was clear she was trying to put a brave face on everything. She had to defer to her husband in all ways now. But having to respect and defend him made her hate him even more.

She was related to a man in marriage, not by affection, but by a system of exchange. He was her jailer—an architect of both prohibition and permission. The debts he paid dehumanized her, the money she took deformed. As she continuously remained the most negative person I'd ever known, why was I surprised? She expected salvation to come in the form of a male or marriage, but while this proved an avid will to exist it was also a dream of annihilation, for no urge could ever speak more directly to a person's sense of inadequacy or self-defection. She was in competition with herself. She wanted success in the person she married but simultaneously loathed the role it imposed on her. The closer she came to someone, the greater the disengagement effected. The very source of her income invalidated her and placed all her sufficiency under the perspective of having been robbed.

There was a labored irony in all of it. The common phrase *to pay attention* contains an unsuspected accuracy. She was a cathected object. An emotional payment was due. And it was this she so bitterly rued, not merely for being an underling or a gossoon, but a commodity, virtually an article of commerce. She was herself the property she was seeking.

I loved her, I merely couldn't cope with the situation anymore. But grieving for the loss of someone we love is paradise compared to living with someone we hate. I saw what she was up against. I couldn't help recall the previous spring when, constantly seeking definition from me, she gave none herself. Now she was looking for an impossible solidity while at the same time committing herself almost irreversibly to a process of disintegration. It was a downward spiral. I envisioned her creeping back to her husband like a pet, a creature of its owner's habits, settling into a life of compromise and mistrust rather than face life on her own. Once more locked in together they would rediscover each other, and it was only too apparent what would happen then. It had happened before.

As Farol never decided with deliberation, she never acted without making a mistake. I thought she would fail—organizers always fail. If you don't know what love is, you don't know what it isn't. The lack of complete commitment to their marriage created a lack of finality in the separation. They couldn't excise what they never finished. She would try to ignore the past. It cannot be done. When you have a bad back it is impossible to lie facedown. She would try to retain beliefs she had given up believing, but that cannot be done either. Her desperation was her pride. In natures so imperfectly mixed it is not at all uncommon to find vehemence of intention the prelude and counterpoise to a weak performance, the willful nature striving with unpersuadable logic to keep up its self-respect in the face of inevitable defeat.

Did that matter to her? I suppose it would have if she had thought about it. But she didn't think. She merely continued to do. Dreams are our temptation, ambition stammering after all it would have like the aspiration of art. I knew what she wanted from someone by what I wanted from her. Whether a shadow pursues or is being pursued, it's the only story Narcissus knows. The imagination wants everything back one more time.

I knew it was time for her to cross back over that black threshold, that final demarcation, neither dragged nor led, but driven by self-impairment into that gaunt, skull-empty house, and she would hear the doors slam upon her.

There is no loneliness like that of a failed marriage. She would crawl between the barren sheets and lie down narrow like a rake turned upward and dangerous, half its teeth gone, the others at uneven intervals counting doubly as sharp spikes.

And then she would try to sleep mating with herself, straining all night to hear something of help come to prevent it but sounding only the fathoms of limitless darkness, her face turned toward the wall to read the handwriting there in that pallet of cold antipathy called a marriage bed.

But then, of course, I should have known better. That's just exactly what she didn't do.

6

Farol did nothing.

She became confused, not by her husband's presence, but by his presence coupled with my absence, and she somehow couldn't fill the unforgiving minute.

The fear of not being wanted enough had actually given the situation she'd formerly found in being free greater assurance, but now she saw herself forced with an even greater fear to have to imagine that which she didn't know or even really understand. She had begun to get things wrong which she had previously gotten right. Her craving for uniqueness doomed her to increasing engagement with everything that only served to obliterate it. The desire to be other than she was now told her she wasn't enough. She wanted to be needed too much.

Delacroix was right. One line has no meaning, a second one is needed to give it expression. She needed me in her life to tell her what she felt about her husband.

I'd had the premonition of such a thing for a long time. But let me first explain. I had to fight the hope for a while that after some costly weeks, at the first symptoms again of her husband's silence and neglect, she would kick the glass out of a few windows and come back to me. I became less concerned as time passed. And finally I didn't care anymore. I wished her loneliness. And suddenly it was as if out of the anticipations of some black privacy, out of some nightmare had of bitter justice, the intercepting witch of fairy tale appeared in a puff of smoke to cry "Your wish is granted!"

Farol began to leave me notes. I ignored them. She came by, knocking. I refused to answer the door. I came across an article in a magazine on a possible cure for MS I'd scissored out for her. Now I didn't care whether she saw it or not. She began to miss me. She was soon leaving me long letters, feeble attempts in the matter of loye at complex reasoning and analysis and redolent with the sort of sentiments one might expect from someone whose reading was confined to pseudosociological books on why women didn't open up more and fat mid-cult paperbacks dealing with the erotic and gladiatorial adventures of amazons in animal skins.

The incontrovertible fact remained—this was my premonition— she needed us both. A clear commitment to one as distinct from the other could only exacerbate the loneliness dealt her, she felt, in failing to have both of us for all she set out to have. To estimate what it was, she summoned each, not so much to have in both what neither alone could give, but rather to see in terms of either all she was given to choose. She was driven desperately over and over again in her double life to find herself somehow redeemed in the chastisement she felt for faithlessly loving one man by an absolution of the guilt she felt for faithfully hating another.

At first it seemed a tremendously strange conceit: if one of us disappeared, he took the other with him—or more accurately, left the other the more hideously visible. When one was gone, the other went missing. I acquitted her of what he couldn't, he what I, and she felt cleansed.

But it wasn't working out that way. As she came physically closer to one of us, he immediately lost the distinguishing quality of distance necessary in fantasy for her to avoid calling up the other missing in fact. For Farol each of us was actually composed of indistinctions. Her husband and I virtually formed one incorporeal man, and she reveled in the image, the balance, informing this phantom figure who seemed truer and more real because he was fashioned of phenomena that by definition could not be present. Distinctions, paradoxically, made us the *less* real, for only by distancing each of us could she stay close, not only to both, though that was required, but essentially to what she wanted of all she didn't have.

Whereas at first I thought she was playing a musical game of love by rules outdated and invented long ago, it finally struck me as faintly psychopathic. She was pitting each of us off against the other, but in doing so rendering herself meaningless by seeking the impossible. It was a mode of equivocation translating itself not only into the mud-dark act of adultery but into a negativity growing from it that finally began extending itself to her own person to reveal the pointless object she'd become. She was annihilating herself, a woman clutching the exception in the insane conviction that it could become the rule. She worshiped lack.

She lived separated from and therefore could care about her husband much more than when living together she despised him. It was counterwishing, affirmation, and disavowal all at once. Simply put, she was never as much mine as when she was with him. And I realized it would never be her husband who'd take her away from me—you can't change a personality—no, her return to him could only guarantee the best way of finding me. But then of course another conclusion was unavoidable: there was a third man in this as well. I knew when she met someone else, she would be gone.

I had often told her I feared that, always to hear her insist she was unapproachable. But now so was I. I avoided her. I wanted *her* to feel what neglect was. The first step in describing silence, to use silence itself, made me keep silent. More and more, passionately, I didn't, in a larger sense, care. I continued working. She came by all the time, rapping at the window, crying at the lock, but I refused to see her. And I ignored the knocking, the knocking, the knocking. *You don't want to be with anyone.* Knock, knock. *You have to feed the cat.* Knock, knock. *You have to start saying no.*

I wanted her to go back to her husband.

She reminded me of my own falsity, for it all came back to me, didn't it? I myself needed Marina to balance my own disappointment with Farol. The faults we're most ready to condemn in others are precisely those we hate in ourselves, and if her fault was not seeing, mine was failing to look. I didn't want to condemn her, I simply found love a cruel and terrible heartache that made me feel sad, vulnerable, and out of control. It had the same annunciatory symptoms of and gave me exactly the same feeling as fear—the pang in the stomach, the giddy apprehension, the wild surmises. What does it mean if one's body responds to dread and to falling in love in the same way?

Anyway, I flung open my door one afternoon in late November, and there stood Farol—her fist raised to knock again—looking doubtful and sheepish and abject. I felt an inexpressible irritation at seeing her and asked what she wanted. She was wearing the gold earrings I gave her. I wanted to ask by what privilege she could come to my rooms but I couldn't go to hers. She asked somewhat tentatively, fumbling up a sheaf of pencil sketches, if I'd like to see some of the work she'd done in the drawing course.

She apologized for being in a rush. Her sisters, visiting for the day, had come with her—moral support, no doubt—and were waiting outside. I was working, but felt obligated to invite them in. For a moment it seemed they preferred to sit in the car. But Farol went out, urgently spoke to them, and they condescended to come in, gliding through the door to honor me with the half-hour audience I was granted and looking around my rooms with peevish consideration until overcome by a pricking urge to leave, presumably to the whelk habitation from which they'd come.

Lucy and Lenore were plain as cats. They inspected the chairs, sat down, and swapped looks. I moved my easels, I'd been working on something, and my hands and palette knife were covered with paint. Several paintings were drying on stiltlike boxes. The place smelled of stand oil, wax emulsions, resins, and fish glue. I set aside some jars of brushes, dividers, and cleared away a tableful of rags. I asked Farol's sisters a few questions out of politeness. They said nothing. Would they like a drink? They didn't answer. Had they ever visited St. Ives before? Hadn't one of them? They quizzically repeated my words, which seemed to stump them. Farol nervously intercepted my questions for them to save face: she didn't think so. No. Sometimes. Oh, they like it.

I had heard a good deal about these twins from their sister, that they were bright, athletic, etc. I saw only two dry rabbity virgins with no poise who seemed deaf and factitious and drained of color. They were fingerheads, spoiled and oddly chinless, their small snipe-featured faces like raptors in duplicate unillumined by any ray of kindness and made up largely of negatives—no grace, no conciliation, no forming intelligence. I'd never seen faces so inimical to imaginative depth. It was the evil of two lessers. Their pinched mouths gave the impression of not working easily, leaving them scowling while looking at you with a kind of stupid, open-eyed lack of cooperation. They reminded me of the tiresome old ladies I met in St. Ives society.

I picked up the sheets of cockled Fabiano, frayed from rubbed-out elbows and hands, and took a few minutes to look over Farol's drawings—six or seven misconfigured nudes of such pagan and fox-footed incompetence and so muddled in anatomy I actually wondered if she was joking. It was awful work, stiff, badly observed, and untruthful. Keep your day job, I thought. I wanted to ask, "Is this your work? Yes? Well, I've seen it, and you should give up drawing immediately. Look at me. You may have gifts that lie in another direction, don't be depressed, but it is definitely not here, do you understand?"

Again I looked through them and tried to find a line or a shape or a turn of limb to single out for compliment, but there was literally nothing to commend in a style as radically antiart as the interests on which it fed were antilife. Why didn't she simply recognize she had no talent and leave it at that?

"What's that?" one of the twins asked sourly. It was a clipped impatient voice.

I turned to find her pointing to a large painting, sweetened with mastic resin that morning and still in its stretchers. It was a portrait of a young girl in her mid-twenties, her head thrown slightly back as if in movement—on her finger sits a dove she's about to kiss—her lips parted in a half smile, her puff sleeves and visible bodice a rich Peking blue with maroon darting, the tips of which I gilded with bole, the folds revealing in their extravagance of detail what I had learned from the paintings of Jacques Tissot. The face is refined to the highest degree of loveliness, its features illuminated by a left-to-right movement of light eliminating tonal contrast exactly where the angle of view would lead us to expect it. I'd hit the target in one shot.

The vision shows a benignly corporeal oneness of aspect, female beauty in a secluded richness and repose so luminous that the viewer's place could only be a benighted one were it not for the fact that the image ultimately draws us into a life emerging into the life of the world, light into light. But it is not the light, not the dove, but the image of the girl, cradled tenderly in a moment of suspension beyond space and time, that provides a still point of balance and stability about which the world not only gravitates but somehow reciprocates by protectively enclosing her in a delicate warmth scooped out of an unfathomable mixture of radiance and shadow that nothing can ever disturb.

I was secretly overjoyed they'd seen it, especially Farol, who looked at it with silent and unconcealed melancholy. There was no doubt what the painter felt for his subject.

> " 'My lady sat within an oaken stall
> Framed as the virgin of Beltraffio,' "

I said. "Frederick Rolfe." I paused. "Do you read?"

Their faces sharpened as if I were exposing them to annoyances they felt they ought to be spared. Each had a red tip to her nose, which twitched, and as they looked at the painting I noticed their skin take on green chloral undertones. I heard sarcasm and strangled murmurs. It was as if they were trying to swallow and be cruel at the same time. But they didn't answer.

I had a good idea where the rudeness and cruelty came from. It was lack of imagination, surely. They had no more of it than sound is sound in echo. I hated the phony hypothecating pretense they had of even thinking they could find the worth in such a painting, and I'm sure I showed that in the offhand way I had them move while I covered it. As if in contempt, again one of them—Snow White or Rose Red, I'm not sure which—stuck her feet up on the short bar of one of the easels until I tripped the castors, and she almost fell. Sorry, dear.

People aren't awful, I thought, families are. I recalled their father, that forbidding man who seemed to me as obsolete as the big-boned prehistoric monsters of Neanthropia he resembled. I saw his rigid prohibitions peremptory and brutally present in Farol's need to be the artist she wasn't. Surely the artist-as-hero represented the family-as-ruin to her, so why should her sisters in that legacy have been spared the same thought? And then wasn't it difficult to be a painter and not appear an attention-seeker? I think that they wanted to disabuse me of their falling for any of it.

I've always hated interruptions, but this was impossible, and I kept wondering when they'd have the grace to leave. One of them yawned. Another asked if she could use my telephone. There were long and uneasy silences. Farol tried to fill these but when she spoke to her sisters it was with an overobliging foolishness of expression that would have served to any observer as a marked illustration of her finding whatever height to which she might lift the discussion too great for them to reach. I remember at the time trying to figure out why Farol seemed suddenly so young; then I knew: she was immature—and in their presence it was embarrassing.

But they were positively juvenile, making the most incoherent, the most unexpected remarks and trying with low repartee, sadly and nervously, to joke with each other at awkward moments in the private language they used to relate like schoolgirls—they were thirty years old—which included various names they called each other like "La La" and "Choocheeface" and "Babycakes." It was hilarious.

Can you see me owning a telephone?

"I've never had such fun," I said.

"Fun," said Lucy, breezing out the door.

Lenore added, "Such fun."

Neither looked back.

Ashamed at hearing an echo of herself, Farol lingered a moment to try to explain or say something to me.

She saw it was pointless.

And they left.

7

I felt bad. I didn't want to leave it like that. I decided that night to stop by Farol's apartment. I drove over and took with me the magazine article on MS. There was a bright moon and cold starlight and under the stark trees the lawns and fallen leaves were silvered over and crossed with shadows cerulean and cobalt blue. The wind smelled of trees, fumed oak. I saw Farol's lights on. There was no sign of her husband's car, I checked. I pushed the doorbell, and after looking down from an upper window she came downstairs to let me in, first peering out the door, left and right—a ghostly white-faced barnowl, slowly blinking—to be sure no one saw us.

I asked if she'd like to go to the movies. She said she would. I followed her upstairs. It was the first time since early summer I'd been to her rooms. She hadn't put in a telephone either. I noticed a new sofa bed. She seemed jumpy at my being there. I thought it possible her husband might come by. She hadn't expected me and appeared nervously anxious to leave.

I knew she felt trapped there. The months had been long and pointless. I saw her, night after night, unable to sleep and fighting panic while all the plans of her campaigns that were once clear faded and disappeared on the blackened ceiling above. No amount of busyness saved her from always having to return from another day, turn down her bed, and wait out the long nights with her lost dreams pressed to her skimpy pillow wondering what she should do not to be alone. She couldn't face being alone. Anything but that. Being alone was death. It left only the memory of her unhappy marriages and the nagging dissatisfactions of watching women with ability make something of themselves while she remained shut out.

She never expressly envied them. She actually *feared* envy—it would be to confess too much. And yet ironically her fear of envy prevented her at the same time from being impartial toward herself and from being able to recognize the several ways, by accepting who she was, she could have measured up.

My subsequent visits found her always the same. She seemed bored and perpetually tired. She sat around a lot lugubriously watching television—I never knew anybody who watched television so much—or maybe sewing a shirt or socks as she listened to "A Prairie Home Companion" on the radio. But most of the time she spent hours doing nothing but sleeping or frowsting about or reading big trashy novels to no consequence, things with names like *Reach for Tomorrow* or *Forever Memories* or *So Lovely, So Dead*. She rarely received mail and almost never answered letters.

Farol procrastinated a lot. She never paid bills on time or easily met obligations. She began to bear an uneasy resemblance to me of Albrecht Dürer's *Melancholy,* the sad woebegone woman with fixed look and neglected habit leaning on her arm and staring into space. I was convinced her incapacitating patterns had their source in the overly coercive but unloving parents against whom she rebelled, her delays and postponements serving as a sort of private resistance to any type of order, command, or expectation. She often said she intended to do something about it all but I think secretly enjoyed the deceptive resistance, failing to understand somehow that her self-reproaches about dawdling or slouching misaccomplishment became only a hoax perpetrated on herself.

I saw her apartment hadn't changed. There was a paleness, a lack of firm outline, to her personality which she gave to the place. I showed her the article I'd brought and wasn't surprised to see it didn't impress her one way or the other; she looked at it, sort of nodded, and indifferently set it aside—we had to leave, she said, and began getting ready. I looked around. There were the usual prints and photographs I'd seen before. Like many rootless people, she was possessive, acquiring what she could in the way of visual art, much of it bought at the gallery on installments and most of it the work of local artists and their advocates in St. Ives who knew each other and bought each other's work, purchases invariably born of impulse and insecurity rather than taste.

Nothing is more subtly destructive than a closed circle of artists feeding on one another. Envy grows from insignificant differences between people, not from overwhelming inequalities, so while the artists in St. Ives were less supportive of each other than envious, it was envy that forced them to emulate one another, not esteem. The curious result was that whenever you visited anyone in St. Ives, his or her house looked exactly like everyone else's, in the den the same photograph, above the mantel the same vaporous print, on the coffee table the same ceramic or sand candle or mammary bronze. You saw the same little objects everywhere, married in one place, committing adultery in another.

I noticed Farol had moved her stereo—her husband's, she said, another concession of his to her during this famous period of deliberation. I looked at her records, idly flipping through various albums, jazz, some classical, odds and ends. I lifted out an album of recorded bird calls just as she appeared behind me. "We mustn't be nosy," she said playfully grabbing it, slightly angry, a blush of shame calling up a spot on her cheek for having been caught with it. I was hardly prying into her personal things, but I'm afraid that in Farol's rooms there were a great many wrong places. She never did a bird call again.

But there was something else. I couldn't help noticing on a kitchen shelf not only something new but what I understood to be, at least in terms of the pretensions to art she always affected, an unlikely acquisition—a cheap porcelain mug with red letters: *St. Ives Country Club.*

"Mixing with the swells, Farol?" I asked, laughing and holding it up.

She grabbed it. I thought: *oh-oh.*

"Did someone give it to you?"

"Ne-ver mind," she said, lilting her voice with unconvincing and painful jokiness, and shoving the mug in the closet shut the door. I knew that lilt, it meant drop the subject. I thought the movies a good idea as she seemed half-cross, half-confounded for having to eat the confused explanations she couldn't digest. But the evening had just begun that way.

Pulling on her jacket, trying to change the subject, Farol began apologizing for her sisters' earlier rudeness as we walked downstairs. They were like that with people, she said, she didn't know why. "If you want to know the truth," she said, "I've never really cared for them myself." *More villain thou,* I thought. We were just stepping out the front door when out of nowhere a man suddenly appeared. He was a tweedy fellow with a large head, puttyball nose, and a shank of care-fully waved blond hair—I swallowed fate: her husband—but he never looked at me, only stepped forward confidently and smiled. "Hi, Farol," he said. "Are you feeling better?"

It wasn't her husband. It was Ted. Farol introduced us. She had no choice. She did so quickly. But her face was pasteboard. She looked like a ghost overtaken by daybreak. The three of us awkwardly stood there for a moment. The silence was like something pressing down on your head. She thrust her hands into her pockets, hastily took them out again. Still she said nothing. It was as if a goblin had suddenly appeared to retrieve something long owed him. I felt embarrassed for her and ex-cused myself.

I went to my car and got in. Farol stepped quickly out of the porch-light. He followed, changing his smile of greeting to something like a reminder of a certain secret, an intimate knowledge between them. They spoke quietly in the darkness for a full five minutes. I couldn't hear them. But I watched them. He was about thirty, jockeyed in the legs, and had a look arch with smiling insinuation. He spoke, she listened. She spoke, he listened. It wasn't a conversation, rather an exchange of explanations, arrangements, but in her something was holding its breath.

There was a suggestive look to them, the awkwardness of unfaith-ful people caught dead in their predicament, and for the understanding they shared, the prompt responses, the nodding comprehension, the amplitude of accord in the way they stood—turned protectively half-away together in a kind of huddled scrum—I no longer had intimations but the real fact of that third man waiting in the dusky future to rob me of all I had to lose.

My tongue swelled and stuck to my palate; it was the first really sharp falsity I had known in her, to touch and be touched by. It was like a bad dream. I watched their intercourse and felt angrier and more jealous than I'd ever felt of her husband. I knew something was between them. The criminal in the dock, the flat-headed murderer bending over to speak to her advocate. A pair of lean hungry mountebanks, a clown and a harlequin unprepared in a prank on their foolish stage. Two adulterers caught horrified in the lime-whitened orchard under a bare moon. I felt as if I had slept through the progress of some dark drama, suddenly finding the curtain had come up but I had lost an act. And as I waited I became as much her husband as her lover, a spectator in a special shade of desecration, looking only at myself but fooled enough to be both.

As I look back I don't think from that moment on in all the subsequent time I knew her I ever trusted her again. I only wonder if I knew it at the time.

I heard over and over again as I sat there the echo of the stranger's words: *are you feeling better?* Better? Better than what? Than when? She had told him of her illness! It was an intimacy—I'd noticed it before—she could share at the drop of a hat with a passing stranger or a chance acquaintance. I began to think her psychiatrist was right, maybe she was a kind of "come-on." Farol tended to treat each man she met as special, an intimacy, I thought, created out of her own feelings of emptiness. It was an emptiness that constantly had to be filled.

I had heard of women who constantly needed to know men wanted them, who were driven to find newer and newer converts to create an image of themselves *for* themselves. It was like looking in a mirror, and if she sometimes ended up in bed it was proof of his adoration as well as her own desirability. To be alone for such a woman is often to have no identity, to be extinguished.

Farol's self-assertion often took the form of illness. She had a bias toward the ill, the bent, the crippled. A hypochondriac as well as something of a fitness freak—not a contradiction—she took comfort in one coming forth to scold the other, the resultant tension between the two, weirdly, giving her a certain identity. Queerly attracted to medicine, the upshot, I'm sure, of childhood needs, she found that the mere act of being given pills, spoonfuls of cough syrup, or remedies of any sort bestowed not only recognition but a kind of love. Pampering meant a great deal to her. She had obsessions about recovery, as someone ill would. But they somehow never made her well. I once thought because she was trying to get better, I soon noticed she gave high publicity to doses, diseases, and diagnosis. She was intrigued by medicine and doctors, of course, as she was by any profession or vocational skill that, mystifying her, drew upon her respect. But, it's true, all patients are doctors, and every invalid a physician.

I felt brutal thinking it, but I thought she exaggerated with harmful effect the momentousness of this illness of hers. I thought she could improve by wanting to. It was not so much her taking an accursed delight in discovering the destructive side of every blessing—although she was one of those people always blowing out the lights to see how dark it was—but rather the desperate need growing out of her deep insecurity of showing herself vulnerable and of finding it congenial to have constantly asked of her by various friends things like "Feeling better?" and "Are you sure you're going to be all right?" and "You're not going to go and ruin yourself again, now, are you, Farol?" Thumping subscriptions to her worth went nowhere. One had to gather oneself instead to the importance of these solicitations before any measure of love could ever apply.

Suddenly Farol's visitor turned and disappeared into the night. I could see some accord had been reached. She got into the car and was completely silent. She never looked at me. Driving away, I was absolutely determined not to speak first. I could tell she was having a quick interval of intensive thinking. You could follow the dots: she began to prepare her mind to define the plan from which she was to make her explanation. She settled that she would be grave. And mute. I said nothing. We neither of us said a word.

The movie playing was *All About Eve*. We didn't stay long. I remember finding, and feeling her find, horrible parallels of deceit as we sat there watching it—the slow revelations, the terrible coincidences, the hypocrisy. The irony was overwhelming. It was as if a mouse trap had been set. From the screen several times in almost documentary fashion seemed to come hideously apt moments of truth and revelation at every moment. Weighted down, Farol began sinking, going even lower in her seat. There is that scene of dreadful recognition where Anne Baxter, the successful understudy of Bette Davis on the night of her triumph, viciously tears off her stage wig in frustration when her advances are rejected by Gary Merrill. At that very moment Farol quickly turned to me and said she felt ill. And so we got up and left in the middle of the thing and heading home there was the same heavy oppressive silence in the car.

Darkness became visible. Grim clouds banked in the north appeared hard in the gathering gloom like mighty steps of granite, east and west the low hills, crowned with gaunt trees, shut out the light. In painting it's axiomatic: how can I tell what I'm thinking until I see what I say? It takes a knowledge of anatomy to draw a clothed figure.

I couldn't stand it any longer and swerved to the side of the road. I took a breath.

"Who was that?"

I remember thinking: *please don't lie.* But she was ready for it.

"Ted?"

"He seemed to know you so well," I said.

There was a kind of gulping embarrassment. She tried to laugh, which gave it a guilty sound. "Why do you say that?"

I was determined to sit there all night if I had to, and Farol knew I would. I turned to her. Her face looked like a rheostat. Slowly she passed a hand over her head and sighed. I was then given a brief story reported in a voice that overstating its calm was betrayed by a small quaver of anxiety. The reply was a reaction, not a judgment. She completely dismissed the entire incident, taking the ground of being surprised I'd actually found anything wrong. The dog ate my homework, that sort of thing. She held her breath every few seconds as if for deliberation to prove she wasn't breathless and was trying too hard to speak sternly to make it believable.

"It was nothing," she said. "He's someone who came into the gallery once or twice. He's almost never around. He travels a lot. He's a professional golfer. I played golf with him once last summer. Maybe twice. It doesn't matter. He knows my sisters. He's a friend. Not even a friend. Only an acquaintance. In fact, that's all he is. A person. Not even that. No one. Nobody."

Nobody? I suddenly remembered the St. Ives Country Club mug, and everything fell into place. Nobody leaves me, she meant. I felt the rebuke echoing from last August, from my neglect of her at the end of last summer. And the truth ticked up like a telegram: *Gone to the links. Have fun with Marina. Happy Birthday.*

Farol continued to pretend not only to see no complication—she had a tendency to talk loud when she was either wrong or lying—her nonexplanation was almost tantamount to her saying nothing had happened, that no one had even appeared at the door. And finally she grew haughty, the pride employed when wit breaks down. The truth I so strongly sensed contained no details, no incidents or events, no real facts of any kind, but I could see a horrified pull of regret in her anxious attempt to believe, and so spare herself, the lie. And the more she went on about it, the more the features of her face only blundered in dissimulation. "I loathed the jealousy I felt. I wondered what it had caused. Jealousy can actually foster infidelity, reminding beauty by way of visual proof of all it can have without so much as lifting a finger."

I asked nothing further. I drove her home. I thought her attempt at handing me over to ignorance made her only the more subject to it herself. There was nothing said to inform, only convince. It was a confession twisted like mullet, with nothing in it that didn't match the weakness and failure of the many other arts she took up. And I knew why. She lacked conscience, of which taste is merely an overt expression. As conscience is the basis of taste, so taste is the correcting and controlling factor with regard to the imagination. And I was certain now some part of her imagination was involved in perpetuating herself only because she had neither.

But I felt shattered. The horror of having found all this seated in all its ease where I had only dreamed of good, the horror of finding this thing hideously behind so much that I'd trusted, sickened me. She said good night. From the driveway I watched her walk to the house with that listing gait and disappear through the peach-colored doors which the moon dyed funereal purple, but not before, upon leaving the car, she turned to apologize for spoiling the movie, and then added, "I'm not well, you know."

8

Suddenly, Farol turned up in commons the next day. The dining hall at St. Ives was always loud, an uproar of bright voices and clattering forks. I ate there to save time and money, commons privileges being one of the perquisites for teachers at the school. It was always crowded. Students sat everywhere, their spirits soaring so high that often, only later, confirmed outside by the peaceful silence, did that noise finally register. I didn't mind it—or the occasional student hanging over me— as it took my attention from the inner sense of agitation I'd been feeling.

She found me sitting at an end table. While she had an open invitation to join me for meals there—and often came, which was a big help to her financially—she didn't like the students. And she liked the faculty even less. The whole experience hung together with too private a gaiety, too manifestly spoiled an air, for her to like the place, and she was one of those people who always kept aloof wherever she felt obscure.

It wasn't merely that St. Ives was rich and exclusive, what bothered her was that she wasn't. And what renewed the obscurity was her strange response to a place she was at the same time using. She made flippant remarks about the students and their parents' wealth and the pampered way they lived. Frequently she'd point out as she ate—failing to see the irony of it—how the faculty members were like welfare dependents who, living off the school, needed in a kind of pathetic communion to be taken care of. I always wanted to ask if she had in mind any inspiring precedent.

Since I hadn't eaten, I suggested lunch. The procedure was to take a tray and file to the front, buffet style, where meals were served by kitchen workers, mostly women, who were slow and incompetent at a most unspectacular job. It took a while to see it but over a period of time, her face putting up little fights, Farol began to show—I don't know if it was a lack of civility or a certain contempt for these people. At first I tried to overlook it, but then couldn't. I could tell they challenged her, not by anything explicit, rather the recognition as she saw it of her own extinguished rights. Pity impossibly misapplied. Their servile and undignified jobs lost rather than won them to her.

And it was the same with waitresses in restaurants. She couldn't relinquish kindness, not to them, for any deference shown in that direction took too much away from her. The result was she always took an arrogant tack with fussy little instances of disapproval, distancing herself from them socially in order to disassociate herself from them in mind. I'm sure she was looking into her own future fears. It was obvious she had a glimpse of herself, lost, luckless, and humiliated—a bag lady, old Granny Sprat, toothless and neglected, down and out, her long greasy hair falling over her shoulders and no one around to care.

I believe Scrulock and Co. were spared this same kind of coldness only because of their spruce efficiency at convincing her they were bluestockings instead of the scrubbers and frumps they really were. The art gallery actually served that turn for all of them. They felt the place gave them a certain prestige, which was why they worked so cheaply. Because they were buying what they sold, they could have been paid in nails.

Farol had no natural manners. They were acquired. She was neither easy with nor informed about the way things were done and lived by standards not especially, or at any rate not continuously, high. It was

clear she had not been brought up educated to grace or the basic consid-
erations of tact. But she was a person with a pair of eyes, a pair of
binoculars, you might say—her unique instrument—which she turned
and focused, turned and focused, attentively observing others and taking away those impressions she proceeded to discipline into a rule-deter-
mined composite for social behavior which unfortunately was limited
for the most part to the conventions of St. Ives.

Seeing is recognizing, perception already a kind of execution. It's
a principle in art. And her art was fairly successful. I saw examples of
it everywhere. She had, in fact, gone very far on very little.

But if she had learned the words, she could not always employ the
grammar. She slipped up a lot and miscalculated. I'd once mistakenly
believed she showed a lineage in direct contradiction to her lot, but I
was wrong—her lineage *was* her lot. She acted exactly as she had been
raised and gave herself away in the small thoughtless ways people do
who never hang up a towel or replace water in ice-cube trays or rinse
out a bathtub after using it. And I often found myself, fatigue in my
voice, reminding her to do so whenever she wasn't around. She was
heedless because she was unhappy and unhappy because she was unsatisfied, and of course what she wanted to do more than anything, but
couldn't, galled her the most.

"I know you hated my drawings."

"Oh, for chrissakes."

"You did."

"I didn't."

"I don't care," she said. "I'll work in my own way. The way I
want, the way I am."

"Do it, then. Do what you want. Degas hated to do landscapes,
Manet ignored fingernails. Vermeer of Delft didn't paint children, al-
though he had eleven of his own." Why didn't she just do *something?*
"All right? The Old Masters wouldn't paint in the open."

"I don't want to paint. I don't want—"

"Then *don't,*" I cried. With clarity and finality I repeated, *"Don't!"*
A cold chill settled around us. I didn't care.

There was a mulishness about her. She urged herself to confidences
which she thought of, when expressed, as being frank. It came across as
rudeness. She was always either too familiar or too cold. I remember her
once turning with painful directness to ask a neighbor of mine, a very
sweet woman—and much to her embarrassment—how old she was. As
I have obsessively mentioned, in restaurants without being asked she

automatically took charge, assuming the right—while often mispronouncing words on the menu—to order meals she never finished. She
thought nothing of scouting through the private papers in my desk.

I've mentioned that Farol was one of those people who took conversation to be a kind of competition. Because she was driven to have
you believe she knew more than she did, she rarely asked questions on
matters she knew nothing about lest she betray her ignorance, fostering
out of uncertainty a pompous but self-defeating attitude which not only
made meaningful exchange impossible but in fact always ended it.

I had thought all along she acted this way with everybody, and so
was especially surprised in the St. Ives dining hall to find how particularly awful she was to those who with little luck in life ruinously reminded her of herself. I remember the incident precisely because I suddenly had a glimpse of myself in the contempt I felt for her. It would
be hypocritical to say my own cruelty surprised me, because it didn't. I
was circling her not as a subject I would nurture but as an object I
would kill.

We had moved to the front of the line, and a serving woman asked
Farol what she'd like. Whereas any comment could be kept from sounding cruel by sounding kind, she merely pointed. And then she murmured, "What's that?"

I heard in that question the voices of her sisters.

"Veal."

She shrugged and nodded. It meant yes. She'd deign to try it.

She never said please. I'd seen it before. She never said thank you.
And me? It was characteristic of my cruelty at the time to notice the
cruelty of such a thing without making an attempt to understand or even
trying to ignore it, but I was trying to stifle recollections of the mug, the
traveling golfer, the effusions of politeness showered on him for his
deep solicitude, generosity, and inquiries after her health. My growing
upset with my anger, paradoxically, made me angrier.

I made a point of letting her carry her own tray and walked back to
the table. We sat together silently in the midst of all that noise, not so
much that of the students hooting and hollering as the loud reverbera-
tions of the afternoon at Dexter's, the meeting at Galloupi's, Ted, and
the amplification of all the misfirings and misfittings—never definite,
always ultimate—that had sounded misfortune over our lives the entire
fall. They all crowded into my head like howls. I thought of her lack of
manners, her cruelty to her husband, her lying to him and choosing for
mere gain to keep him dangling, all the while waiting to make a deci-

sion involving his future with her nose pressed against a balance sheet, and I wanted to bite her! There are certain habits so embarrassing one has to pretend not to see them, and then there are others.

"Do me a favor, will you?" It was hard to contain myself. "Learn to treat people in there with respect. They're unfortunates."

She gave me a stare so blank, so cold and insolent, as to leave no doubt of what she thought of me. But I was thinking about her presumption. And what I was thinking left me almost ill. I couldn't finish my meal.

"I sometimes feel such disdain coming from you," she said. She looked away, her mouth pursed in anger. I made no reply, waiting until the irony of her comment struck her own ear. "Well, whatever you may think of me—"

"But I wasn't thinking of you," I said.

I pushed away from the table.

"I was thinking of a person who couldn't act like you, so must be be someone else."

And I stood up, left the dining hall, and went home.

I remember we went to the squash courts a day or so later, and I played with such ferocity that after three games she never got a single point. "You've taken a quantum leap over me," said Farol afterwards as we walked up the dark stairway of the gym.

But that was the whole point. I hadn't taken a leap over her or anyone—least of all myself—merely fallen into further confusion, for the real bitterness I felt was only a weapon against my own scorned and unwanted feelings.

It was my misery to see that all along I had been speaking to her but talking to myself, despising her less for trying to be free of me than finding in myself what in blaming her for made me even worse.

9

I spent Thanksgiving alone on the Cape. Marina hadn't been feeling well enough to join me. Farol and her husband went to the Wayside Inn, an old tavern in Massachusetts, where they had their holiday dinner. I think her dishonesty at the time began to weigh heavily on her. She said she wanted to be with me but in consideration of systematically easing the pressure of his interest chose instead, either from tact or training, the regulated, the developed art of giving him some shade of attention to lessen the injury and inconvenience the habit of neglecting him otherwise only produced.

The days were gloomy. I spent several of them on Nantucket. I worked some, doing three acrylics in three fast takes, *The Gray Lady* and *Dr. Death* and *Celine's Dark Cat;* a misty watercolor I called *Henry James's Grave;* a painted collage called *Repetition as Insincerity, with White Ruined Earrings,* and a drawing for a later etching called *Scalded to Death by Steam.* When not working I walked the beach alone and nightly watched the stars come up out of the Atlantic like the running lights slung from the masts of old coffin ships. I was trying to figure out what to do. I came to the strange realization that though Farol's presence gave me no pleasure, her absence gave me pain. I didn't so much desire her again as need to believe in my own illogical, self-absorbed way she wouldn't betray me.

I also began to feel around this time that there wasn't enough ambivalence in my love for Marina, not only for me to accept her but for her even to be able to bear what my idea of love seemed to require in the way of misery. Truly, on a deeper level we tend to hate as well as love everyone we know, and I wondered: *could I love only what could live in the light of my reflected glow? And never love what couldn't? But was that love?* I seriously began to believe—neurotic as it sounds—that I had actually fabricated Marina, conjured her up, and idealized her out of my own narcissism and need, for it seemed to me that just as Farol closed me off from my unconscious—I could never paint when she was with me—Marina had become my thwarted unconscious incarnate, allowing my passions to be both idealized and *disengaged.* Was she my mirage? Did I paint her before I saw her and christen her with that beautiful name? Did I begin her as an exercise, a painting of a woman by my demon half merely to use in my fantasies? As a symbol of moral virtues in a world of wars?

When I returned to St. Ives I found a note from Farol under my door asking me please not to give up and to believe that one day in spite of everything—I'd flatly accused her, prior to leaving, of shamelessly encouraging almost every man she met—we would be together. She swore up and down that Ted had been interested in one of her sisters and not her.

I suppose I was both relieved to get this note and not. I'd become frankly ashamed of being so unhappy, there was something deeply immoral about it, and it always left me alone. And yet being alone seemed to me the only way of attaining wholeness, anything permanent. Permanent. I think people should mistrust and never use this silly word. I didn't know what I wanted. At times I even began to wonder in my jealousy if I hadn't myself a strong desire to be unfaithful to Farol, merely accusing her of wanting what in my heart I myself secretly wanted as an escape from the awfulness she made me feel about myself. I remember often wishing her husband would take her off my hands. I used to concentrate intentionally on her tiny breasts and lank hair and broom-thin shins and make dark destitute wishes she'd go off somewhere and never come back again.

As usual, the effect of her being with her husband was followed by a pronounced and immediate interest in me. She came by early one morning before work, let herself in, and came upstairs. She asked quietly, sadly, if we could make love. She said she'd had an awful time with John and missed me. I found an obscure victory in her visit and, making her sit down, grabbed some notes I'd scribbled about her personality and read them to her.

Explaining my reservations about our ever being happy with each other, I concluded by saying, "The love between us is contrasted with— I'm tempted to say safeguarded by—the contempt you have for John, don't you see?"

"Yes," she said.

"Do you care?"

"I do."

I asked her point-blank, thinking of Ted, how she could subscribe to the quaint fiction of claiming to be married to one man while having an affair with another and still find room for yet one more. She became quickly contrite.

"But look, even accepting blame, you do it proudly, as a burden you can lift without thought or worry. Concessions are ruses to you," I said. "Agreement is all on your side."

She turned away, wringing her hands. There mounted a strange corroding shame, the old inner pain, as thoughts began wedging their way in to form a picture of what she was. She began to cry, her face dissolving into a mask of ugly red lines. I had never seen her weep for anybody but herself and because of that didn't even try to help. She stood up and, resting a hot cheek against the coping of the doorway, looked defeated, her eyes stupidly concentrated on nothing. I understood. Staring at infinity makes a person feel so tiny and helpless, and there is something to be said for the pinch of an alley. Maybe that was the reason, even with marriage at its worst, she needed someone, to escape infinity even if in the sting of another's rage and reproach. And yet in spite of it all doesn't it matter what the significance of that rage is or make a difference what the meaning of the reproach is so it won't happen again?

When she stopped crying her cheeks were mottled in patches as though a fierce slap had left a permanent mark. She seemed to descend down her person to those sad plain feet. I felt a flood of pity as she fell kneeling by the bed, vowing she wanted to change and begging me to help her. Would I talk to her psychiatrist? I took her hand and she crawled into bed—I couldn't resist her—and we made love. And we talked afterwards. She appeared less plaintive, less encumbered with unending questions, and said she had mentioned at "group" that she was now seriously thinking of divorce. For the moment at least, she seemed happier.

It was strange. Farol actually lost rather than gained something in her personality when she was happy. She had a strong neurotic suspicion of lasting contentment. Happiness was somehow an object she couldn't find a handle on. She took little comfort in respect of its contents, underplaying its element of height by always holding off a little and showing it only at the most unexpected moments when trying out for comic relief, say, a droll word or expression as if she were testing thin ice. I had to learn over the years the effect of jokes from a dead face. She often tried to be a great tease, especially with children—and of course with me—but it almost always came up flat and limp. What I tried to laugh at should have told me even then of my hypocrisy, but I wanted her.

And conspicuous beyond any wish now, I needed to know where she stood. I wanted one clear *consistent* direction from her. I realized it could come only by means of her being free to know it herself. I had heard of a thing called obstacle love and how certain people needed complexity, barriers in fact, to assure the love that one demanded be proven by it and for the reassurance all was worth it in the many things to be overcome. Or not worth it. I'm sure it explained both of us. I was convinced that was the way with her artwork. Whenever I looked at those drawings of hers, the nerf faces, the childish foliage, the raddled figures, the monotonous scribbles which stood for trees and clouds, all those laborious papery drafts of chalk and stump, I felt she constantly drove herself to the task only to reinforce the overwhelming fact that she not only hated it but that intimidating tooth-sucking father of hers with the unlikable squarish head who in having pursued it abandoned her.

At the time, in any case, a bargain seemed to be struck, a plea for nothing immediate to come between us or interfere, a margin of space where if nothing of consequence ebbed it might the more easily flow. I couldn't explain it, but there was something definite in the midst of all this indefiniteness. I felt her coming closer to me. And one sparkling clear night under a cold hunter's moon, with frosty pockets in the woods, we drove to a party at Rye Beach with some friends of hers, Bill Someone and Anne Something, and along a strand where Farol and I later took a walk, on a dark strait of beach washed by the pounding waves and crashing surf, she kissed me, all but pressed her breath to my heart and told me, "I love you. I want you so much. I love you, I love you."

Snow came early that year. She seemed in much better spirits. Farol always loved snow. She used to jump into drifts and throw snowballs at my window in the morning to wake me and drive into snowbanks for fun whenever she drove me home. When we were alone together she was full of joy. I couldn't fail to be cognizant of the fact that she was trying harder.

She was also given to flus and colds and indispositions. I repeatedly looked for signs in her of physical and emotional deterioration and worried about it constantly. Her demeanor was certainly at variance with any idea of illness or debility, but mine was the fervor of ignorance. I feared one day she mightn't be able to *move*. I wished to save her and everything of me she held within of all I wanted her to love. One evening as were setting out to Boston for dinner she complained of a sore throat.

I decided for her then and there to have a checkup with Derek Schreiner, a close friend of mine—and a doctor—who lived in the North End. We drove over, had a few drinks, and he asked a few friendly questions, how we met, where she worked, that sort of thing. I couldn't forestall the question I knew would embarrass her when he asked where she'd gone to college, for she'd inadvertently mentioned, as often she did, that she'd once worked in a hospital. She wanted quickly to change the subject.

I left the room, and he examined her.

"Have you found anything wrong?" she asked when he finished.

"You'll be all right," said Derek, sending her to the bathroom with some pills to help her sleep. When she was gone I reminded him of her paralytic illness. He said he hadn't forgotten. Hadn't he tested her? He had given her a quick neurological exam, using a tuning fork to test vibrations and reflexes, pin touches to arms and legs, even touching a wisp of cotton to her peripheral limbs, and there wasn't a sign of anything wrong. And the throat?

He said she had a cold.

Driving home, I was tired. Farol seemed better and felt like talking. She asked me about Derek. She seemed to like him as much as I did. I told her something of our relationship, recounting how having met in college at Skull and Bones, we had kept in touch over the years and remained friends.

"Is he married?" she asked.

I said, "He was."

I looked over at her. But she was slumped down and looking off into the night lights as we passed up Route 93 through the falling snow.

10

Christmas was soon upon us. I was hoping the spirit of the holidays would bring more joy into our lives and give us an even stronger sense of direction. Bells. Lights. Carols. Just like the frosted cards. I remember going shopping and buying Farol some leg warmers, a book on Henry Moore's sculptures, and a long white Afghanistani dress, thrilling with the idea of seeing it worn in the splendor of her tall beauty. The electric blanket I'd bought, her apartment was so cold, she needed right away, and the night I gave it to her, I remember, she invited me to an opening at the gallery a week or so before Christmas day. I found in her lighted eyes a private affirmation—a tacit vow I felt an encouragement—of a stronger bond between us.

The opening was of course the same old thing—an outlet for a lot of superficial omniscience in a town where there was much of it—wine, mousetrap cheese, and the usual group of overstated, distinction-making, season-ticket-holding, art-associating punch and judies from St. Ives met to view only another exhibition of pipe-cleaner art or psychoceramics or the latest leaking efforts of someone's drip period, always with some Chesterfield of subheads or other conspicuously presenting himself at your elbow to point out some infringement of style here or there and others full of suggestive stammers and interrogative quavers looking on and saying things like "Strong, strong!" or "I can't claim to understand it, and yet I sense it, see?" or "Positive, but not negative, if you get me" or "It's so, so steeped in authenticity, you couldn't omit one detail without damaging the—the entire concept" and "Oh, that one's *fun!*"

If something was plain, it had a "Shaker quality" to it. If ugly, it was "strikingly contemporary." Anything particularly incoherent fell into the category of "folk art." If it was merely full of drips it was said to have particle trajectory. If it was a single line the artist was said to have stripped his form back to stark simplicity and worked for a delicate balance characterized by a matrix of restrained form. They confused style with snobbery, the artistic with the expensive, and grace with the kind of egregiously condescending attendance paid to the ignominious by the ignorant. Even the ugliest canvases there slaistered in oils like bad greasy makeup elicited comments such as "Rich!" and "Committed!"

The excursions of sympathy for this sappy schematic work were not only insincere but of course entirely dismissive, so that everyone— the Yawnwinders, Harvey Frakes, Gary Woodvile and Cory Wallpoodle, Jolly Jumfries, Neil Ringspotz, and the rest of them—could meet and mingle over drinks and continue measuring the great indifference to one another each secretly felt, which rested on the nimble calculation that only by being familiar could one truly ascertain the proper distance to be kept in order to avoid being close. Farol circled about studying the pictures. Alone, of course. Others were around. But when most everyone had gone, all but the gallery people, she still kept a due distance.

It was customary at the Christmas opening for the gallery people to remain after everyone else had gone in order to swap gifts—not so much generosity as pure form, for all having agreed beforehand that no one could spend over five dollars. I stayed on to be with Farol, whose dutiful, inexplicably obsessive, but continuing commitment to ribbon-tearing Gumplowitz, box-shaking Tweeze, and short fat melodramatizing howling-out-of-her-hole Scrulock left her with no desire to violate fundamental taboos. She spent most of the time that night petulantly sitting on the floor away from me, keeping herself just aloof. I felt the rebuke in her silence.

She had decided to keep her head, reminded of other looks in other faces, and told me so by a slim tentative warning in the eyes. We'd been making love now for almost two years. Mornings, afternoon, nights, in sunshine and shadow, and as recently as the night before when the sleet was snapping at the window with the sound of a million mice cracking grain. And now I couldn't *sit* with her?

At one point I reached over tenderly to touch her, but she slid slowly away from under my hand, stressing some remark to the effect that she wasn't feeling well and moving to lie back against a wall. I asked, "Are you all right?"

Like tinted mirrors, her eyes, colored by the mood of the moment, returned to me in matter-of-fact scrutiny. She said, "It will pass."

I said, "I love you."

She gave me a wan smile. The whole reference to my being there hadn't the slightest hint of consideration, by anyone, merely given in a special shade of their own devising something of a pathetic supplicating note.

I was used to Farol's mood flopping over—sometimes within a matter of minutes—from craven desperation to intense understanding to malign neglect. But this was different. I wondered why she had bothered to invite me only to be so rude. *I'd like someday*—I heard her echo—*to just walk openly down the street in the sunshine with someone who loved me.* My vanity was wounded, of course. I was vain. Part of what I imported from her all along was her admiring view of me and part of what I exported to her I used to validate my own self-image.

She accomplished, of course, much the same for herself when she used, and enjoyed watching herself use, whatever version of her femininity she had made her own.

She habitually told me she loved me. Only I knew it. Her life as lived contradicted every word. She had friends I never saw, saw people I never met, and kept me at a distant hovering regard. She said she always wanted to be with me but rarely invited me anywhere. I never saw her ski. I never went camping with her. I never met her brother. I never heard her use the words "we" or "us," in fact. But it wasn't because of her marriage. She was for some reason ashamed to show in the presence of others what she enjoyed when we were alone together. She had a public face and a private one. And she took immense pains always to keep them discrete.

I was virtually excluded from her public life, but in private she was another woman entirely. And only in private where she was un-observed did she endeavor to atone for what in public she was either unable or unwilling to express, the darkness of our sin, the intimacy of my rooms somehow creating for her an atmosphere of almost primal discovery and arrival in which her uninhibited sexuality always gen-erated a torrent of pleas and promises I found seemingly inexhaustible until none were ever fulfilled. She became in turning to go, almost as if *by* the very act of leaving, another person entirely, and it wasn't so much that the many rueful complaints heaped upon her job or her husband or the people at the gallery couldn't be recalled as I seemed utterly forgotten. There was always that odd ineradicable air afterwards of indifference.

Whether all this was basely calculating or politely deferential or hypocritical I couldn't at the time determine—only because it was neu-rotic and irrational. I only knew custom was maintained in bad in-stances, broken in good. On the other hand, her illness, so absolutely unthinkable, I thought of all the time. And I allowed everything for it.

But while she played with my vanity and my desire to possess her, I couldn't ignore my own self-destructive compulsion to waste my ef-forts in a series of compromises, subterfuges, and deliberate self-delusions by seeking out those who would have nothing to do with me. But the confusion went deeper than me. It had its roots in the very inversion where soul and body react on one another, as lovers come to see in the paradox of adultery, by trying to mix things in order to make a match.

Farol was a marrier. There had to be a need in her somewhere I thought—for *some* reason—of acknowledging something in public, and yet I felt the more she had to play the single woman, the harder she found the role she'd adopted as virtuous wife, and the more resentful she became for being neither. She was not a natural sharer. Marriage taught her nothing. She had acted like a single woman all her life— she gave no dinner parties, had no guests, nourished no fundamental union in any way. She always used the term "wifey" with great deri-sion. It wasn't surprising: being a wife, which she'd failed at twice, was all she'd ever been. It even crossed my mind more than once that in her desperate need for her father's approval she might have been trying to be his *son*. She had womanly beauty, of course, but avoided all her life those characteristics so often thought of as feminine, not simply dresses, makeup, cooking, shopping, and kids but the strong and nurturing hand, warm as earth, that softens all our pain. She may have reached out in gestures of hope at times, but despair was the element in which she took shape.

She was always struggling against a personality not hers, or, I don't know, struggling with two of them that were. She was a *Mischling*. Married and single; evasive, yet painfully direct; abjectly passive but markedly competitive; wary yet wildly, lavishly bold; at once shallow but dauntingly ambitious; diffident in the extreme while burning with an ingrown desire to win; cold yet hot with ruthless vehemence for all she'd lost; an unfaithful wife; possessive, fervent, and yet at the very same time almost devoid of feeling—where did she *learn* all these tricks?

I thought the icon of her sex embodied her, the movements of opening and closing, so sudden and so charged with change that the contrasting image of one to the other continuously became for me a metaphorical extension of Farol herself.

We left the gallery together. She was unnaturally quiet but stayed with me that night. And when later we made love I couldn't stop wondering, in the fusion of darkness where alone we became one, not so much about someone who seemed so ill but never was, as much as how someone who seemed so healthy was so ill but never seemed to be. I remember that particular night very well because of a bad dream she had, when she woke up screaming.

I said nothing at the time of the tension I felt that seemed no longer a question of meaning anymore but rather a substance, absorbing my presence, I could either accept or deny. As I saw it, Farol reasoned that love couldn't last. She fell in love—constantly looked to do so—and then with a furious, dreamy, destinationless locomotion refused to sustain it. I don't know, perhaps she didn't want to seem gullible. Maybe she couldn't trust all it promised. I couldn't decide if she refused it because she felt she didn't deserve it or because she found it, although the most important, the one impossible unreinforceable thing on earth.

We always believe we can change someone, though, don't we? To me Farol was like something familiar seen beneath clear though disturbed water. It was difficult to see a solid view in order to understand exactly what you were looking at, but I wanted to see her. I feared we would fail but, by mistakenly measuring all I was by her, became addicted to my own failure in feeding hers. Our situation was a waste place. Underlying most occupations and even pleasures of mine from early youth was a pain of solitude. I'd escaped it most nearly in those tender moments we call love. I couldn't face the truth now that what we depended upon was illusion. I loved a ghost, and in loving a ghost my inmost self had become spectral.

I was in a way trapped into the belief that irony had meaning, convinced I couldn't live without her morally, that she was a lesson I had to learn, that her faults were precisely what I myself had personally to overcome in a matter that for so long had left us both so inextricably linked. It was positively as if the measure of each took sustenance by the treacherous growth between them in the subterfuge of adultery.

11

Adultery is the vice of equivocation.

It is not marriage but a mockery of it, a merging that mixes love and dread together like jackstraws. There is no understanding of contentment in adultery. The nature of it is its divided aim. It prevents the bond it nevertheless always leaves an anticipation for, dooming you to the agitated vigil of expecting to see what at the same time you are forced to conceal. You are left where in fact you must always remain, not formally committed yet forever engaged in supreme futility to a policy of separation sworn on the very covenant by which you've come together. You belong to each other in what together you've made of a third identity that almost immediately cancels your own. There is a law in art that proves it. Two colors are proven complementary only when forming that most desolate of all colors—neutral gray.

All acts of adultery are acts of thievery. It is a world of intolerable inversion where everything operates from the premise of deceit. What you steal, in fact, alone testifies to your honesty.

There is no union in its condition. It is only a pairing of two cohabitating solitudes, a mimicry of love as it seeks to approximate it, a parody of love appropriating its terms which upon use, however, are instantly found to vouch it false, your words becoming a continual reminder as you speak of exactly what you don't mean. It is impure and like all alloys a bad conductor. It invents affection in its wickedness diametrically opposed to the ways of one's belief. Assertions are annulled. Adultery, in fact, forces you to use a language as uncustomary and outmoded as the word itself has become. In what is spoken of love there is always *simultaneously* something else never being said of doubt and disapproval, something yet audible, a shadow of accusation cast below every statement of affection.

What both recognize can't be said to be seen, and so any originality of feeling quickly cedes to the equivalizing and equivocating tendency in language where your real feelings must be kept silent precisely because you can't communicate them, forcing you to live a lie which like a mask covers the face it also hides. You aren't a couple at all, merely a pair, doubles only in duplicity, not even two anymore, only an elaborate and complicated version of that number, such as:

$$\sqrt[5]{2^3 2^2} \quad \text{or} \quad \sum_{i=0}^{\infty} (\tfrac{1}{2})^i \quad \text{or} \quad 2\cos^2\theta + 2\sin^2\theta.$$

Adultery is the crime that always requires an accomplice—an accessory, not an associate. There is no confidence transmitted, so there can be no trust. How can there be? Who is a thief, then a policeman? It leads to the suspension, not the function, of personality. You have to pretend to be not only what you aren't, but in the strategy of accommodation by which, because you must compromise and relinquish your desires as often as you act on them, you must relinquish part of yourself to the same degree. You are soon lost to a category where you become only a type—archetypal goons out of popular French theater, whether lover, cuckolded buffoon, or misunderstood wife, acting out a farce of synchronized evasion in a corridor of comic doors that open and shut in ludicrous sequence. Adultery is, beyond all else, *undignified*. It wears a nose cone, bells, great flapping feet.

It is not transaction but transgression, a two-way cancellation in a continuous circuit of misexchange. It is the wrong combination, an unstable alliance, an extracontractual snare. Adulterers trust nothing. Nothing in adultery is additive or cumulative. No one wins, all the time. And nothing can stem the torment of what is by what could be, for the memory of what has been contaminates your bed and makes even the very act of renunciation promiscuous. You become but two cold copulars lapping frost off each other's rectitude. Memories, passed on like a body from hand to hand, preempt the present with warnings of further corruption and whisper enough of the sluttish past to make even the most robust promises a joke, which only leads to more promises. And soon you are forced into the vanity of consistently having to justify yourself. Adulterers are notorious egomaniacs and, like them, maladaptive and sadly insufficient. Narcissism doesn't replenish the self, it empties it. It seems like power, but proves only low esteem and a desperate need for attention.

A paradox is that almost to the degree that you come to despise your lover you also come to depend on her for such self-respect as you can scrape together. One has to look for moral support somewhere, and where is one to find it if not in the person whose standards you have substituted for your own? But the trouble is only compounded by another of adultery's legacies, for you soon realize you have become critically disconnected from your former self without any definition of a newer. The despair at the heart of adultery is that it cannot be rescued from the contingency of its origins, and any attempt at total stability is consistently undermined by the lack of commitment taught by the very means it came your way. Every rule therefore becomes an infraction, every luxury a privation, and every privilege a forfeiture.

Adultery is so unheroic, so small, so hopelessly a pantomime of pretended ease and insouciant losing, while being yet paralyzed by sterile emotions built upon the ridiculous inability to assert any claim of recognition, that the crime itself is its own punishment. Its gifts make slaves just as whips make dogs. The sexual acts of adultery, a coarse gluttony, are curiously uninhibited only because they are noncommittal. But in the process of feigning indifference and seeming offhand with the tentativeness of the relationship—bewildered at having to loathe morally what emotionally you need to approve and coldly planning to leave or be forsaken by what at the same time you also feel the need to be loyal to—you soon find yourself ludicrously on the watch for the least sign of unfaithfulness, which is, ironically enough, the very vice in adultery that has *engendered* it.

It smells deviation even at its highest moments, hopelessly trying to bring identity out of separation but leaving you stranded in a paradox of proximity without closeness, where belonging to no one you both merely inhabit an area of negative space in which, hideously, anything at all can be imagined. In its jealousy, physical acts eventually give way to an inner state of such suspicion and turmoil that the slightest alteration of behavior can transform the most insignificant action into proof of monstrous infidelity. Entire attitudes are conveyed in a remembered remark or the turn of a head or a missing glove.

There is a code of substitution, a topsyturvification of moral values in adultery that becomes its canon law. The adulterer constructs his life according to the only logic available to him in an affair that illogically presents itself, for while he rationalizes his usurpation of another man's mate, and she another woman's, trying to believe, each in turn, that a positive, lost, is wrong, both can only conclude that the alternative of a negative, found, must be the only right at hand to address it—and so the breach actually becomes the observance in a desperate attempt to settle a matter of contradiction by means of conflicting evidence.

A rupture has taken place in which two people try to recover in a simulated act of binding agreement what, taunting and jeering them, only aggravates, alienates, and alters. The word μοιχεία—mixing—is Greek for adultery, the promiscuous interpenetration of the parts of two or more substances. And when the contamination spreads, its plume floods deep into the wellfields, for the adulterous mixing of people, places, and things, of language itself, is virtually foreordained by physical adultery. Deep at the heart of its illicitness is a resurgent unrest that reaches everywhere and extends to every aspect of one's life with accelerating surprise. What emphasizes its communion also exploits its anomalies. You have an idea of triumph only by what is being lost. The adulterer is, by definition, the hunter of which he is also the game.

Adultery is finally a fraud. It is envious, proud, gluttonizing, slothful, and angry all at once, and while lustful, oddly impotent, braying with power only until the frightened note underlying it can be heard of its inevitable defeat by the standards its every act contravenes. It is a lie, and the lie creates a myth, and the myth only for a time the pathetic belief in its own conventions. To its way of life society gives no sanction or assurance, leaving its victims unassimilated and quarantined and desperately alone, outcast mortals desperately alone, hurrying away like Adam and Eve in Masaccio's *The Expulsion from Paradise,* stripped to the skin and exposed to the world in the shivering humiliation of their sin, for there is, ultimately, no sense of community in it that ever can be had. You go unmocked only where you go unrecognized, leaving you to brandish the empty arms you can fit to no conclusion and forcing you to create a world out of your own desertion and solitude and uncomprehending rejection.

And it is there, with ominous intimation, that adultery best recognizes itself, skulking and keeping to corners and drawing in until, sick of division and dimmed with dismay, it seeks the only sepulcher it knows, slouching back to its bed of precarious and fatal forgetfulness, where once again in the tired and face-aching grimace of pretense it must assume lust and love—as far apart as hell is from the arch above—fall down.

12

We were invited, Farol and I, to a Christmas party around this time. The majority of the guests had some connection or other with the school, mostly St. Ives faculty, although others, including the gallery people, were also asked. It was a snowy night, blowing cold, and the forecast was that it would mount. We'd gone shopping together a few days before, and I bought Farol for the occasion a pair of black woolen trousers—she picked them out—and an expensive black skirt. She wore neither. It didn't at the time strike me as important. I was happy to be going anywhere with her, the opportunities had been rare, but this night I needed reassurance.

I remember pausing halfway up the walk specifically to ask her, in view of our recent misunderstandings that way, to stay with me at the party. And while with solemn profession she said she would, it was nothing less than remarkable that as soon as we arrived she didn't.

The house was crowded. A sense of the rooms came confusedly through the chatter of hasty introductions. There were people three deep in the parlor alone and a festive air, with candles in the windows and a large Christmas tree sparkling with lights. Farol hesitated a moment—there was always that pause of calculated self-presentation when entering a room—with the kind of decorated face, just the ghost of a question in it, that seemed open to whatever might occur. She struck me that night as taking everything for granted, although most of the people there had never met her before. Few in fact if anybody knew where we stood in our relationship. Some thought she was married to me, others knew she wasn't, but most hadn't the evidence to make the slightest connection one way or the other. I soon realized she wanted it that way. Their uncertainty pleased her. It gave her a secret, and secrets were the props by which she lived. She wore no wedding ring, she used her maiden name, and as she moved about, smiling at everyone, her beauty attracted immediate attention.

"Where do you come from?" asked one instant admirer.

I offered, "Mamaroneck."

"My parents do," said Farol, correcting me.

She would never in all the time I knew her, whenever asked by anybody, ever admit to coming from some one place in particular. I'm sure she thought it gave her an air of mystery, that shadowy thing, a sense of lost origins which expressing need and prodigiously calling out for assurance and protection somehow asked for love. It made her seem vulnerable, made room for the possibility of a distinguished pedigree only because, unknown, it wasn't proof against itself. She tried to pretend she was in the world, not of it, trying to justify her personal life by giving it the sanction of semidivine myth: *I come from nowhere.* In a horrible way, she was right.

The irony was that in the developing conversation, she seemed on the other hand waywardly to have lived for one period or another just about everywhere else, in the very cities and towns of the very people she charmed by that very fact! And by it, inevitably, bridges were made. I offered to get her a drink. She turned from a small group there and said, "Dry white wine."

I got two drinks, quickly extricating myself from several talkative matrons with dopey eyes and cabbages for heads, but when I returned Farol had disappeared. I found her in an adjoining room animatedly talking and charming several people—men—with jokey affability. She was friendly and familiar, smiling and chatting, animated without the slightest nervousness, not only touching strangers' hands with lingering welcome but turning to each new acquaintance with full appointment as if in studious recollection of trying to remember him. I began to realize she was actually trying to impress people simply *because* they didn't know her.

Farol stood in their midst, her fine head with its pale blond hair like a shining star doubly beautiful reflected in the mahogany-framed mirror behind her. She was one of those women with a clean, innocent, almost virginal look who could rut like a mink for a weekend and then appear Monday morning, all scrubbed and holystoned, looking bright as a new tooth. She wore the golden earrings I'd given her and with suggestive sameness her usual attire: a white blouse, a vest, and brown formal slacks. No buttons and bows. She was robust and strong-shouldered and conveniently tall, just a trifle too bloodlessly fair perhaps but with a pleasant, public, familiar radiance that affirmed her vitality that night. Admiration made her face shine, and she seemed the prettier for it.

"Oh, you worked in medicine too?" I heard someone ask her.

"Respiratory therapy," said Farol. She took her drink with a virtuoso deadpan, briefly acknowledging me with a nod, and continued to speak knowingly—in the pretentious medical slang she loved—of chronic lungers, blood gases, hypoventilation, and so forth. It sounded like Galen himself speaking.

"Fascinating."

"I got out of it," said Farol.

"Why?"

"Hospital politics."

It was one of her favorite phrases, one of those holophrastic utterances she used—how often I'd heard them—which, memorized by rehearsal and bearing the stamp of set speech, had long become for her like so many other phrases an obscure and precautionary convenience employed over the years to avoid the risk of the further clarification I swear she herself, if called upon to do so, could no longer provide. A world of knowledge was implied, but what in fact seemed to express or clarify an experience in a single word was literally an attempt to cover it up. It was contour farming. Pure cant. She was frosting an eggshell.

She had been a bed-maker. A nurse's aide. I don't know, some kind of orderly. It was a job she'd failed at, lost, quit, or couldn't handle. I was convinced she switched jobs as frequently as she did and deserted the men she grew close to in order to keep from being found out. Her new lives were actually aliases. She shed identities in reflexive self-dismemberment like lizards. Any explanation unleavened by distinction made the complicated simple, or the reverse, whichever, only because the consequences mattered so much to her, she had to pretend they didn't. The truth was adulterated in the phrases she used, for language, she bitterly felt, had broken its word to her. Words like vows had long ago lost their meaning, and so she found betrayal in the very vows she herself betrayed. And I was always the living reminder of it.

I soon realized how empty had become the promise of Farol's staying with me that evening. She wouldn't even look in my direction, and her contrivances, the intricate ins and outs made in the fashion of moving away constricted my heart. I felt the hurt mounting within me and to avoid the wordless and hopeless pantomime of pursuing her left the room.

I wandered about. I saw Ruth Gumplowitz, who was wearing a hat like a bell hog scraper and looked even homelier dressed up. I was introduced to a blimpish man named Mr. Atkins, who had a head like a bum, to Cobb Something or Other—*Cobb?*—and to several other people with unlikable boxish names supposed to connote all sorts of wasp values like tradition, reticence, and patrician aplomb.

I watched various guests, saddled with semblances of themselves, standing around in predictable pairs. "Have you met"—three couples with faces like piggy banks came forward—"the Shepherds, the Kaisers, the Mills?" I was determined to avoid any autodidact amateur philosophers full of "New Thought" and prosperity consciousness but then ran into several stuporous monologues ("Cornell, in lane two, had just completed its starting twenty and was settling into its racing rate. Ohhh, it was raining to beat the band, and I was calling the settle. Was this '53 or '54? Way back, anyway, and we were three seats behind Dartmouth, now pulling their own power ten, and . . .") which left a black hum in my ears.

And of course I again met a lot of rail-thin creatures with blue hair whose eyes had a knowing penciled tilt and who sounded all the same as they talked on to no consequence. Nothing is ever what it seems to be, dearie. Christmas trees are cellophane, and icicles only fake glass. Flying around inside us is something called a soul, which is fine if you've seen it, but I haven't. Addition is thrift, subtraction is spending, and when you die you're dead which is the price you pay, okay? You takes what you gets, no more, no less. And my husband wants to know if I love him! Wake up and smell the coffee, Terry, I told him, we're not even friends. . . .

I suddenly felt a shadow. I turned and looked up. It was Mother Scrulock with her jingle-bell earrings reaching into a plate of ham buns. When she entered a room it was almost indescribably as if someone had left, and though I never liked the woman, it was hard to take as a serious adversary someone shaped like an egg timer. I watched her dispatch several nuts and olives, popping them out of her fat meretricious fists and thought of Franz Hals' half-cracked woman with a parrot. She lit a cigarette and tittered, making one of her miniature faces in an absurd imitation of flirting.

"Are you here with Farol?"

Her perfume smelled like spermicide.

"In a manner of speaking," I said.

She gave me a side-ogle. I looked at her blowing smoke, chin-whiskered, her hair dyed mother-in-law ginger—it was worse than sad—and almost pitied her, only because I realized she hadn't the slightest idea what it was to be beautiful. It's something no unattractive woman knows. A homely woman who can attain a certain loveliness by self-acceptance is nevertheless almost always driven to act beautiful, which is precisely what no beautiful woman ever does. Tiny Maxine puffed a cigarette and looked at me, a chubby finger touching off an ash as if in punctuation at the drollery of things.

"You're jealous," she said.

"I've a tremendous sense of privation I'm not with you."

Her eyes narrowed into hateful slits. She stuck out her brandy-glass chin.

"You have to be, honest to Christ, the most objectionable person on earth."

"I doubt it," I said. "That would be too much of a coincidence."

Farol meanwhile stood perfectly at ease in the room under a playground of framed photographs on a far wall talking, among others, to a lawyer with frizzy cartwheeled hair and a nose like a grappling hook whom I'd met once or twice before and who, I knew, had several times asked her out. I was disgusted. The almost ostentatiously willed or contrived nature of her refusing to stay with me had the effect of raising the act to consciousness, of enlarging its importance, and I wondered, could it be a petty, calculating villainy? Or a test of some sort? Her husband wasn't there—she needed this balance—so why should she be? Was that her reasoning?

For the present I was struck only that she was playing a particular game. She had repeatedly told me, often at the very moment she was in my bed, that her husband had no confidence in himself and how she hated that in a man. But I should have seen even then that she was one of those people, wonderful one day, awful the next—like a person in a race always changing the finish line—who not only threw the burden on the victim to decide why she was behaving like that but actually *caused* what she disapproved of. And I felt very much like her husband as I looked across the room at Farol and that man. There was a hideous aspect to them. It was the kind of consenting and precipitate familiarity of talk, overshadowed by implication, that had something incontrovertibly wrong with it, something indecent, the intimacy of "strangers on a train."

I found my glances in her direction altogether useless, as various subjects were now accumulating in hideous profusion between me and a weevil named Dale, who was telling me frankly that using people was the only way to get through life. But to see is not merely to look. And I followed the information of my eyes.

There are certain captious persons to be met who find even less

aid to vision than more in the light by which one usually expects it to
be enhanced. Once I thought Farol looked at me. Her glance could often
dismember an object it lighted upon. It was a glance this time—you
couldn't call it hostile, because that would have made it interactive—
drawing me into the realm in which she receded that actually swept by
me, not to acknowledge, but merely to neutralize. I was left invisible by
what wasn't seen and so rendered nonconstitutive of all I, all I thought
I, beheld.

I suddenly realized I'd come to fear her beauty and the casual way
she turned it on other men. I have no doubt that she believed beauty
like sex was a form of witchcraft, giving a woman magical powers over
a man until in the end she could weaken him to a half-idiotic slave. No
one is attracted to everybody, but the way her confidence was shaken by
men who didn't find her attractive was too vivid for me to fail to notice.
She had a common instinct in knowing who thought she was pretty and
duly responded.

But by now this had happened too many times for me to ignore it.
Her image as full presence often doubled as an evocation of absence
and aloneness for me. And while I began to feel both absent and alone,
it became even worse. I began seriously to consider her dangerous.

13

Farol was a fascinator. Her compulsion was to notice every man in the
self-challenging way she set herself—I'd once in passing mentioned a
colleague of mine from school who'd lived in St. Ives for less than a
month when she asked, "Is he that guy who wears red sneakers?" And
he was! But her problem, compounding itself like a cancer, was also to
feel inadequate to the challenge for all in herself she knew was missing.
It was crazy. She wished ardently to succeed, but still more ardently
wished not to be known to have failed. Hints of this double goal, found
in much of what she'd told me, were evident everywhere throughout
her life.

But while her divorces and separations mortified her, they also
taught her over the years how to make use of those experiences and turn

them into assets. Strangely, her sense of inferiority actually made her pompous, her shame and embarrassment not only making her redouble her efforts to be respectable but at times even to assume an overweening moral confidence. She also had sharp instincts, and her manners, as I say, here became superb, for when she tried she could imitate the best of what she saw. She struck me as prepared, as arranged, infinitely to conciliate.

She held herself wholly at the disposition of such fellows who as she spoke—her voice was soft, inquiring, solicitous—turned awkwardly, responsibly red and struggled stiffly to oblige her in whatever appeal she made. When she desired to please she was to me, as to everyone else, the most charming woman imaginable. She accommodated herself, playing up to the exclusively male point of view, her looks inspiring passions, those passions provoking ideas. She knew men well. She knew what they wanted to hear. But while she made no mistake, she had it wrong, for I had come to see just how blank a face such a mask had to cover. The truth was, the very thing she tried to avoid but couldn't was *herself*.

She was a conventional woman. That's not to say she was simple. She wasn't. She was complicated, but her complexity was actually the sum of many simplicities. I doubt there was an element in her personality in itself unfamiliar; it was merely the combination that defied me. The unchangeable given was that she fascinated quickly by her good looks the same people she frustrated by the flatness her personality eventually revealed. This was her ultimate desperation. It left her not only feeling hopeless in the face of all she wanted of what she didn't have, it also made her tricky. She was always trying to justify what she wanted by claiming to decide what was good for me or her husband, paying close attention to detail always but assimilating only what served her memory, not her mind.

What is it with a beautiful woman? The aesthetic, of course, predominates. It's the way of the world. It begins in childhood, increases in adolescence, continues in youth, and remains over the years—"How cute!" "Isn't she pretty!" "What a looker!" "Stunning!" "She's going to break a lot of hearts!"—and simply by its nature exacts a fealty from others as emphatic as the expectation of it subtly grows. The terrible fact is that a personality is often deserted by that beauty. And a void remains.

I took Farol's beauty as largely responsible for her trouble. It left her at the same time both vain and insecure, extremes that not only meet—they are complements, not opposites—but often embrace in mutual recognition and grateful relief to counter the desolation that each when isolated from the other makes only terrifying. All dilemmas have two horns. Her vanity told her she could always find someone else, which made her ambitious. Her insecurity told her she was admired for her looks alone, leaving her feeling worthless with nothing else to give, which made her fearful. The cynical mesomorph who wanted independence hated the coy double who dependent on men was skilled at getting her way through frailty—yet *needed* her!

The result was a mysterious synthesis of the calculating and the disarmed. Her ambition made her willful, her fearfulness made her weak, and if in the latter she was inexperienced, too inexperienced, to be grateful for all she had—which cruelly prevented commitment to anybody—in the case of the former she was too experienced to feel she could ever be happy with anyone, forcing her again and again, as it always did, to cede herself to another.

It was impossible to tear one symptom from the other without damaging the whole personality. The history of one was the history of the other. The two natures seemed only neatly and accurately opposed. The passage from one state to another was not only blurred, it was conducted across a gulf of normality so difficult to discern that, unless you knew her, it was impossible not so much to see one side of her personality ousting the other as to understand there was only one personality in which in fact two states coexisted.

And yet she could fully rely, she knew, on neither aspect of that personality as distinct, for as both were always present, one was called up from potency to chastise the other in act. Perversely, the predominating mood always cried up the mercy of the other to temper it. Each brought the other into being almost by algebra. One was for the use the other used it for. Victim became executioner in logical exchange. It occurred to me that night as to Farol's never wearing makeup that in the curtain-dark realm of our antiselves it is precisely the artificial person who adopts the natural mask. But what in a mask is beautiful that ever *means* anything?

Beauty in its features is only a whisper away from plainness in the first place, and by it a person is often snared and made stone blind. It was no different with Farol. You could almost hear her pleading, "Sex is what I *do!* Without it, I'm nothing! Give me a pimple, lengthen my nose, and I'm lost!" She was caught in the lethal trap of almost always looking better than she was. She was also getting older, and she knew full well of those looks with the kind of underpromotional second-guessing typical of her that there was as little reason for them to be taken as an expression of great intellectual or spiritual endowment as there was for them to last. Beauty fades. Beauty always fades. Beauty, in fact, may be defined as beautiful only because it *cannot* endure. For a beautiful woman to fade is a common event. There is no temporizing in the mind of Cinderella without due reckoning for the clock on the wall. Midnight is always coming.

Moreover, while Farol loved to be called beautiful, she also hated it, for if in reminding her of the freedom it allowed, it reminded her as well with tyrannous symmetry of the freedom it also prevented. Anatomy *is* destiny. The beauty that disarmed her had also made her calculating. It wasn't only that time was running out. The fear in the sexual woman is that anybody can do it. And so how did she cope?

She coped by refusing to cope.

As she spoke to those around her—fatuous phrase upon fatuous phrase—I realized how crucially misleading she was in all she said by what she arranged for others to know, or, to put it another way, kept them from not knowing. Somewhere among us between the educated and the totally ignorant are certain pretenders, half-baked devotees of unconsidered truisms who with a handful of facts and a few threadbare turns of speech manage to rub along quite well. Farol was such a person. She had small conversation, less reference, no range. She was oversimplified, accurately, in symbolizing what she was. But she was also game. She had mother wit, guile, savvy, an intuition of the kind that took pleasure in those very sentiments, conned from the beauty that goes curiously unquestioned, by which she hoped in taking care of matters without elaboration not really to enhance exchange but rather to *encumber* it.

Curiously, the more insecure she became, the vainer she did, her insecurity as it were blacking the very words her vanity polished. But both became an impasse. The verbal formulas she constantly used were only evasions of what deep down she refused to convey or couldn't rely on or was wholly convinced no one must ever know. Always acting as if she were baring her soul, she was in fact doing the opposite, for almost all of her life was a deliberate myth foisted by her surface selves upon the world to ensure public acceptance. When ambition is interlocked with a desperate inner uncertainty which has cut itself off from any nourishing affection and in panic feeds endlessly off itself, however, the idea of failure is not only intolerable, but guaranteed, and so must be covered up.

Farol's phrases filled gaps. Her talk merely sounded like talk. It was, in fact, only human noise, a shorthand—abridgements—entirely uncommunicative and without value, the way people talk about the weather to *avoid* talking. She became dependent on other people and their opinions of her as an insurance against the threatening feelings of emptiness and nothingness she felt within herself. I couldn't figure out if she hated them for letting it happen or hated herself more for doing it. I had the impression that to get what she wanted she would agree with anything, go anywhere, or be with anyone; it was all the same. Always patronized by the men who'd married her, she was beyond something of a no-hoper—she found nothing in herself to give that anyone needed.

But she willed herself to relate. It grew out of her drilling sense of competition, her shouting need to be as good as others. But the terrible fact was that other people's expectations of her represented a violation of the narcissistic image she also had of herself, binding her to their preproprietorial wishes rather than allowing her to acknowledge her own. And so it was worse than craven. She was actually committing adultery with herself.

She lived, pathetically, for other people's expectations of her because she saw herself only from the outside. There wasn't enough within. It was cold windy space. I thought nothing hurt anymore and nobody made her happy. It was the sort of desolation she could identify. Winning men is one of the frantic professions in which success ultimately depends on the opinion you hold of yourself. She didn't feel. She borrowed not only other people's conceptions of her but their language as well. And only because her words came from those around her was she able to go on parroting them back by proxy in the voice they gave her of all she felt they wanted to hear *but she had to omit,* a valueless adoption that drawing her back into the shadow she inadvertently cast upon herself became the embodiment of all valuelessness.

She gave herself away, as if to say, isn't my ordinary life summed up, enclosed, and made pointless by someone else's—anyone's—less ordinary life? Only a pride of such depth and crookedness could masquerade as humility. It was, in a way, the *opposite* of her negating herself in the face of those she judged more interesting.

I was often struck, for instance, that whenever any friends from her past, visiting, gave reports of her no two of them ever seemed to be about the same person, and none of them was ever the Farol I knew. Her beauty gave her tremendous expectations, and yet while she presumed by it all the time, she also mistrusted it. Her melancholy was profound, but at the same time she had a sudden capacity to recognize her own splendor, her meandering intelligence on occasion being able to rise in sharp extreme to high self-appraisal—too high—for when she wasn't grieving or bemoaning her fate it was invariably a balloon flight in which, mistakenly, instead of seeing the rest of the world smaller she saw herself in an overview as bigger, unsubmissively much bigger, than she was.

It was the queerest egotism I'd ever seen—an admixture of presumption and despair—refusing to accept yourself for what you were and yet trying to become everybody's idea of you? Yourself as another's other? It was the legacy of adultery, but was it the legacy of beauty as well? To be what others want? To try to convey you *are* what they want by being so disposed to oblige? She was like a Harvey Frakes photograph—a snapshot, in fact, which was always about whatever it was he acknowledged you said it was. It was trading on others, of course, and it was flirting. But it was worse than that. It was also a perilous and unspeakable kind of forfeit, a soulless capitulation, an admission of such defeat that it defied definition, for she had inverted her nightmares into a mode of operation in which, while her phrases condensed lies and her lying created phrases, neither gave way to truth. Stepping in and out of roles, she was sick from nothing to be true to. Trying to articulate whatever was inside her would only reveal, she felt, the person she could not bear to recognize.

For her dialogue was death. Revelation reveals. Speaking is always confession.

14

I watched from afar for most of the party, a tortured abstract now, as Farol continued to bewitch those around her. I could see in her face she felt sorry with one group for the others she couldn't join. Another glass of wine, which someone had gotten for her, picked up the color of her cheeks. She moved about with a light perfection of assurance that not only had nothing to do with me but recognized no dependence at all. I'm certain I had the look of an object who having strayed outside the boundaries of the human world had lost his conceptual name and function. I was introduced to more couples, the Merkels, the Fishwacks, the sour-faced Wammerings, the Knoblochs, the dwarfed and drunken Monskys, and I tried as best I could to be polite.

But in spite of my parade of vindicating civility I took warning and gave assent to the misgivings in my heart that told me to get rid of her. Still I couldn't accept it. I have to care, I kept thinking, I love her. And yet there was nothing shown by her I saw even remotely hinting of loving me or that was proof against another's blandishments. Her promise had no more conviction than the weight of a feather. And as her back had been toward me all night, I kept wondering: was there really anything solid to choose between a woman who deceived another for me and a woman who would deceive me for another?

Farol was never more familiar. She made free contact, touching men's arms when she laughed, opening a way for their fancy, and so stirring their sympathy that each was led into believing her look was meant for him alone. I thought she felt an unavowed curiosity to see what sort of figure she made when she was under no obligation to marriage or having an escort or even being with someone. Had she discovered in adultery the banality of marriage? Or was it merely once again that balancing calculus she always needed, that since her husband wasn't there, I needn't have been? Was that her reasoning? Or had years of seclusion and prevention, at least as she saw it, only sharpened the edge of her desire?

I knew only that her terror of not being wanted enough, ever, gave the condition of being free greater assurance. Perhaps she loved to do what she hated to continue. I couldn't say. But nothing seemed to stop her. I never saw anyone so artfully selfish while at the same time so vulgarly obliging succeed at seeming neither. Starved for luxury, she found she had a talent for enjoying it. This was her element. She *was* a come-on.

I had never seen such a skillful persuader. She flirted with Harvey Frakes, flattered Snowcone and Frisette, and was now being introduced to the Fishwacks, whom she greeted in shining gentility with the high report of an actress. I suppose it threatened me personally because as a child I myself often held back my true nature to please others and even as I stood there was behaving contrary to my apparent interest, pursuing Farol, chattering away, and wasting my time and energies. Jolly Jumfries then sat down at the piano and played some Christmas carols.

People gathered round to sing. As Farol joined in, others followed. And then she leaned over and whispered something to Jumfries, who struck up a medley of college songs. And there was Farol singing at the top of her voice:

> *"And roll the song in waves along*
> *For the hours are bright before us,*
> *And grand and hale are the elms of Yale*
> *Like fathers, bending o'er us"*

Yale!

And she knew all the words! I was amazed, then saddened, realizing that all this flash about college was her pathetic compensation for never having attended one. Hypocrisy is the essence of snobbery, but all snobbery is about the problem of belonging. Someone then asked Farol if she liked music. And without taking time to clear her throat she said she loved classical music, smiling as if no bleak thoughts had ever troubled her radiance. "I love the *New World Symphony*," she said. And she mentioned Ravel's *Bolero*. "It's the longest crescendo in music," she said.

It was astonishing. She had the trick of keeping her listeners off balance yet engaged, making everything she said seem a metonym for a wider knowledge, a greater breadth, a deeper understanding than ever she had. Her ego was large but almost undetectable. Everything she mentioned or laughed at—or was even *silent* about—suggested depths of experience lying somewhere beyond the shell of common sight. She had no natural conversation, but affectionate and patronizing all at once had a flexible and almost infallible instinct for winning an ear. It was as if she'd learned the rules of selling a product. Speak with the same speed as your prospect. Never disagree. Action. Benefit. Commitment. The kiss principle. Keep it simple. No trade questions. No taboo words. No polysyllables. Nothing technical. Short phrases.

She knew exactly where to expand and where to elide. She never said more than anyone would believe. And because of the slant of her anticipating smile, the vulnerable responsiveness in that face that seemed to withhold nothing, neither desire nor renunciation, men fell in love with her on the spot.

When a squat man who taught architecture at St. Ives was being introduced to her flatteringly pretended to stagger backwards—in exaggeration of being smitten, I presume—Farol recoiled in laughter, double-clutching her breast with joined grateful hands. She had everyone's attention. Almost everything she said or did in the group became a respective assertion to each man that it was her turn for him. And while there was nothing wrong with that, it was as if more and more recognition still wasn't enough. No, she had been hard done by, she'd had enough of it, it wasn't going to happen again. She told some people how she'd once taken the controls of a plane and how she kept in shape swimming and that she was planning to go white-water canoeing down the Penobscot River. Truth is far and flat, but fancy fiery. And what she chose to disclose wasn't so much an exaggeration of facts that weren't there as much as a denial of those that were. She sounded so healthy and happy and in harmony with the world that I honestly began to wonder if I weren't listening to someone else!

But her color was too high, her voice just a bit too loud. Her movement, her manner, her tone were respectively just too free, too easy, and too familiar.

And I was thinking: *I know you.*

I wasn't alone. Several artists who knew how little work I'd done since I met her resented her. Gary Woodvile came up to me. "I *looove* the *New World Symphony*," he cooed with exaggerated theatricality.

"She resents you," said Cory Wallpoodle, "because next to you, dear, little Priscilla Tiebacks over there is d-u-l-l, dull."

"And Bo. Ring," said Gary Woodvile.

"And she knows it," said Cory Wallpoodle.

I heard her ask the lawyer, as his accent sounded familiar, if he'd ever lived in Pennsylvania, which he had. "I lived in King of Prussia!" Farol exclaimed. "And Scranton. And Phoophadoophia." Everyone laughed. Whatever place was mentioned she'd either hiked its trails, fed its bears, or cross-country skied across it. You could see her striding along in her blue L.L. Bean double-seated hiking shorts, you know, the ones with just the right nap and cut, and stopping at intervals to distinguish hawk species for everyone or to explain the international emergency signals or to teach everyone how to make charismola or three-bean mush. "I've hiked some great trails up in Saranac and Keene Valley. The Adirondacks. Getting up at six for the sunrises? Fantastic," she said. She paused. "The region's rich in magnetic ores. Did you know that?"

And I heard her again on fanny packs and toggle locks, sleeping bags and lofts. She was an authority on every subject from wood-range cooking to lock-back knives to toboggan wax to the best route up Mount Chicorua. Olde Town canoes were best, bush beans didn't give you your money's worth, photographs of birds were better for identifying them than drawings.

She was merely repeating over and over again the same set of squibs and opinions I'd heard a hundred times before, which neither many nor complex—although menacingly pedantic—always took the same form and the same shape and the same words!

She knew this, remembered that, recalled this, recollected that. She knew all about it. I shouldn't have been surprised. But I was. But it wasn't only the words. It was the way she worked. To be so self-absorbed, so ill read, so uninformed, so often diffident and sullen and unbudgingly covert and then to be able by some kind of baroque compensation to stand your ground in public cheerfully facing fifteen or twenty unknown people all at once and make each one of them your confidant with the mere thud of a platitude? It struck me that to bring off this juggling act so brilliantly required an almost technical mastery.

The talk turned to boats. Farol said she *loved* boats! Catamarans, dinghies, skiffs, sloops. Wooden boats! She said she loved to row. She used the words clew and strake and gunwale (which she mispronounced). I thought she was going to run out that night, buy a twelve-meter yacht, and single-handedly win the America's Cup. The architect said he owned a dory. She said she'd love to see it! She asked him where he was from and what he did and where he lived. "Near that lovely Greek Revival house in Kingston near Route 111? Oh yes," she exclamed, "I ride my bike there all the time!"

"Well, then," cried the architect, "I find it incumbent on you to come and visit me!"

Bikes. Farol, of course, wrote the book on them. She went on to speak of frames, gauges, custom cranks, and panniers, never without an opinion on each, and all of it a crock of borrowed ideas assimilated without being absorbed. And after a moment, buoyed up from excitement, she began in a flight of breathless duration detailing a plan—an extraordinary one, I thought, since her face turned puce during a simple game of tennis—for bicycling across the United States! Handshakes, congratulations followed.

Farol had to belong. She was a joiner. It is not always to hand oneself over. There is a weakness in the type ambitious to hide. She needed, for example, to be desirable to look mysterious in order to counterfeit wonder. She could never forget that she'd botched up most of her life, nor that to date she was only a mat cutter with a high school diploma. It forced her into the usual overcompensations. Her

parents had moved near New York City, and she liked the association whenever she mentioned it of being thought a native, but to call
her a New Yorker would be to have to characterize a crack in the side-
walk as a geological fault. The truth was, she had spent most of her
life in the tall grass. Big Flats. Hickory Corners. Tanktown. And yet the
craven evidence in her was never absent of desperately yearning to be a
citizen of that prosperous, well-polished, book-lined, magazine-discuss-
ing world which she glimpsed only through windows and felt awkward
among on short visits.

Every boast became an apology. What she revealed told exactly
what she covered up. I'd even seen it several times whenever she boasted
of me to someone else, making me out to be more, and consequently
less, than what I was. She actually *committed* omissions. She wasn't only
emotionally deprived, she was starved—I didn't know whether by her
parents or her husband or what. Her fantasies were invariably half-lies,
which falsely served as a comforting refuge from the emptiness of her
actual life, for the more she relied on them the more painful became
the discrepancy between her romantic projections and what she was. A
person who tells lies knows she hides the truth, but a person who tells
half-lies soon begins to confuse it. The disparity between her phony
exaggerated self and what she knew for the inferior, empty, guilt-ridden
reality was enormous.

I realized that in order to eliminate this intolerable discrepancy she
tried to behave as if she actually *was* that wonderful person she craved
to be. It wasn't so much a matter of choice. It was a question of necessity. Invention's father's wife. Survival.

But it left her with the personality I saw that night that had to go
on lying, fabricating, and pretending lest the illusion these pretenses
created collapsed. It made her not only an imposter, the Wickerwork
Woman, it created infidelity as if literally breeding it. She was trying to
protect herself from her inner anxieties perhaps, but what happened instead was that her posturing and lying simply transformed them to outer
anxieties with the result that any worries about herself were eventually
replaced by the one massive worry that other people would now discover
and expose her lies—which is why, while directing my passage to her,
she also felt an equal and desperate urge to block it. She lacked most
for longing most.

No wonder she was always on the outside looking in. The misery
she felt in failing to accept herself was in not being able to admit it. I
wanted her to be well when not ill, and pleased when not troubled. But

she was too often angry when healthy and melancholy on the best of days. It's *difficult* not being very intelligent—the implications of which, while vast, are still ignored by sociologists—and it's compounded even more when you're stubborn. And Farol remained stubborn. She wouldn't submit to herself. She was deaf. It was worse than wickerwork. She was no more herself when she spoke or behaved with others—it was all dilution—than she was in the way she looked at love. But the closer I came to seeing her behavior, the worse it was for me.

I knew too much. And that she couldn't forgive, not so much for having shown me this or that or even for my knowing it as for my being witness to the very vindictiveness she leveled at me for perceiving it. She was a chameleon. It wasn't compromise, it was abdication. I felt that night to be dragging an increasing load of unsaid things behind me, but knew at the same time that to express them could only alienate her further, for while my knowledge of her constituted the matter of my loyalty, it also strangely confirmed by her own logic what she saw as being held against her. Any originality of feelings she might have had, her trueness, always ceded to a sort of ambivalence in language as well as in attitude. She lost her feelings not only when refusing to communicate them but after having communicated them to you she began to resent you for it.

I think it began to dawn on me that night that I couldn't love her in the way I should precisely because I was afraid to lose her. I feared that as soon as she was sure of one man, she became free to contemplate her future with another. I couldn't get close because I couldn't overcome that fear. You give everything, by definition, only when you have no reservations. And it wasn't only me projecting fear, it was she who inspired it by what she held back.

It was nevertheless ironic. The process of pointless repetition, the void under that premeditated heartiness, the elimination of distinction in the monotone and echo of phrases repeating like wallpaper became the specious if saving half-truths I knew to be false, others yet found to represent a high degree of intimacy.

I remember sitting alone on a stairwell for some time, when the loud sloppy shoefall of someone coming down—unmistakably Charlotte Tweeze and her claw-and-ball feet—made me quickly get up and remove to the living room, where again I circled the group in the midst of which Farol had stood so long engaged. She was still holding court, matching flippancies with her admirers, and didn't see me. The discussion still hung on cycling, and as I passed to the far side of the room I heard someone wittily suggest she sign up for the Tour de France.

Hardly had she opened her mouth to reply when one of those unaccountable stillnesses caught the room, a freak of ill timing that left her speaking an octave too loud in the absolute silence. As a victim with virtue she was right out of central casting, as I heard what she said trail off in the final words, ". . . always a problem. They thought it was multiple sclerosis."

With disbelief and pity, the men around her groaned, I listened in disbelief myself. I couldn't believe she'd told them that. The silence held a moment. But she had looked up. She had seen me hear her. I watched as suddenly an obscure unintending confusion fell across Farol's charming smile, the brick-red shade flowing upward from her neck and congesting her face, deepening into a recognition at last not only of my presence but more significantly of something alone shared between us she had given away.

I shall never forget that look. It was the look of an almost imperceptible instant which virtually dissolved the moment it registered but left me to believe some implacable force striving to pull out of her face a terrible candor imposed, not chosen, demanded she at last confess for once and all to the monumental impersonality of all she was, a mysterious and anxious confession of those inward isolating apprehensions that invited the very desires she at the same time so savagely denied. She *was* her expression, looking at me but looking through me too. I have never in my life seen in a facing presence such an overwhelming suggestion of violation and betrayal.

I have a sinister faculty for catching phrases in a face. All her temporary safety, her hand-to-mouth success grew—were perhaps even encouraged by—Farol Colorado's neither perceiving not divining this in me. I have never understood how for all her peasant cleverness and guarded moves and dialectically overdetermined self-chaperoning she failed to see that. A portrait sublimates in a reparative impulse all that art is supposed to keep at bay. But a face quacks. Didn't she know that? *Couldn't she tell?*

My remembrance of the rest of that evening—I was very tired— is mainly a remembrance of her silence upon leaving. She was almost morbid. She followed me mutely to the car. It was the sort of lame-wing silence she often showed but which in this case I took to be an admission she'd acted badly. Remorse only made her seem guiltier to me. I despised her. I despised the wistful, languishing, seductively acceptant look of comprehension and relinquishment she showed when we were alone together, but when she told me she cared for me, asking open-faced what was wrong, I wasn't surprised, not any longer, nor did I answer her, for I knew her want of adjustment, cover it up though she might with fantasy or fascination or fakery, was a quarrel too deep for any particular condition to have made right. I only felt the day was coming when the little white lies she told would turn into a great black truth. And I had once thought her an idealist. She was in fact pragmatic as a winch. I had finally come to see how she got into her "messes," but by now the noun had lost its definiteness for all it could include.

I wanted to shake the tin heart from her lying mouth.

It was very late, and the thick snow filling the streets, now blowing wildly into drifts—the hedges were buried, the houses spiked and white—took my attention and gave me an admirable equivalent for conversation as I drove past the snow-shrowded buildings of St. Ives to the front of her house. I kept the engine running. Farol sat there in a kind of attention-shedding disarray. Then she turned to me, wide-eyed and feigning ignorance. "Is anything the matter?" she asked. I said nothing. Speaking in a low subdued voice, she asked me if I'd like to go to New York with her for Christmas. She considered her thumbs. "John won't be home." She lowered her head. There followed a long pause. "Could I stay with you tonight?"

I waited until she was finished, not caring or hearing what she said, and then told her all of this was impossible. I reached over and let her out, though I knew within minutes she'd be knocking at my door. I told her through the window I planned to spend Christmas with Marina.

Her face became a cutout pasted onto a human being.

"Good night," I said.

15

Within minutes Farol was knocking at my door. My lights were out. I went downstairs to answer her. I thought she'd be chastened. She often had a way of ducking her head and sighing and looking elegiac that, while it put me off, also made me feel sympathy and look to understand. I turned on the porch light. The cold night had reddened her nose. She wore a pink bobble hat and stamped in the snow. She was carrying some wrapped Christmas gifts. "Can you bear to see me?" she asked. My reply was, "I don't know."

But I did. I did know. I wanted—deeply needed—her apology for *something,* an unenforced compunction or anything even approaching it to find some character fit the person I loved. But if compunction was on her mind, I never saw it.

"You mentioned Marina," she said. I was amazed. She was cocky and primed as a penguin. "I was thinking. She has to let you alone."

"She isn't bothering me."

"She has to let you alone."

I paused. "You must be advising me."

She shifted the gifts. Substituting for her apology, they seemed to give her the confidence of another resolve, the condescension of the wise, worldly woman.

"If you'd like"—she was cool—"I'd be willing to talk to her."

"You? Talk to Marina? I don't understand. About what?"

She shrugged. "Coping, I guess."

My mouth fell open.

"You know about it?"

"Yes."

"You?"

I pulled her in and slammed the door.

"Who the fuck *are* you?"

Farol went pale. Her eyes went suddenly enormous, motionless, in a bracing stare.

"You come here"—my mind raced, reconstructing sentences and exterminating repetitions begging in screaming cadence to deal death—"you can actually come here after deserting one husband—"

She almost swallowed her tongue in anger.

"—married to a man you've been betraying for more than a year—"

She tried to catch the back of the nearest chair but in the violence of her surprise almost fell, spilling her Christmas gifts.

"—and continue, while sleeping with me, to sneak off with someone else only to go on tonight encouraging a roomful of perfect strangers and now have the gall—"

She tried madly to interrupt, biting back her tears.

"—the unmitigated gall to stand there proposing to advise someone you've never *met?"*

"Stop it!"

She began clawing the chair. There was something in her face of a long ugly pull stretching her lips like rubber bands, giving her disbelief a twisted and frozen look, and her nose seemed to grow a point.

"Can't you see you're *ridiculous?* How many men do you want? You have three or four, isn't that your share? Do you want six or eight or eleven more of them? You stink of men, I can smell them on you." She pulled at her hair and almost spat. "No wonder you've spent half your life banging your head against the doors of doctors and lawyers and psychiatrists and insurance adjusters! *Do you ever take any time off?*" I turned, then swung around. *"Do you?"*

Stung with fury, she took a step so rapid that it was almost a spring. Her short hair, matted now and untidy, made her look old and demented and too tall. Looking around madly as if to find something to say, anything, she seemed literally rumpled from the loss of words.

"You grab, you snatch at everything you see! You think it will end with me or a golfer or an engineer or a doctor or an architect with a stupid boat? It won't! Another will appear and another and another and you're going to be telling them the same highly colored tales of injury and pain you've told me and Lloyd and John and Ted—no, *you* listen!—you want this? All these men? And to spend the rest of your life on tiptoe looking for more? But you do, don't you, because nothing satisfies you—"

Her skin seemed to disappear. I saw only two hateful eyes—flaming anger had dried them—burning in a head, detached, as if guillotined.

"—nothing, *nothing,* no one is ever enough! What bothers you is what bothers everyone like you, you want everything—you like those words, you should understand them. I only wonder why the fuck you don't just finish with your silly fictions and accept the fact that you're selfish, and thoughtless and cynical—" She couldn't stand it. "And a goddamn kazoo of self-pity. You're ugly—"

She screamed.

"—and you've made me as ugly as you are. I don't want your gifts, I don't want you, I'm sick of you. I wish you would disappear. Go away," I shouted, "go home! Go home!"

And she did. She went to Mamaroneck to see her parents.

And that was our happy Christmas.

16

I remember Christmas Eve, a dark and freezing night, leaving Boston and racing seventy miles of white lines up to St. Ives to see if Farol had returned. She hadn't. It was irrational of me, understand, but I couldn't get her out of my mind. I wanted to see her and apologize. I gave Marina the gifts I'd bought her, not giving, treacherously taking, taking from her as I always did, wanting something, wishing her tender influence might flow into my dark self, chronically dying for the lack of it. But the gentler she was, the less I could respond and the guiltier I felt for loving someone who seemed so worthless compared to her. The fat meretricious cow who called herself Marina's mother, as usual refusing to address me, made it clear I wasn't welcome, and so I left.

Why did I go back to New Hampshire? Often, nothing has even been plainer to me than what is wrong, illogical, and utterly complex, if not downright contradictory. I'd like to defend my actions by pointing out that I've always been an incorrigible enemy of convention, though I have been, and that there can be found in deep and even in very foolish misfortune a dignity finer than in any success, though surely there can. But the truer explanation is, I am vain, hapless, incomplete, and often unpersuaded. It's the artist's ultimate failure, that he seeks kinship even to a terrible degree of intimacy with the irrational and the inexplicable. And yet I wonder if it's really a question of preference at all, for how else does life finally come to us? The origin of art began with tracing an outline around a person's shadow. To paint a dream is to fabricate a dream. Face it, logic is for accountants, clerks, usurers—and survivors.

I found a telephone booth at the top of a dark hill by the school that night and tried to call New York. It turned out I hadn't enough coins. Stores everywhere were closed. I drove around madly, managed to find a spa open, and got change. I remember the warmly lit houses on the streets, strings of lights, carols being sung. I raced back to the booth and while the sleet was blowing through the open door shoved in twenty or so coins, trying to shake the phone to life. I stamped impatiently but finally got through. One of her sisters answered and told me Farol was asleep. She wouldn't wake her. I recognized spite in her voice. I pleaded to her it was important. My feet were freezing. I begged her, but she refused and hung up. I replaced the receiver. Nothing to trace there. No shadow. Nothing.

I spent Christmas alone. The days of emptiness and regret that followed return to my memory whenever the sky at dusk in New England turns that deadly polar pink behind winter woods and icy ponds and stubbled meadows. A terrible secret seems waiting in it never to be told. A monotonous cold settled in, winter so severe it seemed nature herself was loath to be left out of the general conspiracy I felt all around. A gray pall held. The earth appeared corpse-cold and uncaring in its winding sheet of snow. Crows watched in the trees outside as the brief days faded. It was impossible to think, never mind paint, and I took long drives into the snow-knuckled mountains, wondering over and over what was happening to my life.

I had no dreams in the present, they all belonged to the past, and I dreamed them over as one sings over old songs. But whenever it seemed possible that they still belonged to this life, and might still come true, I woke in my misery with empty hands. I couldn't get over my guilt for Marina. I saw her in my mind going home after dark, a swift shadowy figure with very little money in her pocket. That she should be treated so poorly everywhere, as I for lack of time and attention and my own connivance had to treat her, filled me with a fierce resentment for everybody but myself. With a childish and shallow disregard for all except bare actualities, I could not see why someone somewhere wasn't helping her out and relieving me of my guilt.

Still I drove into the mountains. That whole long winter was full of snowstorms and fierce winds and bitter cold, the snow blowing and drifting and banking everywhere from the glacial peaks to those dried and withered weeds that, lasting through autumn, stayed on their stalks with that persistency of life that outlives death. And I always took the long way home.

When Farol returned nothing had changed. She listened to my apology, but gave none of her own. I mentioned trying to call her, what her sister had done and all, but she only shrugged and said they were always like that. I told her I loved her. I found only vacillation. She was indifferent and wordless and wore the dingy loosely inhabited air of someone not caring much about anything. Dr. Solomon put her on various drugs, Valadol, Sedapop, Emprazil. I never knew such weeks. I proceeded more by what I learned to ignore than by what I took into account. Everybody gets a disease in his own way. My fear of losing her made me lie to her by way of overcompensation and flattery, which fostered in her a contempt for me because she could feel that. In a way I couldn't commit myself at the very moment I most stated I could. My compliments made me hate her.

I have to confess here that my resentment had now grown into a marked tendency toward the provocation and perpetuation of these fictions, and the consequent guilt I felt crippling my creative capacities only compounded it. And where there is guilt, there is a need to suffer, which began to tell me I was not only punishing myself with an attraction to the wrong woman but allowing it to continue!

It was at this point in our relationship that it became clear to me that trying to fathom Farol Colorado had become part of my own personal exorcism.

Whereas I once judged her a complete masochist possessed by the idea of starting a love affair in order to lose it heroically, I soon began to sense it was to her disadvantage to feel deeply for fear of being seduced into choosing a man she might have loved but who was of no use to her. I had always feared her theory that in matters of love one was always taking a chance. Now I wanted to see if it was a fact. I had tried everything else. I couldn't stand it anymore.

Very quickly I let her know I wasn't going to be around much longer. I didn't care. I wanted to break the pattern of fate in which obscurely I found myself being enmeshed. I decided rudely and contemptuously to break her resistance—somewhere—and force her once and for all into either a recognition of me or a détente with her husband. The result was, she was tapping on my door with her car key every time I looked up. At each of our meetings I set the dialogue in such a way that every sentence I spoke became a shaft aimed at her heart and the impossibility of our love. I wanted to get her to face at least the *sensation* of a complex truth, something based on the single fact that our love was hopeless only so that she could assure me it wasn't. I used her as a totem whose tits I could squeeze, whose spit I could drink, whose mouth I could bruise with a kiss. I treated her as she deserved to be treated, as a guinea pig I would inoculate with love before placing it in the center of a maze of traps set to test it, to measure its susceptibility to suffering, to study the evolution of its illness. I pitied her, I bewildered myself, I hated us.

It was a horrible period. She had weeping fits I coldly cut off, and the fatter her face got as she whined and cringed and blubbered, the easier it was to dislike her. Each of her moments of weakness made me more demanding. I ridiculed her job, scorned her friends, and vilified the women at the gallery in every way I could, building up a list of adjectives in an ascending order of emphasis and weight and dropping them on her head one by one. I'd begin long serious discussions of her need for men and money and then just as she was caught up by the spell bring the whole edifice hurtling down with abrupt and deliberate laughter, often changing my mood from a gentle whisper to a deafening bellow in as little as two words. I forced the paint down into the weave, getting a deep grip in the surface of the textile and coating the sides of the stretcher bars.

"What can I do?" begged Farol, her eyes puffy from crying. "How after all I've done"—music by Borodin here—"can I ever convince you how I feel and that I love you?"

She wept, but she was weeping into a windstorm. I tortured her by counting out the months that remained until we were to separate, as I had irrevocably decreed. I alternated tenderness and violence the better to keep her off balance and soon had her weeping every time we met to see if beneath her sloth and self-indulgence she had any passion, any conviction, any grace, any goodwill, any kindness, any loyalty, any sincerity, any principles, any love, anything at *all* worth believing in.

And I was amazed. Servitude, far from decreasing her love, made her even more devoted and confirmed to me that her feelings of guilt and inferiority raised even higher the level of her unrequited desires. She became not only obsequious, but oddly and incessantly reborn out of my heedlessness and indifference, responding to my whims with willing passion and immeasurable docility: show me your body, lower down, lie down, kiss me, take me into your mouth. She became waxen, sorrowful, and almost desperately love-hungry. She needed help and wanted to talk and began to turn to me. And soon I began to wonder if there wasn't something in achieving power that didn't involve the regret for having attained it, for I was finally so deluged with her repentance, her desolation, her confession, and a list of promises so mercilessly bright that when she begged me once again to save her, to stay with her, to help her against herself and her husband and everything else I honestly think all of it frightened me more than the idea of losing her.

I had the saddest, strangest scene with her one leaden afternoon. There was a Breughel sky outside, glaucous and cold. We were sitting in a booth in a St. Ives delicatessen—a waiter with orange-colored hair and loud blue eyes kept looking at us—and she spoke only of her father.

She confessed that when she'd gone home she went to hug him but that he turned coldly away. Everything had been wrong! Her whole family! She said everyone sat around in different chairs reading different things and saying nothing! No one seemed to care that anybody else was alive! She pressed to her lips, while staring beyond me, the small tight knot into which her nerves had crumpled a napkin. Apparently her father had said almost nothing to her the whole time. He wanted nothing of sentiment.

I recalled her once telling me in a lighter mood how her parents first met—her father had jumped down from a tree to offer her mother some gum—but there was nothing of that reverie now, not a trace of affection, only her drawing breath out of pain and rejection. I always felt uneasy when she talked about her father in thinking of my own, which is not the only reason I was quiet.

I was becoming depressed. It was almost impossible not to realize that every man in Farol's life was an improvement on her actual father. I tried compassionately to stifle thoughts of the men she herself had hurt, and yet at the same time I was wondering in asking what I was about to if I myself wasn't betraying the same lack of compassion he in showing her not only caused her to show him but was now forced to see in me.

"Can you accept the need for him?" I asked.

Her laugh was like paper tearing. "Accept the need—I love the way you put that."

Farol was bitter. With her eyes averted she spoke of him with a clearness that proved the steel surface she had in a few minutes forged from her despair. Her voice had become shrill, and I spoke in the hope of restraining it. I don't think she knew herself if she loved or hated that man. A child hurt by a parent cannot tolerate the hatred it comes to feel for someone so necessary to them, and often repressing rage will cover it up. I thought she hated her father. I saw much of her life as a sustained act of protest against her mother's fate. I thought he was the repulsive truth behind all her cynicism, her contempt for so much, her suspicion, even her dismissal of religion, for wasn't a child's attitude toward God often colored by the experiences with one's own earthly father as lord of the circumscribed world?

I subscribed to the theory that although the freedom to hate her father was bound up with discovering herself, it also carried with it an enormous feeling of guilt, and if deserting men reenacted somehow the feeling of her father's continued abandonment of her it was also a killing she had to pay for with her own happiness. I stared outside at the pewter sky, thinking of father and daughter locked in this duel and wondered, what newborn dread did he see in her caress? What in that figure of refusal with a heart of pumpkin wood, even if he was her father, did she need? And what of all she needed did he so represent that not having it had prevented so much?

And then it struck me. I realized I'd taken on her voice in my own concerns, the instant echo, the visual quotation of herself. What was absent in her father for her was also missing *between her and me!* I had appropriated in contaminated sequence the very questions toward her she'd asked of him and was afraid to hear the response she'd already received. I looked at her, and I asked, "What about the love between us, Farol? When it comes with such authority why isn't it like other authorities a guarantee?" I asked earnestly, "Why when the struggle is for success hasn't the success at least some serenity in it? Why feel so much about love in order to feel so little about its responsibilities? Why, in short, is such a passion in proportion to its strength after all so sterile?"

She tightly grabbed my hands. I looked at her stricken face. It was as if at last she heard my words and recognized the miserable irony of it all. I think she was suddenly surprised, not so much that I loved her, but at my actually having called up such a force of that feeling in *her,* in a nature so often taken, as indeed she took herself, to be so cold and unfaithful and lost. Her face for a moment almost relaxed from its pistol point of cynicism.

And it came to me in that elemental contradiction from which something positive springs, odd but perhaps part of that misfortune, that she was thinking here we are at least trying again, here's someone willing to listen to me, here's someone who cares. Her father had cast her down, she hadn't seen her husband for weeks, and I had been dismissive and cruel. But she needed to trust someone—*someone*—and to feel it, to see it, to know it, to have it. It was a remarkable if bizarre coincidence that she who believed in nothing still needed someone to believe in her.

The extremity of her collapse was brief and in a sudden gust of passion she instantly showed the effort to recover. Gone was her false unreasoning pluck. I looked into her green eyes, misting over, and felt something of need expand within her. Oh, she said, she'd gone about everything backwards. Couldn't I forgive her? Didn't I see? She told me she lived in apprehension not for her husband, not for others, only for herself, and that it was easy to talk to strangers only because she was not emotionally involved. Didn't I know that? Wouldn't I help her?

I was convinced, at the time, I had the power to make her happy. I wanted it to be a generous, not a vain thing to feel. I wanted to make things right for her, to make up for all the things she'd lost or didn't have, for whatever it was she wept for in my room night after night. I wanted to get away from those tears and from the bitterness that bound her and her husband together more closely than the most enduring affection.

I wanted to alleviate her suffering, and I wanted her to stop bringing that suffering to me. I was determined now more than ever she had to be freed. I can't fully say by what reasoning or on what grounds I came to believe this, but I honestly had begun to think of myself as the agent of her deliverance.

I also wanted to know if she loved me. I wanted our love to be unconditional. People in love often lack imagination, but love is an energy that has to be nurtured, fed, entertained. I asked her if she loved me. It wasn't merely that she had an answer. It was merely that for the first time—there in that empty delicatessen—she was willing to hear the question. "I do, oh I do love you," she pleaded. But I was still skeptical. I had the experience of finding that her contrition was almost always in direct ratio to her being deserted.

"I love you," said Farol. "I know it's hard to believe that, after all you've been through. You know what I am, and it's the thing that I am, whatever that is, you've had to put up with for so long. It's the thing that I am, whatever that is, I ask you to bear. I want to be better, please give me the chance to show you? You've been so patient"—she was holding my hands, rubbing them—"and I've been selfish and blind. You've made me look at myself, and I hate what I see. I *hate* it!"

I had heard it before. She often said things out loud that most people generally preferred to think, trying to make of the assertion what she could avoid in the act, but this time she seemed different. She told me of a letter she'd recently received from some distant uncle of hers. It seemed as she mentioned it to have upset her terribly. I asked her why. She paused and passed a hand over her hair and leaned forward.

"Ten years ago," she said, "he came to my wedding. I think my mother asked him to write to me. He was one of the few relatives there from my side of the family."

"And he mentioned this in his letter?"

Her lower lip started to tremble.

"Tell me. Please?"

"He wrote, 'You were the saddest bride I'd ever seen on her wedding day.'"

And if it all made me understand why, insidiously, from the first she had struck me as a creature of tragedy, it was as if now in dropping from her strenuous and capricious height to a sudden conceivable honesty she was at last willing to show me the real thing. I told her she was never in one place in our relationship, that she zigzagged, that nothing could ever be planned on. I told her I wasn't as patient as she might believe and mentioned that once when we'd first met and after work had gone to a restaurant with some of her friends and she took over, ordering for me, never asking what I wanted, even snapping at me when I offered her a taste of my food—doing everything, in fact, but paying— I actually considered never seeing her again. *Didn't she realize that?*

"Please don't leave me," asked Farol, "not now, not after all we've been through, no no. I want to start again and this time mean it. I know I've given you cause to doubt me. I know I've done all the wrong things. But can you not give up?" She had the shrinking look of a dog trying to understand. "Please? You're my best friend! And I love you so much. I love your face. I love what you are. I know, I'm no Pollyanna." Tears filled her eyes. "But I never said I didn't love you, never. Never."

She squeezed my hands.

"Please promise you won't give up on me? Please," she begged. "Please, Christian?"

I looked at her. I thought people aren't perfect. The only unfailing rule is, if they seem so they can't be. And I promised.

I looked at her.

I made a promise.

We came out of the delicatessen and left in a dull moist snowfall— she was driving—and after turning onto the main street, not having gone three blocks, a distinct look of penalty suddenly stole into her face. I asked what was wrong.

"That was John."

I quickly turned to look back and saw a beige station wagon heading in the opposite direction and pass out of sight. "Did he see us?"

"I don't know," she said, blushing in angry confusion and lowering her head like a child caught stealing.

17

Their marriage was soon becoming impossible. February passed. We were into March. It was about her husband now that Farol had to make a decision. I had a lively unreasoning hope that somehow all would be well. It was not a hope, I should add, that in any way met our difficulties, rather a hope that avoided them. The question remained still obscure whether the bitter or the sweet prevailed. I was content with a certain chill and despondent with occasional lifts, confused and assured and alarmed, divided between the joy and the pain of being with someone I loved but without even the remotest sign of the possibility of permanence.

Farol was unable to resolve anything. There was still no separation agreement. It soon become sadly apparent she couldn't make up her mind. So how could I?

Our fulcrum was hypothesis. While her husband told her repeatedly not to leave him notes or contact him unless she was ready to return for good, she often returned to their house—frequently upon just having left my bed—to sweep up, feed the cat, put out bird food. It's the way with adultery. An urgency to care for him became not only the direct result of seeing me so often, but the implication of his refusal to take her back without her total commitment made her behavior the more reprehensible for the very same reason it gave his greater dimension. His jealousy had long ago turned her into a liar, full of excuses, lame explanations, and deceit.

John Colorado had her loyalty only because she neglected him. In a very real way, she could be loyal to him only when she was unfaithful to him. A grudging respect for him, however, frustrated her with an anger that left her ashamed and, because ashamed, obligated. Finally, she knew he was better, morally and ethically, than she was on every front. And so they met once a week at "group," and talked. And deliberated. And analyzed. But it wasn't working out, not for him in any case. When one ox lies down, the yoke bears hard on the other who's trying to stand up. She usually told me what took place. But there were also confidences closed to me. And I knew she was telling him things, as inevitably she had to, she couldn't tell me she told him. It's been pointed out that if you've got two pitches and one delivery, you've got only two pitches. But two pitches and two deliveries—that's *four* pitches. That was Farol. And that was me. It was a nest of rats.

I remember once driving with Farol to Concord to buy her husband a birthday present—a cooking pot—and having to listen to her criticize him up and down the entire trip. And then one day he surprised her with the gift of a new racing bike. I got the full story because without the slightest reluctance, or the least concession to taste, she promptly rode it over to my house to show it off. It was a Fuji 21 twelve-speed racer with clincher-type tires, counterpull brakes and pedals—"toe clips," she corrected me—like the jaws of a barracuda. She proudly proclaimed it cost $1,000.

"And you accepted it?"

"I had to," said Farol, with a significant look. "Don't you see? If I didn't?"

I couldn't believe it. Accepting the gift, she thought, was actually her way of *giving* a present. Refusing it, according to her way of thinking, could only have increased her guilt, not only in his eyes, but in her own. And I realized it's the way with many vain people. You do what you are. Somebody once remarked that the day the Bastille fell a matinee on the next street over was not interrupted. Farol parked the bike by the porch and within five minutes was in bed with me.

The gist of such circumstances, of course, she inevitably felt taxed to explain. Several times she confessed, rather circumspectly, that she loved both of us in different ways. It was obvious she didn't love her husband, merely recognized her own precariousness. But I was the same, rating my crimes against Marina by measuring Farol's criminality to John. And when I saw her praising him to his face, manipulating him to be patient the better to exploit him and pacify the situation, it only served to show I held Marina in the same light so I could do the same.

Our sense of fair play was a system we invented loudly to exempt ourselves from it. Farol declared almost by fiat whatever she decided was best for us and then proceeded to depend on our sense of honor, not only not to pry, but to accept whatever she did in consideration of trying to be fair to both. She of course did nothing. She couldn't. She needed his security. She asked for my love. She wanted everything. She couldn't chance upsetting the delicate balance. The unthinkable alternative was to have nothing, you see. I mean, what if I deserted her? Where would she end up if she couldn't go home? But then what if her husband threw her out? And so the longer she deliberated—it was the survivor's night-mare—the more time she wasted.

It made her desperate. She began to measure nothing by the consideration of others, only by herself. The more attention she got, however, the less it meant. She seemed to feel, increasingly, the more she had, the more she deserved, the more she could have, the more there was. It was, ironically, an almost Aesopian selfishness: acquisition became loss. It was as if, starving with her jaws full, she chose to be poor by making her wants so great. By having each of us, maddeningly, she had both and so neither. In consequence, she had to equivocate, and remain extremely alert, always keeping us both apprised of what she was doing next.

Where she was amiss nothing counted, and where she was right everything did. She became contradiction itself, justifying her actions simply by their being done. She seemed in a queer self-crippling way to have perfected the habit of setting two halves of herself arguing, sometimes obliquely, disguised, sometimes I felt in open schizophrenia. She saw herself as a total failure. She couldn't submit to the imputation of a flaw. She should go back. She shouldn't go back. She wanted to move in with me. She thought it best never to see me again. She wanted to know where I stood. She didn't dare ask. She'd tell me she'd go anywhere with me, and then at another time I'd hear ferocious compensation fantasies in her nonexplanations of just dropping everything and going away alone to some place where nobody knew her. To sculpt. To draw. To do woodwork. To find herself. I don't know. To *lose* herself.

Often before she could realize one idea another dispelled or displaced it, and her utterances, incapable of keeping pace, became confused and unintelligible without scrutiny. I began to think she suffered from the fallacy of misplaced concreteness, fashioning agents or forces out of impressions and generalities. Her mind was like a door, its hinges twisted, swinging and banging with every wind. And each successive blow at her sense of impermanence and instability—each unresolved day—drove her in upon herself, her schemes becoming the premises to the very conclusions she never reached. Choice itself made her change her mind. And yet nothing signified. I always found out the next morning she was someone else.

I feared her impulses. It was disturbing on the one hand to find I could think of myself only in relation to her. At the same time, because I wasn't happy, I felt a gnawing sense of guilt for not being satisfied with someone I loved.

My doubts about her kept her bound to her husband, and her husband's coldness toward her kept her bound to me, but the incontrovertible stony-hearted fact remained that being the cause of both she was forced as time passed to take the medicine she dispensed. She habitually thought of herself as tracing a plan of judgment, some plan profound and airtight, never of course without projecting some ultimate punishment, obscurely terrible, returning from seeing her husband either drenched with precepts about how it was all over between them or confiding to me in another mood that it was probably best for all if she simply went back to him to try to make something of it. But whatever it was always came to nothing.

She was always moving and constant change became the law of her days. Dodges. Plans. The terrified person's attempt to organize. There was in her abruptness something of the stock market, up on anticipation, down on news. I couldn't know half the time when she came by whether she'd be in high feather or hysterics. She went on Haldol. Again she needed to know ahead of time how I was spending the weekend, where, for example, I'd be on Thursday night, when I planned to stop by, and so forth. She developed headaches, complained about depression, and now began taking Zomax for pain and Valium for sleep. She was seldom not tired.

The winter days held. And our lives continued this way. Farol went from a sort of punishment from one hand to caresses from another, one day one of us consoling her when the other was cruel, the next day the reverse. No consecutive weeks were ever the same. There was me, there was her husband. There was classic opposition everywhere. She had managed to turn us into competing lovers, confidants in our concern for her who could by definition never meet. I knew she was using both of as counterpoises, but whether it was to fill her needs or initiate conflict or have us cancel each other out, I couldn't at the time determine.

She was soon asking me to tell her what to do. But how could I? It was the plea to the therapist: act, choose, decide for me—*you* be responsible for my mistake. At an earlier time she believed me to have some kind of magic capable of making things come about as I wanted them to. This conviction became suddenly shaken. But I didn't know them *together,* so what could I do? They'd begin fighting the very moment I'd become resigned to their inner harmony and then find light the minute I'd acknowledge their tragic demise. They expanded and squeezed their feelings like a concertina. High thoughts degenerated swiftly and inexplicably while plans for revenge gave way to sudden reconciliation at the last minute. But that wasn't the point.

The point was, I didn't want to tell her what to do. I only wanted to know her decision, one way or the other. Who did she want, and why? What did she need and for what reasons that someone might be able to identify? Romance comes to people with optimism, with a sense of possibility. I tried to exercise the middle of my range, not to lose my voice.

The greatest poverty, I felt, was to feel that one's desire was too difficult to tell from one's despair. I weighed over and over again the worth of waiting, of watching: not to be realized because not to be seen, not to be loved because not to be realized? No, no, I thought, and so kept on trying. But she was always asking me to decide about us exactly the same moment she wouldn't decide about them. She seemed in her pessimism to have no conviction anywhere—that either of us would do, or neither. Or both. That was love? It wasn't a search, but a survey.

I tried to talk to her. I told her that she directed but simultaneously blocked my passage to her—had she forgotten last fall? Sending me on a park, shuttle, and fly to Plum Island? The day at the Dexter Shoe Outlet?—and that too often she seemed to need me only to balance her disenchantment with her husband, to need him to cushion the betrayal her mistrust constantly made her think me capable of. I was always facing someone escaping something and never coming to me.

Weren't these reflections worthy to consider? Hadn't she by the aggravations of refusing to reflect on the meaning of things committed downright blunders? Weren't they the very things that drove her into the messes—her primal scream—she constantly spoke of? Wouldn't she at least think about it? I even tried giving her some drive satisfaction, gratifying her masochistic need for self-pity in order to bolster her confidence. "But the thing is you're very successful in making a mess of your life. You show a strong will to go to the dogs," I said. "Think about that, turn it to your advantage, maybe that will help."

But thought frightened her. Reflections she couldn't bear. She didn't have the reproaches of thought, only the reproaches of disappointment. She was not only intimidated by complexities she never used the proper means to avoid—she avoided them. It wasn't a case of stupidity, but stubbornness. It wasn't only egotism, but emptiness. She refused to think. She hadn't the art or ability to reach conclusions by means of the usual premises which involved steps of thought and demanded language, whether interior or interchanged. The cliché here applied: she *leapt* to conclusions. She reached conclusions by determination alone, excluding middles and hopfrogging the logic of thought.

An idea gave her a scheme, and scheming replaced thought. She was merely determined to have whatever object in the distance she marked down. This can look like courage, but is in fact cowardice—a sort of anti-intellectual quietism—which is why she had to suffer the embarrassment of always having to discover what sequentially she'd all along ignored. She had to know, paradoxically, what in fact she refused to learn.

We each wanted her exclusively. She finally met this appeal by doing nothing. It wasn't a question really of whether she wanted me or wanted her husband simply because, considering only herself, she needed *us*. Less wasn't enough. She couldn't settle for some one thing of the nothing she felt she had in the everything that passed her by. It wasn't only an inability to distinguish priorities. She wouldn't bend to resolve problems. She wouldn't think. And where she refused to think she couldn't learn what she needed to know. So she continued to brood and suffer, standing flat as Buridan's Ass between equal bundles of hay and listening to the mad dialogue within her that stumbled out doubles in a profusion that by reminding her she had nothing suggested she have all.

And so she tried to stave off all matters of consequence, keeping up the delusion and choosing in preference to the real loss she couldn't face the apparent gain she could. It was always with a lavish mind that she opted for everything and with a hoarding mentality that she lost it. But it didn't matter. She ended up deciding not to decide. To decide for her was a kind of suicide. She wasn't going to be left high and dry, not her. To do nothing was to commit no error. She reasoned that it was better to be loved by two too many than one too few. And so she kept us in a parallel procession, two by two, a duplicity blinding her—and binding her—to the constant but inconclusive folly to be safe, to keep the form, trying by some miracle to hold all the pieces together where she showed no trust and to build upon something where she gave no support.

I don't think it finally mattered to her. Anything was better than being alone. I honestly think that for Farol Colorado to be sentenced to a lifetime of freedom was a much worse fate than to be sentenced to a lifetime of slavery.

18

We regarded each other, meanwhile, as husband and wife. When we went to bed—never without her birdlike alertness at night for each shifting minute—it was always with a feverish sense of pressure, of a tight blankness into which crept shapes, questions, insistent images. It was always the same: Edmund waiting in bed, Goneril setting out a glass of water, taking off her earrings, placing them on the table next to her contact lenses, and after making love both falling asleep in a darkness that rolled over us like the long distant past into which everything was the same except our relationship to it. It would be false to call it intimate. We had nothing in common but doubt and suspicion. It was hopeless.

She saw her husband as well. Curtain to curtain, however, it was the same old story. Things didn't cease, they merely climbed wearily backward to what they were before. They fought all the time, and their domestic quarrels became nightmares. Oaths, tears, recriminations. I took her as a woman claiming to care for a man she deeply hated, not an unfamiliar phenomenon. It was shocking, for example, to rediscover her competitiveness with him and the part that money played. She avoided the word. But it finally dawned on me that's what she meant whenever she spoke of her fears.

At times she seemed almost rigid with greed. I had never quite believed her feelings were so conditioned by material interests. But as she thought she was always one man away from welfare, it became impossible for her to hide any longer her regrets about who had sacrificed what for whom. Most of her worries now were of the financial sort, with a touch of the legal thrown in. Could she leave him voluntarily and get back in? Would he close her bank account? Would he take advantage in the settlement? And then what about insurance? She had begun to hate the hand that fed her, the more so because she could not afford to bite it too hard. Although she never forgave anyone who helped her, especially if the help came in the form of money, she literally couldn't *afford* being without him—or someone whose belief in her had as much of finance as it had of faith. The motto on the New Hampshire license plate suited her perfectly: "Live Free or Die."

It became even more complicated. The emancipation she couldn't face because it deepened the conflict sharpened her dissatisfaction. She not only resented her position but unwittingly made the burden even heavier by comparing it in an invidious way to her husband's and mine, which left her nothing to look forward to but a working life where she saw only further lack of privilege. The need for security set against a vision of herself as a common worker angered her, and her eyes always grew raw with hurt as vehemently she vowed, again and again, she would not die a weak and beaten creature. I didn't understand. She was *living* that way. But then so was I. There went but a pair of shears between us.

I wasn't sure what to do. I tried to endure it, submitting reactions to one wearier refinement after another, but everything began to take too long for my taste. I couldn't paint. It may sound like an exaggeration but an artist's inspiration is always present, the one thing necessary for expressing it being concentration—not to have it blocked. But then that's what was happening and there was no getting around it.

We were alone together a lot. Sometimes she went shopping, buying drapes. Fabrics. A blouse. That sort of thing. She had difficulty buying clothes to fit her figure—the combination of hefty shoulders, large hips, and pencil-thin calves exasperated her in front of a mirror—and her exasperation often left her moody and listless. She complained of bony ankles, narrow shins, thin hair, and a small head. It was all true, including, to be pedantically thorough, little ears and a flat bum, and I had to keep reinventing a vocabulary of encouragement to humor her. The sad woman I approached to console always became snide and insufferable upon cheering up, even vain, often referring to her first husband's second wife ("She looked just like me") or her second husband's first wife ("She looked nothing like me") and somehow, by a feat of prodigious ingenuity I'm still trying to figure out, always comparing herself favorably to both.

Nothing ever seemed to please her anymore. She seemed constantly annoyed. There was always this defeated shrug of hers, a kind of lounging insolence that always reminded me of a spoiled child. I was seeing instances of her melancholy every day now but felt inadequate in dealing with it—thinking of her illness—which made me try too hard and say flattering things and buy her too many gifts. I once thought her merely ungrateful, but it wasn't that intricate. She was only a jerk. I began wishing half the time I was with someone else—someone, anyone, who could glimpse a promising spark where Farol found only smoke. I know she sensed this, and I'm sure she felt the same about me, for I myself was becoming silent and discontented and very unhappy.

Ritual ousted belief. We took refuge in habit and with morbid wariness were both put on retrospective guard. She was often depressed. Sometimes seeking to alleviate her depression I would succumb to it myself. Although I tried talking to her, I didn't even like the things I seemed to be *right* about half the time. We were both living a lie over so constant a period, I swear, it was becoming a truthful fact. I began to look forward to long winding drives after school when I felt a saving peace in being alone. It occurred to me that maybe that madman Dr. Trinity had been correct about me—I did want to get out of the world. Whenever I returned, Farol would ask in a featureless way where I'd gone. And did I want to do anything over the weekend? And why I was so silent? But I was half the time too unhappy to know where to begin. It was diamond cut diamond. She cheated me. I mystified her. And the days passed by.

I couldn't sleep her out of my mind. Though I prayed to be rid of her, my prayers went unanswered. I began to think her depression my failure, my failure a lack of understanding, my lack of undertanding the want of love in me letting her down. Her blandness, which I thought to be a quality of the absolutely modern, the new emotionalism, could have been—or so another possibility seemed to me—the effects of newer, more exotic prescriptions she got from her doctor in Boston: Movicol, Surbex, Filibon, god knows what. Tryptophan tablets were another, I remember.

I actually became apprehensive of her visits to me. Her work hours were cut back. She gave up drawing class. She had time on her hands. There's nothing like Monday to foul up a weekend. That was her day off. When not lymphatic and drooping she could be an even bigger pain in the ass. I became familiar with her whole repertoire of caustic and belittling remarks. My smoking bothered her. I told her I intended to stop. "You won't stop," she said. "You'll never stop smoking." One evening she invited me to the Yangtze River restaurant in Lexington, Massachusetts—she overordered, of course, ate half the food, and left me the check. Another time she tried giving me a haircut, insisting she knew how to do it. I couldn't believe it, it was a perfect mauling, and I got angry. But it was typical. Every challenge drew a boast, and every boast left a failure. But why if she could accept her failure, couldn't she accept her fate?

"I'm good at big things," she once told me.

"There's no such thing as big things," I cried impatiently. "Big things are only small things. What are you saying?"

Doubt, disbelief, skepticism, defective humor, mistrust—I had never found these qualities so pronounced or powerful in a single person. She clung to the past, punishing herself out of a guilt she refused to acknowledge and acknowledging only the pain she felt as the result of it.

Several times she suggested we go for walks—you know, a stick, Old Shep, happy wanderer shoes—and always grew irritated when I couldn't, or wouldn't, or didn't. But, I mean, *walks?* With someone who didn't talk? Who was so negative? Who in her peevish ignorance remained so fixed upon such a brooding internal study of herself that she turned afternoons black? There are things harder to take than boredom. It wasn't only that her appeal had worn thin by the overcontact that invites fatigue, her impenetrable self-absorption was unbearable. It wasn't so much that for her every idea had to have a face—a male one, preferably—every face was also expected to turn away from her faults as if they didn't exist. I was fed up with her litanies full of excuses and aliases, "I am not me," "I'm better than me," "I'm a different person now," "That was someone else," etc. I was sick of her and felt confused in ways I never had before. Nothing is quite as bad as being without privacy and lonely at the same time.

I could stand neither her arrogance—she was never in the center—or her displays of grievance. Oversimplified in the way she thought, she couldn't help but oversimplify others: all were either with her or all against—exactly what she expected from others, precisely what she wouldn't give of herself. It seemed to be only her own convenience that counted with Farol Colorado, and I soon found myself mounting silent but monstrous accusations against her for what in assuring me of loyalty she merely wanted to be accepted for. It was unpleasantly instructive to learn, for instance, that she was not so egregiously self-defeating as she appeared. I discovered about this time that she had never said a word to her husband about me. "He knows nothing? Not a thing?" I asked. She explained in a remorseless and measured tone, "He suspects there's—someone else in my life." "Should it matter to me that I am he?" I asked. "Obviously it's not so simple as that." But Farol merely did an about-face and on the verge of angry tears questioned me about Marina.

"And what have you told her? That she's worthy of you and I'm not?" The pitch of her voice was almost unrecognizable as every few seconds she wailed, "What else could she think? Nothing? Or don't you even mention me? How do you think that makes me feel? Who is she anyway? Where does she live?"

I told her what I'd told her before—as much as I felt she should know—that Marina was a young girl with a complicated family and a simple way of looking at the world. I explained that she had nothing, and expected less. I felt superstitious about speaking against her, which irked Farol, who proceeded in turn to tell me her husband was brilliant, which of course immediately convinced me she felt the opposite. I had to downplay all I loved. It infuriated me that I wouldn't allow myself to be proud of her. I wanted to tell Farol everything, that Marina was the only person I'd ever known whose dreams were untouched by felonious ambition, that she was someone who loved animals, memorized poems, worked hard, danced in my dreams, and wore what growing up we used to call Catholic skirts, plaids and pleats, someone whom I loved but through some incalculable changing fate still beyond my understanding I no longer desired.

It was a matter so bewildering to me I began to wonder if sexual attraction didn't actually require a degree of tension and even *dislike* between partners—some disparity, a note of antagonism, even a certain enmity. Our intimacy, the closeness Marina and I felt, not only failed to strengthen our passion for each other, it began to dissolve it. It was precisely the reverse with Farol and me. The extraordinary thing was that whenever we quarreled, weakening the negative side of our ambivalence presumably, the result was usually revitalized affection. In a sense the more alienated we were from each other, the more passionate we became. Were barriers bridges? And did they serve disturbingly as reiterations of our need for them? I could never get over it. Did passion cease as love grew? Was intimacy attained only at the cost of discord?

I had to confess, finally, Marina knew nothing of Farol. I told her it didn't matter, which wasn't strictly true—not until Farol could show me, without changing, a single consecutive set of feelings. Dupery for dupery. But I wasn't married, I rarely saw Marina anymore, and I was committed to Farol.

At the same time I couldn't help think of the story of the two barbers who lent each other their services, one with a good haircut, the other a bad—and which of the two one should go to. And it made me wonder about my own choice.

I can explain it only by saying that Farol had a dazzling, irresistible shine with a marked vulnerability. Once this image was established it wasn't so much that it was impossible to discern her true character and habits as much as one didn't *want* to.

I suppose the sad truth was, I could be satisfied with very little if I was only delivered from the dread of losing it.

We went for drives in the rain. I don't think there was a dogtown or dorp in New Hampshire we didn't pass by or see twice over, odd out-of-the-way places in the mountains with names like Loon Cove, Madbury, Donkeyville, Quail Trap, East Lempster, Blodgett Lodge, Goshen, Shuttle Meadow, Goosewich, Kettletown, and Pigsgusset. I remember another trip we took to Cape Cod. Farol was never more sarcastic than she was that day. It was as if she were turning outward a mockery she couldn't direct on herself. First, there were the usual observations about my car, and then we stopped for a bowl of clam chowder in Hyannis at Mildred's Chowder House, a spot famous for it, which she said rather shortly wasn't as good as it was at The Grog in Newburyport where *she* once took *me*. She took a pill of some sort. Extreme irritability is a typical effect of amphetamine abuse. I didn't know half the time what she was taking.

I remember as we rode along once shutting off a radio station playing country music. I made a derisive comment about square dancing. "What's wrong with square dancing?" asked Farol with a nasty rebuking snort. "I've done it! I like it!"

I thought: *particularly changing partners.*

Farol never liked my house. She felt no compulsion anymore to hide her feelings about it. I merely thought to myself: *it's better than the none you have.* She disapproved of a great number of its points—the water pressure was too low, there was no kitchen space, the bathroom was too small. Why was this room pink? What good was an oil stove? Where were the fireplaces? And much of the criticism had to do with me. Who needed so many jackets? Weren't there too many books? How could I like that Cahoon painting? Why have a garden so tiny? I felt such disdain coming from her, to use one of her phrases. I thought at times she was jealous.

Can you fathom someone jealous of a happiness she's supposed to be part of? Can you imagine someone actually jealous of the love you feel for her, for being unable to return it in kind? What was even worse than that was not only the disrespect she showed for me in loving her but effectively proving it day in and day out by the very decision she refused to make. I sometimes thought she actually disliked me *because* she was in love with me. Envy often passes for love. And competition only feeds it.

There was a painting that hung in my library, a portrait, one of my favorites, I had once done of a young man whose sweet alabaster face, lit directly from the front, emerges from a shadowy background of Courbet black. Farol never once complimented it. I recall her several times standing before it and almost strangling on her silence. It struck me only upon later reflection that the neurotic and the artist are similarly driven by an intense longing for immortality, a desire to transcend the anxiety of the human condition. But whereas the artist ultimately accepts his solitude, anxiety, and mortality by giving his longings expression in an external medium, the neurotic in a desperate effort to compensate often tries to overcome uncertainty and anxiety by perpetually manipulating him or herself, which is an impossible, crippling enterprise.

Aren't people turning inside that way like aspiring artists wasting their talents producing symptoms? Or are symptoms substituted for the lack of talent? Is neurotic suffering artistic creation gone wrong?

"There's nothing at all to the house you like?"

"I'm only giving you a piece of my mind," she brusquely replied.

I wondered: *but can you afford it?*

I hated her fastidious pessimism and found it uncomfortably disingenuous of her, under the circumstances, to be so queenly. The whole day passed that way, with her remarks as she drifted from room to room confined to exiguous and monosyllabic quacks of disapproval, devoid of variety, wit, and compass. One had to go far, believe me, to find a more exemplary fusion of insecurity and snobbery or dependence and resentment. And it was very easy, I remember, to criticize her on the way home for accepting under false pretenses the bicycle her husband gave her. But who trades in contradiction will not be contradicted. "I took the bicycle," she replied—her eyes cold as high-shoe buttons—"because it was incumbent on me to take it," she said, "because I'd have seemed guiltier," she snapped, *"not to take it, do you understand?"*

Incumbent.

She stayed away the following four days but of course came back, mewling some excuse. I began to understand that for her being alone meant being left alone, which frightened and angered her at the same time. Sleeping with me, she often woke violently as if from an agonizing jolt of pain and then, sweating and angry, went stumbling about in the dark for the garnet-colored Placidyls she now started gulping to calm herself. She was unhappy, and her unhappiness continued to make her aggressive, but I'd never seen such aggression so thoroughly transformed into such cynicism and moral superiority.

We are driving to Groton: "Let's eat there," I say—I love doubtful little restaurants and diners—"it looks like a Spruance print." "No," says she, "my father was always going into places like that. Can't we find something better?"

Bed-dear.

We pause in a field by my house. "Did you know you can use a watch as a compass," I ask, "by holding it faceup and pointing the hour or small hand directly at the sun? One half the distance between the hour hand and twelve o'clock will be due south." She lifts an eyebrow and says, "My hero."

Innumerable examples. Mankind, for instance.

We are sitting on a sofa at a party. "Wouldn't it be nice ('Nice,' she echoes), all right, at least pleasant if we could always be to-gether"—I take her hand—"just you and me and no one else?" She shakes her head. "Oh no, that doesn't work. That's idealism. Married people need a life away from each other as well. (*Right,* I thought, *look what it's done for you.*) Separate interests. And even separate friends. You have to protect yourself. You may want things to happen in a cer-tain way, but they never do. Mankind proves it. Look at history. Look at today." *Christmas trees are cellophane, and icicles are fake glass. . . .*

As the days passed into weeks, she was always one plank deeper in the water. It wasn't merely cavilling. She had no passion, no belief, no saving principle, nothing positive. I was no better. She had to pull her-self up all the time, which began to irritate me. Resentment succeeded bewilderment, her withdrawals evoking my reproaches, my reproaches her distrust, and time and time again I would end up paradoxically in-sisting on my loyalty with wrath and on my love with anger.

I inevitably began to see other implications. Who you want always tells you who you are. And I remember thinking at the time that a per-son finding himself in love may be only trying to understand that which is most strange to him. So strange, opposed? And if opposed, then to be avoided?

"Why are you smiling?" she asked me, returning once from a drive.

"I just realized I'm going to quit smoking," I said.

"You'll never quit smoking."

There was no communication between us, which left traces now of an obvious rift. Although I avoided questions about her husband, I did try to learn something of her plans. She always hinted at extenuating circumstances, but I was tired of things being true "by extension." She spoke as if she were a split-brain patient, repeatedly telling me, "I think in pictures!" It was routine twaddle, of course, a meaningless phrase, but it became a defense mechanism for Farol, immediately solving and settling two matters for her—it not only asserted that she was artistic but absolved her of the conversations from which, lest she expose her-self, she now began to shrink. But she did nothing artistic if indeed she had the talent and said nothing if indeed she had the thoughts.

Beyond that she resented discovering how little she knew. Even questions she framed she herself hadn't the answers to. She took questions as an affront. Her competitive sense made her terrified of appearing stupid, which I thought stupid of her, for doesn't truth impose the imperative to enter language? Mustn't questions be asked to have answers provided? Isn't not-thinking a form of moral cowardice?

Repeatedly, I tried to talk to her. I saw it was our only hope, for speaking presages change and prevents that gray ongoing silence that gives itself up to inertia and permanent precaution. "I can't verbalize!" she tearfully shouted at me. "My father never encouraged us to talk!" But that wasn't all of it. Farol couldn't face the painful ordeal of having to speak with the continual risk of having her speech mock her. The girl with the bat in her hair was screaming so loudly she couldn't hear the screams of the bat. Her deceptions had become too elaborate.

She merely brooded in her apartment. I never saw such self-pity. Her television set was never turned off, merely lowered to the point of near inaudibility, a generator of mindless white noise.

My affliction is perspective. I was usually carrying on a conversation for the two of us, prodding, trying to suggest, even taking the side of what she wouldn't—or couldn't—say. I wasn't trying to talk her into anything, merely talk *with* her. I wanted her to confide in me. Explain. Give me a picture. But words didn't work. Nothing did. She was the little girl again with cotton in her ears. Her stubborn refusal to share anything but that mood of portentous dread wasn't only a handicap, it was a breach of trust. There was something of semiliterate hostility and philistine suspicion about her reticence and refusal. She not only mistrusted the requirements of communication but with sinister dexterity actually communicated that mistrust by the very silence she maintained, which became the perfect equivalence in form and feature of that criticism.

Gesture alone seemed important to her. She was a physical person. Group therapy was an activity for her, in fact, not at attempt at analysis at all. She feared words—talk itself for her was a kind of overstatement—and was suspicious of what she wasn't curious about. That insatiable curiosity about how life is actually lived was absent in Farol. She was not inquisitive about the customs, manners, and habits of people in the way an artist must be—searching, observing, absorbing, and mastering them. She lacked, most of all, the fictional imagination, insight into the heterogeneous world of various shapes and sympathy, tongues of colors, and the jargon of trades. It was this she never had in either its active or creative form—and that she thought she did made it all the more tragic. She merely suffered her wounds to bleed and her resentment to cry out.

And so she drove on and on, staring straight ahead, watching one dark street succeed another. Where she was going, she wasn't sure. Where it would all lead she couldn't say, for she was a creature of disastrous impulse, cold to information she needed to know but needing to know had first to learn with the foretaste of some exchange, and that she couldn't abide.

How could such a person stay married?

19

Farol couldn't bear that question.

She was nevertheless becoming desperate. It took all the running she could do to stay in the same place. Marking time, she found her mutually neutralizing thoughts created not only severe pressures but with crippling irony left her a person intolerably dedicated to her own worst interests, forcing her to turn inward the full anger she couldn't express without consequence, and this became the source of even blacker depression. One night I found her in the bathroom with a bottle of pills and, fearing the worst, confronted her. It turned out she had a yeast infection, and this was a prescription called Nystatin, vaginal inserts. I could feel the sense she had of my apprehension. There was a sullenness in her gloomy dismissal. "Don't worry," she said. What she meant was: *worry more.*

Her husband was, meanwhile, growing increasingly exasperated, and as his exasperation grew into escalating threats she became frantic about what to do. A separated wife imposes enormous problems. There was his pride. He had become a figure of fun, and he knew it. I had come to know him. When you sleep with a woman you in a sense sleep with her husband as well. He was neither king nor custard. He was a weak man who only pretended to be independent, and the weakness he conveyed by his patience made her look strong. He was also a man having to face the inevitable fact that there was no limit to the deceit his wife was ready to practice—the worst of which, clearly, had to be the small guilty efforts she made in his direction to placate him in order to keep sleeping with me. The irony was that aggression often feeds on appeasement, and weakness can be provocative. John Colorado was expecting her to return, and because she hadn't the continuing effect was confusing him. And he was getting fed up.

I realized that all along he'd been carrying the stove, she the stove pipe. He'd gotten her an apartment. He paid for it. He didn't do it with his eyes shut. It had been a test, but she was failing it. He had waited, but the time had long passed for her to return. He didn't need her, he wanted her. The only trouble was, the reverse was true for her. Now he was through coaxing, and I had the sense even then, I don't know why, he no longer wanted her back despite the fact that at "group," or so I was told, he still kept impatiently screaming at her, *"Decide! Decide! Decide!"*

He began drinking again, growing even more truculent and suspicious. And he became spiteful. I was fully informed of all his faults. He started seeing other women and was soon betraying her with someone in particular named Cheryl, whom he openly boasted was a companion far more obliging than Farol, which couldn't have been far from the truth, for once upon stopping by there she'd found lying around the house several pairs of panties. I heard she was looking for me at the academy all that day, knocking on every door and fuming (my colleagues had witnessed several scenes like this) but couldn't find me. I got a firsthand account, later, when she came by vowing with almost unpronounceable disgust—while gulping some Haldol—that she'd never go home again.

The poor fellow was perpetually under fire, and it was inevitable that he should respond with some precision of aim. But Farol was one of those people who heard little of what she didn't want to know, choosing to understand only the facts she wanted to hear, like simple words, say, but without the grammatical complexity so crucial to comprehension into which they were often woven and without which meaning was often lost and truth often sacrificed.

I despised both her hypocrisy and her lying. I said, "I thought you said he hated sex."

"He's got a big problem," she snapped.

"You're not that big," I said.

She shot a stern glance over her shoulder at me. I wanted to hurt her out of my own bitter disappointment because I realized this affair her husband was having meant he wanted her in ways she had all along denied.

Farol became famously familiar with these affairs, and although she'd been the specific if indirect cause of them, they sorely angered her. Similarity sat in inquest of similarity. She refused nevertheless to shoulder the blame. Never mind that her husband had merely substituted her standards for his own. She was superior to the very idea of prosecution. She felt he degraded her. She had at last found a means by which hatred could satisfy itself with persecution and railed against his vices—he was an egotist, a shit, a know-it-all like her brother Bart! But of course it was impossible for her to admit the full extent to which he was responsible for her feelings of degradation without having also to recognize that she'd not only once given herself to someone unworthy but, if things didn't work out with me, might have to do so again.

She was caught in her own snare. With feigned valiance she tried to direct her hatred against him, but she hadn't the liberty of self-realization not to see it ultimately impeded on her tenuous dependence of him. In panic she realized that dependence was suddenly put in jeopardy. Now she was losing *him!* She was in the midst in several ways of a sort of serial polygamy. Everywhere, to everybody, she was becoming the other woman, and each new plot was ruined by thoughts which like the functions of celestial navigation actually gave her the exact measure of her *mis*judgments!

I watched her with mad ineptitude flinging this way and that, digging, calculating, triangulating. Half involved, everywhere, she was committed nowhere—and proceeding in bounds like a kangaroo. Coming by at all hours, interrupting me at school, appearing in the unlikeliest places, she was in a fury. She was now taking a drug called Derifil. Biographical narration necessarily smooths over the raw guilt and sheer raggedness that such a downward-turning life produces in its unhappy subject. She was at the mercy of her greed and ambition, which after driving her to an inspired activity suddenly withdrew its energies, leaving her listless, blank of mind, weak of effect, irritable, and empty-handed.

At times she seemed crazed, seeking me out everywhere to fill me in on various unredressed wrongs of her husband and cursing the day she married him. How different this was from the cool, sharp Farol of party fame cutting the chorus of repartee with her high glassy laugh. She even looked different. There were deep blue dents on either side of her nose, and her hair seemed somehow disassociated from her head, as if it were a shapeless batty wig she'd put on carelessly. She left in my doorway long, incoherent letters—composed like punitive writing assignments in their misspellings and erasures and run-on sentences—asking me what to do. Everything she did came back to bite her. It was a litany of woes.

But I asked her, was it up to me? It was as if she hadn't heard. I kept forgetting that little of what she said was ever connected anyway. It was typical of her. Whenever a solution was not forthcoming, she changed the problem. She begged me again to see her psychiatrist to tell him what I felt about her. She gave me Dr. Varion's phone number. I tried to call this time, again and again, reaching only his answering service. I left messages, but he was either too busy or unconcerned to call back. I didn't want to give up. In a way, I couldn't. I almost began to feel it was my *assignment*.

Sometimes I thought she should meet other people. Sometimes I thought only if I were able to meet someone else could I love her more. Sometimes the freedom that allowed me not to love her terrified me. And sometimes the idea that either of us could meet and love other people made the whole enterprise between us look ridiculous.

Farol and I talked in cars, at the gallery, on the athletic fields, in gyms—everywhere—and wore the question to shreds. But all our discussions were circular, like discussing *pi,* and we always ended up where we were. She rehearsed over and over again what she felt and didn't feel about her husband, speaking to me now but without divulging the specific truths of what she'd promised him lest she be implicated unfavorably with me if things didn't work out for them. I never really knew what was between them. I was both a part of and apart from the whole conception of what they were. But this is finally the untold story in almost all lives from which, while existentially involved, we're essentially excluded.

I realized her marriage had been crucial in the development of her fierce determination to achieve a social place from which she could never again be dislodged and that once sufficiently secure she felt she'd never again have to suffer condescension. What did or did not arouse emotional response in her, however, was now plain enough. Of real and lasting remorse for having left her second husband she obviously had no more than when she'd left her first. She was at bottom wholly detached from it: she could list the details of his infidelity and reprisals and suffering without a quiver of feeling. She spoke of going back almost as an execution. What alone stirred visible emotion in her was self-pity.

I was always asking over and over again in my mind how much

of her problem could be explained by her illness. I began to think her indecision possibly a symptom of the thing, maybe even the cause of it! I wondered if the illnesses we suffered from, expressing a larger and deeper imbalance in our lives, if the very sickness we dragged after us like baggage somehow didn't instruct us in the participation of our own healing! Symptom as metaphor: people in bad marriages who developed "splitting" headaches. The bronchitic who couldn't "get something off his chest." I wondered: *was the paralytic only a person who couldn't proceed?*

She cast about everywhere to countenance that indecision. Whenever faults are established on one side, the common reaction is to assume virtue on the other. I hadn't the luxury. I had to hold two negative judgments in my mind at the same time. It left no end of questions. First of all, was Farol's difficulty with her husband either proof she should leave him or that I should be brought in to precipitate it? And then was it any more logical for me to assist her in making a choice against him than she should in the act of leaving him therefore choose me? What finally had I to do with this loveless marriage? Wasn't it dissolving long before I ever got involved? Hadn't that been told me in the very room, on the very bed, where its dissolution took place? And by whose decree was it given to me to rectify this wrong?

On the other hand, it was clear that mere obstinacy against her husband could not have held us together so long. I thought she must have cared for me. I thought the folly she showed in their direction was no more than a symptom of her seriousness in a much more important one, ours. As for me, I was still convinced that I loved the person Farol was before she became what it was perhaps impossible for her not to become. And so I held on. I tried again, in vain, to reach her psychiatrist. Meanwhile, I felt two urges: to expose myself to the force of life as it came, and to try to hold firm to the commitment two passing years so largely indicated we'd made.

I kept pushing for that awareness, nothing more. At times she assented to it. The irony was that her awareness was always the product of the moment and never a prelude to change. Always she'd reset her pace to a series of switchbacks and shifts. The only constant was change. Even if she said of a morning she'd made up her mind, it was impossible to believe any process had ever proceeded. I knew at the end of the day she'd transform once again into a mistress of mixed messages, speaking to me in a language that always meant more or less than what it did. My questions about what she wanted she never answered in the same way twice, and the answer was always the same. I've given in to my fears. The cards are stacked against me. I'm standing in my own light. Nothing's clear. What's the use of anything?

A prudent archer always has a second bowstring. And that was the disgusting thing in the whole business. It wasn't a romantic problem, but a practical one. I feared in the face of this that whomever she chose wouldn't be selected, merely opted for. A connivance to care. Survival.

A decision of any sort, even a desperate one, would have had something of a lift in it. But there was no decision. She's anesthetized herself. It was nothing, a nonyielding, a kind of blind and impersonal postponement that carried no glory of resolution. She protected the intrigue because the intrigue protected her. I thought part of her simply wanted to get rid of—or perhaps more accurately be gotten rid of—the person who most reminded her who she was. But which of us was it? Which of us between her husband and me could possibly know what we were to her? To both of us the real thing was always only an approximation of the real thing.

It was astonishing to discover the degree to which she conspired, for example, in her husband's hard treatment of her. She seemed at times to be under instruction as audible as a towboat whistle, actually cooperating in her mistreatment by fostering his mistrust! Her assaultive conduct, never mind her sexual, was almost guaranteed to make things unsatisfactory. And I'd already begun to see there was enough about Farol's behavior with men that its nature was almost counterphobic. The distinction between suffering endured and suffering invited, and perhaps even unrecognized, was not to be ignored. I began to think she actually temporized with him precisely to *taunt* such a dismissal! A true definition avoids using the word it seeks to define. Cancer *cures* smoking.

But with me it was no more positive. The same circuitous misery prevailed. She became more and more unsure of me: I would do nothing to help her, I wouldn't tell her what to do. At first I thought she failed to understand not only that I was available to persuasion but that a requisite amount of thought must be part of that persuasion. We existed by virtue of each other—it was a gruesome contradiction—as well as at each other's expense.

For example, I remember needing desperately to get away. I'd been looking with relief toward the end-of-term spring break and went to the Cape alone for a few days. It turned out my sister, Daisy, was staying at Tarquin's house nearby. One afternoon, visiting her there, I heard a knock and looked up. There stood Farol. She was twitching with nerves. She had driven two hours to see me and then I wasn't there. She let herself into my empty house, meanwhile, walked around, and came across a photograph of Marina on a bureau in one of the bedrooms. Breathless with anger—and fully expecting to find Marina with me—she raced over to my brother's house to confront me. She knocked on the door, looking bereft and windily indignant, her breast heaving. There was nobody there, however, only me and my sister and her children. I took Farol outside and explained that the picture had been there for years and had nothing to do with us. I told her I loved her, repeating it enough to believe she was convinced of that real truth before she headed back for St. Ives that same night. But the next day, I later found out, she had called Daisy (who was completely bewildered) asking all sorts of crazed and personal questions. Did she have a chance with me? Had I been with Marina down there? Would she tell her the truth?

Confront. Found out. Crazed questions.

Dissemblers create a double they in speaking to never believe. Those who personally deal in mystery and duplicity themselves are disposed, more than anything, to find in others only deception and nothing else.

Farol and I, in a way, understood each other too well, fatally well. We could neither of us protect the character of the other against itself, for the other in each case was also, equally, the very self set against the conditions that protection was called for. But that wasn't it. Her egocentricity made it impossible for her thinking on the subject to moderate the simple belief that she couldn't trust anyone but herself. She was no longer able to indulge in grand Aladdin-like sweeps of the imagination, for I represented, as she often pointed out, the potential for her third failure, which was rather a direct confession, in terms of our failure, of her being as indeliberate as I had to become *because* of it. I then began to think out of my worry, and the more I thought the more thought became incompatible with action, even the will to action, the very thought of action. The process of identifying with her, coupled with the dread of doing so, left me as paralyzed as she. I couldn't act.

I seriously wonder if I was even myself at the time. It occurs to me that people who fall in love often reflect what they have repressed in their own nature, for I remember, when trying to give helpful advice, speaking in the voice of a logical positivist as if I myself had only survival in mind.

"There is no authority except facts," I told her. "Facts are attained by accurate observation. Deductions are to be made only from facts."

I knew *that* needed improvement. I took hold of her, hugging her awkwardly, and said, "Try. Be patient. Whatever you do, be truthful."

But I had it all wrong, and should have known it. People like us didn't want advice. We wanted approval.

20

And then came that day in late March.

I've been trying to remember whether our mood, Farol's and mine, offered something more positive than usual that morning we set off for Deerfield, where I'd been commissioned by some historical society to do a series of sketches of the old town. Memory challenges me to want to think so, for I recall having felt upon leaving an unexpected sense of release as we drove into those low picturesque hills which stretching over undulations with a kind of rhythmic value reached past the countryside filled with the sweetness of washed air and led one to believe in a new sense of promise.

That promise went unfulfilled.

I did my drawings. We walked around streets of old taverns, museums, saltbox houses. I did some quick sketches of Mount Pocumtuck. I won't recount the places we visited or how in the ensuing hours we tried to make something of having this time alone together. It's enough to say that as the day proceeded the possibility of enjoying it became less and less distinct. It was not as if anything happened, simply that nothing did with all the palpability of something. No, it was, quite to the contrary, an experience rather like an occasion missed, and my lifted heart subsided painfully.

There was something obstinately elsewhere about Farol almost immediately. If at first she seemed oddly distant—it didn't come simple and singly, but with an attendant shade—she soon seemed not to be there at all. She wasn't merely a tight fit. I had the impression, despite her presence, she was never in sight, as though her being near me had itself become a preemptive action taken to best convey how far away she was. I can make no attempt to describe this configuration of shapelessness. Simply put, her very appearance was not understood by the eye. She walked in a hunch with her collar up like a gloombag and had a face a mile long.

I recall trying to start conversations. I don't remember her saying much of anything. There seemed little spirit in her body. She was lethargic and slow-moving, her speech passionless and flat, traits I thought characteristic of schizophrenia or of a person on antipsychotic medication or both. She seemed to me like one of those little exhalations you see on clam flats—*ppblnff*, and a bubble—and when you look again you have no idea where it issued from! She did with sniffing and blinking what others did with the spoken word. She'd say something, and I'd look up and wonder, did it come out of her mouth? And when I replied she sort of disappeared.

She was finally walking openly down the street in the sunshine with someone who loved her, and it meant nothing. Not a thing. Her company was to the day what a body cast is to ballet. It was as if, causing failure to forfend its miserable surprise, she was trying to *make* me resent her. Why, I wondered, was there never a middle ground between the high triumphant siren and the lost embittered soul? Perhaps confronting the two faces of her situation again, and suffering the desolation I had in the fall, she herself began to feel invisible. I kept asking her if she was all right. She would only give me a weak smile and mumble something completely inaudible. Try, I thought, try, at least try! But she had fixed her eyes very hard, it seemed, upon some secret to which by a barrier of some unassimilable and tiresome self-consciousness, tensely formulated, she refused to give the slightest access. She lagged. she delayed. She renounced, I felt, the very attempt at making herself acceptable.

But there was no secret. She didn't love her husband, she wasn't satisfied with me, and she couldn't bear being alone. And yet all remained options she had to keep open for all that was missing in herself. What's a boomerang that doesn't come back? A stick. She was living in the confinement of unfulfilled dreams.

We ate lunch in silence. She eventrated the afternoon. It was not the same day at all but a different one, a pale solution of sunlight coloring the sides of things that were now unalike, the sky a diluted blue without distance, neither near nor far. A streak of alizarin crimson across the sky reminded me in its synthetic hue of her. I thought in some wide-open space in some far distant world there had to be people who could talk to one another, who had ideas worth exchanging. There had to be people who played with thoughts, running them back and forth on colored strings, not thoughts necessarily brilliant or profound, merely provocative, people whose speech was the result of thinking, who laughed from humor, who made you come to life because they were alive.

I thought of Marina, funny and feminine, magically alight and alive with the joy she brought others, like the floating lover in Marc Chagall's *Birthday*. She who was so much what she was! I saw her in my mind somewhere dancing free, swirling with blue ribbons in her hair. Suddenly I missed her terribly. Against this pointless emptiness she posed such a sense of well-being, a moving embodiment of life itself and what is given to us in it, for in the living center of that mysterious equilibrium that held her world in place she was constant, even fulfilled, in serving anonymously as its fulcrum. And I was losing my life.

We drove along the Connecticut River. It was late in the day, and the hills had the same odd light I'd seen in the Loire one autumn visiting the Château de Beauregard to see the seventeenth-century paintings of Ardier. How long ago it seemed! How far a joy to recall! I tried again to talk to Farol. I never saw her more like her sisters. Blank of mind, weak of affect, irritable. *Enthusiasm wanes,* I thought, *but dullness is forever.* Her eyes were almost moronically dull, her delicate face cast in the vacancy of low intelligence. A charisma bypass operation. It was even worse than her unsmiling talk which filled with non sequiturs and dead words left no point of view from the secondary sources she strung together. She sat stiffly, her eye on an outdoor gloom. I asked again if anything was wrong. She took the line that nothing was. No, nothing was. All was not. All not sure. All not. Everything wasn't.

She was impossible, it was no good, and I turned around and headed back. I looked at her. I felt she was playing a game whose rules I didn't know. And yet I found the closer I looked, the more I saw, and the more there was to see.

I remember at first thinking she was neurologically damaged. Then I began fighting the hideous possibility in all I thought of there being a purpose in all this. Farol never estimated her trouble, she couldn't, but I swear I saw in her vanity and insecurity a method of madness, the necessity of choosing precisely those men whom she determined would fail her even as she tried to change them into the kind of men who would never have charmed her in the first place. I became convinced that she actually kept her husband and me around by *rejecting* us. It was the ultimate possession. She banked on us as the means of absolving

herself of her own lack of commitment for the very support she by simultaneously preventing was able to dismiss us for *not* showing and so
could hold us both blameable for the decision we therefore saved her
from making.

I told her so, out loud.

She looked stung.

"I love you," I said. "But I really don't think that matters anymore.
Your husband loves you as well. Having both has left you dissatisfied
in having only one. You've canceled us out. But you haven't defeated
yourself."

She looked miserably away and bit her lip but said nothing.

"You're waiting for someone else."

Farol seized on this, looking wildly indignant, and made a storm
of protest. Declaiming made her imaginative, not forthright, and stirred
her memory only for the hurt and harassment done her.

I was speeding now, caught up in all the thoughts she'd come to
regard as unthinkable. I didn't care. I'd had enough. I hadn't been com-
muning, only conspiring with her. Both of us were afraid of the same
thing, both of us were awaiting the same punishment, and both of us
were getting nowhere. It was as if while I was waiting for something
to happen she was waiting for something not to. It was going to end.
I wasn't going to spend another day like this, not anymore. Always her
worst fear was to be unmasked, I realized that, but it was the only way.

I turned to her—I told her to look at me—and poured out everything that was on my mind of what she refused to face and why I
thought so and how in trying to deceive others she was betraying only
herself by failing to accept what she was, for good or bad, that others
might do the same. I said, "I once thought you were fearful. Your husband thinks you're irresponsible. But we're both wrong," I said. "Doing
nothing is your expression of power." I went on, "If indecision hurts
and frustrates you, it's at least better than acting without conviction, but
finally even marriage isn't at issue, no, merely that the bond between
us that you severed be mended," I cried out to her before it was too late
to think.

I wanted her so badly I told her point-blank to go back to her husband so that she'd refuse to, once and for all.

Suddenly Farol looked trapped. Working her hands in unproduc-
tive dismay, she seemed halted in a mood of cataleptic rigidity: *what
shall I do?* I wanted her to hug me, to kiss me, to say something. I felt
so disappointed that a lump of incommunicable poignancy swelled in

my throat even as I spoke. She was clearly unready to be with anyone, yet what would her terror mean if not, in spite of what I said, she had to be? But the interest rates were rising and as we rode along I felt her slowly draw in. Shadows began to lengthen. She closed her eyes, putting her collar up as she slouched down, and soon there was nothing but caution in the voice that offered at intervals—and only when I asked—something or other, but phrases only, empty half-truths.

I had said too much. Being known to her meant being found out. And that was not to be borne.

I heard only omissions. Her omissions were lies. Badly undermined, she buried in evasions the unwelcome facts she couldn't face. She needed to lie to spare herself the confrontation of truth, avoiding it until by an alchemy all her own lies actually reached her consciousness as truth in a strategy to protect herself from self-awareness.

By the time we reached St. Ives it wasn't any longer that she showed merely a sense of being enveloped, overwhelmed. She'd grown pathologically silent. Her face itself had altered, her eyes having changed from deep translucent green to a veiling gray, fixed now to some still point beyond time where no present mattered, no past made her sentimental, and no future inspired. I don't ever recall her getting out of the car, I suppose because she never got in.

I remember the rest in detail.

Later that same night I heard someone knocking at my door. I looked out into the night. Farol was waiting there on the porch, and facing away when I answered. She turned, hesitantly. She was standing back in the darkness, nervously jangling her car keys, looking at me like a person trying to memorize, to frame somehow, the perfection of something she yet couldn't arrange, couldn't quite understand. I looked into her face.

There was something of the shoplifter about her.

"I know," I said. "Don't say it. You won't be sleeping here tonight."

She went defensively box-shouldered and tried to meet my eyes to challenge them with false bravado as quickly, childishly, she tilted her head and asked why.

I couldn't help smiling at her, not without some pity. It was clear she was not the sort of person to be trusted with the contents of another's heart. Her oafish underground invention was the product of a mind that fed upon the mechanical and the lethal, solely concerned with bringing about somebody's death in the most elaborate way possible and then proceeding to ask in the blithest way imaginable why they weren't alive. I was lucky to have escaped from her preposterous cellars with my life.

"Because you've gone back," I said.

How long we stood there looking at each other I do not know. Years or minutes could have been swallowed up with equal ease in the indescribable and unaccountable interval. She looked leaden with a kind of motionless hope.

"Haven't you?"

But I knew.

There was nowhere for her to go. She couldn't look into the past. She couldn't look into the future. Her only hope was to remain still. But necessity can make even the timid brave.

So I wasn't surprised at her answer.

"Yes," she said.

Part
THREE

1

Farol Colorado was mortal.

Although she often made plans with a view to variation, where her needs were concerned she had considerable skill in turning theory to practice. Love was a fable. Her decision was a fact. Such experiences, repeating in her, put any sentiment by. The move she made, with its grave directness, had the distinction of leaving no wandering spark of fancy or memory to charm her out of an undertaking she didn't have to go far to defend and could at least find sufficiently coherent. It had the merit of being perfectly plain, easily apprehended, and definite, encouraging her in the reasonable belief that her shrewdness was a virtue. She gave up her apartment—there was nothing to misunderstand—and took refuge in the reflection that once having returned to her husband she could now guard her integrity if by no other means than the very good one of not looking ridiculous.

That's where she belonged. I knew that. It was only where she shouldn't be.

I had lost her. I found I was able this time, however, to look impartially on all that confronted me—any other way of viewing the situation now seemed false—and simply accepted my fate. She was a figment of my pretensions that had somehow acquired reality, which was all right. Justice is, more than anything, a process, not necessarily a result. I had been living for more than two years by proxy, an echo, a shadow, a figure swallowing regret what had served without attention and for the most part without effect. I felt I knew Farol. I don't suppose I loved her less, but merely felt she didn't love me enough. There had been focus in none of it, redolences, in the want of a central sense, that mocked my fitful exaggerated self and recalled in a curious way various paintings of Manet, who in his habit of giving equal emphasis everywhere, in the exaggeration of widely separated details, kept one's eye jumping in search of a unity that remained often elusive.

Choosing abruptly showed not decision, but despair. I was humiliated that it was a despair of me, but she'd been unable to say "I love you" with even the slightest conviction for so long—even in the grip of passion it became a false note, a puppet's voice, I thought a liar's voice—that I couldn't help but feel I'd become what she got instead of what she had. Lovers dance, shout, sing at the top of their lungs. I heard only muttered whispers in a room. I couldn't change that, but her weakness saved me from cynicism, and her willfulness only made me smile. Proximity had been fatal to all her relationships.

I felt she would fail again. It wasn't that she wouldn't try and even try hard—she hadn't been a high jumper for nothing (one of the few sports, I couldn't help but note, that always ends in failure)—but that was the very pattern I knew her by. She was not only reckless, she was small. It was small greed, small ambition, small deceit. At first I thought her compulsion to return a desperate and reckless effort to indemnify herself for her deceptions and the heartless and fornicating cheat she'd been. I knew it wasn't from love. I could have understood her returning out of compassion or responsibility. But for *security?*

My blindness hadn't let me see it. But while love is blind it can tragically have its eyes opened. I had no trust in her competence, I had lost faith in her judgment, and I was not impressed by her flamboyant displays of urgency. My future died into regret. But I wasn't thinking of the future anymore. My impressions were really nothing more than that and had value only insofar as they were destined to be confirmed by the larger and longer opportunity of seeing them so.

Whatever, I was determined at the time against waiting around for Farol to present herself to me in some showy display of felicity for performing an office which, while honoring her, made me only superfluous. I was tired of her false promises, her disingenuities, her vows that were like air blowing on my cheek, leaving no impression. I figured on the one hand if I didn't get everything I wanted, I should think on the other of the things that I didn't get that I *didn't* want. I decided not to return to St. Ives in the fall and that week formally notified the school of my decision.

I quit smoking, thoroughly cleaned my rooms, and—amazing for me—even began to run two miles a day on the school track. I felt a profound desire for wanting to live wholly without violence even of the emotions. And I passed the days after classes, often late into the evening, doing some tiny oils of the Berkshires from sketches I had made. It was pretty much straight ahead. To that period I can trace three watercolors of mine, *Leg Bells, Memory as an Aviary,* and *Blues, Sticks, and Lights,* an oil on canvas board called *The God with the Replaceable Head,* a large gobby reification of a woman becoming a puppet, and several gouaches and India ink, *Cats Wearing Lockets, Firegreen Cake,* and *Strange House in the Snow.* I also went to Rhode Island to paint a portrait on commission, on the way back stopping by Peace Dale to visit Fritz Eichenberg, the greatest living wood engraver. I decided to take a trip, called Marina to invite her, saw friends I'd long neglected, and took various groups of students into Boston several times to visit the Gardner Museum, all of which had the requisite effect of persuading me that while I probably wouldn't be quite the same again, at least where Farol was concerned, there yet remained for that very reason and by that very fact a right and graceful appeal for improvement. I was surprised less at the amount of time I now found than to see how much I'd squandered before.

I got my old car fixed, wrote out several job applications, and for the first time without guilt was able to hang on a large wall my *Virgin of Beltraffio,* finding it there every morning, all its features perfectly placed, the eyes of a child beneath a woman's eyelids, the nose a region of beautiful parallels, the hands dreaming up a dove on the tips of those gentle fingers. Things were beginning to make sense again. I felt young for the first time in years.

The academy in the meantime had given me a small room in one of the buildings to work in, so taking up Van Gogh's habit of painting a picture at one sitting, I threw myself into a hell-rate of production and finished, among other things, my "Infidelity" series, three paintings—long on my mind—of two figures each, male and female in whispering collusion: lawyer and murderer in the dock, clown and harlequin on stage, adulterers in an orchard, figures not presented but arraigned, darkened over with the bosky colors of shoemaker's black, Rookwood stone green, and touches of burnt ceruse, indispensable for representing shadows, their drab dress wrapped around them like straitjackets so effectively depriving them of any interiority of embodied presence that it is almost impossible to fight off the impulse to turn away, the inter-folding space pulling you in, the anticomposition kicking your teeth out.

I calculated it to offend perception, to be viewed as a voyeur might read a novel, the characters no longer allowed their secret but splashed up piping hot from hell and fixed to their inessential and belittled faces. I also finished during this period six other canvases—two I threw away—*Gubbinal, Scarred Feet,* the nightmarish *Ancora Mental Asylum* and *Mischief Night*. These paintings still remain among my darkest work, and I recall the overwhelming feeling, even as I made them, of doing something unholy. I fought many dark thoughts, and though I was seeking deliverance, I would reel about at times light-headed, feeling blank, feeling the need to run away, I don't know, hoping to leave behind in the place I was fleeing all the intolerable memories.

I went to Maine the first weekend in April and took Marina. At the time I was studying the work of, as well as taking notes for an article on, the American painter John Marin. Against the lurid drama I'd left behind at St. Ives, Marina seemed so bright and unused and trusting. Her beauty (which like all beauty had an aura of inaccessibility about it) hadn't diminished. She who was constitutionally unable to look behind anything was such a comfort to me. But what was I— what had I been—to her? She would never say. But I knew. A failure. Her faith only heightened my faithlessness. Her love was like a secret that I had stolen from her, and my deepest consolation in being with her, which was also the source of pain, was that the less I felt I deserved her the more I felt she deserved.

The sea coast was cold and beautiful. Smooth sails, rough water, warm textures, cool surfaces. We rented a boat and went sailing along some of the wonderfully named Maine islands, from Tumbledown Dick to Big Pot to Ten Pound Island to Jordan's Delight to—I tried not to think of Farol—the Hypocrites.

Marina was reassuring in laughter but seemed tired, I thought unwell, the unmarred beauty of her face with its soft flesh tints showing too delicate a transparency, too pale a cast, for me to think it only the effect of working in darkness at the hospital. The lightless room. A tiny pod. The X-rays. In a way her goodness *allowed* injury. In making it easy for herself to be deceived she had helped in her own betrayal. She paid for not understanding hypocrisy, or the duplicity at which I was past master, and had to absorb our direction, our corruption, our foul secrets, Farol's and mine.

She made no inquiries about any of this. Unlike most of us who merely knew some of the answers, she knew all the questions but never asked them. It wasn't that she refused to survive by guile. She simply had none. Nor was it that she didn't care. She cared too much, about everything, more mingled things, I'm sure, all difficult, than she could speak of. I remember one morning she seemed even for her unnaturally silent. When I looked there were tears in her eyes. I cradled her face, holding it close to mine, and asked what made her so sad. She said it had been so long since she'd been to my house on the Cape she suddenly couldn't remember where one of the doors was.

I felt, despite her simplicity, there was a deeper gravity about her, but then I always did. Somehow her innocence overrode that gravity. True virtue never publishes itself. Its transpirations, so free and open, are never even reckoned most of the time. After a few days Marina became enervated—a long walk along a rocky shore brought her down considerably—and we came back a day early. Before leaving I remember writing a postcard to Farol from Stonington Harbor: *"Scenery is here. Wish you were beautiful."* I never mailed it. I still have it in my desk. And when I returned I was busy again.

2
——————

My room in the school building was a perfect place to work, and I rarely left it. There was a skylight in the roof that sent down one clear ray I lived in. I put in a cot, on a hot plate cooked omelets, beans and rice, Brunswick stews, and hardscrabble oatmeal cakes for breakfast, and even brought along my old record player. I did two watercolors, *Andover Spires* and *Gloucester's Eyes,* and a synchromistic tour de force, held beautifully flat on the canvas, of only natural colors—sinopia, ruddle, paraetonium, orpiment, and earth itself—*Jesus Christ, the Apple Tree.* I also did *Prayers On Fire, The Black Shutters,* and *Woodrow, Molly, and Max,* all acrylic on canvas board. And finally I painted my *Two Sisters,* perched black rooks with machine screws for faces and eyes a poisonous chrome green, their bodies scarcely more than a surrogate for the overupholstered backing of a twilight, dark as the purple of Canosa, I banged shut like a door behind them.

I worked quickly, with speedy notations, and jumped feet-first into spring, squeezing onto my palette a sunburst of yellow ochre and cad yellow, always tough tight little paints. Several boxes of OB Super Plus Tampons Farol left behind came in handy for flocking and varnishing, and I discovered a wonderful means of cleaning my brushes in her pickling brine, pitching out the beans and rotted kraut that had developed a mother during fermentation and finding the wine vinegar and iodized salt she'd mistakenly used, along with the overuse of alum, a perfect solvent.

I thought of Farol. Her trade-off, her dependable husband, the knowing, hour in, hour out, it was too late. The two were strangers, assimilated but unconverted, strangers who merely knew each other's most intimate habits. She trusted him as one might trust any mechanism. It was an infinite loop. He was a man without imagination and she a woman with less. Imitations of emotions, the saddest hand-me-downs. Recollections left visions, visions not from a pious funeral but a mean tomb. I smelled an odorous divorce. I slathered the yellow paint around on my palette and thought: *Farol is shine, but Marina is light—a different thing.*

I remember once asking Farol when in one of her guilty moods she told me her husband was so good-looking why she had chosen me. "I'm into character," she said. It was typical of her and almost made me smile. She never thought to ask of course, no doubt because it never occurred to her, why *I* had been with *her* instead of Marina. It was impossible for her to know that while she was striking, Marina was beautiful, but, strangely enough, it was a presumption that was actually part of her meagre knowledge, her inflated ego, that temper at once so closed and continuously self-indulgent.

My repeated joy was to find Marina in these yellows. She belonged to the day. I threw open every window, finding Bonnard's yellows and golds as light and color streamed in, and caught her fragrance in the sunlight. And I wanted light! Nature is full of yellows—it lights up road, wood, marsh, and meadow. I melted it over four or five canvases, catching her in one mood after another in singing gold, in the warmth of fire and the luster of lamplight. I listened to Mozart, putting the *C Minor Mass* up loud as I worked, all fast takes, off-square formats, and my brush fairly glimmered. I first painted *Persephone,* spring's daughter in a cascade of gold and phthalo green and another with Marina wearing a madder crimson and cornflower-blue jacket by a covered bridge. By working quickly I reduced to nothing the margin of reflection between the canvas and myself.

And it was as if the work I did, rising above its own intensity, became substantial on its own. I wanted to paint her with the same sense of the eternal that long ago the halo used to represent. I had the requisite music, Marina and Mozart—the *D Minor Quartet,* the Hoffman *Serenade in D Major,* the *Fugue in C Minor* for two pianos, the most beautiful of all his piano works, and, what seemed to light up my fingers, Mozart's longest chamber work, the *Divertimento in E-flat Major* for string trio—forty-four minutes exactly—perfect for doing a painting in one fast take.

I did my *Girl with Blue Eyes,* knifing lights into a stiff buttery yellow paint that filled the canvas with hard sunshine and unbroken repose and then glazed it with aureolin, a special rapid drier and permanent. And in *The Church at Camden* she changed the season to fall's music, the crowns on the tree leaves trembling in the wind like the golden scoops on Norwegian bridal pins. I wanted light! I followed that with *Yellow Night,* a blind girl in coal-tar blues and yellow lake with jonquil hair rising between two threatening umbers.

Beautiful Ophelia, who couldn't will, my memories of love are all of you.

I tapped the violent surging of my emotions and executed *Rhomboids of Sunlight,* a girl dangling a prism, and the voluptuous *Wading*—bought off the wall in Boston at the ICA the hour it was hung—Marina catching her uplifted skirt to her thighs and stirring the dreaming yellow hearts of pond lilies lying open there as limpid and unaffected as she. I worked quickly as I say, wet-in-wet, suddenly transfiguring gray-brown ground to luminosity by opaque white and brilliant yellow. Quick scumbled designs. Thick white impasto gave me silver bracelets and gold rings at a stroke. More light! More light! I used colors from natural ingredients, grinding them with the glass muller and slab I'd brought along and mixing them with distilled water and gum arabic. I got some great effects by dragging the paint out in layers. To give plasticity to the red and blue lakes and umbers I even added a little sugar candy.

At one point during this period I developed a feverishly high temperature, and often when this happened stark mental images came to independent life. I came to *Waterfall as Burning Hair* in flame, the rapid brushstrokes I used literally unable to duplicate in terms of either rhythm or speed or rowdy love the fugitive, high furnace feel in my hands, wet with vision and fever and dreams. I wanted light! Finches' wings! Birds with topaz-colored eyes! Gingko trees raining down their glittering golden fans! Matisse's sunshot certainty! And I found them all in one last good effort, a fight between three-dimensional and flattened forms, the pellucid neutral light in *Blonde in Pinafore Among Giant Tulips and Cowslips* her body color, pure as a Correggio Madonna, set off by the richly colored flowers, full of calculated scumbles, and that sun-washed yellow wall which is a part of heaven I borrowed for the angel standing before it and which I shall never give back.

I was rarely home anymore.

I usually ducked over to my house before dawn to shower and several times a week to get my mail. (One morning I found the packet of information from England I'd sent for—the AIMS material on multiple sclerosis—and read it all.) Sadly, when I look back now I get disconnected pictures of a time when the commonest events seemed to hint that simply to be alive was the sweetest and dearest gift possible, and yet all in all it was one of the most fertile periods in my life. So why wasn't that enough for me? I'm hard put to know. Life's dimensions, reaching from the abyss to the heights, stretching between terror and hope, touch truth at both extremes and no doubt must be accepted on those terms. If the worst and the best visions are true, I've often wished I'd known less of either to know more of what's between. What's between, however, doesn't separate but join, and it's *there* things are adulterated.

As I say, I was almost never home. My absences I can only conclude had the drawback for Farol of not enabling her to measure the operation of her ingenious policy of trying to save her life by losing it— and she needed, of all things, to know where she was successful—for the preliminary appeal I made to fate and fortune to find my own again was soon followed by the light of another appeal which for its precipitate arrival, in the unbuckled moment of its suddenness, I tell you, I found almost funny.

There was a note I found under my door one afternoon.

I slipped out of its pale blue envelope a folded sheet, the burden of which, one sentence written in enigmatic request of meeting with me, was borne on the back of the correspondent in question signed "F." I put no construction one way or another on it, merely drew a face on it, doodled the letter into an obscene word, and threw it away.

How many subsequent notes I received, each one precisely dated, I can't say. There were several, but I ignored them all. I didn't care what might have been, what must have been, what may possibly have been, what was very likely, what might well have been but perhaps wasn't, or even what in fact *was*—because for the very first time in years this, or anything related to it, had nothing to do with me.

3

Farol Colorado couldn't seem to comprehend that. I remember hearing a car drive up early one morning and looked down from an upper window. It all seemed rather portentous. She sat in the car for a few minutes and then got out. She wore the same green jacket, the same blue jeans, and the same white face, dim and vacantly remote, but she looked older and pokenosed and had a thumbed look to her. There was that list of tribulation in her walk. She hesitated at the foot of the porch stairs, but when I invited her in she moved past me wind-quick with embarrassment and a lowered head.

A bad haircut, making her head seem even smaller, gave her a handicapped look. She wasn't wearing her wedding ring. But I didn't have to ask what the matter was. The whole picture, as painters say, composed.

We went upstairs in silence.

Standing there, she said nothing at first, looking only rueful and gazing at the foolishness of her feet. She sighed and sat down, trying to muster sufficient composure to speak. She had a transitory air, an aspect of weary yet restless nonarrival. And then she spoke low of having made a mistake and of being miserable, and I saw the two of them like captured raptors in a cage. A tone of impatience heaved in the beat of her breathing, but the impatience wasn't with me, not this time. I asked no questions. What had happened was all too clear.

A mere thirteen days had elapsed since she'd walked away from me. Now she was here again. She had made a go of nothing—merely tried to tidy up. People alone like her, in the end, turn into enormous ears. Perhaps she had heard I was seeing Marina. I only knew that one result of trying to organize confusion is often to find by oversimplifying it that things often return in new and even worse forms.

I watched her sitting there, knitting and unknitting her hands. She had returned to her husband, but hadn't gone back. She had tried to buy in. But she wouldn't submit to either the recognition she was given in marriage or the lack of recognition it implied in becoming reconciled to it, for she'd lost her identity long before she'd lost her love. She had high expectations and low self-esteem, which even when reversed, as often they were, broke no patterns but only reassigned the symptoms of the same disease to continuously added-on behavior. The closer she came to someone the greater the disengagement effected. I believe love for her was impossible, for when it became possible it was almost by definition no longer love.

In her case it was even worse, for she had not only returned for security but the blind psychotic necessity, I could see as she spoke, of further assaulting her husband with the incestuous loathing she felt for him by way of feeling it for her father, two authorities she was literally bound to hate in a deathlock as fierce and arduous as any I'd ever known. She seemed mercilessly exposed, preferring to have her revenge rather than her liberty. She was committing suicide on her enemy's doorstep.

And then Farol looked up and stared significantly into my eyes. I couldn't believe it. "We shouldn't make love," she said quietly, warning herself as much as me, "not yet." My jaw dropped. I looked at her. What was she telling me? *I had given up the very idea of even seeing her again!*

At that instant there was pleading in her face as with hands clasped she began to pour out the train of a new argument accumulating in her heart. I was almost too taken with her intense driving concentration to hear what was being spelled out. I didn't want to see her, I didn't want her back, and I was in the process of telling her so—she heard me begin—when she announced she had to go to work and left. The very next morning, early, I heard the clack of the mail slot in my door, went downstairs, and found a letter filled with cramped and troubled handwriting.

> *Dearest Kit,*
> *I know what you're going to say* [she said] *and I deny it. I've done a lot of thinking these past few weeks, and I will be as frank with you as possible even though it is frightening. I've missed you more than words* [illegible]. *I love you, Kit. I don't say it lightly, but with the very truth of my being. I loved you long before I knew it—before I presumed to know it. I was thinking of you when I seemed to myself to be thinking of other things. It's strange, I know, there are things in it I myself don't understand, like so much else. And all I've done has been a perfect failure. But I've questioned my heart and now I am sure. I am certain. I want to make a commitment to you. You are the person that I love and cherish, is that so wrong?*

You once told me I wasn't giving us the time we needed. I was a fool not to listen. I've been selfish and unfair and don't even feel fit to be loved. That night we came back from Deerfield? I can't even explain it. John stopped over—I felt so discouraged—and convinced me to return. I should never, never have done it. I gave in to my fears. But it's been awful without you. It's not only that I love you. You are my best friend! [illegible] and to be with you now and twenty years from now. I don't doubt my feelings for you. I feel like begging you to ask me to be with you. Please don't let me prolong the agony. I don't want to learn to live without you again.

For me, I feel that time will prove nothing new, all the cards are on the table, I see, I feel, I know what I want. For the first time things have finally made sense. Please don't give up now that they have? I remember telling you once that if we should be together, you'd never get rid of me. I mean that. I feel alive with you. I feel more like Farol. I think I have much to offer you, loving you, supporting you, discovering things with you. You've taught me so much, and I have a greedy little mind. I'm not unintellegent. [sic] I realize I am taking a big chance expressing my feelings this way. But I feel I've already waited too long and done too much sidestepping, so here I am point-blank and can tell you only again, and beg you to believe with all you're [sic] heart all I say.

How's that for a game of soldiers?

4

I couldn't comply.

Farol understood that. I allowed no interval for thought, reminding her quietly of the numberless times she'd said as much. She listened. I advised her with a fine tissue of reassurance that she'd done the right thing in returning to a man she'd loved once and surely could again. I tried to imagine Marina writing that kind of letter and almost laughed. I couldn't even picture her *thinking* it. I couldn't take Farol's extremes anymore—I was either dying of thirst or trying to take a sip out of a fire hose—and so I proceeded to use all my efforts one afternoon at

lunch to dissuade her from believing there was any other possible way
of our being together.

She stood there and calmly met my eyes. There was an element of
relief for her, I could see, in the simple and straightforward attempt
in what she said to falsify nothing, not even the expectation any longer
of winning tribute but a final thankfulness, even if I wouldn't believe
it, of at least having made the disclosure. Even agony has its beautiful
aftermath, and if agony is a purging of the soul she must have had the
cleanest soul on earth. It was as if a sound, at her touch, had come back
to her from within, a circuitous sound leaving an echo that seemed to
say she'd imposed on me only to the point of asking what, having once
asked, she thought better to spare me again.

I loved her for that.

I felt the force of her words, the inquiring tenderness, the shy
brave hope so open to all possibilities that it included even the pain of
having it refused. And I remember the nights of longing that followed
when turning through multiple shades of decision and indecision and
unable to sleep I felt lifted aloft as if floating, carried on the warm
swells of a tide high as the reveries of my heart. I either loved her—
I couldn't say which—or hated myself. And yet I fought her, I fought
her, I fought her. I received letters from her I never even opened, and
entire days went by when I couldn't be found merely for refusing to
be seen. I thought any answer would be inadequate just because it *was*
an answer.

Weeks went by. I saw Farol at intervals, briefly and usually with
each of us going in a different direction, but she never took a step backward. She asked for nothing and with love in her eyes, always placing
her hand on my chest to do so, inquired about me only for the satisfaction of knowing I was all right. Which I was. And busy? I had been.
And happy? That was harder to answer, I suppose because so much
that way depended on her, but my reply in always asking the same of
her surprised even me. I felt that her concern for me reflected by way
of some strange parallax everything she'd given to him. And yet whenever I inquired if she was happy, she denied it. Taking my hand, she'd
invariably look away, her eyes misting over, and shake her head. "How
would you feel if I found someone else?" I asked her. She lowered her
head and said, "I'd be crushed."

She repeatedly told me she'd not stop loving me, and while the
very breath of that utterance reached my heart, the strength of her conviction told me only how much I myself was holding back. It was some-

thing I couldn't help. She came to see me very often, but she had come to see me often before. I felt her ambition, and knew about her over-heated dreams. I'd never known her when one hour wasn't unperplexed by the next. I wanted a real person, not a fake artist. And beyond that I had to contend with the still inescapable fact of what Farol was doing to her husband. A man needs a woman, pathetically or not is not the point, who will support him, enjoy his success, affirm his masculine power, and in her husband she had scorned this and tried to destroy it. I had seen it not only in relation to myself, I was proof of it against him. I had an acute sense that I was living more than ever between the real and the unreal without enough knowledge of either to be able to tell one from the other.

What I kept finding myself return to, disturbingly enough, was the reflection, deeper than anything else, that in forming a new and intimate tie with her I would only be abandoned again by reducing to definite form the idea of what alone together we'd become. Losing someone who didn't love me was easier to accept than winning the love of someone I might fail, worse by far than the insolence of the bleak and empty canvas one has to face—and she for me resembled—that remains, one tends to forget, as much an *obstacle* to art as an op-portunity for it.

I had come to live with these paradoxes. I had often wanted to be with Marina on the very night of a day spent with Farol and rarely spoke to Farol when I wasn't immediately thinking of something I wanted to apologize for to Marina. It was insufficiency, not abundance. With a single clock you know what time it is—with two you're never sure. I had a handful of infidelity every time I had a handful of love.

And yet it was obvious it had been the same for Farol, who'd rarely been able to be with me without having to ask herself what had become of her consistency as a wife, thinking, as long as she breathed no change, she could keep hold of a remnant of appearance that would save her. But now she wanted her husband no longer and said this time she meant it. She told me he was cold and selfish and dull. I wondered how much of this she was saying for dramatic effect, but then I be-lieved anything. "It's crazy to be married to the only person I'm afraid of," she said. "No, that's not true. I'm not afraid of him. I hate him."

Admitting to being a fool doesn't keep one from becoming an even greater one. But one lives more by memory than by truth. And the very act of loving stops thought by making it dependent on action for its expression.

About this time she became ill, I remember. Still working at the gallery because she needed the money, she went in day after day with a fever. It was the flu, she thought. I took her bottles of aspirin, lozenges, throat sprays, and cough syrup, but nothing helped. Acknowledging it might have been a bladder infection or mononucleosis, she nevertheless gave me pause. I drove home, thinking of MS, and raced back with the AIMS papers I begged her to read. She merely leafed through them and shrugged, which bothered me. Didn't she care? I worried about her terribly, picturing myself half the time if ever we got married pushing her about in a steel wheelchair or carrying her with the fireman's lift from one room to the other. Leg braces! Crutches!

"You don't want to—to *die,* do you?"

"No," she said.

I rattled the leaflets. Didn't she want to talk about it? Didn't she care?

"What good would it do?"

"I don't know," I said. "It might suggest your diagnosis was wrong. It happens all the time, doesn't it? I mean, was your doctor's name in an alphabet you recognized?"

She looked at me and smiled. What could I do? It is almost impossible to rebel successfully against those we understand perfectly—we tend to think the opposite is true—just as perhaps it is impossible to love those we come to know too well. The heart, as they say, has reasons which reason does not know and only the heart and the heart alone knows what those reasons are.

Slowly, imperceptibly, in any case, a strange sense of closeness crept into our lives, perhaps because I was soon to be leaving for the summer. It was formless, substance only, shaped perhaps but with a gentle structural looseness of intentions no longer spoken—in notes, in letters, in meetings at the unlikeliest times and in the most imaginable places. We were back where we started, I suppose, but the fact made us frank, and that frankness brought us closer. Knowledge for her wasn't any longer a fear but a fascination, and I began to learn more of her hopes and dreams, more of her thoughts and feelings than ever I had before. I was still skeptical. We had made such poor use of our chances together. And having my hopes dashed again, along with the thought of my dashing hers by failing in whatever way to meet her expectations, wore such a forbidding aspect that I merely kept counsel, even though her simple willingness now, her acquiescent grace, her levelheadedness, contributed to enrich each passing day with an odd precious intelligence.

Sooner or later one must inevitably head down an unknown road that leads without assurance even beyond the range of the imagination. The only certainty is that the trip has to be made. I remember thinking if the same returns not, the difference could be prevented.

There was a party given by the Yawnwinders one night to which Farol invited me. We went together. It was one of those late spring evenings, clear, with a lift in the air of warm earth and the scent of lilacs, a quiet dusk settling over the motionless woods where deep within birds could be heard chattering in trees touched with the delicate leafage of Corot. Farol drove to my house, but because we couldn't chance being seen in her car, we took mine. Our ride there called up considerable misgivings in my memory. And in hers, I thought. She was very quiet. She had a kind of quiet that gave me this anxiety. Something could always have happened to her. "Are you all right?" I asked. "You're so quiet. Is marriage that awful?"

She replied, "Not marriage. John."

But once we arrived I remember little different about that party, except us. It was of course the usual factitious meeting of coarse-grained stupidity and default. Mr. Menageranium and Ruth Gumplowitz were arguing about the worth of Pakistani rugs. Several of those women with three names, all shanks and bangles and slatted eyes, stood in a gather defending the making of nasturtium chutney as art. "What about single parenting?" asked someone. "Or the application of cosmetics?" *Or shooting someone,* I thought, as I saw "Tiny" Maxine across the room loudly barking at someone. Drink had given her the look of a flounder with migrating eyes.

She was insisting Neil Ringspotz pay her a dime after giving him a cigarette. He called her a bitch. She called him a bastard. "I love your gold earring," she said. "And I your red, white, and blue dress," he replied. "If you were standing on a street corner and yawned, someone would drop a fucking letter in your mouth."

I saw him see me with Farol and, smiling, took the occasion to suggest that if he should say anything of the kind to *her* it would be his last. In the meantime, Harvey Frakes was passing around a series of recent photographs he'd taken—each one of which he'd personally copyrighted by hand against any possible infringement by the growing contingent all over the world, no doubt, desperate to have them—showing frizzy-haired hags with deteriorating breasts and playgrounds with empty swings ("Those are symbolic," he said) and naked little girls with chicken legs on their stomachs. And the hosts, Snowcone and

Frisette, were showing off their latest piece of pipe sculpture, which caused a brief spell of chin stroking and pen taps at the teeth until everyone more or less judged it their best work to date. "Don't you see?" said someone. "In order to keep reality true to recognizable form, they've sculpted what is fake and illusory. It's positive negativism. I love it." I heard mention of everything from Cubo-Futurist grids to Whimsical Modern, Hard Edge, and Op—odd, because what I saw looked like an abdominal belt with an attached unguinal protective appliance. I was waiting for Farol's usual sycophantic commendation. It never came. And I was waiting for her to disappear.

But Farol never left my side.

She kept touching my thigh as we sat together and her hand repeatedly sought mine. She several times kissed my shoulder. No longer showing that desultory sense of indifference, she seemed to act with a horror of any accident or public ugliness happening that might menace our brave but still contingent regard for each other, and when several questions rudely asked of me about my future plans produced in my face a shade of embarrassment, questions obviously posed in the light of Farol's recent remove, she couldn't contain her exasperation. It said a great deal to me. I was wondering if she'd had a fight with her husband before coming. But I didn't care.

She was fairly militant about having no one—not Scrulock, not Tweeze, not even overopinionated Frisette with her mouthful of bad teeth that went every which way but loose—miss the opportunity of seeing us together, not merely for one clinging evening but in the splendor, she seemed to say, whether they knew it or not, of a bond, of a deeper secret, of a commitment between us, they could no longer contest and she would no longer hide, and in my defense she let show the intensity of consciousness she'd not only reached but wanted others to know as to my personal privilege with her.

She was not only handsome and affirmative and inconceivably kind, but funny. I couldn't help but notice, for instance, the effect our being together was having on the women from the gallery and mentioned it when I had her alone for a moment. I pointed out that Mother Scrulock was about to explode.

"The Original Dirigible?" laughed Farol. And she kissed me.

It was prodigious what in the way of suppressed communication passed between us that evening, although I'm certain no one was fooled. Farol stood by me. And I think in spite of a good bit of skepticism all around she won from most a grudging if amused acceptance of everything, determined on, she tried to conceal no longer.

And I remember later that night when back at my house I kissed her good night through the car window before she drove home, how remaining quiet for a moment she looked at me and asked for a favor. I asked what it was. She nodded toward the house and in the softest voice asked if I would mind taking down that painting.

That painting?

The girl with the dove.

And I did.

5

We began to see more of each other.

She often met me in the morning when we went for breakfast at a place called Al's Diner—no snobbery anymore—and saw me later whenever she could. I was still off cigarettes and kept up my jogging every day. Farol had her own activities. She joined a woman's exercise club. She even began to read, mostly self-help books, I'm afraid, though I distinctly remember feeling heartened at the time that she seemed interested in a biography of Alice James I had been reading and which after I described it as a book about invalidism she asked to borrow.

And it turned out that way back in February she had enrolled at the Cambridge Center for Adult Education for a course on wood carving—I remember secretly thinking *oh no*—though she hadn't wanted to tell me about it, she said, until she'd done something good. Another mine, I feared, another vein.

Unfortunately, still, I couldn't call Farol at home and so tried as often as possible to take her lunch to her at work (she liked cheese combos on pita bread with sprouts, no mayo). Telephoning the gallery I always got Tweeze or Gumplowitz on the other end ("Farol," they'd call out in a sarcastic lilting singsong, "your loved one is on the *pho*-one.")—on a real bad day raising Scrulock, her great goose honk of a voice telling me to call back—but nothing deterred us, not anymore. We managed to find each other, Farol either calling me at school or leaving messages at my house. Sometimes stopping at a red light, I'd

look up after suddenly being rear-ended with a bump, only to see behind me a blue car and laughing face.

And soon neither of us went anywhere without first telling the
other where we'd be, and if for any reason one of us couldn't meet.
I was waiting for the inevitable rehearsal. But it never came. She was
never abrupt anymore, or abject. There was no plan to this—not one I
saw—no policy of resumption, it seemed to happen naturally, and the
direction for us was that of greater freedom and the opportunity to
love each other without being under arms.

The strange thing was that outwardly not a thing had changed
for Farol and me. I was living alone in St. Ives, and she was married
and living with her husband. His long hours protected us. She had to
synchronize everything, telling me either where she'd be, which was
usually where he wasn't, or where he'd be, which was always where I
couldn't. Pity us that though we looked at this as a condition, we hated
it as a fact. For although we wanted to be together, the complication
of having to act in a community from which we were truant, while it
created an even deeper dependence on our part for each other, nevertheless left many problems. The burden was clear. We had to find our
own logic in order to have our own beauty.

We saw a few plays, went to the movies—one about boxing, I
remember, she claimed to find too violent to watch—and spent hours
on the squash courts, games, though still competitive, no longer played
as if between Right and Wrong. And we tried having dinner together as often as possible, ethnic restaurants she especially liked,
Mexican, Chinese, even Middle Eastern, the lamb and hummus at a particular restaurant called Bishop's always evoking from her a delightful
"Yummo!" Farol loved to eat. I began making bread, reading cook-
books, learning sauces, even fixing things like exotic breakfasts in the
hope of her coming by: banana sautéed in maple butter served with
walnuts on French toast and a splash of brandy. And I made a distinct
effort in the way of serious cooking—we went shopping together at
Galloupi's—fixing meals of Mongolian Fire Pot and Chinese chicken
baked in a clay robe and lobster thermidor, her favorite.

"I'd better watch out," she told me, "you'll become a better cook
than me."

Truth, I thought. *The opinion that survives.*

At a certain mysterious point, separated as we were, we seemed
no longer divided. An element of continuity was all I expected, but
her tactful consideration, the full consciousness of her sense of union

with me, swept away so many obstructions that it left a vast expanse of discovery in which everything seemed not only decently possible but now good and true. I don't mean to say we had no worries. We were not clear of anything. She was not separated now, but a married woman in every sense of the term. I worried that I made her so deceitful, and she worried in the wake of her deceit that I might give up or decide upon Marina or even find someone else, but our mistakes—we'd made them all—told us at the same time all we had overcome. It was the strangest thing. She became less mysterious, and the more human she became, the less ideal, the more I found to love.

And soon she started to talk to me. She communicated in touches so close, so fine, so frequent. She'd never been so voluble, so charged with contributing assurance. Whereas once she was merely reverberant, she was now resonant. I saw sides of her I'd never seen before, and late at night when she could stay awhile before going home she sat on my bed, rambling on about edelweiss and going barefoot and sea otters and Arthur Rackham's drawings. I was treated to a long account—I heard the sweet peal of rollicking laughter again—about how in her early teens she wanted to wear cotton T-shirts instead of a bra! I'd never seen her happier or more sentimental. She was like a new person. She gave me head rubs and left tiny wind-up toys on my desk and one night even confessed how as a little girl she cried watching the movie *Bambi*.

As Farol began to share her thoughts and feelings, I came slowly to depend on her advice, which became allegiance, and on her loyalty, which at the time became larger than love, and soon her perceptions, her blunders and felicities, her bad grammar and good health, her laughter became part of the familiar human sound of our small world. She now seemed to want nothing more than that to flourish. She mentioned divorce and spoke for the first time of quitting her job and finding another. I thought: *doing what?* She made applications to several large electric plants along Route 128, hoping to get some kind of assembly-line work.

Art still teased her to test her talent. For the wood-working course she bought more rifflers, scorpers, V gouges, U tools, and files than I had ever seen. I asked what she was making—an ark?—but she said it was to be a surprise.

She began repeating without qualms what the women at the gallery said of me, mimicking them herself and even calling them Trey, Blanche, and Sweetheart herself. She returned to signing her letters

"Fat Lips." She even started wearing her large horn-rimmed glasses—no small step for her—without being self-conscious about it anymore. She brought me candy and made pesto and once or twice baked cookies, bags of doorstoppers which I appreciated even if I couldn't eat them. I began to notice other changes, flattering ones, for she began mirroring me in small but insignificant ways, taking on the habit of using my words, talking like me, assuming my opinions, even *sitting* like me. She mirrored me in the smallest ways. Amazingly enough, I thought she was even beginning to show interest in my work!

"Paul Jawcelf wants to buy one of your paintings," she said. "He says you're a genius."

"Genius"—I smiled—"is the faculty of clever theft."

Farol laughed and clapped her hands. "I like that," she said. "That's good. That's good. I'll have to remember that."

We tend to know perfection through the reason, not through the senses. Beauty, it's said, alone is revealed to us through the senses. And yet the inviolate statue that was Farol had grown human, and taking on the imperfections of her humanity without apology, accepting herself for what she was, made all the difference to me. I was touched by a vulnerability in her that let me reach out with what might be called the rationality of sentiment.

It was so much better than before. I think I could have taken her in almost any incarnation but that of pedant. She used to *tell* me I needed her. I realized I refused her help me not so much because I suspected the impulse of her trying to be near me without being with me but because I couldn't stand her high gibes or that humbugging presumption of hers for having abilities she never had.

But that changed too. And when in late April I had things to do at the Cape, grass to mow, planting trees or flowers, or whatever—among other things, a roofer had advised me to screen over my chimney, against bats—Farol understood it all to be part of her concern as well, no longer out of a vague sense of condolence or condescension but from something we shared together this time of a mutual celebration growing out of our happiness and gathered out of our hope.

Our hope. Why after more than two years did I hope for such a different end to the story? I don't know. I suppose I found myself destitute of the materials for a final judgment.

I had her word. She was bright and handsome and so convincing that it was impossible not to think well of her, and yet it still seemed there was something impudent, terrible, almost vicious—somewhere—

in the remote, stern, uncaring father's daughter I'd known who could so quickly, so efficiently, so easily become again mine. Wasn't it but compromise?

But of course resisting the way life comes to one, no matter how strange, is also a compromise. And this became not a rejoinder to her but an admonition to myself. There were times when I felt she asked too much of me, to wait, to trust, to continue hoping. And contrasting her constancy to me, while married, to my doubts of her, while single, left me truly confused. It was something really more to feel than to calculate. But what we wish, that we readily believe. And I thought at the time that after so long if I rejected her love, it could only be the worst, the most fearsome thing, I couldn't even find the word for it, I had ever done. I felt in facing the same thought two feelings. She had been given a lot of opportunities. But I felt she had never had a chance.

I think in that alone she reminded me of Marina. Whereas Farol had the success of determined directness, of course, Marina was timid. As she was afraid of being fired, she was also nervous about being telephoned at work. I had less and less time to drive to Boston to see her. And because it was impossible to reach her at home, thanks to her mother, who constantly stood in the way of our ever being together, I rarely saw Marina anymore. She was never there for me, nor I there for her. Farol was meanwhile coming by all the time.

On those rides to the Cape—Farol took French leave every Monday—I saw her face open like a window thrown wide. She'd sing in the car or make the sound of a lapping dog in my ear or begin whistling, interrupting herself often either to talk excitedly or to tell me of a dream she had or simply to exclaim with a sudden squeal on something we'd just passed, like "Cranberry bogs!" or "Look, deer!" or "I tot I taw a puddy-tat! I *did!* I *did!*" Sometimes she did her gorilla whoop at the top of her lungs. Regression is one of the great keys of freedom, and to me our very silliness became a confession of trust and a test of goodwill.

She never seemed happier. Her face lost the impassivity it once wore, and its angular outlines disappeared. Her green eyes, always lovely in a lapidary way, grew softer and came alive with animation and delight, and she began to show the attractiveness again that had been immured for so long and so impenetrably behind that cold imperturbable shell.

"Tiny Maxine wanted to bring her bathing suit," said Farol, mentioning that the women at the gallery envied her getting away and

wished they all could come. I pictured them snorfling in the surf, bob-
bing about like bottles, which put me instantly in mind of hippos and
walruses and the winter reveries of the emperor penguin.

"Her idea of interior decoration is an enormous meal."

Farol said with impish eyes, "One thing you can say for her size
is that a great deal of her would be having a good time."

"If she ever wore a white dress, you could show a home movie
on her."

She jumped on me with raised claws and cried, "Vulturefeet!"

"The Mares of Glaucous."

"God, I'm tired of all of them," said Farol, sliding next to me and
kissing my shoulder. "Every Tuesday morning Charlotte wants to know
where I've been over the weekend, with whom, for just how long, and
why. And Ruth is forever sticking her nose into someone's business."

I thought of Gumplowitz's nose.

"What choice has she got?"

Farol burst into laughter and hugged me. When we got to my
house there was always too much to do. Farol helped me with various
chores. Our projects often tired us—she looked so funny at times in
dusty jeans, her nose smudged, spitting a weed off her lip and laughing—and I could see the tomboy she once told me she'd been, the tall
gawky girl of ten, eleven, twelve, combatively joining all the other kids
in the fields of Big Flats, romping and shouting and, I don't know,
tearing the frock she wore, if ever she wore one.

The arbutus came in April, loveliest blossoms of spring. I knew
where the largest clusters grew and the pinkest blossoms with the longest stems—a hint of this fragrance still proves to me that reality can
live up to the imagination—and once by an old road, finding a spray of
full-grown blossoms, I picked them for her.

Taking them, she held them to her and grew serious.

"Will you listen to me, if I say something?"

It wasn't clear what she wanted to say. But I wanted to hear it.

"I love you. I want us never to—"

I stopped her mouth.

"Shhhh," I whispered. "Be sure? Be certain this time?"

But this was a confirming stroke to a resolve on my part already
vaguely taken.

And that love Farol feared to lose. I never saw it more clearly than
when, wistfully looking at her watch as each of those days drew in, she
had to remind me it was time to leave. Her husband expected her home.

Her face always became an oval of anguished concern lifted to mine whenever she had to go. She would look at me and shake my shoulders. Did I know she loved me? Would I promise never to give up? Could I truly see, in spite of everything, that we'd always been meant to be together? Or was it all wrong and hopeless?

"See those trees," I told her. "The branches of a tree should balance the roots. By transplanting a tree you've given it a shock and because of that you have to give the branches one as well, pruning the laterals and leaders. And so, you see"—I squeezed each of her buttocks—"two wrongs make a right!"

"Oh, you're a caution!" she laughed, punching me (her monkey-bubble punch) and wrestling me to the ground where we kissed and rolled downhill and could have rolled downhill and kissed forever. But time was always pressing and before the smoky darkness fell like disenchantment around us we knew in the sudden silence as we lay there we had to call it a day.

She had to get back to St. Ives in time, before the clock rang the change.

6

There was something at issue now we both had to face, something that could neither be hidden nor denied. When previously Farol had told me we shouldn't make love, I understood that. And it wouldn't have mattered to me, for being loved seemed sweeter by far than being made love to.

But we made love all the time!

We virtually lived in bed. She slept with me on the very night she said we shouldn't! And it had been that way now for months. I'd be with her and no one would know. Or was I wrong? Perhaps everyone knew, even her husband. I didn't care now, and I don't think it mattered to her anymore. She referred to her husband with muffled contempt and said he tried to play the martyr and continued quite openly to speak of divorce. Her every confrontation with him became a détente with me.

And so it was all spring. Stolen afternoons. Early mornings. Sometimes whole weekends when her husband left her alone to go bicycling, she reported, with a group of friends. (Hadn't she once told me he had none?) Otherwise she came and stayed as late as possible, lingering as long as she could. Whereas the urgent passion we felt often left us before drained of the higher force of love, that somehow changed as well. Sex and love now became one. Her lingerie became more transparent—she looked healthier, more fit—and she began wearing teddies, silky camisoles, and garter belts with nylons, teasing me in the darkness as slowly slipping out of them with a coy half-smile she revealed in her tall nakedness a body shining as bright as her sunbeam-gold hair.

A dangerous hunger excited Farol. She'd tug at my belt, kissing me, fighting my kisses, relenting, fighting again. She'd bite me, slide down to take me in her mouth, and then we'd be in bed, kissing and working up to a heat that grew uncontrolled, even rough, with Farol at first struggling with all her strength, twisting almost inside out, writhing to free herself of my restraining hands or arms, until with her lips moving as if in prayer she'd abandon herself like someone accepting a well-merited punishment and then with frantic whispers nuzzled in my ear of "Spank me!" or "Just a little longer, just a little longer!" suddenly give in with a sob, wrap her long legs high around my waist—her hands, her arching force, pressing me more deeply into her—and rise to a shuddering climax.

I thought there was something to her need for sex-as-eager-punishment, the subconscious guilt in her both wanting and deserving what found its perfect embodiment in spanking sex.

Afterwards if I fell asleep I'd always wake up to find looking down at me a face making the noise of a toy rubber pig. As I've mentioned, she liked giving rubdowns and massages—clup, clup, clup—proud to show her abilities in respiratory therapy but more than anything looking to linger awhile. What was rash was that we often overslept. She always had to hurry, gathering herself together to go back home, taking pleasure back to penalty for before having done the reverse, often misplacing an earring or a sock or a shoe and then having to search the floor for them at the last minute as I straightened the bed table we invariably knocked over making love or swept up the shards of a broken water glass that might have fallen. And then ducking into the bathroom—or the "biffy," as she called it—she'd wash thoroughly before leaving. She often had no money for gas, which saddened me, and I'd slip money into her pocket, which she always gratefully accepted.

I remember late one afternoon watching her dress. I saw how love put light in her eyes and rings on her fingers and a sense of joy in her heart. She positively took my breath away. There was no denying anymore how I felt. "I love you, Farol," I said. "Oh I love you too." And she fell back onto the bed, kissing me and my eyes and my mouth. She drew back to look at me. There was such a fixity to her face that I felt I'd never known what conviction was before. She was suddenly everything I wanted, and I told her as she continued dressing that if she wanted the same we must fight for it and struggle and never stop.

She peered over the mask of ther half-pulled-on blue jersey—her bandit eyes wide—and spoke through it. "Would you like to live together?"

"I want to marry you," I said.

"Do you?" asked Farol. "Do you really? Could you be happy with me?"

She pulled the jersey down.

"I'd go without chocolates. I'd go without sugar in my tea," I said. "I'd go without tea in my sugar."

Laughing, Farol tugged on her jeans and zipped the fly and began tying her shoes—the pair from the Dexter outlet that reminded me, whenever I saw them, she might once have walked away. I never wanted that again. I held her sleeve as she went to put on her jacket, dragging her laughing onto the bed as she tried to hold her watch in front of my face. But I didn't care what time it was, pulled off her clothes, and we made love again in a struggle of passion as strong as our confession, as confessional as our need.

Struggle.

Farol had her own sense of it. Her doubts and fears became a consideration now, for she knew the longer she stayed with her husband the stronger his expectations grew of what that commitment meant. At the same time she saw the implications elsewhere of my being left to find another person to form another life. It wasn't that I merely sensed it. I saw it. The fact of Marina in my life was now more than ever a hobble to Farol's trust; just as I once wondered if I could love an adulteress, the very woman I was betraying for her became the source of her doubt. She felt everything in my interest in Marina of obligation—it was a mirror image—that she herself felt about her husband. Maybe she pitied her. I wanted to feel she understood and sympathized. But what's understood in the mind often puzzles the heart. The hidden effects of confidentiality teach from the cause. Our doubles are always our devils.

It was late, and Farol had to go.

"I don't want to lose you, Kit," she said, hugging me. I smiled. I promised it would never happen. "But I worry about you and Marina. I do, I do."

"I never see her. Anyway, she knows," I said. "I know she knows."

"About me?"

"About you, yes, I'm certain."

"Have you told her—everything?"

"Everything?"

She smiled sadly.

"What I mean to you," she said. "What we are."

In her concern I heard myself speaking, for she was echoing in her love everything I myself meant in loving her, and I suddenly felt in spite of the implications—one of which stood out prodigiously—that we'd become truly one, at last. She deserved the truth. And so did Marina.

We must fight for it and struggle and never stop.

"I will," I said.

And it was this that determined what next I must do. Marina had to be told.

7

I dreaded this, I think, more than the day of death, dreading it more so now for so long having believed it would never come. But it was a death. I'd watched it loom slowly from afar, and the grim task await-ing me at the time left a chill that could only be completed, I knew, in the coldness of my conscious perjury, for I saw that to confess to the truth was, by the very same stroke, to have to confess to my falsity.

My stare as I drove up to Boston was a refusal to see, not a pro-jected fear, my controlled stillness mocking that primitive wail—crying out to me again and again of incalculable error—I impatiently stifled as yielding nothing to my purpose. I followed logic and called it truth. I didn't want to do it. But there was no other way if I wanted Farol. It wasn't so much someone else playing in my heart, however, as my deceiving it myself. And I think I felt that most of all. I wanted to spare Marina myself. Us. The whispering conspirators. She was infinitely better than we were. But I was also sick of lying. It had gone on too long.

And so long had I lived transmuting right from wrong that soon the quality in the taste of wrong, converting the sense of it, hardened my resolve. The humane and the advantageous I calmly identified. Memories I did not ponder, only denied. I found necessity instead of deceit and guided myself by the simple expediency of one forgiving the other. It was as if our love to Marina was a sacred law or sacramental, the general holiness of which she took for granted so thoroughly that it never occurred to her to investigate its particulars. Her fault lay less in not seeing than in failing to look for the mysterious footprints, the thoughtless tricks, the smiling hypocrisy, the cavorting and fugitive figures who lived up there in the mist-thick shrouds of New Hampshire. I blamed her innocence. I saw it was easy to reason, with immense advantage, against someone whom I could represent as the cause of not having tormented me with the shrewd and insistent notions by which to me, at the time, passion made its exertions.

All love demands a witness. But in the irrecoverable dark a shaft of light strikes blind. And she would be sacrificed to that.

We were sitting that night in the Bay Tower Room, high above Boston, the lights of the city playing below. I remember Marina's delight as she looked out across the spacious night-expanse. The view was breathtaking. We sipped our drinks. I said that something strange had happened and that she ought to know about it. I asked if she could bear to hear something sad. She took my right hand and asked me not to worry about so many things. A smile came out of someplace in the center of her. I couldn't speak suddenly, swallowing the words that formed. And then I ordered dinner, and we talked of other things I never heard.

I had met her earlier that afternoon, waiting at the hospital until she got off work. Walking along the Charles, her arm in mine, she stopped on several bridges, leaning over them with laughing eyes that dazzled at the sailboats gliding along. I watched the positive sun-play of her smile. And then she saw a dog. And oh how beaming she looked, and how glad! How she caressed the dog, and how the dog knew her! How expressive that spontaneous manner, that heightened color in her face, her irresolute happiness! Then came a mild shower, and she hugged me and with a sun-bright smile said it didn't matter, that she loved me in the rain.

We stood there on the esplanade. She gaily held her hand up to the drops. I couldn't bring myself to tell her what was on my mind. I thought, as I had in Maine, that she also looked tired, not low in spirits, but subdued and frail like the scent of a flower dying even upon the sense it charms, and even as the day went down something of her ethereal substance seemed withdrawn with each lessening gleam of light. At sunset the earth became a succession of great stairs, falling from a high rim to a lost horizon. I wanted to mount them with her and disappear forever. But then darkness fell. And I became part of it. When I mentioned dinner Marina chose a favorite of ours—on top of a building—with the high report of a child.

I remember I couldn't eat. Nor could I look away. I watched the candlelight in her face, the lavender shadows lost in her hair, but couldn't stop contemplating the blue of her eyes. They seemed to ask why, why I was so alone, why I was troubled, and yet all the while renouncing themselves, accepting distance, in what seemed a demiurgical act: they incorporated horizons, bore the space of the world. I saw her solitary presence across the table, an image looking back at me from the other side of the metaphysical divide I alone made. But the evening was passing, and she had to be told. I had to tell her. My troubled spirit again broached the subject of what I said she should know and which she again met with that quizzical and laughing face, that irreducible eagerness to please, please still, please even as she heard me begin.

I looked at her for a moment, hesitating an instant as she moved forward. It was as if she suddenly needed to share a thought or had some lingering hope that I might take her in my arms and kiss her. I felt a thousand impressions within me and presently the one that was uppermost found words. "I've met someone else," I said.

Her amputated body no longer counted, lost in her jacket. "No," she said. She colored to the eyes, and then became almost transparent. "You didn't, did you?" I saw her straining to understand. She tried to speak but couldn't, for the child hadn't yet enough logic for the heart's defense. She smiled though there were tears in her voice as well as in her eyes, and the white face, the small hands, shone like crumpled flowers. The tears that stood in her eyes as she raised them quickly to my face were frozen by the expression it wore. She smiled until the smile went numb under the affective horror, but did not vanish entirely, to let me behold the most heartrending thing that can ever be seen—the smile of despair.

In spite of all the pain I had already given her, her face was so guileless, so unprepared, that my cruelty was at once hideous. Grief, I thought as I spoke with a mouth dry to smacking, couldn't have altered the shape of her face; it was just as round, as childlike, as ever, and yet before my eyes the features changed. It was like a pumpkin with a happy face, mouth tilted upwards pleasantly, suddenly and senselessly attacked by a madman cutting away at it: the eyes were gashed, her mouth stretching, stretched in painful agony beyond repair. She was defenseless and disfigured and now crying, blinking incomprehensively through the tears running straight down and dripping off her chin. She turned her eyes from me like a lacerated angel's, facing the wall in humiliation, pressing her clenched hand tightly to her mouth to try to stop, but she couldn't stop, and we had to leave, and though I recall her later walking unsurely, and unsteadily, up the back stairs of her house in the dark that fateful night, I remember little else.

I drove back to St. Ives in a black light, barely conscious, entering another life I didn't recognize. I who had left her alone couldn't bear it myself. I heard screaming in my heart. I hadn't had a sense of such abject isolation since I was a little boy. Immediately everything around me seemed but an improvised satisfaction. I felt lost and cold, a partisan of the unfixed with such a sense of fundamental trap, the perception of even a moment's discrepancy from it so utterly gone, that I suddenly wondered how other people lived, how I myself had lived, so unconscious of the pit yawning beneath the ramparts of this sad, unequal world.

Everything said good-bye as I drove through the moving darkness surrounding me, good-bye to Marina, good-bye to the life put second by second behind me, good-bye to myself. The deed was done. Finished. The swiftness of action had only mirrored Farol's with her husband's. Anything not loved immediately becomes the brutal victim of what is. I raced along recklessly, fighting back tears and indulging in such sharp deprecations of myself and this miserable world where the nature of choice itself seemed so crude and profane that it could only have been a kindness to me, were it not the last refuge of my cowardice, to hop the median and aim my car directly into the oncoming traffic.

We were committed once more, Farol and I, to our piratical secret. Except that I was alone. Free, if you will, but alone. The most intoxicating passions even when there's suffering are often fermented like spirits out of the worst complications and the most impossible conditions. Now that the conditions had gone, so had the intoxication, but the suffering remained. Adultery *is* mixture. I wasn't only alone, I felt suddenly servile to Farol in the shame of what I'd done to Marina, the difference between what I still felt for her and what I could say of it giving Farol grave suspicions. I wonder if she knew how often afterwards when we were together I literally held my breath for fear of showing the extent of what I'd done.

I could never indicate, nor could she have understood, the line of division I had drawn.

I shall never forget the mixed feelings I'd had waiting for Farol at dawn on the steps of the gallery after the dreadful rainy night I returned from seeing Marina. I had wandered the streets of St. Ives all night, following the river out past Newfields and roaming for miles in aimless quest of a companion no longer there. The passing hours had seemed almost imaginary, removing me from a sense of time and space with everything I'd ever known increasingly lost to evidence. I kept seeing the almost chloroformed pity of Marina's large eyes and her face as white as a signal of terror. Something told me by the minute to go back to her.

I had desperately needed to talk to Farol but couldn't telephone her, not at home. There was no way to reach her. So I walked. I walked, it seemed, until I could walk no longer, and then found myself in the early morning fog waiting for Farol at the gallery long before it opened. I had nowhere else to go. When she arrived and saw me—I was disheveled enough to frighten her—I told her immediately what I'd done, explaining it in detail. I remember how astonished she looked, caught off guard, listening with pained eyes as I spoke but nodding with the understanding of a person long familiar with the letter and law of the broken word.

I remember looking to her with a kind of adolescent hope to comfort and stand by me. But it was strange. She'd so abruptly had her way, and with such finality, that the look of momentary but singular disturbance crossing her face revealed to me the unavoidable responsibility I'd placed on her. I realized how frightened it made her. I could see the burden she bore in my sudden appearance of the just as sudden dependence it pointed to in what I expected of her. And I'm certain she saw in it the inevitability of what likewise awaited her in having to face the same difficulty with her husband. At the same time she couldn't fail to hear in my voice the constant strain of regret I felt for leaving Marina, and while she had fears she also had her pride—and an inward and different need of her own.

Farol vigorously urged me to consider the duration of my own case, proceeding throughout on the ground of the immense difference between me and Marina. "Don't reminisce. Marina will get by," she said. "Women do. What reason is there to go back and start rethinking the whole thing over again? You can't pity everyone, and you shouldn't try. Forget her, it's the only way. Marina will find someone else." I may have nodded. But I prayed she wouldn't. I couldn't be with her. Oh, but I prayed she wouldn't, ever, ever, ever. Never.

I remember staying in my room for days, playing over and over the cavatina of Beethoven's late quartet, Opus 130, a movement of such haunting sorrow and beauty that Beethoven himself supposedly wept while composing it.

There is something in a person who is a perfect example of a type. It passes the understanding. We believe she'll never change but always remain the same, just as she is, eternal and immutable and permanent, offsetting, in the endless succession of all she is, our own precarious and meretricious selves. It is inexplicable. But in this light, for some reason, we are able to let her go. I felt this way about Marina. She had an aura, an inert and motionless and sovereign tranquility, with no ratiocination in it, no design, that left me behind. She lived where I only sojourned. I knew I would never forget her. But she was beyond me. Then she was far away. And soon she was out of the range of reflection.

Over the next few weeks, however, Farol seemed to draw strength from the way things had fallen out. She became almost a symbol of what she had never encountered before; it was almost as if she were surprised she had fallen in love. And once she began to let herself go, the movement took her off her feet, the relief of it something like the cessation of a cramp. She shared all she felt and in doing so shifted her sharp pain, following me day after day with care and concern. Part of it may have been panic. She became apprehensive in May, for instance, about where I'd be in the fall, and constantly asked me about it. I wanted to be with her. She expressed a yearning for me to stay. So I signed up—once again—to teach another year at St. Ives.

There was something else in which she seemed fulfilled. Was it the contentment of having me and her husband finally the way she needed us both?

I wondered. The strange thing was that although she lived with him she now seemed to need my help even more. Ironically enough, she needed it foremost to sanction and support her in having returned home—which she yet regretted having done! I never saw anything like it. She sought my understanding only until I showed it, and urging me to wish her well without the willingness to undermined her very own needs, for in the precarious state of our affairs when love meant allowance, allowance meant indifference and both meant failure. What it came down to was that she was listening for precisely what she couldn't bear to hear and was angrily forced to recognize the very thing she had to ignore to be happy. Going back was wrong until I told her it wasn't. It seemed never to vary. If I went along with what she'd done, I gave the wrong impression, and if I didn't I clearly failed to give the right one. It was as if, paradoxically, she couldn't be there unless I was around to tell her *not* to be.

But censure was senseless, wasn't it?

I merely tried to be what I meant, she to show what she felt, and we both tried in the face of it all to win each other's belief. It made us generous. I helped her pay for various things she needed, gas, tune-ups, parking tickets, clothes she hadn't the money for but wanted, and several times she framed a painting of mine at a discount, plain frames mostly. (A running joke at the gallery was the women lending their name to various frame styles: "Little White Farol," "Thick Scrulock," etc.) And out of a superstitious need to please we often gave each other gifts. Farol gave me a pair of lederhosen, a paperweight rabbit her father designed, some handcuffs (!) tied with a little green bow, and several loaves of banana bread. "I wish I had my old Blickensderfer typewriter to give you," she told me, "but it was one of the things I left back in Syracuse with—you know."

It was simple shorthand. *Back in Syracuse* meant her first marriage, *you know* her first husband. And of course *I wish* was the topic sentence of her life.

I bought her countless books—I could never inscribe any of them with love lest her husband notice—along with a malt-making machine, an original Frisbee pie plate, leg warmers, an old Fanny Farmer cookbook, eggbeaters of all sorts and sizes, a pair of binoculars, several jackets and sweaters, black leather riding boots, an Edward Gorey poster (signed), several of my paintings, and, in view of her current interest, a lot of carving tools.

I wasn't painting anymore. I tried to give Farol my full attention. I was always with her in ways that rarely let me do anything else— doing, as I saw it, not making. I've often wondered if the urge to live well makes irrelevant the desire to create, even robs one of the chance for it. At various times in my life it became a contest for me, except when I was with Marina, who inspired me in ways impossible to explain, not only with the motivation but as a subject. I never painted when I was with Farol. Well, that's not strictly true. I once helped her paint the walls of the gallery—she needed the extra money—a stint under bad light with rollers and trays that took a long time but in a way showed us we could work together well. We spent two full days and several long evenings playing housepainters, talking and splashing about and singing songs and ditties to stem the boredom. Again, her favorites were always college songs:

> *Hail to the victors valiant!*
> *Hail!*
> *Hail to the conquering heroes!*
> *Hail! Hail to Michigan!*
> *The leaders and the best!*

I remember taking the opportunity to ask her, while reminding her that most artists earned less than housepainters, whether she ever worried if I could support her the way her husband had. Support her? Her husband? "He gives me *nothing*," said Farol, not indignantly, but with the grave necessity of setting things straight. "I don't even know what his salary is. He doesn't tell me. He won't. He never did. He said it was none of my business. He never gave me an engagement ring. Not that I care, I don't like diamonds anyway, it's just a good example of the kind of life we lead, okay?" And she unpocketed the paltry amount received for doing the gallery walls and asked, "Why do you think I have to do extra work?" And it was then that she mentioned a friend of hers had found her a job for $58—which she decided to take—as an aide working every other weekend.

"An aide?"

"At a hospital," she said. "It's only a half hour away."

Farol greatly feared one day finding herself penniless. She said that even if she had the chance to live with her husband in luxury, she'd prefer to eat bread crumbs with me. She kissed me and called me "Cookie Puss" and made an irresistible duck quack. I laughed. "What would you have done last fall if I had gone to Iowa?" I asked. "Gone into the evergreens and puff up?"

"That'th *ridiculouth!*" said Farol, going comically cross-eyed and doing her imitation of Sylvester the Cat. "That'th *prepothterouth!*" And then she came up to me with a sly look, tapped the tip of my nose with a spot of white paint, and said, "I'd have found out your address. I never give up. I would have come back to you."

She smiled coquettishly.

Then she became serious and putting down her brush came over to me, looked me in the eye, and said, "You'll never get rid of me."

It was the oddest thing. She never doubted I'd *take* her back. It was one of those presumptions of hers about which she never thought twice. No special pleading. No cap in hand. No worry about the way to or from. I suppose I was flattered. It gave her conviction of a kind, to say the least. A clouded look took hold of her. Didn't I want that? Didn't it matter? Did I want her to stay with John?

She knew I loved her. But she also knew something else, and it became very unsettling to her—I wasn't jealous of her husband. I pitied him. I disliked him, I'm sure, I feared him, I know I opposed him, but I also understood him and commiserated with him. I mean, I felt everything—*everything*—about him I felt about myself. I saw in Farol's coming closer to me not only what he was losing but inevitably the reflection in my having been left for him of everything he now had. We were merely different chapters on the same subject. I was his closest secret, as he was mine. Empathy is the source of moral behavior, isn't it? And truthfully I knew, in a kind of bizarre chiasmus, that if she didn't care about him she could never really care about me.

There was never pleasure without penalty. I often thought of him as the adulterer. I followed the principle of transitivity, which had become the code of my life with her, and figured that although he'd once had Farol's affections he had no more claim to her than her first husband had when she left him for another, the logic as algebra by which passion reasons. But passion doesn't reason. It rationalizes. And what gave me pause was that each of those men had in good faith loved her, courted her, married her, and in promising all finally gave it, which left only one variable in the equation: Farol. No, I wasn't jealous. I was only doubtful, and afraid.

But Farol could explain. She'd been afraid herself, she said, and doubtful as well. She told me that over the past few years when she'd had nothing to do she only pretended to be busy, never coming by in order to avoid being *rejected* by me. She spoke of those people at "group" who had both advised her to return to her husband and those who had warned her not to. It had all confused her. And she added, significantly, she didn't want to become ill again. I understood that. "I felt guilty and responsible," she said—I heard in her speech the echo of her current reading, books with words in the title like *me, you, how, self, growth,* and *healing*—"but in going back, believe me, I simply wanted John to find out for himself what I already knew, that while both of us might care for each other, nothing in our marriage can possibly be saved." She took my hand. "I at least owe him a period for this recognition. Don't you agree?" I did. I thought of Marina and of what all along I'd expected from her in the same way, and I did agree.

Farol had loved other men, and she'd left them. I knew that. But I felt I was the exception. Was it therefore wrong of me to worry that the only thing an exception can possibly prove is that the rule is faulty?

9

School ended. I packed, left for Cape Cod in early June, and was soon busy. It all had the effect of a rapid interval. There was such a sustained happiness, a closeness we felt, that the days we were apart never seemed to count. The air lost its bite and dawdled warmer and warmer over grass and meadow and sea. Farol lost weight. Carefree bangs fringed her forehead, and a boyish haircut emphasized the childlike and rather poetic quality of her narrow, hollow-cheeked face.

I had the lawns cut, flowers in vases, and something by way of a surprise whenever she came down. I'd become by now a confirmed bread-maker, making brioches, crumpets, potato doughnuts, and drop scones along with various loaves, and even something of a cook. "Roast duck," I'd announce, serving up my new specialty. "America's unique contribution to gastronomy! The greatest delicacy, according to Josef, the famed chief of the Café Marivaux in Paris, known to the inhabited world!" Farol was grateful, though sometimes made wistful, and always said she wished she could cook for me.

My aim was to make her happy and include her in everything I did. Picnics. Barbecues. I looked for antiques for her and bought her clothes, books, and interesting old eggbeaters for her collection whenever I saw them. She went barefoot all the time and had a perpetual sunburn across her eyes. We played tennis. When Tarquin and his two boys came visiting for a month, we did things together. At times things became strained. As I say, Farol wasn't at ease with children, and the boys found her weird and aloof and indifferent to them. I heard them several times refer to her in private as "Disturbo" and bawled them out for it. "She calls whimbrels terns and never even says hello," they complained. "And why does she boast?" I denied that she did. "What is occlusion then? She said she had perfect occlusion. But she hasn't. And her teeth aren't even straight. She's a wonk." I told them not to be rude.

We swam. We went scow-banging along the beach and worked in the yard. We played golf, and tennis, and several times went to a batting cage and hit baseballs. Once or twice we dug mussels in the mudbanks in West Dennis. The marshes and fields were a glory of blooming locusts and wildflowers, the ponds alive with arrowhead and golden club and floating heart. Lone herons fed in the marshes. I finally got a telephone so she could call me. There were strange complications, the strangest of which was not so much the two lives she was living as our not mentioning it. But I began to get an interesting picture of her attitude toward her husband, who was being at once protected from the truth and at the same time being denied it.

I wrote her virtually every day. I sent her prints, packages, and several postcards of sea otters, her aquatic soul correspondent. And I drove up to St. Ives whenever I wasn't having trouble with my car. One morning we went to an auction. I bought a cuckoo clock and a white lollipop scale for her—a six-foot-high antique—which she loved. "What a wonderful thing!" cried Farol, kissing me. "Thanks, Bunky!" She reciprocated by driving me over to their house—forbidden ground—stepping into her husband's garden, and giving me a paper bag full of vegetables. Most of the time that summer, especially as her work hours were cut back, she'd drive down to see me in Sandwich, stay as long as possible, and then hare it home at the end of each visit.

But what, I wondered, was she expecting from her husband all this time? I feared the progressive and continuous claim on her she was

slowly being forced to return. "You can't change a personality, Farol,"
I told her. And her reply was, "I know, I know, but I owe him just a
bit more time."

There was also duplicity. I was put in the dubious position of having to admire her for what she took from me to give to him. And while
in a strange way it became her, this temporizing care for her husband,
it turned my own logic against me at the same time, for whenever I
thought of what in having he deserved I could only conclude that what
in not having I didn't. I became the adulterer in this light, I'm afraid,
and in consequence began to pity myself as once I did him. And it
wasn't any different with Farol. The remnants of that thwarted desire
to please I'd so often seen at parties seemed to linger on in the bright
wired smile with which on occasion she regarded me and by which she
seemed to confess in all she had to hide the falsity I feared. But that
particular pretense, which most of the time she carried off famously,
once or twice became even too much for her.

We were sitting one July afternoon in a restaurant named the
Sandy Neck Lounge when I noticed Farol go suddenly and eerily silent.
Although at first I couldn't say why, I soon realized it was a song playing on the jukebox called "Desperado"—I'd heard it before—that gave
her that faraway and troubled look.

> *Deeeeesperado,*
> *Why don't you come to your senses?*
> *Why don't you come down from your fences?*
> *Open the gate.*
> *It may be raining,*
> *But there's a rainbow above you,*
> *Better let somebody love you*
> *Before it's too late.*

And then I remembered it was the same song, making her cry, that
she'd been listening to on the radio the first day she'd moved into her
apartment. I said nothing, but listening carefully to the words suddenly
realized where I'd heard them—she was constantly quoting those lyrics
herself! And finally it dawned on me that they reminded her of her
failure. And of her infidelity. And above all of her husband, whom I
could no longer avoid mentioning.

"Sometimes," I confessed, "I feel inadequate compared to him."

This found a mysterious smile in her. It was conscious, that smile,
confirming something in a moment of private amusement like a seal

intentionally applied to make the commonest thought appear absolutely inscrutable.

"It's funny," she said. "He said the same thing about you."

"You've told him about me?"

She nodded.

I wanted to say *that's why you feel closer to him*. But this time she surprised me.

"You're the one I love," she said. "Everything feels right with you. You shouldn't worry. It may seem strange to you, but I think of you"—her jaw seemed set in a grudge against him—"I think of you as my husband."

"Have you told him—everything?"

"Everything?"

"What I mean to you." I looked into her eyes. "What we are."

"What we are"—she shrugged—"what we were."

"What we were," I said, "isn't the same as what we are."

She said she intended to tell him.

"I have to," she said. "I will."

Summer was upon us. I couldn't go back to the mind of winter, so refused to press her. Conversion is a process of unification. Those who experience it have often been suffering from a divided personality that has allowed them no peace. I subordinated everything to reconcile all contradiction to that peace, and so did Farol.

Or so I thought, for something now came up that actually made me wonder. I knew she was not only restless but still felt personally unfulfilled. I suppose I'd known it all spring. It wasn't only her husband. That false start had been accompanied by several others. She'd briefly taken up photography, then dropped it. She had looked into modeling but gave that up after a week, claiming she hadn't the right clothes to wear. (Harvey Frakes later told me she wasn't young enough.) For some reason she lost interest in the exercise club she'd joined and quit. And although she initially seemed excited by the job she took at the hospital—running out to buy nurse's uniforms, white shoes, and even looking for a stethoscope!—even that finally lost its appeal.

I remember at one point her rushing about to find a Grandma Calico kit to make a doorstop doll. Jaunts for paper patterns. Strips of ruffle trim. Candlewicking designs. She showed frustrations during this time, I tell you, that evade conveyance. She wanted to be remembered for something she'd accomplished, for to be forgotten was only to be remembered for everything trivial and worthless. To me her about-face maneuvers spoke volumes, and I have to confess I've since come to wonder if people who think they see the whole meaning of something, or even come under the heading of those who try to, actually have any conception of it at all. There was a faculty missing in Farol, something that simultaneously told me in my preferring her over Marina was also missing in me. I recalled the octagonal wall at the Prado hung with pictures of Velasquez where, at the sketches of the Villa Medici Gardens, was written: "After hot, bleak Spain he loved Italy as one who has known passion loves a passionless girl."

There was something pathetic in all of it. Deprivation makes people selfish, and she seemed to try what she couldn't do in the same way she wanted what she couldn't have. I thought they were the operations of a mind completely shut on reality, 180-degree course changes (they'd become something like her insignia now) made in compensation for the reckless compulsion she had of beginning everything with no real idea, ever, of seeing it through, with yet a deep and abiding need for success of some kind, one thing to be proud of—something, I shouldn't forget to add, other than her car. That she loved. It was the one thing she'd bought and was paying for herself. Anyone merely tapping her car, for example, while opening his in a parking lot, infuriated her beyond reason, and I mention this only because it was about this time that she began badgering me again to buy another. Couldn't I afford it? Wasn't mine useless? Didn't I care?

I was thinking of buying one, but that wasn't the problem. I had come to know Farol by now. Myth, after all, is what we believe naturally; history is what we must painfully learn and struggle to remember. And the competitive edge to her needling spoke entirely to something else.

It was this wood-carving business and—was she aware of it?—the essential dissatisfaction in having taken the course up of finding herself deficient. She viewed art as a kind of waiting, properly, if not always, to be understood in her case as procrastination. And the pattern never varied. I remember all the grizzling she'd gone through before I left for the summer. At first she said she had no tools (I wanted to tell her Goya painted with a spoon) or working space (and that Bonnard owned little more than a tiny bamboo table on which he kept his brushes), but I said nothing and over the months bought her chisels, wooden planes, C clamps, spokeshaves, squares, draw knives, and no end of carving tools, gravures, and gouges.

Most of all I tried to help her with the best advice of all: don't try to be new. I told her it was more pertinent to be better than to be different. "Didn't they tell you this in high jumping?" I asked. "Jump at the height—not with the technique."

But it wasn't the equipment.

The trouble was with her. Driven out of the house by the miserable situation there, she constantly sought relief—purposeful activity—in a continuing attempt elsewhere to find something of self-worth. Somewhere in the same void where free time terrified her, she also demanded she create, to balance all she found she had destroyed. I think that's what attracted her to art. It remained somehow an ideal and an incomparable constant for her that could recoup the losses of the world. The problem was, she had no gifts for it. But what was typical of Farol was that in trying to compensate for her inabilities she devoted her most intense efforts to the very things she was least fitted for attaining.

She suffered watching others succeed at the kind of work which she could pursue only with lavish subvention. And that was the hobble. For her, art wasn't form. It was a disguise. She didn't want to make, she strove to compete, and the competition that made her envious became the envy that made her fail. It was the very reason nothing of the many things she tried could ever please her. We were discussing painting once, I recall, one of the few times we ever did, and she pointed out, almost accusingly, that I loved to paint. I told her she thought I loved to only because I could and that people are always patient with what they're good at. I was talking about painting, I remember, but thinking of her penchant for divorce. "Art! Art!" she angrily exclaimed. "Everybody's an expert on it but me, right? But what is art? Tell me! What is it anyway?"

It was ironic. Her life more than anyone else's should have told her.

"Can you imagine an imaginary menagerie manager imagining managing an imaginary menagerie?"

She looked at me.

"That," I said.

Farol's woodworking project, in any case, had been to design and carve a kitchen tool. She had worked on it for months, but when the day finally came for me to see it—I remember her telling me at the time she could do so many things it was hard to concentrate on one!—I seriously began to wonder, holding it up, whether she had done it wearing mittens. It looked like a Fudgesicle. The mallet bought to chisel the thing was actually a better work of art! My silence made her defensive—

she looked at me doubtfully—I mentioned something about wood being a bitch to work with. I hadn't the slightest idea what to say, so I said nothing. It was wrong of me, and thoughtless, but if I had spoken the truth I'd have ended up telling her to drop what she was doing, and was that fair?

She became superpolite that night at dinner, meaning she was furious. What struck me so forcefully was that she was not blaming me, that she was *deliberately* not blaming me. She was suppressing anger at me and everything about me so badly it was just about killing her.

But I realized that the sense of discontentment she evinced during that whole period embraced every feature of her life. It was a rebellion fueled by all the pressures, frustrations, and disappointments that repeatedly drove her to tasks for which she hadn't the slightest talent. Above all, it was incited by the disgust she felt reviewing her once hopeful life. The problem was that as the years wore on, instead of the goal becoming clearer, it was becoming even more difficult to perceive. And Farol began to suffer from the thought that she wasn't going anywhere, while at the time having to declare she was. The rancor of someone ambitious feeling her powers dwindle is savage enough, but what of having to watch others rise when you yourself have done nothing?

The self-hate of a narcissist is among the deadliest of all emotions. It is a sadism turned against the self, I thought, which carried far enough, I thought, could lead to—paralysis.

With that thought in my head, and looking at that warped tool, I suddenly had an idea of what to do to try to help her. No, not advise. Advice she hated and I'd done enough of that. And theory? No, Farol wanted cash returns immediately. Well, someone was being paid—*had been paid for six or seven years!*—to help her. The idea, so completely wonderful to me, was just sitting there resting on its oars. The strength that suffering confers on a person, I realized, is contingent on her learning the truth about herself.

And that very night, after a series of repeated and frustrating calls to his answering service, I finally spoke to her therapist, Dr. Varion. He said he was busy, which was unfortunate. For him, I mean. I told him I was coming.

I wanted to talk.

10

Farol and I spent the weekend together. I drove up to St. Ives and because her husband, along with his brother, who was visiting him at the time, had gone on a camping trip and left her alone, she slept over at my house. There was more than a hint in his refusal now to have her with him that reconciliation was quite unlikely. The days became very warm. We took a few drives into the countryside. Again we looked at cars. And again it was a pointless activity.

I remember her talk, the usual stuff about cars, of course, but with an increasing reference now to subjects that came under the heading of broken things, like maimed lives, the gallery people who were completely ignorant of themselves, Scrulock's rudeness, and as always her own parents and their insufficiencies. She seemed to be crumping out again and spoke with slack automism in light of getting a divorce of going on unemployment compensation.

Let me add, I myself felt I should be earning more money now, for both of us, and mentioned I'd made an application for work as a commercial artist for the Boston *Globe*. We discussed our future, meeting the subject head-on with neither of us unaware of the pass to which we'd once been brought by near failure and by it realized no less an unexpected wish that in the autumn we might at last be together. I paused a moment, smiled, then told Farol I was going to see Varion.

But she made no objections, indeed she thought it might help. It was the very thing I had banked on. It was not only a shadow move around her husband, she had in her dependency a need to have two minds meet over her, and there was a touch of secrecy to it all. Farol had an unexpected and infallible instinct for intrigue, often revealing the curiosity of a child about forbidden subjects along with a tireless and detached interest in wanting to know what people made of her. It might perhaps be thought strange she didn't get along with children only until one discovered she was a woman, as too often I feared I was a man, with the very same needs.

There was in her importunate conceit a child's insecurity—something I'm sure I also needed to observe to feel above it myself. At Farol's age it seemed a cruel penance, no more pitifully confessed, I thought, and no more resonantly, than in those automobile showrooms (how aptly named!) where she walked around asking in the shrill voice the same shrill questions she had asked before. Her confidence, growing as she did so, seemed to take complete hold of her. But it wasn't confidence. It was pretense, well-meaning no doubt, the desire to show in all that biscuit-crisp efficiency what she could offer as a wife and helpmate, but those weren't questions, they were answers, one desperate response, in fact, charged with a crying need for recognition, to all she'd failed at, the divorces, her missed education, the lack of foreign travel, her menial jobs, and all those pathetic attempts at sculpting and drawing and wood carving thrown in on top of her ignorant sisters and disapproving parents and threadbare braggart of a brother. That was the tragedy, and it was there she needed the help.

I remember just turning to speak of it as in the putty-colored twilight we drove back to St. Ives when I noticed she was smiling, somewhat cryptically I thought. I asked her why.

Farol gestured forward with her head.

We were riding behind what to me looked like an old fruit truck on the back of which was written the name *Dzundza*. I looked at her.

"That was my husband's last name."

"Your—"

"Not John." She paused. "You know."

"Your first husband?"

She nodded. "Lloyd."

I went silent, subdued, momentarily closing my eyes. Quickly passing the truck, I pronounced the name to myself: it sounded like an anagram or the quack of a loud sneeze. And it reminded me her husbands were like face tissues, pull one and another came up. Pick a name, I thought, any name. Come seven, come eleven.

She looked at me with a secret smile and said, "Don't fall asleep."

11

No fear, I was awake.

I was dressed, out of the house, and on my way to Boston before dawn. I entered the high-rise building on Stanford Street and following directions went upstairs to Dr. Varion's office, which was decorated with ferns like a funeral parlor. I waited an hour (from the window, sadly, I could see the Bay Tower) and then finally he appeared. He was a man of unforgiving bell-shaped fat with big pegs for fingers and a nose like an oncological knob. He had big raw ears. Out of shape and perspiring, he walked with a waddle exposing a huge potbelly—he weighed over 250 pounds—and black pointed shoes. I shook his damp hand.

"Well, well," he wheezed, dropping into his chair. "The painter."

There was a look of sleepy cunning about him. He had the offhand manner of the busy man, distant in the way of fine thought, as he surveyed me with mock appraisal and asked me if I had insurance.

I said I didn't know. "But what about Farol?" I asked. "We have to help her."

Dr. Varion chuckled. He wagged his head and held up an ugly hairy hand. "Wait, wait, wait," he said, "not so fast. What about you? What's your psychohistory? Why are you involved with her?" I was supposed to call him Dr. Varion, but, typical of doctors, he used my first name. You know, roll over and play dead, all that. His angry eyes, intensified by strong spectacles, were black and protruding. He had a voice colder than a dead man's nose and gummy viscid lips that plapped at each other between pronouncements.

"I love her," I said. I told him right off and unequivocally—circumventing, of course, the fundamental rule of analysis—that I wanted to marry her. He said he wondered about that. "Why have you waited so long? Why haven't you simply walked into her house," he asked, "and carried her off? Why have you procrastinated?" He talked loudly and was suspicious when he was not talking. He spoke of reverse contrapuntalism (wasn't that puntalism?) and of various preconditions of mine (wasn't precondition redundant?) and a lot of psychobabble, but the questions he was asking, which were cruelly direct, I suddenly realized I couldn't answer.

I tried to explain my feelings but couldn't even convince myself. I also saw he wished to avoid that notorious innovation, the short session, choosing to avoid destroying by means of his profession the very reason for its existence. But I'd been there before, having met his ghoulish double and venal counterpart years ago in another hell. When I finished talking he bent a paper clip, stared out a window, and said condescendingly, "I think you could use some help as well."

I laughed at him. I stood up and paused and thought to leave. Clearing his throat, Dr. Varion swung off his glasses—candor—and pointed out with weary authority that Farol's parents were the basic source of her trouble. (The one-punch diagnosis seemed to belie the complexities he wished to emphasize with me.) I agreed, but that seemed obvious, and, sitting down, I pointed out for him that to me analysis had as its major task the repairing of a relationship that people have, a living relationship, not one with the dead, which was effectively what the Pratts were to their daughter, what in fact her husband was to her.

"Farol is engulfed," I said. "Don't you see, she is struggling against a personality—*not hers*—she nevertheless insists she retain?"

I thought of all her names: *Farol Ann Sprat Dzundza Colorado*. It was devastating. She was completely obscured by the very names she thought differentiated her. Stamp a name on something, it takes on an identity but at the same time loses one—and is altered. She was adulterated by identification. It was a compound label of nomination and renomination joining lethal overabundance to radical insufficiency all at once. It worked only to efface her in increasing diffusion and disintegration. Identification became annihilation. The mixture of names formulated no one. She was smothered in description, and rendered meaningless.

"She won't submit to herself," I added. "It's made her distrustful, particularly to those closest to her. Doesn't she tend to see as rivals those whom she has to reject before they learn what she knows of herself? Isn't that one of her games? Look, you've talked to her husband. She says he hates sex. Do you believe that? You don't believe that, do you? He doesn't hate sex. He's afraid. He's come to fear sex with her," I said. "He knows she's unfaithful and—dangerous."

Dr. Varion stroked his huge nose.

"Dangerous?"

"She gets rid of men. She feels no one can love her for what she herself can't *become*. And yet consistently all she isn't becomes everything she tries to be. She repudiates what she is while insisting she be recognized—talk about reverse contrapuntalism!—but is actually jealous of the ideal by which she nevertheless strives to shape her own life!"

"Farol and her husband have been seeing me now for several years, and—"

"And have you helped her? I think she actually *comes* here to fail!" He looked about indignantly this way and that. "The fact is, you—"

"I think she trusts me. She says she does. I've become like her father."

"That's my point."

"What?"

"You cooperate in her failure."

"How?"

"By failing to see she cooperates with you! She's the perfect patient," I said, "because she's not a *committed* one. She expands like an ideal gas to fill any available space—it can be compressed into a very small area, but the pressure increases! Can't you see that? She wants everything because at bottom she feels she's nothing. Everything tempts nothing!" It was frustrating being watched instead of listened to. But I could read his doubt—hadn't she waited, I delayed? She planned, I postured? She adored me, I tolerated her? And I began to wonder what she had told him. "Haven't you ever wondered why she never stays with anything or anyone for any length of time?"

Waving his hand, he conceded she was immature. I said she was vain. He said she was weak. "You're right, but she's vain *because* she's weak."

"Listen to me," said he from the lofty pedestal of long experience, "she's looking for something. For the last ten years she's been trying to decide—"

"No, she's *afraid* to decide," I said. "She's afraid to decide what she wants to happen. She tries to make happen what she fears to decide in the hopes of finding what she refuses to seek." I seized the desk. "And why doesn't she find it? I'll tell you why. She works at relationships only to prove them failures in the same way she takes up crafts to prove she can't do them. Resistance is the opposite of escape. She fears constancy can only come to prove her false."

He leaned on his hand and puffed air.

"You don't agree."

"My business is reality," Varion told me. "I have no time for paradox and no time for euphemism and no time for hurt feelings."

"But you're right! The proof she's looking for something is she walks out on everything. Jobs, cities, husbands. She leaves them flat," I said. "She decamps to avoid one mistake only to compound it elsewhere by making another. Don't listen to me, look at her life. She's her most arrogant when she's most abject. It's the defeated alone who become vain. She's trying to become someone she isn't."

Dr. Varion's impatience approached contempt. He folded his hands. "You know this."

"She aspires to what she can't do. She won't accept herself. That's her problem."

"And what's yours?"

"Seeing it and being unable to help." I hated this man. "That's why I'm here—I think."

"You think?"

"How long has she been coming here, six years? Six *years*," I said. "And all this time you've been encouraging her to artificial and self-conscious urges for which she has no qualifications."

He looked disgusted. He's going to shout loudly, I thought.

"Urges?"

"Creative urges. She assumes them like names. Dzundza. Colorado," I said. "Art is only another."

Dr. Varion leaned forward and his jowls shook. He asked blackly, "How have *I* encouraged her?"

"By not discouraging her," I said.

His lips pursed like a blowfish.

"She's no more an artist than you," I said. "Her dreams are her temptations. She competes to disadvantage, throws up her hands, and then despises herself for it. She tries to live through others, marrying to emulate what she hates to admire, and only comes to despise herself the more. There are too many contests and not enough prizes," I said. "I think her negative feelings have been too long held in check for fear of losing her father's affection."

"It's possible," said Varion.

"But he has no affection. Her rage festers. And other men are made responsible." I paused. "It has to do with her father, of course, her need to excel, but she has to learn to face the world with these deterrent objects there. They won't change. But she can. You have to tell her that."

He heard, he didn't hear, it didn't seem to matter, it did. We talked on pointlessly for a while, and I could see he was bored or hungry or just wanted some peace and quiet. He looked at his watch and asking for my phone number scribbled it on a pad, holding the pen halfway up the handle with a doctor's—with an illiterate's—indifference.

"Will you tell her that?"

"Yes, yes, yes," he said. "Now I'm afraid your time's up. As to payment—"

"She can't compete. The point is, she shouldn't try. She seems to know it herself. It's as if some phantom double, one half of her—some antiself—won't let her get away with it. She checks herself." I thought a moment. "Don't you make something of that?" My mind felt suddenly on fire. "Her failures that way are only a sign of a deeper disease." I was looking, trying to see something still unclear. "We cling to our symptoms, don't we?"

I leaned forward.

"We punish ourselves, don't you think? Isn't that her illness?"

I paused.

"It is, isn't it?" I looked at him.

Varion closed his eyes.

I asked, "Does she have MS?"

He shook his head and, shrugging, made the sound of a pip.

"When did she get it?" I asked. "How? Tell me! *Tell me!*"

"I don't know," he said defensively. The words, his lips, sounded gluey. "Do you?"

I sat back wearily.

"No, I don't," I sighed. "I only know that she manages successfully to prevent everything she unsuccessfully tries to propagate. Maybe to ease the pain of separation. Separation is all she knows."

Dr. Varion stood up and told me other patients were waiting. "But let me get this," he said. "As it stands, you feel Farol's incompatible with the things she wishes for, is that right?"

"Yes."

At this he brightened, a gloating smile spreading across his face, and leaning forward he patted five little fingertips against five others in a prissily judicial manner and asked, "Then where does that leave you?"

"She loves me," I said. I felt a sudden chill, a hollowness within me. "She believes I love her. She told me she loved me."

I couldn't really believe Farol's behavior had anything of the abnormal or cruelly unbalanced. To me it seemed at worst a reckless extravagance, a generous if confused expenditure in the direction of self-identity that set the possible above the probable. As I got it, she thought one's generosity entitled her to do as she wished and in their gratitude her friends would make allowances. I felt she could be helped. She'd come around. Wouldn't she?

Dr. Varion whooshed air and with a sense of exasperated anticlimax summoned me to within an inch of confidential distance. "There's a female patient of mine currently living with a man she says she loves, all right?" He plapped his lips and hunkered forward. "But she told me this week she's leaving him for someone else, someone who takes her out, I don't know, gives her money."

"And you approve?"

"We don't assign faults here." He walked to the door and opened it. "People are different. You paint, I'm a doctor. I'm Jewish, you're not. Who knows why? This woman has to live," he said. "She wants to save herself." I saw it coming. "She has to—"

"Survive," I said.

He smiled at me. I smiled back at him. He had a dreadful smile. He found me insolent. I found him impatient and fractious and dull. I found him peremptory and smug. I found him silly and temporizing and fat.

And I never went back there again.

12

As the summer went by all seemed warm, timeless, and peaceful. We were happy to stay as we were, afloat on the tideless, hypnotic day-to-day. It was a sort of growing regard, a happiness of which it seemed that the balance became every day clearer. There was an element of guessing, but the plan of love had gone on unfolding itself. The testing time, ever to be expected, had never come. There showed no sign of its coming, our avowals held, and the unscrutinizing hope of that love continually banished anything foreign to it.

Our best avowals became familiar. And everywhere, at every opportunity, at my house, in cars, twice in an empty dorm at St. Ives, at the drive-in theater, and several times in the sunlit, sense-intoxicating surf of the sea, we made love. My love filled me with desire. I felt unpardonably happy. I even bought a new car.

One hot day we went swimming at the Head of the Meadow beach in Truro. I took my camera and got some beautiful pictures of Farol. It was the loveliest of memories, no talk of therapy or threnody or theory. The afternoon was waning, I remember, the light growing deeper in the western sky. We were returning on the mid-Cape highway, and Farol was just sliding down in the car, slipping off her bathing suit to change. She went to put on her shirt and was reaching for her panties when I quickly stopped her hand. And as I drove I began lightly touching her between her legs. She responded and lay back, her eyes half lidded with pleasure, almost hypnotized in fantasy, moving slowly up and down as I began desperately looking for a cutoff or a wocky little islet with impending dunes, a sandy redoubt, some isolated place. But in our urgency there was no getting farther than Eastham. She rolled up, biting my neck. I have a vivid memory of kissing her salty body and tasting her damp hair. I swung off the road by the Eagle Wing Motel—she was whispering *hurry*—and in a wooded glade there near a path called Kittiwake Lane we forgot the motel and devoured each other on the spot like spring cats. I remember her head snapping sharply sideways as she climaxed, her neck drenched with perspiration, and her saying, "That was the most beautiful moment of my life."

And I recall driving home closer to her than I'd ever felt, watching the sun sear the horizon and dip swiftly into the sea detonating the sky in a series of gold, pink, and vermilion explosions.

There was a definition growing certain, and a wait within that certainty we took in stride. Farol was the first thing I thought of in the morning and the last thing I thought of at night. "I love your face." I heard her words all summer. "You're a wonderful lover." "You make it impossible not to move." "Make me suck you." "I love your mouth on my breasts." "You make me feel like myself." "You're my best friend." "I want to be with you the rest of my life."

Along about mid or late August she seemed more preoccupied than usual. I confess there were times when still she became melancholy—I rarely knew why—and for that a bit wearying in long stretches. But sharing demands a touch of pain in its joy, there is no music without frets, and I wanted to show her the unconditional love I felt. She'd been a dream. Now she was real. Real is not always easy. I knew she hated the job at the hospital. It was a real headache now, she said, and she couldn't do half the things asked of her there. I could feel her panic.

"Am I supposed to be able to draw blood, run machines, calibrate gases?" But she owed money. And of course she felt the pressure while living at home but loving me of being continually split into two radically different personalities.

But there were frustrations strictly of her own making. I recall one afternoon in particular. My stepbrother owned a rowboat, which we took out. We took along his boys. I began rowing. Farol naturally insisted on having a go. Boats. One of her things. Six-liter lungs. She manfully grabbed the oars, I remember, then abruptly sent us in circles, dubbing the water so badly with such a poor scat and slapback, trashcanlid-banging series of mismaneuvers—talk about catching crabs!—I couldn't believe it. My nephews exchanged glances. If previously they'd found her sullen, it became confirmed by her silence the rest of the day. Farol never did go bicycling across the United States.

Instead, she took a long sullen walk by herself halfway to the end of Sandy Neck.

I caught up with her miles down the beach sitting lugubriously on a boulder. I said hello. She felt hurt and embarrassed and said everything was a mess. Wet hair always made her look homely. There was anger in her sunburn. I looked at that small head, those sad weak ankles, those heavy thighs sloping to shins thin as a pen-and-pencil set, and thought: *poor girl*. I sat down and explained to her that she need only be herself—she didn't have to *try* so hard—adding that it was what I'd told Dr. Varion. And then Farol began to cry. I told her he was a fool. No, she said, it had nothing to do with him. Something else was wrong. I told her the boys often laughed at me. No, it wasn't that either. I asked, "What is it?"

I waited there in silence.

Terns were dropping like stones for fish. I watched the salt waves curling in and crashing onto the beach. What was it about them, the movement, that reminded me of Farol? Something. I couldn't say what. "Please?" Then going suddenly tight in the jaws, Farol said, "I've had a terrible fight with John." But was that new? I asked. "This was worse," she said. Neither was that.

Like characters in an allegory, she and her husband had long ago become for me hypostatized ideas: Farol, the endlessly distraught prisoner; her husband, the grim intolerant personification of power who wouldn't let her go. He was a misanthrope, a nervous and unimaginative man, and although a person to my mind profoundly averse to marriage, the hard fact remained he wanted her to live with him, right?

Wrong.

"I have to tell you something." Farol looked at me anxiously. It was as if she were seeking one phrase out of several slaughtered possibilities. "John has asked me to leave." I couldn't believe it. Irony had come full circle. He couldn't stand it any longer. Suddenly he wanted *her* out! Now I understood what she'd been thinking of all this time. I could see she was ashamed. Another divorce! Repeated failure! Cut off! Tearfully she looked out to sea and keep repeating she needed time to think. She apologized. There were natural regrets, even in this, she said, did I realize that? I daresay I did. I recalled her casual advice for Marina but tried not to think about it. She said it was like a punch in the stomach. She was confused. But was she afraid? I'd stand by her. I felt a sudden rush of joy. I loved her! I told her she could live with me! I wanted her children! But her face was eventless. She took my hand and with a wan smile said, "Oh, you've seen me with children."

"I mean *our* children! They'll be cute, round and fat as pinwheels!"

"Cute," she repeated.

It was one of her phrases, of course. I found it sinister, her not forgetting them.

"I'm sorry." She lowered her head. "I sometimes just feel I can't do anything deep."

But I was thinking: *children*. She had curiously little interest in them. They weren't notable presences for her. She didn't seem to have any direct human rapport with them. She didn't hate them. She was indifferent to them. She merely stared at them as though they were strange creatures from another planet, not humans at all. My nephews disliked her, my students were doubtful. She herself reflected the child's own incapacities for the conceptual—she couldn't *say* things to them! It was interesting. The child often can't convey in words the procedures it carries out in acts. I always thought that Farol embodied in a way the very child she didn't have. The perverse thing, however, was that she retained the child's most petulant characteristics, not its most engaging. She wanted total freedom and no responsibility. I thought of her desperate need for attention whenever she'd made something; she behaved in fact like a ten-year-old. But it was more than that. A woman whose intuition is geared toward men is seldom any good with children. The flirt is always the bogey of the mother.

Farol was just on the cusp of childbearing. But nothing had come of it. A woman who is childless suffers a strange inferiority. The primal question—whether she will or won't, can or can't, does or doesn't bear a child—is the central crisis of a woman's life, for it reaches to the core of what almost by definition alone makes her womanly. Sex and marriage don't. Independence certainly doesn't. Neither do affairs or careers. The lost experience lingers. And it often finds her hopelessly neurotic. You can't despise children. It is impossible, for one thing, to convince anyone you don't want them—no one will believe you—and the feeble attempt at affecting to do so makes the most robust efforts only the more pathetic, for it sounds like sour grapes. And then it is socially unacceptable.

Childless women are seen as pariahs, outcasts of a kind with too much missing to shrug away. They have been excluded from the mystery. They are taken as incompetent. They know nothing of bassinets or Carter's snap pajamas or an infant's milky breath. Babies remain forever strangers to them.

But the problem goes much deeper. A woman without a child never really knows whether she can have one or not. She remains unproven, inadequate, and secretly sees herself as defective. A hollowness has not been filled. The curious thing is that she becomes less envious of her childbearing sisters than actually doubtful of herself. She is unperformed: over her potential maternity stands a question mark the shape of her uterus. She has missed something she herself finds unforgivable, which is perhaps why women without children are among the most ferocious hypochondriacs. It is the formal equivalent in women of being impotent. It calibrates a kind of selfishness where, empty and recessive, she is either left alone to sit on a paradox and brood or to try to find solace elsewhere, which explains to some degree why women without children often see in the childless man a natural ally and confidant and are always among his best friends.

Strictly speaking, all men are childless. But he is born without the gift. She forgoes it.

Farol's fears fit the form. I think the whole generative concept repelled her. She transmitted the idea that in some sort of fruitless transferral children but perpetuated in being what she herself in becoming never had. They incorporated a kind of negativity for her. In a way, procreation was taboo. It was also typical of Farol's conceit: hugely self-deceiving, she'd chosen not to do something she wasn't sure she could do anyway. I thought of her father. It was as though his power, anger, and indifference had somehow reached into the latent future to eradicate the life she herself refused, in not becoming a mother, to engender. I suddenly realized she was never a mother because she was always a daughter. Her father canceled his grandchildren in refusing her the childhood dreams she needed to have come true to grow. It was something she'd have seen herself had she taken the time to look. A childless woman, in her predicament, has all the time in the world to study her limitations.

But there was more. Shouldn't we at least admit, on the principle that the greater includes the less, that the personality of which the disease is the expression is also to some degree inherited? I thought of her father and the great moist weight of that forbidding man. His independence of her and hers from him was as a kind of reverse adultery, almost unthinkable, although it was a fact. It called back to her like an echo. And yet Farol couldn't bear to reflect on the very rejections to which she nevertheless always reverted to rectify the wrong she was.

I was reminded of her constant bladder infections. To prevent infection, urologists tell little girls to wipe themselves from front to back. But Farol was always wiping herself from back to front! The past was her infection! The past! And the past she wouldn't relinquish!

I helped Farol up and we began walking back along the beach. I stopped, held her face, and using her own words told her I loved her. I assured her she was my best friend. I said I didn't want to learn to live without her again. I promised everything would be all right. But would she only believe in the future we could have? She hugged me and said yes, yes, yes.

We wandered up along the dunes and walked through the springy clumps of shadbush and dusty miller and poverty grass. Out on the marsh a black skimmer was hanging around and several gulls had taken up residence overhead. I picked a salt-spray rose for her. She touched my cheek lovingly and brightened. She turned and nimbly turned up a slope and stood there overlooking the ocean on those high palisades where it seemed one could almost jump off into the world. "Look," I said, pointing to a spot on the far horizon, "the ship." "The thip!" she lisped, laughing and taking me around the waist.

Together, we sniffed the clean salt air and cooled our eyes with the purple sea, a tint of mallow touched with French blue as beautiful as the wide sky above with its one stroke of a mare's-tail cloud. I loved her as she stood there, her hair blowing gorgeously in the wind. I leaned past her to point out one of those dark green areas of woods and landscape near Sandy Neck that looked exactly like a Cézanne. But she was looking at me, and I took her in my arms and kissed her.

I couldn't stop kissing her. She seemed to flood my heart with warmth. And then what happened was like a dream. We slid down without a word to the shoulder of a ridge through the cascading banks to an intimate space, found a whimsical pause in a haphazard gesture of the dunes—I remember fumbling with her bathing suit in a sort of voluptuous rage as she licked the sea salt from my body—and we made love in the hot white sand. I have a distinct memory of looking back as we walked away. I saw something in the concave figuration of sand. It was her forgotten rose lying there.

When she left for home after that final weekend I felt as if she'd taken all the warmth of those long lovely months and placed it in my heart forever. It was a feeling of longing that seemed to go on renewing itself within me in an infinite loop. And I remember the very last thing I did when summer ended was to mail her a penny postcard of the Cape Cod dunes, with no message written on it, only the mark of an X on one special dune.

13

I returned to St. Ives in September. There was nothing else for me there, except Farol, but the chance to be with her again made the meagreness acceptable. She was my only companion. When not teaching I tried to be with her whenever I could. The occasionally rueful mood that took something from our familiarity during this period I traced to her wretched situation at home with her husband. There wasn't even megaphone diplomacy between them anymore. They merely lived cold and guarded, avoiding each other all the time, and I became nearly ill myself thinking of her locked in the small madhouse, her feet drawn up, her eyes staring over her knuckles in misery.

I didn't see much of Farol that month, wasting a lot of time negotiating that job with the Boston *Globe* only to find the job fall through. I felt that not getting it, facing the changes we were, took something definite from me, even diminished me in Farol's eyes. I remember finding in her surprise when I broke the news a marked discouragement. But mine exceeded hers. Money with her always seemed to clear the way, I couldn't bear to think for deeper sympathy, but for the larger opportunities we'd been so long trying to realize.

And so to supplement my small income I contracted to do a mural (for $1,750) in the St. Ives dining hall: *Paul Revere Sheathing "Old Ironsides,"* a project undertaken in the midst of more scaffolding and noise than I had ever imagined. It was pure hackwork, but I set aside the money for a reason. I remember casually mentioning why one night after playing squash with Farol. "Now we can get engaged," I said. "The only reason I didn't bring up the subject before was that I wanted to be sure I had the money."

"You don't always have to explain," she said.

"I'm not explaining," I said. "I only wanted to buy you a ring."

She smiled when I referred to one I'd seen. She bit her lip thoughtfully but to omit no precaution repeated, I can't quite add diplomatically, that she always thought diamonds were conventional. "I'd love an emerald," she said. And she added she believed it was something we should pick out together, which only confirmed something, elsewhere, I'd been thinking about for a long time.

Autumn was soon ringing in the air, with the poplars and aspens turning gold and the crisp winy days of wood smoke and apples indicating an early season. So we took one of Farol's free weekends from the hospital, drove to the Cape, and went house hunting. It was no secret that she never liked my house. It not only preceded her, she had nothing to do with it and always felt another woman's presence there. The whole situation footed up to the conclusion that I should sell the house I had and with her buy another one we chose together. There was no complication in that. And it wasn't merely that I loved her.

I realized part of Farol's unhappiness all along was that having nothing herself she'd always had to adopt the surroundings, every time, of whomever she married. Sadly, it always took more than it gave. That couldn't happen again. We were given some brochures and shown several houses. The first one, a newly built garrison with a few ugly saplings in front at the end of a dead-end road, she said she hated. The next was a likely seventeenth-century saltbox on Sandy Neck Road in West Barnstable, one not far from the beach. It had large old fireplaces, a root cellar, and a studio. But could we afford it? I said I could, I told her I'd sell my house, which had a detached garage, including a summer kitchen, an orchard, and four rolling acres with a hundred different trees. She said I wouldn't get much.

But didn't she think we should have it appraised?

There was a long pause. "Here's a Greek Revival for sale in Chatham," she said.

"Do you think we should get an appraisal, Farol, or don't you know?"

She went on flipping through the brochures.

I laughed. Her idea of tragedy was a deduction killed by a fact. She knew nothing of real estate. My efforts to convince her that my house, built in 1895, was worth more than any we looked at were in vain—she shook her head and said, "I doubt it." I swear, I never knew half the time whether what she said was a contradiction, an assertion, a denial, a taunt, a confirmation, or a joke.

Poking about through the upper rooms of that saltbox, Farol assented to its possibilities, but absently, and seemed almost lost in her thoughts. Looking back, I believe it came over her with sudden horror that here was another place she saw fixed before her for life. She stood there nervously, suffering the strain, I imagine, of already having done this twice, with two other men, and not so much learning anything new but actually seeing in what she hadn't learned before repeated. She walked around the rooms silently in that dark blue nylon jacket of hers, her hands deep in the welt pockets, and one could almost hear her thinking: *what about me? What will I do here?* She seemed determined to express a commitment in the proposals she made by use of the plural pronoun of what we might do to fix it up, how we might improve it, but it was as if all along something came up to veil the view.

And it turned out there was.

When Farol got back to St. Ives her husband was waiting for her. He ordered her to get out. Although for weeks he'd been dropping hints for her to leave—advanced communications management—she'd ignored them. Now it was too late. This was it. And I was, perhaps fatally, given the whole account. He ordered her to go. To pack her bags. To blow. It sounds odd perhaps to say so, for all the time that had passed, but it all happened quickly. There was nothing specific that precipitated it, and she protested this vehemently, but he refused to listen to another word and told her to go see a lawyer. She insisted he give her more time, saying she had nowhere to go, but he became enraged at this and began throwing things and shouting that her time was up. I asked her if he meant it.

She shook her head and said, "He threatened to throw me out bodily, and slammed the door in my face." The proceedings were closed.

She was gone.

I could only conclude that her second husband had as closely studied the particulars of the first as he had the possibilities of a third and, almost jumping to get there before her, chose to act rather than be acted upon.

There was a cheap apartment available on the top floor of a rickety old gray house in St. Ives around the corner from the gallery and right next door to the Gumplowitzes. Farol, who didn't want to jeopardize her chances in the settlement, decided to take it on a temporary basis until her divorce came through. Rain, drizzle, soft fall weather. I recall the day in October she moved in, her neck long in an attitude of defiance as she unloaded her belongings from a car filled to the top like a tinker's van.

I remember going to see her there the first time and taking a small present to cheer her up. The place smelled of mice. It was an inexpressibly drab, ill-lit single room, a sort of emotionally barricaded pillbox at the end of a dark cloistral passageway. The walls were gray and unpainted. Hot pipes. Sooty upholstery. A stained filthy stove in the kitchen and cracked linoleum on the floor. Off on one side almost as an afterthought the cramped bathroom looked like a pot closet, and there she'd put the white lollipop scale. I noticed she had removed whatever reminded her of her marriage as ruthlessly as she edited Big Flats provincialisms out of her speech.

I saw again the familiar boxes, a few corded bundles of books, an oak-framed mirror leaning against the wall in the walkway. The red bread box. Plants. Her sofa bed lay open and sheeted to an improvised mattress one had to step over. A back window gave an ugly view below to an overgrown weedy yard with a gray broken fence. There was no shaped space. You could hear people downstairs. It was dreadful.

My gift was a small wooden pull toy, an antique yellow racing car with red wheels. It did little to lift her spirits, I'm afraid. She gave me a glassy kiss and thanked me. Her hand felt as flat and gray as the morning. If at first there was a baleful intensity to her white set face, the shadow in which she stood fell like a gloomy veil across her forehead, and a certain worn expression met mine only to look away. She didn't cry this time. She was only silent, and bitter, conveying it in her cold attendance to the few duties she saw to while moving around me with a reserve more deadly than violence. She pushed this and lugged that. There was the print, empty chairs on a summer porch. And then she began sweeping, scaring her cat as she worked the broom into corners with a snapping action like repeated bites.

I tried talking to her. It was almost as dark inside the room as outside. A makeshift desk lamp on the floor cast a poor light, but one could see that this old place with its gawkish features and gloom reminded her of her own failure. Come on, I said, please. Everything would be all right. But it was as if I myself were part of a suspense composed of more elements than she yet knew. And the suspense was prolonged, with many other thoughts that were part of it, I supposed, crowding in on her, at the same time, however, giving me a glimpse of someone I found, ultimately, more coldly analytical than fearful of her fate.

I wanted to believe, on larger grounds and not for the mere ironic beauty of it, that consonant with her rejection by one party she could find acceptance in another and come to nuzzle gloriously in my arms. I wondered why in loving me she couldn't find something positive in what had happened, as all along I thought she would. But I saw the prospect unlikely, then the possibility lessened, and finally there wasn't a chance of it as she began to speak of her husband in hateful terms— that was her concentration—and of all the lost and wasted years she had spent with him. Most verdicts are compromises, I realize, but I couldn't for the life of me distinguish between what he'd done to her and what she'd done to her first husband. I didn't pursue the matter, only because I was still trying to determine how in being no longer either's she was in fact any more mine.

Farol threw some cleaning rags into a box. I saw she felt it useless to do anything more. Clothes were everywhere. She kicked her shoes and hospital whites away. "I'm fed up with all of it. Jobs. This place. Everything." She wouldn't look at me. "You don't mean—everyone," I asked, "do you?" The mistrust that made her ignore me gave her memories. "I remember those years alone when I was working at the hospital. It felt just like this."

"Are you talking about"—I couldn't forget her catchphrase—" 'hospital politics'?"

"Same feeling."

"What exactly do you mean by that? I've never understood."

"One time I wore some striped panties under my uniform. Some jerks found that very funny. Interns." I waited. I tried to make sense of what she was saying. I said, "You mean some guys at the hospital where you used to work once made some snide comments about you?" That was hospital *politics?*

She stared into the darkened windowpane and nodded. She said, "So I quit."

She sat sadly on the mattress, and turned. Wearily, she pulled the blanket over her legs. I kissed her cheek but got no response. I touched her arm and left. I could hear the light in the room snap off. Then whatever she had to cry was too far away to be audible. I went downstairs and, pausing, looked back at that dim apartment. The shut door. The narrowness. The isolation. This was where all her shrewdness had landed her. A musty room. It was a pity.

But it was long in coming. She knew she deserved to be out. Her husband deserved to have her out. And while I deserved what I had, I can honestly say that night I wasn't sure what it was. But my deeper concern was with her. I recall only trying to take heart in the idea that you can put up with any place if you have to be in it. It was small consolation. A better one, one I hoped would help her, was one that she herself had taught me.

A person in the process of change soon comes to find additional change easier.

14

Farol now demanded money.

Her husband flatly refused and told her she wouldn't get a fucking cent. I was given full reports day after day. She knew what he suspected and didn't dare ask for alimony. They fell to mutual accusations and made good their deficiencies. It was all self-interest, battle, and greed. Violent inferences were surmised from the simplest remarks, and execrations followed. She betrayed him, he caused her to betray him, she was the force behind the cause of that betrayal, and so it continued until these distinctions became so proverbial and so limber that they could be freely turned in several directions.

The following month their problems became even worse. He wanted everything, money, marbles, and chalk. She haggled and he wrangled. He insisted she return a cookbook she had taken. She wouldn't give back a sofa. He refused to keep the cat. She called his lawyer. He threatened her with reprisals. She warned him she'd sue. I tried everywhere to disabuse myself of the notion that all of it was the unmediated vindication of herself. In love we seek the image of our own significance, and the partner whom you've won, who cares about you, who loves you, is your mirror, the measure of what you are and what you stand for. But she was intransigent. I saw she was a manipulator in this, and I felt fairly certain she was litigious.

"You don't like what I'm doing, do you?" asked Farol, wearing a rather hard smile. "I'm not stupid. I feel your disapproval. Well, thank John. If that's the way I am, he's made me that way. I'm only doing what I have to do to get by."

I found her actions less offensive than her excuse.

March was set for the divorce. She screamed at him for compensation and insisted that her insurance coverage be extended beyond that time, and he shouted that he'd take her to court if she asked for anything more than the token amount she'd put in as a down payment on the house. But she saw a lawyer. And soon his back was up against the wall.

She kept repeating, "I'm not going to die a weak and beaten creature."

As the omens markedly developed, Farol and her husband eventually dealt with each other according to the same rules by which they'd lived. She mistakenly assumed he was in her power, and he'd failed to credit his wife with any sense of discrimination or ambition. But the forces of greed suddenly changed all that. I couldn't finally decide whether he was cheap or she mercenary. One's vice only exaggerated the other's. But the vices are actually identical, and if it wasn't the only thing they had in common, it was the only thing they really shared. Farol thought like an accountant. Her ultimatum amazed even her husband in a way it shouldn't have, but she had learned something from her first divorce. She had already ended up with nothing once. It wasn't going to happen again.

I watched them separate, watched them quarrel, and finally watched them negotiate, for it all gave way in the end to a final sterility, a muted two-part apathy and lack of feeling exceeding even their usual measure and so imperfectly synthetic that I thought them two of a kind. Dead. Not even hateful. Merely supremely indifferent to one another. It was the least emotional separation imaginable. They cited "irreconcilable differences," that vague euphemism devised to keep the dirty laundry hampered, and the scales fell to balance. You get the bookshelves and the stereo, I'll keep the slow-cooker. You get the chairs, I'll keep the table, and neither of us need bother about the child we never had, okay?

The house became the focus of their fight. She was not in a position of making a discretionary move, but she was sitting on her equity as long as her husband was locked into that house. At one point he decided he was going to sell the house and move away. This lent itself greatly to Farol's advantage, allowing a proposition of settlement the women at the gallery told her to pounce upon, and when I converted some of her fears, as she couldn't afford a lawyer, by asking my stepbrother to defray some expenses by drawing up the separation and property agreement, she obviously figured that in as added compensation for the tribute her husband on his end continued steadfastly to refuse, until, forced to it, he settled on her a grudging sum as a hedge against the court fees he'd otherwise have to face, and she took $20,000—never bothered to thank Tarquin—and walked away.

I remember the click of pleasure she made in personal triumph at the sight of the agreement, the spiteful delight she took in beating the man she had married at his own game. I also remember the feeling I had of being placed in strange fellowship with her exchanging sense of accommodation. When are weeds not weeds? the riddle asks. The answer: when they become widows. But she was now my jurisdiction. And I was hers. Her husband never spoke to her again.

I tried to comfort Farol during those dark interim days with the promise to be fulfilled of all she feared might never be. We slept comforting each other more than anything else. A luminous amber pallor, the shadow of last summer's bathing suit, set off the agile shoulders of that tall body that so often seemed even too listless for itself. She watched television all the time. I thought it was absurd for a person to sit around being offended by her own meaninglessness, trying to force everybody into the same hole with her, but I have to admit my resentment was in direct ratio to my feeling directly responsible for her. Her depression, I thought, took from her looks. It was struck by the cruelty of what remains when glamour fades. The caricature of beauty is of course homeliness. She scowled. She was flabbier. There were frown lines above her nose, and the question in her mouth that seemed forever forming was, "What's in it for me?"

The anger and humiliation she felt in going back to her husband only to be summarily dismissed was exacerbated even further by an even greater dislike of her job at the hospital. Farol hated the long weekends—I offered several times, without her ever taking me up on it, to go with her and stay overnight—and complained at being given the night shift when left alone she had to perform various tasks for which she was unqualified, like drawing blood and reading the blood-gas machines. There were problems compounded by the divorce she felt only "group" could settle, but she complained to me of having no time to herself anymore and spoke with an injured air about her need for creativity. She hated her apartment. She was also having trouble with her car about this time, and we spent several days off and on at a garage getting it fixed.

"Do you need those?"

She began taking pills again of ten assorted kinds.

"Do you need to ask?"

I said, "Yes."

"Then that's my answer too."

Stress, as I came to learn, is the worst thing for MS victims. I watched for signs of illness. I didn't see a lot of her. There was always an errand, always a doctor to see, always "group." I sometimes thought by her absences she was trying to save me from herself. As I say, much of the time she was never around. It seemed she always had to get away.

At Thanksgiving she went home to New York. And she would go home for Christmas. I'd noticed it before that under oppressive conditions Farol was repeatedly driven to visit her parents. I never saw a dependence this way in anyone else so prodigiously sounded. It wasn't so much a search for love as for significance, for she wasn't seeking them as much as an identity for herself. She seemed to *demand* they respond to her, if for no other reason than to gain time in order to reverse it before the danger increased of losing more. It was as if like a foundling she'd determined on finding the true biological parents who in deserting her long ago severed her from a meaning she needed in preference to accepting the adoptive ones under whose uncommitted regime she remained so halfheartedly even if legally acknowledged. But the results were always counterproductive.

I thought sadly of her going home, facing those two people in whose eyes she'd always found such a want of approval and passionately asking—even as she knew the answer—won't either of you ever recognize me? Admit I'm worth something? Accept in all I'm not what you've made me I am? It was almost too pitiful to think about, for she was only returning in disgrace again, retracing her way in routine steps back to the old dark horrors, the failed bride actually coming *back* down the aisle in defeat to no less a formidable presence waiting for her there than the stern unappeasable father who'd given her away.

And so I wasn't surprised that cold day in late November when calling New York I found her loving response a near presence, an immediate and unashamed immolation making me feel, in spite of the distance, her arms around my neck, her face gratefully pressed there, holding me in a clasp of desperate possession that like a resistance to something unseen put soul into the passionate but pleading whisper in her trembling voice when she said, "*You* are my family!"

There were over the years many times when upon reflection I had often wondered why I was with Farol Colorado. It was at times like this I thought I knew.

After returning to St. Ives after Thanksgiving, Farol threw herself rather madly into a new interest growing out of that small gift I'd given her of the wooden pull toy. She wanted to start making them as Christmas presents! I thought it significant that she took up this project hard upon visiting her father, that this flattened atavistic need of hers, sprung from impulses repressed in earlier years, secretly shaped her later life in health as well as disease. To me it had ominous implications. She was not only abandoning any attempt to work out her problems but defensively turning in the envy of aspiration to some sort of child's world which, to my mind, reached past her father into the stolen past and all those lost probations that dying there she sought to resurrect.

I grieved that she hadn't the artistic means to come to terms with all of it. I was not necessarily more worthy because my art saved me from that exploration. My art *was* that exploration.

It wasn't long before Mother Scrulock joined her in the pull-toy enterprise, and together they began devising several plans to market them. But on the basis of the three treacly sentimental woodcuts I saw—a bird, an animal, a car?—I wondered. I never saw anyone so engrossed in anything so little. Farol went out looking for what I believe in the craft are called "findings" and bought more wood, paint, tiny wheels than I could imagine she'd use. She said she needed a special kind of saw. And tools. And more room. *If only I had more kitchen space. If only I had a draftsman's table. If only* . . .

I took the opportunity of asking her in this context if Dr. Varion had ever spoken to her about my visit. She shrugged and said, "He told me you were an idealist." The inescapable fact of course was that next to him everyone was. "If love isn't an ideal," I replied, "what is?" I wanted to sit her down, intercepting that thought to explain it, and lingered an instant for the purpose. As it was—

As it was, the days went by, cold weather returned, and only well into the month—Farol was busy at both the gallery and the hospital—were we reminded we hadn't made plans for the Christmas holidays. I wanted her to spend them with me. She asked if I wanted to go to New York, at the same time expressing certain reservations by way of preliminary warning as to whether I'd find it tolerable. She said her mother got nervous having visitors. I deliberated longer than I should have, and it nettled Farol, but the invitation was unconvincing. And I hadn't been feeling well, having fallen prey to a stomach infection in mid-December. I spent much of the next week in bed, becoming irritable and ill disposed to go anywhere, especially when one night upon being invited to Scrulock's house for her annual Christmas-tree trimming we were asked—I *detested* the idea—to bring our own food.

To me it was easier doing it than not doing it only by approving the kind of coaxing vulgarity I'd so often seen at the gallery and which to my annoyance somehow never interfered with Farol's inclination to oblige. I went to the party anyway, objecting vigorously as we drove, until Farol's agitation, matching mine, led her to estimate point by point how we could never be happy together if such things had to matter so. She was right. I knew she was right, I apologized, and by the consideration she showed me later that evening I felt that if she had been angry with me she had gotten over it. And the next night when I stopped by and made a point of assuring her that I wanted to be with her in New York, I remember her nodding solemnly. I paused. Didn't she want me to? It seemed to touch a fact in her that brought something else to light in a quick second thought.

She looked detached without looking indifferent but said that was fine. "Wearing corrective shoes?" she asked as I went to leave. She pointed.

I looked down at the old pair I'd put on to go shopping in the wet snow.

"Dashing," she said, sarcastically.

I have always loved Christmas shopping. I tried to make up for the emerald ring I couldn't afford—among the most expensive gems, I found out—with a profusion of gifts. A day or so later I took them over to her apartment, climbing the stairs of that old house with its musty smell that always made me feel lonely. There were noises below. The family living downstairs, most of whom were out of work, came and went like rabbits in a warren. Once inside, I noticed a wonderful photograph on Farol's shelf I'd never seen before. It was a picture of her, wearing a green jacket and jeans, clinging halfway up a knotted oak tree and making a comic rubber face. I gave her my gifts.

She'd once given me a painting by a local artist we both admired, and I'd gotten him to do one for her, a bright watercolor called *Farol's Shirt Circus*. And then she opened the other presents: books, clothes, and jewelry. I mentioned the ring was beyond my price range. It didn't bother her. She was happy with what I gave her, she said, although she was secretly hoping, she added, that her parents and sisters would give her a short-wave-cassette-radio, something she really wanted. "This is yours"—she pulled out a large marble slab—"for breadmaking." She said she'd have gotten me something better but hadn't the money either. I loved it. I kissed her in thanks and said the only other thing I wanted, and asked her for, was a copy of that photograph on the shelf. She said her brother took it. It was as if, suddenly reminded of him, she began to wonder if he'd be home for the holidays.

But she hadn't seen her brother for more than a year, had she?

"Are you coming to New York?" asked Farol, abruptly changing the subject. "Yes," I promised. I saw she was already packed. "I plan to leave tonight," she said, "and pick up Lucy on the way." "You'll want some time with your family of course," I said. "I'll come on the twenty-sixth," I said. I smiled and lifted the photograph from the shelf.

"You're coming then?" she asked.

There was no hindrance in our talk to make me believe she wasn't frank, but why did she keep asking me if I was coming? I took it as tact. The reticence I'd shown before had given, I felt, a sense of dawning complication to my word, and then I began to think it was perhaps all contingent, the success of my visit, on something that didn't depend on herself. I wanted to be with her, but I'd spent so many holidays alone, so many nights alone, so many years alone that I'd actually begun to think it my lot in life. I remember when kissing her good-bye, her lips felt weirdly indistinct. I assured her I *wanted* to come and felt she wanted the same, but hesitated to push it.

My thought was that she didn't want to pressure me, wanting me to meet her parents but of the step she was about to take only toying with her power over it in anticipation of the courage she was about to summon.

Once more I looked at the photograph and asked, "Not even a print?"

She turned away as she spoke, and this time her voice was softly reproachful as she said, "You can't have everything you want."

15

I took the train from Boston the day after Christmas and that afternoon under a dark overcast sky Farol met me at the station in Stamford. I hugged her. Her father was waiting in the car. It was damp and windy, the weather-bearing clouds hanging over us and drizzling down gray light as we turned out of an area incoherent with ramps and highways and drove mile upon mile past outlying suburbs into a section that in its monotony left a depressing lack of suggestion. What completed the effect was the silence that fell among us. I made several observations. Mr. Sprat, with one or two expressionless replies to his daughter, was the same plethoric man I remembered, the fat vacant face giving nothing away, the thick lips, as it were, seeing to it.

He wore a hat pulled down that gave him monkey cheeks. He seemed even more overweight than before, although it may only have been the effect of his dullness. I saw little in those gormless eyes that told me if he was a man of many moods happiness was one of them. I asked something about Pugwash. But the man who rarely reached above that kindness didn't answer. I quietly reached behind the car seat and Farol took my hand.

The Sprats' was a small white house. It was set back, with the blinds drawn, in an unimposing middle-class neighborhood—crowded and terminally genteel—where narrow yards and extemporized struggling terraces functioned only to separate. But the lack of variety everywhere fell away in the gratified suspense I felt in being there. It began to rain as we arrived, my hair was wet, and I looked a bit disheveled upon entering. I met Mrs. Sprat. Farol with a queer childish squint introduced us. Her mother was thin and gray-haired with little reindeer's eyes that revealed a shifting alertness. If her husband looked like a bread truck, she looked like a canvas pail. A small, somewhat defeated-looking woman, she showed the traces of lost prettiness and had the shriveled look of a doll made from a dried apple, her lower face caved in around a slight overbite. The jeans she wore to look young only made her look older.

I gave her the gifts I'd brought. She seemed exceedingly diffident in my being there, most visibly in her bunched hands, and with pained dishonest eyes asked Farol if there was anything I wanted.

I was shown into the house. There was a spareness to the living and dining rooms, with little in the way of ornament. A manic neatness held from which seemed removed, as if in formidable defense against any sort of irreverent inspection, every last trace of anything personal, original, or descriptive. There were a few books. Several stern plants. Mediocre reproductions were set in scanty preference on the walls at exactly ruled distances from each other. I remember seeing a metal animal or two on a shelf. Lucy and Lenore, breezing by, noncommittally acknowledged me. I was told their brother wouldn't be coming.

"At least Farol's had the chance to see him recently," I said. Everybody looked at Farol. "No, I haven't," said Farol, coloring.

We sat down to dinner in a muddle of formality and silence. I made a lighthearted remark or two, but it well might have been separate tables. Conversation was subject to selection and restriction, and I found a check constantly at hand in our exchanges. I considered the first rule of table talk, that the seriousness any remark receives increases exponentially according to the number of people present. Six people, six divisions. But even that explained nothing about this family. They reached understandings with one another by brief looks. At first I took it as a fine scruple against insistence, but I soon felt an indefeasible gloom. A rigid prohibition seemed to hold, a state of apprehension poached of any consequence or value. "The food is delicious," I said, commending the lamb chops, and was given a strained smile. You heard the silver, chewing, coughs.

I immediately felt I'd made a mistake in coming. It seemed a family of ghosts. Farol's appeasement became unease, while her sisters sat like primitive Smiberts, subjects with faces like puffed-up balloons and inflated masks. They were all of them so composed of countenance they did not talk, did not complain, did not laugh, did not exclaim, did not question, in short did not resemble any people who were alive I'd ever seen before. I drew a breath of relief, getting up, as we adjourned to the living room to have coffee. I said, "It must be pleasant to have the family together." There was no reply. "It's a treat for me. I usually eat alone."

Still there was no reply.

As the evening wore on this remoteness became more acute. Mrs. Sprat, who seemed both distracted and observant at the same time, penetrating, on the watch, paced back and forth with squeezed hands.

She spoke once or twice—a kind of peevish, strangled hiccup—and arranged things in the room. Her face was tiny and pinched, her hair trimmed like the head of a safety match. I thought her a particularly correct, apparently normal, and totally uninteresting person. Across the room, filled from head to foot with a sort of chamfered squareness, Mr. Sprat sat reading the paper, his mouth tightly closed upon some secret of an unbreakable determination, glowering as if he were perpetually staring into the causes of some disastrous mistake. He was moody and disappointed. Surely Farol had told them of the divorce. He sucked his teeth. I pointed to the shelf and asked, "Did you make those animals?"—Farol watched with a look of worry on her face—and got no reply.

I fought the impression, growing more and more distinct, that guests were borne with resignation in that house until, struck with the inescapable fact, I realized that my presence there wasn't only repetitive, it was anticlimactic. It smelled of precedent! I suddenly saw in their faces tacit references to this having happened before, to other men having come there, of my visit in its repetition having no special significance. And then of course I understood. There weren't only six people there—the phantoms of two husbands had come back to visit with me! And it was then I understood that Farol in coming here had always wanted to show her parents she'd married well, but she never had, and I'm certain they thought she never would.

I set aside a magazine. Mrs. Sprat picked it up and put it away. Weather was mentioned several times. A horse-faced friend of the family dropped by and talked about his sore foot for what seemed an eternity. It wasn't long before my hope of staying a few days completely vanished.

But there we sat. An hour passed, the effect of space in the room as we sat separated, leaving an even larger effect of sterility. A real black frost seemed to descend. Neither of the sisters, common as I had never seen the common vivified, had anything to say but rose and stole about quietly with shrugs and whispered remarks. They were the type who actually entered enthusiastically into the art of making an unfavorable impression. "We're going to a movie," one of them said.

"Now?" asked Mrs. Sprat.

And both got up and left.

I tested a question or two with Mr. Sprat about mobiles. I didn't want to talk about art. I might have ventured to tell him what I hoped for Farol and myself had not his coldness made of the situation more than my efforts could overcome. "Art shouldn't be necessary," I blurted out. "It's a tragedy that we have to create. We poor dabblers need a second chance in life only to respond to a kind of world we're basically *dis*satisfied with, not the reverse. Art is a need that expresses faith only because it's missing, and because for such an activity everything is without basis except itself, there's no canvas on earth as good as the least talented person trying to make it better. Creation's not prayer, but worry, the rebus of all we make for a picture of who we are. But the more we paint, and the more successfully, the more questions we have and the less satisfied we are of getting answers."

Everybody's mouth hung open. I have no idea where it all came from, though I felt so pent up I wanted to talk. Was I somehow trying to tell Farol I loved her? Or was I trying to tell Mr. Sprat something? If so, I failed. He looked at me. He revolved a little finger in his large fungiform ears and shrugged.

It wasn't only aloofness. His very spirit was inert and unpersuaded. I could see he was a seriously flawed man. He was a dull man, duller than any man I had ever known. I once thought him only vexed, but his heart was not so much broken as just not there. A family had grown up around him almost to his surprise. He had no heart to touch and seemed to wonder with studied peevishness why the rest of humanity was subject to such an affliction. He was literally soulless, harshly stern of nature yet consumed by his own eccentric folly, an appalling figure in a household that as I saw it continued, as best it could, to keep up appearances. I don't think it an exaggeration to say that anyone ever came into that obdurate presence with its Nova Scotia stubbornness and malcontented stare who didn't immediately desire to escape from it on the spot.

Mrs. Sprat was no more giving. Fundamentally, every mother wants to give birth to an artist. This woman had long had her doubts. There seemed to be a sense of stifled injury about her. The twins were nothing but goons, but Farol, who showed some hope, had been a real disappointment. When missing exceeds chance, when a record of failure was so complete it approached perfection, it reflected on them, and they knew it. And yet all the while Farol looked on them with borrowing eyes, hungry, sharp, and speculative. I couldn't say whether she embarrassed them or they embarrassed her, I only know to them she was a source of discomfort. She bewildered them, kept them guessing. She exasperated them as much with her vagabond air as with her career of mismatched marriages, double reverses that left them startled and helpless, her foredoomed and angry, and everyone involved in a state of isolation.

I remember it suddenly coming to me, as I looked around, that no one there was *married!* Not me. Not Farol. Neither of the sisters. And her parents were married only nominally and in the most remote way. Every once in a while you'd hear a remark that showed the little rapport they had—in fact, Farol several times confided to me that one of the gloomiest prospects her mother had to face was having her husband around the house once he retired.

There was a streak in the family, worse than diffidence—for they were also meek—of hardness, of what might be called affectlessness. They were philistines. And in this I found a secret sense of satisfied logic in their not liking me. Their emotions were switched off, their temper seldom tried, their disaffection assailed by forces in comparison with which changes in health or fortune or place were as nothing. It wasn't a family that could help, only hurt each other in the drab, tired, baffled, and parsimonious way they did. They seemed to want nothing between them, merely to live compartmentalized in a cell bounded by its own walls, a prison of perfect formality, neatness, and abnegation, with everything in its place and every emotion warped. There was no joy, no celebration. It was the prerogative of their faith to ask nothing, to give nothing, to want nothing which having been given might necessitate a response in return.

The visit in its untenanted gloom was like the gape of fatality of someone near death. I had to get out of there.

Farol suggested a walk. They were all big walkers there—it passed the time and was inexpensive—and so we went out into a black drizzle that night and silently circled the neighborhood by way of a hill. The twinkling Christmas lights in various houses we passed seemed incongruously out of concert with my regret. I sensed that Farol was aware of the strain by the few questions she asked of no consequence that belied her real interest. She knew her family was awful, but what she wanted clear was whether there was anything worse about it all, almost to have it confirmed, than what she herself had seen. She seemed guarded, but it would have interested her to have the larger impression that tactfully left to ourselves I could have given but on grounds of delicacy didn't—I felt bad for her.

But I felt oddly divorced myself. The emptiness of our meeting, I knew, could only give her parents a calamitously wrongheaded view of me, and nothing done to counteract that impression could have mattered only because nothing said in my defense, if indeed anything were, seemed to have. We were met on sternly practical grounds, not even met, thrown together by some sort of irregularity, and my having gone there, instead of proving anything new, merely recapitulated for them what they'd already known of other men long before meeting me. When we returned from our walk Farol showed me my room, bade me good night, and disappeared.

We decided to leave the next morning. It couldn't have been too soon for me, and though I hadn't planned on it, jumped at the chance. Farol said she would work at the hospital the following day. To me it seemed a slim excuse to give her mother, but I felt no obligation as there wasn't a trace of my having been a guest. And so on a cold day darkened with fog, the damp winds and clouds matching in their slow accretive growth the buried decisions we pondered, we headed back. Almost immediately an impossible preoccupation settled over Farol. The opportunity always came to her easily. She said nothing, and said nothing for miles, and even lunch, the only interruption, dwindled away into silence. It grew darker. Please, I thought, no more of this. Couldn't she confide in me? I was not concerned with mistakes, they didn't matter, still less with bad luck, which can befall the best intentioned, but with not talking? Saying *nothing?*

My questions irritated her. "Are you all right?" I asked. "Is there anything the matter?" There was nothing in the way of response. I asked, "Have I somehow offended you?" She merely gripped the wheel, shook her head, and said in a voice shoe-box flat, "It just wasn't the right time to have invited you." At first she had seemed guarded. Now she seemed bored. I thought it best to leave her alone.

It was a long silent drive with cold rain glittering in the white beam of her headlights. We passed down the highway, two strangers, and there was a sign for Deerfield. It seemed almost the plagiarism of another time. I glanced at her several times. She was only a recessive presence who had become increasingly unwilling, then incapable, of reflecting upon the past in any perspective unrelated to hysteria or glossy falsehood. I felt angry with her—more than once, in fact, being with her I wondered why I loved her. She sometimes had this effect on me, that I often felt lonelier in being with her than in being alone. I became engaged for the rest of the trip in a kind of internal migration.

But she seemed lost in thought. It wasn't so much depression as a look in her composure of settled regret, the resignation, as I saw it, of having given herself over with shrugging inevitability to some gloomy prophecy come true. Once in a while as I looked at her I kept wondering what her thoughts might be as she stared out across the darkling light through those big light-shelled, plastic-framed eyeglasses with an almost clinical deliberation.

16

After we returned, some days later, Farol explained this grave mood to me. I had wondered what suddenly made her so busy and distant, and waiting for her one night after work I said, "I haven't seen you." She said she needed to be alone for a while, expressing the strong conviction that if left to herself she could finally produce something. In the way of? Art. Again, it was a reprise, a summary, all the old themes and obsessions hauled up by the single rope. "I want to do something, not end up like Maxine and Charlotte," she said. "They don't think I'll get anywhere. Nobody did. Nobody does. But I'll show them."

I left her alone. I complied only because outward assurance seemed far better than inward uncertainty. But as usual this unhappy obsession gave a serious and abstract cast to her behavior, and I connected it to the period that followed where almost everything seemed unregulated between us, beginning—inauspiciously—on New Year's Eve, a wet blustery night.

I cooked dinner, and we ate in haste, Farol having promised the gallery people she'd stop by at a party they were giving. We agreed to meet at 11:30 in front of her house. I waited for her in my car on her dark side street until midnight, but she never appeared. Gloomily, I opened a bottle of champagne and drank it down. Shortly thereafter she drove up, rolled down her window, and said, "The driving is treacherous." But there was only the merest dusting of snow. And I knew she was only pretending to be unhappy, for she was never unhappy when she wasn't expressly dependent on me. What it revealed was interesting, what it concealed vital, but I was too depressed to care about either. And I went home, somewhat drunkenly stumbling on the stairs, and fell and broke my glasses.

A few days later I drove to Boston to buy a new pair and on the way back stopped in to see Dr. Schreiner. Among other things, I mentioned Farol's behavior and how erratic she had seemed lately. "Are you still with her?" he asked. He seemed surprised. I couldn't bring myself to ask: *do you mean is she still alive?* "She's not well, Derek," I said. I gave him a few examples but mentioned there were things I thought she wasn't telling me. "What if this thing is serious?" He shrugged and asked why I didn't find out for sure. I looked doubtful. "There's a way to check," he replied. "There are medical records, you know. Reports, lab tests. Why not write to the doctors who diagnosed her?"

"They'd tell me?" I asked him. "They wouldn't tell me anything." He looked at me and smiled. Then I understood.

I shook my head.

"No," I said.

Weeks went by. Farol was working hard on her pull toys. At least her car was always in her driveway. She occasionally left me brief notes now and again explaining she'd come by when she had a chance which she seemed never to have, but I never knew half the time when they'd been left: she never wrote down the date or the time anymore. I saw her one Friday afternoon. "This weekend I need sleep," she said. I had a relapse with my stomach infection, spent a night in a local clinic, and was growing thinner. My energy flagged. One night I stopped by her apartment—I'd seen so little of her—and she met me at the door stupid with sleep. The television was blaring. She looked cross. I waited a moment for her to invite me in. But this time her inattention wasn't even cordial.

"Why don't you get a haircut once in a while?" she asked. "You really need it." Then she said she was sorry. "I just need to be alone," she said. "Do you mind?" I told her I understood, and went home.

I returned the next day—she hadn't expected me—and knocked on her door. It was a gray Saturday afternoon. Again she'd been asleep and stood in the doorway, groggy, wearing only a sweatshirt, pink panties, and knee socks. But I'd become afraid for her. "Don't give up," I said. "Don't go back to where you were! Please, just hold on. Trust me. I want to help you, Farol. I love you so much. I *ache* that you are so lonely."

I followed her inside the dark and poorly lit interior, finding again the dismally clouded ceilings, that floor so sunk and settled. She sat edgily on the bed. There was no sign of any woodwork she was doing, no tools or anything, but I noticed she had gotten a telephone. I was surprised. She had never mentioned it to me. "I need it for work," she exclaimed. "There are times when the hospital has to get in touch with me." I crawled into bed, snuggling up to her. She'd put on weight, her torso had thickened, and her waist and thighs, noticeably ring-straked with bandlike wrinkles, had lost some of their tone and firmness. I slipped my hand under her shirt. "We shouldn't," she said in the low voice she'd learned to adopt in this room, "they'll hear us downstairs."

She said she hadn't been feeling well. And she said she was tired. She had the night shift this weekend at the hospital, and she told me she'd been up late working with Scrulock on the toys. She seemed nervous and suggested a walk—to a place called Weir's Hill.

I was quiet on the way. I thought she was desperate for love but didn't have a clue how to find it. My blundering attempts at intimacy rose before me like a kind of rude giant, mocking my impulses. I wanted badly for things to be right with us, but always doubt followed certainty as closely as a shadow. We drove out some miles, parked, and began climbing up a scrubby, boulder-strewn trail to a spot over-looking the countryside. Farol was again in one of her small chilly moods, no sense of whimsy, no freshness. The mystery of her expression seemed to denote inner thoughts of a cold vague complacency, a world of ideas absolutely closed to me. She'd begun to say less and less about more and more. I thought of the joy we once shared, transforming life itself, where rain loved me and snow became a lady.

Now I'd become the bad hiker, walking too fast, walking too slow. I cut through some branches, negotiating the muddy watercourse at times on all fours, and found her at the top. She asked why I disliked walking so much. She said I should be stronger. She'd also said recently, at different times and in different moods, that I looked younger when I was thinner, nicer when I seemed older, and older when I seemed dissatisfied, which was slowly becoming the case. "I don't like your glasses," she said.

I had heard seriously ill people were brutally frank. But what was all this?

I asked her what the matter was. She sighed and threw a stone. Oh everything. Distractions. Work at the hospital. She gesticulated disgust. "And the toys," she said. "I need a band saw, Maxine isn't co-operating, and as far as space goes—well, there's just no room." But I had already heard the false note. Hadn't she just told me she'd seen Scrulock last night? "I didn't say—I mean, I did say—no, not *seen* her but had planned to, that's the point!" She became suddenly cross with me and began talking in a high-pitched voice, flinging out vituperations and becoming almost cross-eyed, a look her face characteristically assumed when she was lying.

I haven't mentioned this. She had begun to lie. They were not vicious lies, only small pointless evasions brought in on matters she for some reason no longer even wished to share with mute appeal. I thought what she blamed on me was only a version of the kind of defiant malingering she was actually trying to defend herself against. But it was at times like this that the deepest of all my fears announced itself, that if I poked my finger through her I'd find nothing but loose dirt.

Farol sought shelter in a pout of mist. And I wondered if such a change was connected in any way to various whispered hints of unease I'd lately begun to notice. My car, my hair. And were those corrective *shoes* I was wearing? She also criticized me for reading all the time. I wasn't surprised. Books call for self-examination and try to make sense of life. Now it was my eyeglasses—I didn't wear them right, one side was lower than the other. I began to ponder, in light of all this, the many things incurred but not recorded. But I knew it wasn't in her nature to be satisfied. She saw very little in the many things she was given of what in having once wanted she was ever grateful for. I thought if you don't know what you're looking for, you don't know you've had it when you find it.

She made the charge that I resented her pull toys. "I don't understand your work either," she snapped, her eyes flashing. "In all these years," I said, "you've never once asked me about it." She looked morosely away. "You told me not to try to be different."

"I told you it was more pertinent to be better, that's all. When you get better, you become different."

"You hate the project," she said, "you hate my working at it, and you hate Maxine Scrulock."

"Work is done alone, Farol," I said, "not by collaboration—the final result of which will inevitably be a compromise between two people, a doomed average, a rational number distilled out of the fusion of irrational ones." I was speaking of art but felt I couldn't have stumbled upon a better definition of who we were or found a more cogent argument for leaving her right then and there.

I didn't want to leave her, but I was getting more than a sense of what she felt about me by what she now told me she disapproved, and I recalled enough of her tact in the past to feel frightened. I knew it wasn't like her to say something awful merely in the exigency of the moment. Words said betrayed what she knew she could never take back. It was precisely why I held my own tongue, even though I now felt a return of the oppression I'd known before.

Farol, who always had a hidden agenda—who often had a mistaken sensitivity to a discord that wasn't there—now became expressly discontented. At times I wanted to forget the civilized approach and punch her lights out. It wasn't only that her husband having left her left her curiously indifferent to me, she'd become ugly, and I was seeing put into fact what before I thought I'd only theorized.

"Tell me," I asked, "did anything happen back in Mamaroneck to make you resent me? To make you harbor some sort of grudge? Have your parents said anything?"

"No," she returned. Her response was polite but had a rude edge. "My father only said, 'Hair must be very important to him.' "

I thought: *certainly more than hypocrisy and bad manners.*

She shrugged. "You were quiet."

"They were quiet," I said.

I wanted to scream at her that they'd all pulled their heads within themselves—I'd been their guest!—and slammed the door like turtles.

I wanted to shout hurtful and pointlessly cruel remarks at her, as she had been doing to me:*"Read a book!" "Wear a skirt." "Say thank you!" "Talk!"*

"And you're quiet now."

"I don't feel the need to talk," said Farol.

"That's what worries me. There isn't a need." I paused. "Is there?"

And of all the stupid responses she ever made, there followed one of the dumbest, most stupefyingly ignorant remarks I ever heard in my life.

"No," she said.

We sat on awhile in silence. Once or twice I broached a subject, but I could see her attention was only given to it from duty, not even courtesy. The gray day fell around us, then she said she had to go to work at the hospital. Another weekend was gone. We descended the hill by separate but adjacent trails without speaking a word. And then she drove me to my front door, and I got out. "I hate this street," she said, and drove away.

17

Although Farol had begun telegraphing messages to me with decreasing subtlety, I hadn't the faintest idea what they meant. But of the day following that walk to the hill—it was January 23—I have some precise and disconcerting memories. I remember walking over to her apartment with the Sunday papers after a night of fitful dreams. When she answered the door, immediately upon seeing me she wanted to go out for breakfast. And at that instant the telephone suddenly rang.

She stood motionless a moment. She had to answer it—there was an awkward pause—and picking up the receiver did so with a voice at first flat then quickly and quietly modulated to a party on the other end with whom she seemed clearly familiar. I thought she laughed, a bit too obligingly, at something whoever it was had said. His mode—I knew it was a man—was questioning. Her replies, giving nothing away, were confined to monosyllables.

My presence there gave her a guilty swallowing look. I was infected by her embarrassment—she kept turning to me in an ungainly way—and so excusing myself walked home. Within a half hour she came by. She brought along the paper. She asked if I still wanted to eat. I said no. We read the paper together in silence. A strange discomfort passed between us as if, having already eaten, we were suffering the same indigestible meal. Farol, like her sisters, had developed frown lines above her nose, and seemed falsely absorbed. Dread rubbed the floor of my stomach, and I began to feel the sickening sweep of a descent into something I couldn't see. Nothing fixes an event in the mind so fast as the wish to forget it. And as I listened to the silence it was a hundred years hence, and I was dead, and someone else was there about to be lied to whom I pitied. Eventually she spoke. I sensed the fake insouciance. Without looking up, she said, "That was John."

Was it her voice that entered my ear or her thought? I don't know. I only knew the sight in my mind that began to stir made me wonder if my love for her was more a stay against chaos or merely a part of it. There's a truth to the idea that a person does not suspect faults he himself would not commit. I didn't have that excuse. I'd committed the kind of fault I feared, and the fear alerted me. But I was tired of the vanity of our separate consolations. And coming events do what we all know with their shadows.

I looked at her.

"Do you want"—my throat went dry—"do you want to see other people?"

There loomed in her face a look that frightened me; it was charged with something so forbidding that for an instant I held my breath. Her jaw shifted. She said, "There have been times when I've considered it."

My gasp was not contemptuous, or indignant, it was simply that she'd succeeded in taking my breath away.

"Not *people*." She pushed aside the paper. "*I* don't know. I need to be alone for a while. I haven't told you this, but I went to the Museum of Fine Arts last week just to get out, to get away, and found being on my own was something I enjoyed. I just walked around, no big thing. But I felt like myself!" She spoke in a stilted speechy way—it was the voice of the gallery women—as if asserting a privilege I'd somehow long denied her. "You remember I told you of living alone those two years after my first divorce?" I did remember, and she said she couldn't bear it. "That was something I needed then. It was good for me." My heart heaved. She had told me exactly the opposite a thousand times. One lie meant there were others. "I don't know if I want to see anybody. Anyway"—she blew air—"I've had the chance, if you must know."

A chill suddenly stole through the room.

Farol was looking away, but she couldn't repress a smile. She coyly touched her tongue to her upper lip and became unbearably demure. "Do you happen to recall that day at the garage a month or so ago? Getting my car fixed?"

I didn't. I couldn't think. And the process of trying to understand all this, coupled with the dread of doing so, left me speechless.

"There was a man there, anyway. He spoke to me. You were waiting in the car. Well, a few days later—I was on my way to Galloupi's—and he pulled up in this Mercedes and asked me out." It gave her a smiling but casual memory, as she momentarily leaned her chin on one hand, but pulling herself together she recounted the rest as a matter of course. She said it was nothing. But something of an amused scrawl in her eyes seemed to mock her own remark. "He's a lawyer. Curly hair," she said. "He's been divorced himself."

"And you assume this interests me?" I sharply turned her toward me.

"Don't, please," she said.

"Don't touch you?"

"Don't invent quarrelsome things and talk as if I'd said them."

She had no idea of the effort I expended to keep calm. A stranger? On the street? How long had she talked to him? And why? But he wasn't a stranger. She'd met him before, see? The *he* and *him* in her mouth sickened me. I looked at her. It was as if, relieved, she'd been waiting some time to tell me this. She had the story already formulated; she knew its pauses. I asked what she would have thought if I had done that.

"Now I know how John feels," I said.

"Don't make him out to be a martyr!" said Farol, turning to me shaking and black. She harshly set aside the paper and I thought she was going to cry. "I'm better than you think I am."

I wondered about that. But I realized now who had called her— I knew it wasn't her husband—and that she had given this man her name or phone number or both. A lawyer. Was there no end for her need for attention? I asked in a voice I did not recognize as my own, "Why didn't you tell him you loved me?"

Her lower jaw hung loosely like the mechanical part of a toy woman. Then she sighed.

"Why?" I repeated. Her illogical reply was that he didn't know me. What did it matter anyway, she asked, it just wasn't important, and she wouldn't have told me all this, she added, if she'd known I'd get so upset. I had the weird feeling of my voice not being linked to me. The words seemed to come from somewhere else, my memory or unconscious mind. She became sniffish and said she was only trying to be truthful and look at the reward she got. She stood up. "And there's no need to look at me like that."

I don't even remember being able to see.

"I told you, I need to be alone," she declared, with an edge on her voice. "It's not what you think."

"What do I think?"

As soon as she asked that I began, eerily enough, to see that what I thought of her all along had actually become a part of what she was.

She had a way of speaking in three-quarter profile, as if half to herself. "I haven't the slightest intention of going out with him."

You, him. You, him. Yourself as another's other. I was becoming too tired to put my disappointment into words. I was not only tired but discouraged and confused. Why had she even bothered to tell me this if it meant nothing, why had the matter come up?

"Or going out with anyone?"

I wanted to be with her, not follow like a duck or a dwarf with a ring in his nose. She went visibly tense as she heard my question, glaring at me, one eye a drill, the other a slit, her lips compressed like a person tasting bitter seed.

There was something self-contained yet apparent in her posture. She weighed me for a moment, but said nothing. Then I understood— I had been told something deeper than that story, and she had wanted more. She had moved to a certain limitlessness, the strain at constant stress, continually developed, allowing for a permanent strain as long as that stress was maintained. She would hear neither what she didn't want nor what she wasn't waiting for at the time. I found her silence more cowardly than cruel.

"No"—I hated my hesitation—"no, of course you can't promise that. You want to be alone. And visit museums. And go on walks alone." She turned nervously toward the door. "And in the meantime you want to consider seeing other men, is that it? That's it, isn't it? That's what you want."

We'd moved onto the porch. Her eyes were no longer smiling. They were gravely searching mine. She spread deprecating hands. "I've been thinking about it," she said, and vanished.

A rubber-gray sky was darkening early with the promise of a storm. I went for a long walk under snow clouds, my head hammering, and late that night found myself standing in the darkness of the school gym. There was a telephone in the lobby. I thought of Farol, the rise and fall, the forced grace and sudden despair, by which alone she came to me, and I had to know where we stood. I dialed, not having the slightest idea what I was going to say, and reached her at the hospital after some delay. When she answered I went silent for a moment, not trusting myself to speak, so wrenched was my heart. And then I said, "I love you."

I strained to listen. There was nothing on the other end.

"But I've been thinking about what you said." My anguish spoke for me. "Maybe it's best if we didn't see each other"—I closed my eyes and thought of the very last thing I wanted, the very last thing on earth if she loved me she could bear—"until July." I tightly pressed the instrument to my ear. There wasn't the trace of a sound in the phone.

And then quietly she agreed.

My throat swelled as she hung up, and I remember nothing else, only the weight of the empty receiver in my hand. I tried to follow my thoughts down to the bottom. I had no idea whether I could trust what I would now see. I knew her spirit of contradiction and her eagerness to excel in argument would not easily allow her to yield.

But I wasn't sure what to believe. I only knew I didn't believe she didn't want to see me. We never know what people might give us that they don't.

I thought she was ill.

18

Snow fell all the following week. It passed as one long unclear solitude to me, sadness and melancholy smothering my thoughts like the heavy drifts in the cold incorporeal stillness outside. My actual experience was of an indefinite duration or alternately of a perpetual present made up of one continually changing apocalypse. And along with an indifference to space there came an even more complete indifference to time. I didn't see Farol the entire period and couldn't bring myself to wonder where she was. I stopped jogging. I couldn't listen to music and started smoking again. I woke up at night and raked over the past and saw amazing things. I left the light of my lamp burning night after night in the hope that she would come by, but she never did.

A friend of mine had asked me to mind his dorm for a few days— a house not far from mine—and for the change of scene I obliged. Most of the students had gone for the weekend. I wandered the rooms, I stood by the windows, I watched the houses being plastered white, the cruel long-skirted winds swirling off the rooftops and blowing into the black misconfigured trees and bushes along the walkways out front. The snow was three feet deep, the tall vines hooped with snow and set fast at either end like snares. They were queer lost days. A sepia gloom in the afternoons invaded the rooms and deepened them in darkness.

I couldn't sleep at night. Nothing consoled, no book, no friend, no event, no plan, no perspective. And as the days passed into nights I couldn't stop missing Farol. But what her secret interests were, for what occupations she trotted off, I did not know. I was thinking only of the man at the garage and why she told me about him.

As I began pondering it all it was as if the repeated question suddenly gave me the answer I sought. Wasn't she trying to prove by recounting a tale of ignoring him that she wanted to be alone? I felt the breeze of a promise. She'd mentioned her name to him; so what? And her phone number would have been easy to get. Within moments I felt remorseful; my thought was not only that she had merely embraced a mood rather than an idea, but that I had been heedless of her needs. And I felt perfectly miserable for what I had done.

I called Farol impulsively on Friday night, very late, and blurted out all I felt for her and how much I wanted her in my life. I told her where I was staying. She asked if we could meet there the next evening at seven o'clock, and at her words my soul virtually swooned. There was hope! I slept by a window that night looking into the darkness. A thousand great orchestras, more wonderful than anything I knew, broke into mighty strains. The chant of a marvelous cantata rose to the stars like a hymn of life. Now the color-organs burst into full flower, throwing strange patterns on the sky, which was filled with powerful singing. My blood was singing. To me not a man or woman or child—nothing—was outside the communion of that night. The world seemed never so wonderful!

And I woke up early on Saturday with a delightful idea. It was a dark sword-cold morning, the large drifts of snow hovering high and throwing blue swollen shadows everywhere. But I'd never felt more alive. I spent most of the day shopping and buying Farol a cashmere scarf, several jerseys, and then with some money I'd set aside, the short-wave-radio-cassette-recorder she had wanted. I hurried back and, cooking a special meal—makloubeh, an Arabic meat pie—set the table, put out candles, and made certain everything was ready. When she didn't appear on time I wasn't worried. All the streets and highways had been plowed. Eight o'clock. No Farol. Then nine. I called. No one was home. I called the hospital. She had already left. Ten. Eleven. The tension of waiting for her gave me a scared childish feeling, the kind one trusts, always in vain, never to meet with in mature life. Twelve. And then it was one o'clock. There was no sign of her. I waited through most of the night, but I never saw her. She never came by.

Early the next morning I went home and found a note, left not where I'd been staying but shoved into the wet mail slot of my empty house. It has been hastily scribbled, with no indication of the time it was left, and read:

> *Please please forgive me this evening. I've been stuck on the road with my damn car. I'm frozen to the bone. I'm bullshit to say the least especially since your phone call last night. I wanted to be with you. I'll explain and make it up to you. What has gone right in the last week—nothing. I'm sorry. I'm just so angry at this whole stupid everything. Life is absurd!*
>
> *I'm so embarrassed.*
>
> > Farol

At that moment, I was her husband.

I closed my eyes and felt the future in an instant. My first thought was that all along what I'd thought false in him, so real in her, was reversed. It was intolerable, it was impossible. But she'd known where I'd been! Why hadn't she called? Or come by? Even in the morning? Or left the note where I'd been? A dead spot in the note, as in a painting, was the giveaway: there was no mention of love. It's not imagination that causes the mind to become unhinged, reason does. She was false as water. I fought back my tears, recalling advice Picasso once gave a student—whenever you see nothing, use black. For the first time since I'd known Farol I had to face with conscious recognition the fact I could no longer avoid: she had been with another man, and though I knew it, I merely couldn't accept it.

And I was afraid to ask.

My hope of seeing her that day, a day filled with malevolent green light, went unfulfilled. I couldn't eat. I hadn't eaten for days. I began to weep in a lost weary fashion, almost without thought, looking for her through the windows. I recall wandering around the rooms, straightening objects that were already straight, moving a chair an inch or two only to replace it. I didn't dare leave the house in case she came by. I kept asking myself over and over whether in truth I loved this woman—what was missing in me that over and over I did? I know she didn't want to be alone, she wanted me to be. And her husband. It's not your enemies who condemn you to solitude, it's your friends. I longed to let her know the cause of my anger, yet perversely looked forward to seeing her face. I didn't know what I'd say when I saw her, only yearned to let her know she was forgiven.

I was going mad, not by the hour but by the minute. It was torture to try to sleep. I got in my car and began blindly driving, heading

down the deadened wintry highway to Boston. I parked my car by the
Charles and sat as my throat filled with sorrow watching the bridge
where a thousand years ago I'd once stood with someone else. Not a
sky. Mere indications. Distant flaughts on a canvas. I started walking
the empty streets of the city—I had nowhere to go—and after several
hours, to get out of the slow wet coldness chilling me to the bone, I
entered a theater and sat sick at heart in the small close darkness watching I have no idea what kind of farce and remember only that I broke
down in tears watching a clown trying to extricate himself from a piece
of flypaper.

It was very late under a high cold moon when passing through
the North End I stopped at Dr. Schreiner's. I knocked loudly, and when
he saw me he found me hard to recognize. I'd become thin and attenuated enough in appearance that he thought me ill. We sat down and
I explained what had happened. I told him about my trip to New York
at Christmas, of Farol and her family, and the other presences I sensed
there. I knew I had reasons to doubt her. There were reasons everywhere to disbelieve and to doubt. I just couldn't *invoke* them. I admitted she'd been through a lot. Marriages. Divorces.

"Maybe she's been lying."

"About what?"

"Everything," said Derek. "Her husband. Men."

Inexplicably, her behavior didn't seem to confuse him.

"A normal individual can feel love and hate toward the same
person, and will express it," he said. "Not so others. Neurotics. People who choose and then blame their victims—husbands, say—to whom
they assign qualities they don't like in themselves, pettiness, for instance." He looked at me. "Or infidelity." He was pacing now. "To rid
themselves of that quality, they project it onto someone else as a way
of getting rid of it. Do you follow me?"

I did.

"I'm concerned about you."

I told him that I'd changed my mind about getting to the bottom
of Farol's illness and asked if he was still willing to help me. He
laughed and said maybe she was suffering from dactylic quinarity or
cervical heptavertebrae. Did I know if her condition had changed? Not
really. Why did I think she was ill? Her behavior, her mood, everything. Could I tell him what kind of medicines she'd been on? I
couldn't think, I couldn't remember. But I promised to let him know
and gave him the name of the hospital in Pennsylvania where Farol had

once gone. Could he do something? Would he help? And agreeing to, he outlined a plan.

"I think you should know why I'm doing this," he said. "I mean, there is an ethical side to it all. You know?" I saw his point, but hadn't he agreed there was something wrong with her? He'd wondered about her himself, hadn't he? Hadn't he only a month or so ago asked if we were still together?

Shaking his head, he went silent for a minute. That wasn't why he'd asked, he said. I didn't understand. What was he saying?

"Do you remember one night a year or so ago," asked Derek, "Farol hadn't been feeling well, and both of you stopped by to see me?" He had crossed the room and was speaking to the window. "And I gave her a checkup?"

I nodded.

"She rang me up the next day." He turned. "I've never mentioned this to you because she specifically asked me not to, and it was none of my business anyway. Ordinarily I'd have kept my word," he continued, "but I remember even then it struck me as odd, her calling on the pretense of asking me, since I knew you, if there were other women in your life."

"On the pretense?"

He looked at me.

"Please?" I asked.

"I hate to mention this," he said. "It seems so long ago."

"Go on."

He shrugged.

"She was flirting with me."

I drove back to St. Ives, my head racked with conflicting swing and spin. The more questions I began asking, the more I found parts of the story way beyond my reach. I didn't want to believe it, and yet I recognized her in all of it, the presumption, the easy familiarity, the medical fixation, the phone calls. I recalled her calling my sister, reading my mail, the day she entered my house when I wasn't there. Infidelity. The bare idea of it—and here was a measure of my self-delusion—struck me dumb, the very concept for a moment seemed impossible. She'd been so intimate with me! But it was incontrovertible. I knew her, and I heard again: "The best revenge is success." A doctor. Money. Prestige. Social attention. Everything. The fulfillment of therapeutic and psychic needs. I remembered her childish, rather mad desire to own a stethoscope. Something to crow about. The dreams of Farol Ann Sprat.

I thought of her note, the car trouble. I wondered how she'd try to explain it to me. She'd tell me it was a flat tire—no, that would have been quickly fixed. A fan belt. The carburetor. A frozen engine. Something complicated or esoteric. A torrent of remonstrances rose to my lips, but they were sealed by the incomprehensible reflection that deep in the dimness of what she said may have been a particle of truth. And yet I knew a way of finding out. It was merely a matter of eliminating the impossible—whatever remained, however improbable, had to be the truth. But either way, she herself was going to show me.

I spent the entire night, my face in the pillow, praying bewildering prayers which while they asked for different things somehow all made room for her. I love her, I thought. If I know that, I thought, I won't have betrayed her and I'll still be worth something.

And in the morning, after writing down and mailing off to Derek Schreiner the list of medicines Farol had used at one time or other, some remembered, others copied from scraps of paper and notes in my wallet—Allimin, Doxiden, Vistrax, Pathilon, etc.—I wanted nothing but sleep. I don't remember how long a period elapsed, hours or days, before I became conscious of someone standing beside my bed and looking at me. At first I thought it was an apparition, my mind being stopped by the sensible externals of sound before I could arrive at any meaning.

It was Farol Colorado, and she was talking. I sat up trying to sort out the image from the ugly strings of circumstances tying her to the nightmare from which I was trying to awake and that now stammered down to reality. I blinked at the pale-light windows. It was another morning. Another full day had passed.

She sat down by the side of the bed and said, "It was a wild night at the hospital."

There was a desperateness to the fixity of her eyes, as if she were tracing the outlines of an issue that couldn't be met. She was nervous— a sense of something unspoken came as a slow ache—but by circumventing the subject she only drew attention to it. It was obvious she would say whatever would save her the trouble of saying anything else. But what she didn't mention, she'd only leave exposed.

"And I realize you were busy at the hospital the night I waited for you," I dissembled—she looked up surprised—"but you should have called." I gave her the excuse she quickly accepted and my deceit became hers. She almost couldn't contain herself. I repeated, "Don't you agree?"

"I do, I do," she said quickly.

At first she became intentionally naive, assuming a look of injured virtue. She tried to explain. The faint but sickening silliness was for a certain time concealed by a maze of complex machinations. She said she'd been stuck in Amesbury that night. The fuel line. Something stupid. She wasn't tempted even by momentary circumstance to tell the truth but still managed to speak in a sanctified low tone of what happened. "It was late," she said, "I was tired, and with all the car trouble I decided to spend the night with Sue." She became helpful. "My friend? Who got me the job?" I nodded, catching her unawares by being so agreeable. This gave her a pleasant turn, and for a moment she was cleverer than her face and revealed nothing.

But she was cautious—and couldn't look at me and suddenly moved across the room with that one-sided crablike walk of hers, her face safely averted, as she chastised herself a bit too vehemently for being so thoughtless. "I know, I know," she said, "I should have called. I feel foolish because it's not like me not to have." I listened to what she said and saw it wasn't ingenuousness but ingenuity. Who comes from the kitchen smells of smoke. The words came haltingly as she monitored them to step around potential traps and deny contradictions but all she said was mocked in the memorization. I saw she was relieved—her former apprehension could be read in her delight—but gratitude made her contrition too bright. There was almost luxury in her self-reproach. It looked like mime.

But it wasn't mime. Mime tries to make the invisible visible. She was doing the opposite. It was clear she had no idea what her face looked like when she was talking to me. I knew she was lying, I merely didn't know why or for whom. I also realized not getting caught in a lie for her was like telling the truth and whether she broke her word or not didn't matter because it was always meaningless when she gave it. Mystification is simple, clarity the hardest thing of all, and trying to be honest only gave her a look of comic dishevelment. But the longer she went on, the more she explained, the less there was to believe, and this she couldn't allow.

The disadvantage of lying is that if everyone does it, it loses its usefulness, so she had to be certain of my belief the more definitely to establish our honor. It was important she insist we value truth together, for only if we both loved truth could she alone afford the luxury of lying and deceit. And I was going to make her prove it.

I decided to test her. I did what I had planned. I had not forgotten the $1,000 bicycle she took from her husband the day she was fucking me. I went to the closet and took out the short-wave radio cassette I'd bought her. Sitting on my bed, Farol brought her knees together nervously working her fingertips over them. She was watching me very intently. I set the cassette down in front of her and said, "I wanted to give you this the night you couldn't make it." She regarded me with the same pitying expression that always confessed more of her guilt than her concern and then lowered her head into her hands. She muttered, "I feel undeserving of anything." I wondered: *but are you?* The liar can follow only her own logic. I thought: *if she takes the cassette, she's unfaithful.*

She looked up, hesitating a moment. I knew her mind, I could feel it nibbling the possibilities. With her face sugared over with devotion she said a few words of thanks. And then kissing me on the cheek, as if overcome with emotion, she picked it up, put it under her arm, and went home.

It had always been an act of discretion for me, continually demanded, to determine when speculation sank under its own weight into suspicion, but the death of air becomes fire, and now I understood. The shock of recognition for me lay somewhere between self-realization and self-pity. It suddenly came to me that I craved the same approval from her that she craved from her father and was given the same response from her that she had gotten from him—nothing. I realized a daughter who has been in opposition to her father will eventually reproduce in herself many of the traits she has most rebelled against.

An artist, however, paints not what he sees, but what he thinks about what he sees. That was her mistake.

She was mysterious.

But not unknown.

19

I remember the next few days, assuming I was sane and awake, only the chilling confirmation in fact of what I thought had happened as myth and dream. Farol was involved with someone, but not the man at the garage, that was only the canary in the coal mine. To be so portentous one would be deeper than that. Only now did I see that she had mentioned that simply to see my reaction, confessing that truth through misdirection to hide a blacker lie. I felt the foreboding, but in my desperate need to salvage something of meaning for all these years I felt there was nothing I wouldn't forgive.

Farol came by to visit. But she came by only when she knew I'd not be at home and then tried to prove her loyalty when seeing me later by asking where I was, a ploy that after quickly giving me hope immediately made me feel useless and undeserving. When people say that they need to be loved, they often mean that they need to be seen, and there seemed no echo left of my existence. I felt worthless not because I didn't love her, but because I did.

I began to see how love murders the actual. A lover is never a completely self-reliant person viewing the world through his own eyes, but a hostage to a certain delusion. He becomes a perjurer, all his thoughts and emotions being directed with reference, not to an accurate and just appraisal of the real world but rather to the safety and exaltation of his loved one, and the madness with which he pursues her, transmogrifying his attention, blinds him like a victim.

I was convinced she didn't believe in my love only because she knew she didn't deserve it. Still I deluded myself. It is always more difficult to fight against faith than against knowledge, for one thing. I also couldn't bear feeling suspicious. I thought by being suspicious you often made happen the very suspicions you fear.

My obsession was grief. I began waiting for her after work, looking for her, finding only cold inattention each time she saw me. Once she kept me standing in the gallery parking lot, refusing to introduce me, while she conversed with a friend for twenty minutes. The days passed in galling impotence. It was a nightmarish rhythm of promises broken, expectations dashed, conversations unfinished, and appointments not kept. Rushing off, she always had something to do somewhere, but whenever I drove by her car was there in the driveway. Her self-assurance grew out of and then virtually became her contemptuous response to my desperation.

One gray afternoon I took her lunch and though she said she had no time to talk at last reluctantly agreed, almost by way of a bargain to prevent my lingering there, to see me that evening. I suggested the delicatessen, but she refused to go there and chose a Chinese restaurant nearby. I went home and put on a tie and jacket.

When we got there Farol became nothing more than single messages. She'd recently developed a taste for hats and sported a gray fedora. I noticed for the first time in years she wasn't wearing the gold earrings I'd given her. She seemed arrogantly offhand and settled without deliberation before a platter of food, which she began to eat freely. "I'd like Perrier water," she said to the waiter. "That's what I drink now. Better for you. Salt-free." She asked me between mouthfuls why I wasn't hungry. I couldn't eat. A bubble was developing in the pit of my stomach. I couldn't even gather my thoughts.

I wanted to tell her I loved her. I told her instead what I'd been doing—to my horror I began to talk too much—but quickly discovered by a not very oblique scrutiny that she wasn't listening to me and that these weren't matters of grave importance. She explained that she'd been alone. I said, "I think you've been unconscious of avoiding me." She met this with somewhat amused tolerance, but in my experience suffering always seems unreasonable to those who cause it. She forked in a mouthful of food and said, "I've been busy."

"I'll be working at the hospital almost every weekend now," she said, "and I have to go to Syracuse sometime to visit Penny." She sipped her tea. "A friend of mine." She told me there were so many things she had to do she couldn't even list them all. I made no rejoinder, only took some cassettes out of my pocket I'd bought for her and put them on the table. Setting them aside, she exhaled strain and asked me not to give her any more gifts. It wasn't from kindness. She was trying to save face. It wasn't so much that she didn't deserve them, but that she'd have to take them. But it wasn't from guilt. With her gifts never made you dearer, merely convinced her she was more worthwhile. No, she simply didn't want the obligation of having to encourage me with thanks.

And as I sensed that, a wedge of pain replaced my heart. I asked her if I could tell her something. She compressed her lips and brought her hands together in her lap in conscious mimicry of the gesture of a child waiting for a lesson. I said, "I've missed you."

Farol nodded. She could commiserate here. It was all right to have feelings as long as you didn't have to show compassion. She shook her head and becoming hard and trite and vapid said, "You should seek other friends." It saved her the trouble of saying anything else. "I didn't do that for the longest time," she said, "and it was a mistake. Everyone at 'group' agrees. Why don't you go back and talk to Dr. Varion?" Giving advice made her smug. She was visibly pleased with her own objectivity, and leaned back, detached, compactly satisfied, as if measuring that sad benighted ghost of former years with her new self.

I could see she was almost as pleased in pretending to nurture me for the crime she perpetrated than in having committed it in the first place. She sniffed piously. "I was like you. But I realized I owe something to myself. I had to get in touch with my feelings and learn to plumb the depths of all I myself could be and do."

The contradiction she encouraged of her being alone but my needing friends went by her—along with the irony of her having prevented other friendships I might have made by almost exclusively taking up my time all these years—but the odd mixture of audacity and self-delusion by which she sought a substitute for truth simply flowed on.

She was a liar on the most profound level. Without a passing thought to principle, she sat there with that sweet irrecusable face merely sounding once again all those feeble familiar fictions for the detection of which not the slightest shrewdness was required. She resumed eating. Her overconfidence gave me hideous insights, and it was a struggle to recall anything she'd said over the years that seemed honest and good and decent. My memory worked backwards, and, queerly, the further back, the more distant an event, the easier I could remember, but it was the strangest thing, by committing myself to trying to recover the past I felt almost immediately divorced from the necessity of making the present act of perception a condition of it. Something had already been lost.

But all the time I wanted to, somehow *needed* to, tell her that I loved her. I wanted to believe that while pessimism of the intellect was perhaps inevitable, optimism of the spirit was still possible. I had thought of so many things to say, but all I could get out was, "Don't you remember our promises?" Failing to touch her heart, however, it merely appeased her pride and flattered her vanity.

She assumed a quiet sculptural attitude.

"That's too much responsibility," she said.

We sat in silence. I could hardly help lowering my voice and speaking as if in a sick room. I whispered, "I'll wait for you."

Farol put down her fork.

"It wouldn't be right for me to ask that," she said. She became stiff, stately, and offended. "I told you what I needed. I want to be alone." Every time she said that I saw the face of another man beside her. Of course she didn't believe a word she said, which didn't make her saying it a bit less unspeakably base. "And I don't want to be sacrificed for. It's something I've asked for, now I've told you that, haven't I? Haven't I asked you that?" She shoved her face forward. "I have a hard time with commitment!" She moaned and pushed back from the table. "Oh what's the use."

She stood up and said since I hadn't eaten she could take the food home in a bag. I paid the check. And we left the restaurant almost as soon as we'd come.

As we drove back the sense of sulfurous secrecy she gave off became virtually an odor. I realized in what she said of wanting to be alone—it was almost for a minute as if she believed it—how the habit of lying begets credulity in the liar. A bad conscience can find comfort in vague memory only for so long, however, and clearly because the more she divulged the more she felt trapped she grew sullen and silent. There were always several ways of understanding her, but between what she said and what she meant there was always something that was neither.

Recalling that dreadful Christmas party the year before, I watched in my mind those men whose vulgarity, whose credulity, she accentuated by parading familiarly through their midst her inaccessible life, and now I was a stranger myself living on a plane of experience informed by even worse pain and disillusionment. And yet I found nothing in her to respect anymore, I couldn't share it, I couldn't believe it, I couldn't *feel* it.

My heart wouldn't obey my head. I knew everything now but why I wanted her, but I was afraid if I began asking that question, never mind answering it, I would hate myself even more. I'm certain part of me was trying to punish her by letting her see what she was and maybe somewhere in me I wanted nothing more than to have her cruelty confirmed over and over again to rid myself of the rat.

At her door I paused. I waited, asking to stay awhile. "There, you see?" Farol said, flushed with annoyance. "I asked you to understand. Now you want to come in." But it was still early, she was trapped by circumstance, and she had to brook the inconvenience. She wouldn't let me inside. She found an excuse by saying she needed some air.

We began walking slowly around the block. It was almost dark, the dusk sharpening the cold air, smelling of deep pools of rain. At first terror made me silent: not courtesy, not charity. I tried to speak. My voice unused for five minutes, almost cracked when I tried. I didn't know what to say. I tried to suggest she was making a mistake. But she only smiled angrily inward like a teenager who knows it all. She wouldn't look at me. Her face was locked. She walked along beside me, determined to give me no assistance. At one point my shoulder chanced to touch hers, and she drew back with an instinctive aversion that told me she wasn't bad at making commitments, merely not good at keeping them.

Presently we came to a gate, which was closed. I laid my hand upon it, but made no movement to open it. I stood and looked at her. "You are—very much absorbed," I said, swallowing. Farol lifted a hand and dropped it again. She edged away from me in the manner of a person with a guilty conscience. I was near her. A complexity of passions tormented me. I wanted to be kind. I wanted to be cruel. I wanted to help. I wanted to hurt. I saw what she was. I knew what she was. But purpose is but the slave to memory, and the very mind that knew that was the mind that wouldn't take heed. She said glumly, "I just want warm weather and birds."

A precarious balance was struck. It was exactly because I was frightened that I could bear this, and yet I knew if this condition increased I would surely go mad. I was walking, in short, on a high ridge, steep down on either side, where the proprieties, as I moved step by step, reduced themselves to my keeping my head. But wasn't she on that height as well? I wondered why at her age she'd go and get entangled again. I thought she was operating on impulse. I loved her too compulsively to acknowledge her responsibility. I believed, still believed with that sort of belief which the fear of a thing engenders, that she loved me. She'd *told* me she loved me! Who picks a person's pocket and then tells him he really should be more careful?

With a complete liar you know where you are, but when a person mixes some truth with her stories you're lost. The galling difficulty was in trying to distinguish what pathetically she'd invented and avoided from the need I projected for her to have to do so. I wanted her to be responsible to me. I saw that a great deal of her calculation had been done on my account. But to me her lies were insulting, and I wanted to catch her in them. I wanted to find out why she was lying and for whom. Like a dog, she was always on the wrong side of the door. Whenever she went to bed with whomever it was, compounding adultery upon adultery, she had to remember each time that the incident had to be translated to me in disguise; it was only a question of time before concealment implied more than mere omission. Sooner or later she'd have to tell the truth, if only to avoid once again tricking herself into the subterfuge by which in sleeping with two men at the same time she could only lose both! And so I thought the only hope was to strengthen her authority, to force her to recognize her responsibility to me.

Farol was a coward, like all terrorists: it was too risky to allow her to experience the feeling of failure, to believe in—and so accept—her own deceit.

As we walked I had to allow her to exult in her own grandeur without risk of her losing face—her authority couldn't be put in danger—and yet at the same time I had to prevent her from believing she was what she was. She'd lived alone before. She said she understood everything she'd now be up against of course and spoke to it, a lot of ponderous gambols around a few elevated ideas, but it was obvious she was lying. I was thinking: *keep your friends close, but keep your enemies closer*. Pretending to believe her, I followed the tactic of "superior objective," retreating to be in a better position to advance and flattering her with a lot of naive and ignorant questions. Valor is not the only thing discretion is the better part of. I tried to emphasize how much I understood her plight, pointing out what anyone living alone had to contend with, using the very words by which she'd so long argued the same. I ran ten possibilities past her of isolation.

But I touched what was without substance and within what was not I was left. She remained true to her falsity, and it took no act of acrobatic reasoning anymore to see I now had to relinquish the slightest claim to represent anything she loved. She repeated she wanted to be alone. She said she ought to have been able to say that long ago. Her lying pronounced emptiness habitable. She projected a vacated site of belief and optimism and became almost enthralled for my benefit speaking of the difficult unknown things awaiting her, things in having to face alone she'd bravely overcome. Mordant gilding. Palette-knife impasto. It was literally a picture of everything she never believed.

She tried to conceal the guile on her face, which alone spoke the truth of the lies she hid. She didn't have the burden of reflection, but her lack of conscience was only a help. She never faltered, and what she was thinking was clear: *no one can disprove me, a person can say anything she wants, I can get away with this!* But it wasn't only lying, it was a disregard for accuracy that positively verged on inspiration, a spate of such nimble deception and so astonishingly representative of all she didn't mean that it was almost as if one half of her was actually in a visible fervor to enlighten the other of the very hoax it perpetrated. Her disappointment fairly burst into song—she became abstract as a way of appearing profound—and then turning to me with perfect seriousness she said in a high-flown voice as if reading aloud, "I know it will be hard for me. There will be difficulties. But where the rewards are enchanting, the dangers are real."

I asked her to repeat that.

"Where the rewards are enchanting," she said, "the dangers are real."

Smiling beatifically, she told me it was a quote from a book I'd once given her.

"Good night," I said upon reaching her porch. And then I said, "I love you." The words were no sooner out than I realized, not so much that I didn't mean them, but that she wasn't worth them. Her spaniel eyes shifted. She hesitated, unsure how to respond. "Thank you," she said. I backed down the stairs and left her standing there.

Thank you. It was her way of trying to be faithful, not to me, but to someone else. But as fidelity wasn't possible for her, I now understood what her first husband knew, and her second, and all the men she'd ever been with. It wasn't so much a small head, but a small mind. And a smaller heart. She had all the characteristics of a dog, except fidelity.

I remember the incessant rain before Easter vacation and the gifts I left at her flat (a turtleneck sweater, bottles of wine, a wooden sculpture I'd made) so that in keeping them without acknowledging them she could have repeated evidence of what she was. But the gifts were not only reminders of her fraud, but my own, for I was literally giving things to keep from killing her, strangling her in her own bed, thus employing a defense to keep at bay the sure promise of prison. And then one morning—she'd waited until the day I was to leave—I woke and found a note growing cold under my door.

> *Please don't make things more difficult for either of us anymore. I need to end our relationship. I apologize for all your heartache and pain. I have learned a lot from you and grown in many ways. We'll call this the last of it.*
>
> *Farol*

Five lines. After three and a half years, five fucking lines. I went to see her that night, bent as I was on appearing as a phantom of her own design. She was immediately mistrustful, and from this sprang a harsh, jerky, and overemphatic manner—she was almost humming for me to be gone. She asked, "You got my letter?"

Led-dear.

"I did," I said in my best manner.

Farol waited a moment. I looked into her eyes, not deep with open passages but showing the surface of a shield. "And I understand. I wish you everything you deserve." It sounded so earnest, she seemed relieved. She had been won over enough that on her face, once slightly dazed, now appeared an expression through which shot a gleam of amusement. Her wistful hug gave a stroke of paradox to her wiliness.

She felt safe, buoyed up by the skill she had of claiming to leave someone for a while without so much as a pang for parting forever. But deceit like love is also a convenience, and because I knew her I now knew one from the other.

"You're wonderful," she said.

I smiled.

No, I'm not.

20

At this point I have a deeper interest to declare. A week before, on the morning following that ponderous walk Farol and I took, I returned to the store where I had bought the radio-cassette-player and made another purchase. Driving back along her street to be sure she'd gone to work—I saw her cat outside alone—I pulled over. I had dramatized the spectacular contrition I felt, made my pleas, but now that was over. The verdict of not guilty does not mean innocent, it means not proven. Her abstractions had grown perilous, her moves indistinct, but that vagueness in relation to me which working in my favor made her responsible for omitting a certain precaution now gave me a distinct advantage over her.

Farol never locked the door to her flat. I hadn't forgotten her walking into my house on the Cape and spying from room to room when I wasn't there. And so I walked into hers. It was dark as a crypt inside. The rooms were crowded and messy, and the kitchen sink, stained and miniature, was filled with dirty dishes. The low bed was still unmade. An empty box for Chinese food lay open on the floor. And on the mantel sat a card on which the sententious slogan she'd quoted me that night was written out in her cuboidal hand. But the rewards weren't enchanting for me, and the danger no longer mattered. There was only a riddle to solve. I wanted a figure.

I quickly called the telephone company and, using Farol's androgynous name, inquired with a view to straightening out my own records when the phone had been installed. I waited a moment, then was told January 13. Figuring service would have taken a week or so longer, I looked at a desk calendar. She'd been as double-faced as the month! It was like a frost-clear bell. The whole enterprise with her lover, despite the appearance she wanted to give of being alone, was as premeditated as her lies had to be with me. She had to be sure of him before she cut me away! I rifled through her desk for a letter, an address, a name, but there was nothing but the dark thought that became my advice to myself. Tease a fasciculus into its fibers. Tease a fiber into fibrils. A fibril requires a microscope. Tease a fibril into micelles. What's left is the filament. Find that.

I set to the task at hand. I quickly unscrewed the phone, popped the disk, and wired in the pezio transmitter I'd bought, a micro-miniature transducer no bigger than a cough drop, balancing the instrument and checking for extra weight. I then found a perfect spot in a corner behind her bed for the FM receiver, which, taking the signal the second she picked up the phone, would reduce it by a heterodyne circuit—not perfect quality, but it would throw—and retransmit it to my house less than a mile away.

What's virtue in man can't be vice in a cat, right? Two magicians were at work. She'd perfected sleight of hand. The French Drop. Nice. But so had I. The Boston Box. Nicer.

But then I did nothing. I immediately went to the Cape and stayed there. Everything had been set to intercept her, but my resolve to go through with it still hadn't hardened. I hadn't even bought a receiver yet. Was it to convince myself I didn't want to go through with it? That in not having done so I yet had a chance? That I still cared? To tell the truth, I wished I were no longer alive. I can't even put words to the depression I felt, ringed around by meaninglessness, as I was, and forbidden even the death of the darkness that surrounded me.

While everything seemed buried in the sleep I yearned for that wouldn't come, I felt a fear that wanted even coherent thought. Dread has no object. Dread is precisely the fear of the unknown, the unknown possible, the fear not only of what can be but of what one can become.

I was lonely, but not alone. When someone leaves you it's not that there's nothing there—something was there and then it's gone. Minus two is the *opposite* of two. A flat shadow was cast, but nothing stood above it.

And while there was something of haunting emptiness in the
clanking buoys, the faraway foghorns late at night, that told the unforgiving truth, I still hoped in the same way she had, for it's the blind
above all who embellish their dreams, and I was just like her. I stayed
on for three or four days, my fitful sleep broken at nightmarish intervals
only by a ringing phone—but every time I picked it up there was only a
click. I'd fall asleep only to hear the phone ring again and again. I woke
each time in cold terror, and I was soon awakened by the pounding of
my heart.

I began to feel serious evidence in those calls where no one spoke
of coldly brilliant malevolent intelligences of who knew what origin,
advanced psi powers, a sort of distillate and concentration of the col-
lective unconscious, grown free-floating, of all human fear, anger, and
hatred.

Only one time did I ever hear a voice—it was Dr. Varion, who asking for my social security number wanted to be paid. The rest of the
calls were clearly Farol's, calling—to assure herself for her peace of
mind I wasn't in St. Ives—and then saying nothing and hanging up.

I became the watchman in the night. Day and night represented no
more than segments in the overall cycle of my interminable fatigue. I
felt I was no more than the vehicle of its functions and sensations, but
in that feverish interval I spent alone I began making an estimate of all
her manipulations over the years. It was true, the things you forget are
the very things you should remember. I saw with a sinking heart how
she'd been with me this way always—photos given her she mislaid, gifts
went unthanked, notes unacknowledged. The same thing more bluntly
put, and irrefutable in the light of her deceit, acknowledged the criminal means by which, making me less a fool than an accomplice, she was
never anything more. In a sense we deserve the person we need. I suddenly saw her silence upon returning from the Christmas trip meant she
had a secret, and her silence was her guilt. It was clear she couldn't have
said anything to me she could be frank about that didn't involve the lie
that she wanted to be with me, and so she was silent to avoid talking in
order to avoid lying while blaming me for asking her to communicate
the very things, to save herself, she couldn't. She'd already been to bed
by then with whomever she was fucking. And maybe long before.

It dawned on me that if, as it's often said, a criminal often holds
his or her family responsible for what she has or hasn't become, the legacy was clear. Since she couldn't prevent my coming to New York, as
clearly she had tried, I'd been, as it were, contracted out to her family

on that trip, linked in a conspiracy, in the same way I had been with her husband. She didn't want to see how I'd respond to them or how they'd respond to me, she simply wanted me to witness what they had done to her in order to defend what she was about to do to me.

I'd calumniated myself for her to save face all these years until she didn't need me anymore. But I wasn't merely a witness to her infidelity. I *was* her infidelity, a co-partner who in seeing her lie and cheat and steal had become a living reproach to her. Water returns to the idea of water. I think she took the measure of all she was and thought: *if he's satisfied with me—with that—he's not much better than I am.* The consequence was that I had to go. It was revealing that no one had ever left her before, that it was she who'd always been in a position of leaving. It had nothing to do with courage, only cunning. She was a passenger. And her game was sex golf. She had left Lloyd to be with John and left John to be with me and left me to be with whatever man was in the middle now. It was hard to keep remembering that not for an instant had she ceased to practice the actor's gift, a shadow dressed up to deceive, canceling me and her husband out only by finding someone else. Her method was simple. She began to revenge herself on one man the moment she laid eyes on another.

There burnt in me a rage for all I wasn't told, I hated her so badly, felt such overwhelming anger at being so manipulated and postponed that I leapt up in the black gloom and madly wrote a letter to her husband asking to meet with him. I suddenly realized it was a letter filled with the kind of questions which, when asked, only become answers, like the tormented echoes out of the same silence he himself had come to know—always I was (as he) at the center of two images, the identity of another man—and yet as I wrote I remembered more upon reflection than if I had it all before me at the moment.

I saw with horror her remorse had only been for the riddle of what to do with me. It was my humiliation to see that all along I'd believed she loved me only because I had loved her. Her life was only a mirage, a miracle of my own making, of my own mind! In the sum of the parts, there are only the parts. The world must be measured by eye. And to punish me for my contempt for facts, fate made me look at them in the fire storm I suddenly heard of all her criticism. My shoes! My eyeglasses! My long hair! The very street where I lived! And then suddenly a telephone there in her room! Isolated details went off like bombs. It was all part of the ingenious cowardice by which she tramped forward to tell the truth by lies, the vilest of which, I finally saw, was not her single refusal to make love that time—"They'll hear us down-stairs"—but rather her having done it so often all along to allay my sus-picions. Everything, *everything,* had been doctored to fit the present re-quirements of what was then the future! And I suddenly recognized everything I should have known. It's in the first anatomy lesson. The heart is a hollow muscle.

I had failed to understand the value of whatever Farol said could never be determined by one who listened that didn't also know her. But know her how? The liar cannot only be as comfortable as anyone who tells the truth, provided she keeps on lying, but can actually proceed as though she were honest, whereas it's the honest person who in having to remember the truth becomes miserable once he begins to lie. And yet all along her deception was my desire, and I encouraged her deceit by believing it. I not only feared her lies but saw I had never been able to question her without shattering the basis of my future with her.

But the future was now a fiction. I concentrated no longer on the will to believe but rather on the wish to find out, which is the exact op-posite. I knew that she had already told me too many lies to be with me any longer. But what else did I know? Anything? Anything at all? I jumped into my car, posted the letter to John Colorado, and kept on driving. Faith is air; facts are iron. And now I wanted the truth.

21

I crossed the Sagamore Bridge. I drove through the rain with a red riding-light in my eyes, and it seemed but an instant before I was stand-ing once again in front of that raw gray house which, closed to me, only loomed in the dark like only another secret. I went upstairs through the echoing desolation and knocked several times. Farol answered the door, after her surprise, with a look of open exasperation, and I immediately felt the current of ill will.

"Nobody listens to me," she said, almost stamping with uncon-cealed fury. "I'm tired of this. I'm tired of people banging on my door."

"You mean me."

"Yes," she said directly.

Walking indignantly to the far room, she began to descant on the futility of never being believed and said I should now call her first before I came over. Her voice was correct and malicious, and the anger that gave a twist of meanness to her face made her look homely. I saw the tension in her narrow nates as she turned and quickly took the telephone receiver off the hook. I said there was something I had to ask her—I put the receiver back—and waited until the glare that answered mine had passed its paroxysm and come to a conquered pause. "You've been lying to me all along," I said. "Haven't you?"

She tightened defiantly.

"Haven't you?"

And then she became frosted with self-respect. She turned away to begin again one of her absorbed revolutions, but I stopped her.

"You told me you loved me. You said you'd never give up. At Thanksgiving you told me I was your family. 'I'll always be with you,' you said." She looked away, her lips pursed and white. "You have a very easy conscience in such matters, it seems." Her attempt at laughter—stress release—was hollow. "I want to know why. I've never lied to you."

She swiveled around, her eyes flashing, and bitterly said, *"You've led me to believe—"*

She stopped.

"What? Say it." It was as if she suddenly discovered in her mouth, between her teeth, a lie she couldn't utter. "That I want to be with you?" I paused, waiting for the echo to evaporate.

"That I love you?" I clutched her sleeve, felt emptiness. "Why else am I here? Why have I come? And waited all this time? This long?" I felt silent cries come tearing their way up out of the very ground of my being. All I wanted was her to acknowledge what I yearned to forgive, for even love when tested in the extreme carries more than a measure of forgiveness, but she was determined to say nothing. She was fish-cold. Her sigh, like her art, was manufacture, not creation.

Her cat rubbed along her leg, and she bent over and made a kisslike whistle. I could see she was waiting all this out, aloof, unconcerned, inert.

It was an indifference I found too much to bear.

"You've been seeing someone else," I shouted. Farol gave me a look of open and terrible disclosure and then her face seemed to constrict. She straightened up, and her eyes went unnaturally still. But who cuts is easily wounded, and the readier you are to offend, the sooner you are offended. "Don't pretend to be shocked. That's too cheap a defense."

Disturbo. I *hated* her.

"And don't lie," I warned her menacingly. Fear made my voice thrash. "There's another man."

She stood stonily silent, matching my stare, her eyes suddenly withdrawn and opaque. Although she'd relinquished the whole game of being partners with me, her control was acquired habit, and still she couldn't forgo the pretension she'd given out of needing solitude.

It was almost as if I had to remind her she was lying through her teeth, for the gray but feigned stupidity of her face did not change as I drew near.

"But it's not the man at the garage," I said.

The weightless paw of a shadow descended on her as, backing up, she looked suddenly smaller. She seemed to wonder why she couldn't speak, why two kinds of speech wedged in her throat as if the two were strangling each other. I heard a loud braying echo from the past—*the best revenge is success*—and drew a breath of pain.

There's a fear that is a kind of exhalation, the hiccuping horror of one about to be executed whose eyes shine with the terrible thrill of finality.

"It's a doctor, isn't it?" She suddenly changed color, and the blood drained from her face in seconds. "Someone from the hospital."

Farol's face went white as a miller's, and she couldn't for a moment flutter out of the question by a premature scare. I seized her arm. She paused, virtually immobilized, lowering her head.

"*Tell me the truth!*" I screamed.

But her consternation hadn't been given enough time to produce the right effect, and she could only be herself.

She looked at me sidelong.

And then she nodded.

22

Scalded with fright, I dropped to the edge of the sofa. I thought I'd been prepared for it, but I wasn't. I was thunderstruck. I began to tremble. My legs were literally shaking. I had been removed a long distance and heard someone speaking far away, a remote voice from an eternal void involved in a tangle of pale and shuttling elisions making no sense. But there was someone sitting beside me, and I asked, "But why? Why did y-you begin seeing him?"

"I don't know"—she shrugged and tossed her head as if pretending to be disgusted with herself—"I guess you could say I was flattered."

I looked into her face, and at the exact moment that the false bottom dropped out from under me like the trapdoor of a gallows I remembered all I'd forgotten. It was as if in response to the antagonism of a chance tug at her arm I had pulled out her entire soul. But she had no soul. She was always what she was, it was I in my blindness who'd changed. I realized that she had never loved me, that if the largest part of falling in love is believing in the possibility of it, she was even further from love than she was from me, and it was here she showed herself her father's own daughter. To know a truth you also have to recognize a lie, and it was as if I were looking at her for the first time. She couldn't trust, for while trust is the basis of love, she lived merely to survive. Her feelings had been intensified solely by my response to her fantasies, which were only mindless games her repetitive self-absorption played with itself, the would-be publicist of an ignored cause.

Thinking herself in love never failed to flatter her vanity. I saw that for her to deny herself was just as exciting as indulging herself, that to long for a body and then in the end relinquish it gave a twist of drama to her diseased sense of romance. And at last I understood how her belief that happiness was impossible became the strange source of consolation for someone with fishhooks for hands and a hole for a heart who appreciated nothing of what she had, only what was lacking.

She stood there, calmly considering me, like some ruminant with its bovine look of stupid disdain, desperately trying, forcing herself to find explanations pointless in order to save her own skin.

"I know, I know, I should have told you all this before," she said, exhaling irritatedly. "But it's not like it was planned. He was around a lot. Everybody knows him at the hospital." It was a way of talking that tended to preclude discussion, which of course was its intention, but I was unsure in whose favor the dialogue had been resolved, or if it had been resolved at all. As her concern was only for herself, she was angry at my surprise and arrogant in defense of what she'd done. Didn't this happen all the time? Couldn't I understand? "It was very difficult for him to ask me out."

There was a tone of self-congratulation as she spoke, a high imperiousness that showing no softening memory of sorrow proved her incapable of seeing anything more than what she felt she deserved. She had forgotten I had seen her this way with her husband, defending her falsehood while taking advantage of him by blaming him for making her take advantage. It was her way of feeling superior, for the less of a man she made him out to be, the less of a wife she needed to be to respond. Look what he made me do, he deserves me, he allowed me to be the way I am, he didn't deserve any more than I gave and was lucky he got that.

And it was by seeing this in her that I knew she had already blamed me to another for my never accepting her. It had always been the way with her, for somewhere in the deep demented reaches of her ruefully inept but blame-shifting mind the very people who worked hardest to approve her always—astonishingly—*failed* to. And yet, strangely, those she had the least use for always saw her best.

I attempted to control myself, trying as much to breathe as I was to understand.

"Is he married?"

She hesitated. "He—was."

"Divorced?"

She became sniffing and proprietary. "He's separated. His wife asked him to leave last fall."

"And you've been with him"—my throat almost went out of business—"all this time?"

Farol made a fishy inward motion with her mouth and kept shaking her head as if unable to find an answer, a mercy more to herself than to me. I couldn't bring myself to repeat the question. In that moment, however, I realized no one ever kills himself who has not first wanted to kill another.

"But you like him. Don't you?" I bit back the tears, feeling ashamed and humiliated. "You want to be with him?"

She leaned forward, with crossed wrists, coldly weighing, calmly balancing her words, and then a small smile of triumph flickered momentarily over her lips as she looked up at me. "I guess I would have to say"—she sighed—"yesss."

"No, no," I cried, groaning so loudly that she raised a hand in warning. I felt a tearing, ripping sound inside me, and bent over as though from an abdominal operation, my arms pulling tightly around me to hold what was left together. I kept repeating, "Why, why, why?"

Farol suddenly stormed up, her face mottled with anger, and would say nothing more. Insincere herself, she never expected others to be anything else. Suspicion made her alert. She had said too much already. Her cowardice alarmed her, and I think she was afraid of what I might do.

But it's the weak who are cruel. Knowing herself to be a traitor, she read in my eyes the very blame by which through feeble wit she sought to be absolved. Guilt hardened her heart. She shook her head.

"You never accepted me for what I am," she said with soft deadly finality.

I was only staring at her, eyes frozen, and wondering: *what are you?*

But then something happened that shouldn't have. The telephone rang.

Farol's face suddenly had the dead-white look of a clock at the end of a hall, a look that told me everything—we both knew who it was—and the moment of ugly coincidence bleaching her itself became a notifying act in which she glimpsed her divided self. It was the one thing she had all along been trying to prevent. She stiffened, squeezing back an impulse to scream, as the phone kept ringing and ringing and ringing. She didn't know what to do. It was clear she'd been expecting the call, even clearer that she was waiting at home to answer it. She guardedly lifted the receiver, listened a moment, and said she'd call back in five minutes. Chillingly matter-of-fact, she turned to me and folded her arms. Her eyes narrowed with venomous disdain. I had to remember it was this tall, stiff, cold pragmatic bitch who cradled hurt birds and wept at *Bambi* and flinched at the violence of boxing films. Looking at her, I wondered how I'd ever come to love her.

I thought of the lengths she had gone to carry out her elaborate deceit and said, "He must be some guy."

"*What about me?*" she screamed, her face almost purple and reptilian. She advanced her face tomcat-fashion until it was almost touching mine. Her malignity left me faint. "*What about me?*"

I felt the bitterness and gibbering suspicion that lurked in every gesture. There are certain natures that only in times of crisis rise to the

occasion; it's what they know best and alone understand. Farol's whole
history had been one of confrontation, and she was now breathing her
native oxygen. But her fury was mounting, and her eyes had the look of
rapidly eroding self-control. What was terrifying was her hatred of me
for seeing what she was, her aversion proportionate to the lies she'd expected me to believe. But she was intolerable even to herself, and what
I found even more incredible was her terror at the image of her I might
continue to love, *not* what I might come to hate. She shifted her feet
and continued to stare at me. She stood waiting. When would I *go?*

The tension was almost unbearable. But not another word was said
in the strained silence lest anything more come to reach the threshold
of my undeserving conscience.

It was only seconds before the phone rang again. She looked at me,
her face still ashen and pulled shut, her cheeks twitching. But I wouldn't
leave. Alert as a jackal, however, Farol quickly saw how the unthinkable moment could be turned to her advantage—she was as cunning as
she was desperate—and grabbing the phone this time immediately put
the sound of fear in her voice, purposely pretending that she was scared.
There followed a breathless hiatus, beneath which I heard the same
short but pleading whispers to her lover once given to me, as speaking
with muted appeal she imparted what she could, her omissions becoming the very lies by which she fostered faith. But who lies for you will
lie against you.

And I was suddenly awake in her bedroom three years before,
standing in the same darkness, watching the same charade, listening to
the same violations.

I thought she'd panic. She had to prevent me knowing anything of
him, and having told him little if anything about me she had to protect
that. And all the while she had to protect herself, defend herself, transform herself, in fact, upon the instant by some indecipherable and fastidious magic from the pathologically loose commodity of mistress, ex-
wife, and whore into a simple honest woman suddenly in danger. But
this time she was prepared. She began working her voice, pretending to
falter, and struck just the right emotional throat notes where each half-
utterance haunted by broken inflection only served her turn, and yet the
wincing words, the wimicking exaggeration, was all of it the sheerest
hypocrisy, for in the room where we stood she was clearly clocking the
interval, glancing at me once or twice as if stepping back to inspect
what in the process of walking forward she had to be certain she could
afford to lose.

But her maxim was: never lose a chance. And now I saw it employed. What her objectives were at first I wasn't quite sure; then they became clear—she was not only trying to convince her lover she was in the very danger he suspected but protecting herself from showing what she prevented by telling him in so many words what I'd caused. Literally unable to divulge anything that wouldn't also compromise her, she immediately realized what she couldn't say could convey even more to him than she'd hoped—she could act in spaces thin as a minute—and appearing not only helpless but actually threatened began to answer with the guile of jittery equivocation the questions hideously supplied for me by the responses she gave. *Can't you talk?* "No." *Something's wrong— is someone there?* "Yes." *Your next-door neighbor, quick, what's their phone number?* "I can't remember." *Give me their name! Hurry! Their name!*

Again she looked at me. It *was* a kind of panic. She was trying to get the job! But swift and ready and resolute, she caught the flying opportunity—I'd given her just what she wanted—and in the course of a single moment that instantly won his favor by acquiring his protection was able to communicate in the perfect innocence she feigned an image of vulnerability as frail as the quaver in her voice as she spelled out, "G-u-m-p-l-o-w-i-t-z."

And this time her look, cutting into my soul, told me all: I promise until I don't, I wait until I won't, I love you until I don't. She was becoming almost minute by minute a mistress of shades.

I once thought the word *dumfounded* was a bit of poetic license, but standing there, my voice failed me. I had to look twice at her who seemed not there, who seemed as incompatible as cruelty and compassion, a specter not a shape, not a shape but only a shadow or substance of a sort, yet each seemed either as I blinked and saw the unsubmissive ghost of what I loved fade in the very air I breathed.

She was there only in her emptiness, a being scarcely human parting forever with even the very worst of what I knew of her. I gazed at her with the intensity of one who does not dare believe the validity of what he sees. And disbelieving I backed slowly into the dim hallway, walked downstairs—Ruth Gumplowitz came rushing past me at the door—and stumbled blindly into the night.

23

I found myself almost unconscious driving through a lowering February fog, circling the wet night roads of St. Ives, wondering how something that was almost nothing retained enough being to feel the anguish of its own nothingness. The person who robbed me of what I loved was the person I loved and who taking it away left me to die impaled on promises unfulfilled, questions unanswered. I don't know how long a period elapsed before, long past midnight, I became aware of standing dripping wet in a phone booth and speaking almost incoherently to someone who under the circumstances had to be the most unlikely person on earth. The illogical became the logical. It was absurd. But I had absolutely nowhere else to turn.

While the betrayal was complete, I felt cursed to know more, and yet it was a measure of the shallowness of my life with Farol that after all these years there wasn't a single soul we shared as a friend.

"Well, well, well," came the voice from the obscure doorway. I was met in the darkness and let into a hallway by a woman pleased less by a knowledge exclusively hers than by the irony of my sudden dependence on her to have it. "So Farol's finally told you."

Maxine Scrulock's house sat on a dark hill. I almost hadn't been able to find it in my confusion and despair. The road was poorly lit and seemed only part of the continuing trail of wrongs unwinding before me that led so inexorably to the reaches of that suburban dead-end street. I saw she had been asleep, her nose was shiny, and the nightgown she wore looked like four sides of a house. She stood smiling at me for a moment and then excused herself, but not before pausing on an upstairs landing to add, "And now you want my advice, is that it?" Her laughter ceased with a slamming door and the sound of a loud flushing toilet.

I sat down, exhausted and weak from not having eaten anything substantial for almost a week. It was a small living room, crudely paneled in pine, that ran around to a kitchen of exposed brick hung about with antique cooking tools and utensils. A cheap reproduction on the wall depicted an alpine torrent with a fallen tree across it, and the polar-white shag rug looked feral and faintly obscene. There was a gift-shop fussiness to the room. A maple hutch held lots of flatware, stemware, tableware, leisureware, and barware. The whole place, full of collect-ibles, was a selfish and acquisitive person's, with the same figures, fig-urines, prints, and paraphernalia from the gallery I'd seen in so many other houses. I leaned back and closed my eyes.

And then I heard someone come thumping downstairs with the tread of a grenadier. "My advice is"—Scrulock breezed into the kitchen on one side and reentered through the other with a bottle of wine—"forget it."

She had disappeared to put on some makeup and returned, losing ten years in the process but somehow looking worse. Her eyes were buffed ice-blue, and her mouth like a thumbhole ringed in sealing-wax scarlet gave her face the look of a used palette. She poured two drinks and handed me one. She took out a cigarette and flopped into a chair. The jeans she had put on bunched her flanks into sausagey rolls and made her look spinnaker-fat.

"Let me tell you what I told Farol, okay? Why get involved with anyone—why bother?" she asked, gulping her drink. She sat back satis-fied, wobble-headedly surveying the contents of the room, and mentioned her ex-husband. I had of course heard every detail of this story a hun-dred times from Farol, who had repeated it to me often enough to make it a saga. Scrulock's husband had divorced her almost immediately after they were married but left her enough money, she felt, to outweigh her lack of charm. Now she was alone. Her collecting instinct was of the kind that often compensated as a friend in certain lonely people. But acquisitive people are never grateful, and because she was deeply bitter, I knew this could only help me. "I spent five weeks facedown on the bed when that B for bastard left me, okay? Never again," she said. "No sir. For-*get* it! But you won't listen," she snorted, "no one does. Farol didn't. You want to know why?"

She pulled a huge cheap onyx ashtray onto her lap and lit her cigarette.

"Ask me." She was enjoying this. "Go on."

I was betrayed into having to seem effectively kind. I was as hard as nails, as keen for the bitter truth as formerly I had been for illusion. But immediately I saw I had to beget a temperance and make seem at least casual, if not offhand, every point of inquiry to shake from this simpleton's head the facts I needed to know.

"Why?"

"Simple." She snapped her lighter and sat back, eyeing me with a look of unsleeping guile. "Farol has to sleep with men. I could have told you this a long time ago. She has to have someone in her life. She needs men."

I saw my chance. "Like—this doctor?"

She breathed smoke at me.

"You said it, not me."

But I was thinking: *would a doctor be with her if she were ill? What if she hadn't told him? But wouldn't he know? Or find out?* Then I thought maybe she was with him precisely because he *was* a doctor.

"When did she meet him? Not before Christmas." I looked at her. "Or was it?"

Coyness didn't go with her jutting chin. "I don't think you're going to like the answer," she said.

"I don't like the question."

I moved forward.

"Was—was it last *fall?*"

There was a male's growl of satisfaction in her scratchy laugh as she cleared her throat of phlegm and with flabby arms that looked like they'd been made out of Neufchâtel pounded out her cigarette. She shook her head and sat back smiling with her hands in her lap fitted together at the fingertips exercising malicious no-comment.

I tried to be calm. "What's his name?"

It's not important. It doesn't matter in the least. But still you ask it.

Scrulock plucked a chin hair and with a shrewd and pawky eye gave me this closet smile. By hinting at nothing, or by at least trying not to, by enacting the prudent and unclamorous part, I almost had to bite off my tongue. I could see she was watchful. Ugly women are very clever at knowing what it is you really want from them. And she was no exception. She was *the* no exception. But I could wait.

"Is he handsome?"

"No," she said. "He's tall, and humpily muscular with sunken eyes." She said he liked boats and had gone to some third-rate college in Connecticut and that according to Farol his wife had asked him to leave. She shrugged. "He's heavy. Big in a, oh, lumberman's grunty way."

A trace of mirth glimmered in her eyes—I saw she was dying to talk—and she polished off her drink. "He wears a toupee, all right? But that's it. That's as far as I go." Of course I knew she'd go much further. The bale was open, and the cast would fly. She smiled hideously, jiggling her shoe, and sang out like a doorbell, "Someone's *jea*-lous."

I admitted to it. She said she pitied me. I quickly took that measurement. Going on the premise that the enemy of my enemy was my friend, I told her how much I loved Farol—to beguile the time, look like the time—and by praising her inordinately depended with a kind of juxtaposed psychology on drawing out of this overcosmeticized, middle-aged trot the deeper resentment I not only knew was there but felt she couldn't disguise. The meditative route is sinuous, not so the active. A cynic's heart is always blacker than its tongue. I poured her another drink.

"But she's in love with him, isn't she?"

Scrulock sneered.

"How could she be in love with him—she's only been out with him, what, nine or ten times?" *Nine or ten times!* A great wave of anger swept over me. The facts seemed to come like my own malice, my own disbelief.

"He comes to the gallery?" I asked.

She lit another cigarette, snapped her lighter shut, blew a puff of smoke at the ceiling, and said, "When he can." She pulled a flake of tobacco off her tongue. "But, face it, he's a busy man. He has his practice. His kids—"

"He has children?"

"Three." She burped. "School age. One's only six. Now you see what I mean."

I listened with anticipatory horror. My thoughts were scurrying to and fro in an effort to take stock of the situation. A multiple divorcée? Who disliked children? And perhaps now to become stepmother to a surrogate family like one of the prep-school parents she once so merrily mocked?

Scrulock was an envious woman. The more she drank the more I hoped she'd divulge. She was smoking like a train, her face becoming fire-flushed, and her hair looked as though she'd mopped it around in a barrel. She kept asking what more I wanted. I thought: *keep talking, butter mountain.* But all I got for the next half-hour was a laughingly irresponsible account of her own misfortunes. I had to listen, of course. We didn't talk. It wasn't conversation, only the pertinaciously stupid monologue once again of another hard-sell, disgust-effecting careerist who thought life unfair, women ill-used, and men unnecessary in every particular, including one in which until her revelation I'd always believed the male had been employed at least as intermediary seminiferent.

Nothing could change her mind, though I tried to speak—and steer her back to—Farol and the inconsistency between the two of them of what each deserved in relation to what both wanted. Still I regulated my deportment and put off the features of my genuine face, allowing myself to be joked with mummying tact into adopting a mask of civility to make genteel use of my foe. Scrulock's aggressiveness gave me an advantage, I knew that, but I had blundered in drawing a parallel between them even if it was to suggest a difference.

"I get nothing free," she grumbled. "Where did you get that from, that son of a bitch Neil Ringspotz, whom you've always seemed to find so fascinating? I can't bear fools."

Odd, I thought, your mother apparently could.

"Look, I work with Farol," said Scrulock, temporizing. "She's a friend—and a survivor. I know her, I talk to her, I give her advice, I see her every day, and I don't intend to run her down, all right?" It was interesting. When she was acrid and fulfilled the promise of her face, she was not so appalling as when she became velvety and concerned. I thought I had blown it, that the drink had made her maudlin, but I was wrong.

"But let's face it, she's sick," said Scrulock. "She's a man-killer. You know it, I know it. Everybody does." I was waiting for this. I knew those smiles meant to communicate she could understand Farol's situation as only a woman could were false as hell. Farol's way with men was henbane to Scrulock, and nothing would change that. "Take this doctor." "What's his name?" I asked, but ignoring me she transferred the cigarette to her mouth and its red tip bounced as she spoke. "I remember the first time he came by the gallery Ruth and I both looked at each other and thought, 'This guy has no idea what he's in for!'" Ashes were dropping into her lap. "But it's been like that with all of them. He's no different from the others."

A silence. It was like a degenerate parody of confession. I leaned forward.

"The—others?"

"You. Ted. Same with John," said Scrulock. "Her husband was no different." I thought my heart had struck its last sound.

"Ted?" I gasped.

The stranger she said all this time she'd known but a slanting *minute?*

Scrulock dismissively waved her hand. "Farol couldn't make up her mind the whole summer about that guy. It was ridiculous. Happy one week, down the next. It was just a physical thing anyway, so what does it matter anyway." She stuffed out the cigarette. "But now that you mention it, she often spoke of another guy in Maine." I felt suddenly nauseous. I asked if I could use her bathroom. I was dazed. And yet why after so much time had all this come as such a surprise? The bathroom with its bottles and lotions, while merely another example of this person who pampered herself in such a superficial and self-deceiving way, only reminded me of my own vanity. I thought of Scrulock standing before these mirrors, looking at her own awful face. It reflected my own presumption. I leaned over the hopper and threw up.

When I returned Scrulock continued talking—she had her feet up and was still drinking and smoking—and casually told me of the days Farol and Ted spent together playing golf and swimming. I closed my eyes, though the more the mind takes in, the more it has room for. And the unimaginable now edged toward the routine. I was looking into a basket of adders.

"And then there was that Ernie jerk. The guy with red hair—what's his face?—from the delicatessen. Talk about a creep!"

There are shades of color in black itself.

For a moment I couldn't speak. My tongue and lips felt baked. I felt ripped with shame and humiliation. "I knew she went out with him," I dissembled.

I wanted to scream. Trust itself blasphemed. She'd gone from man to man like a monkey swinging on ropes!

"But that was all over before it began," I said. I tried to control myself. "Wasn't it?"

"That's my point," said Scrulock, shrugging. "It's always been that way. She'll leave this doctor, too, so what else is new?" Again I asked his name, but she only leaned back and stared at me. As she relaxed, a wimple of flesh folded under her chin. I couldn't bear to look at her anymore. I stood up to leave. She felt suddenly superstitious. "I don't care, I wish her luck," said Scrulock, lying. She rose and seemed to swell to double her natural bulk; her hair bristled—one could almost imagine a sound of crackling sparks. "And that's where we come in at the gallery." She blocked my way. "Something you never understood," she said with a nasal drawl like nylon ripping, "something men can't. She needs *us*." The Mares of Glaucous. Lear's spaniels. They were never more or less than what they were. But Farol—she wasn't worthy of the energy required to form the words that sentenced her.

I withheld my rage with a effort that whitened my gills and gave my voice the refined attrition of a file.

"What's the doctor's name?"

But the secret stayed clenched in her teeth. She folded her arms and fixed me with a hateful smile that said: *you get nothing more.*

I felt lost driving back in the weirdest way. The black windy night gave me a feeling, with no one else on the roads, of unrelieved indirection. Shadows of torn clouds raced one another across the sky, and the forests I passed, dark and silent, appeared like armies of the dead frozen upright in a last stand against the ruthless night. I heard in the distance the sound of a clock striking some unknown hour. Turning slowly down her street, I saw Farol's car was gone. I knew it would be. There was no doubt anymore where she was. But that was no longer enough. I pulled over. Much will have more.

I got out of my car. I opened the front door of the house—it was too late to care, too late for everything—and walking upstairs to her flat flipped on the light. I looked on the table—it couldn't have gone smoother if I had planned it that way—and found an envelope lying there that had already been opened. There is nothing more incriminating than a telephone bill. I studied it. Farol's charges for the month of January alone were $220.46, *excluding* all collect calls, which most of them were, and every call made to the same number. I wrote the number down, then quickly dialed it. A man's voice answered. And I hung up and thought: *snap.*

I checked to make sure the bug in the instrument was still there. But nothing had been touched. The transmitter behind her bed hadn't been moved. The only thing left for me to do now was get some kind of receiver, even a radio would do, and wait in my house to listen. I stood in the room, trying to organize my thoughts, wondering just where to begin, and then I knew. It was late, but I didn't care. I picked up the phone and called Derek Schreiner.

"Do you have a beeper?" I asked.

It took him a moment to find his voice, groggy with sleep.

"Come over," he said. "I have more than that."

24

Clouds rising gray in the east left the sky damp and vapor-smoked by the time I got to Boston. It was bitter early morning winter weather, and the streets of the city were empty. Dawn was still hours away, and no one was stirring, no one was up. Derek was waiting for me when I arrived. I looked ragged and in a hampered state and apologized, quickly filling him in about the bugging—why I needed the beeper— and of Farol's involvement with this doctor. "Another doctor," he said, but wasn't surprised. He said she wanted money. But I'd been thinking about that and, in trying to be responsible for both of us, aimed for a different perspective.

"Wouldn't she specifically *choose* a doctor," I asked, "the cure itself a symptom only confirming what her sickness hinted at?" Derek said nothing.

"Isn't she ill?" I prodded. "Mightn't she in her illness be guilty of the act but unconscious of the crime?"

I felt his silence. There was something that glimmered out of his look that in the perception of my distress made him pause as if before committing himself to some matter put before him he yet hesitated directly to touch. He only shook his head and said, "Her pills. Several are for depression. Elavil. Haldol. The rest are only coated tablets with fancy names. Surbex, Zypan, all very impressive. Derifil, which contains chlorophyll, is used to control fecal odors for people who smell. Movicol, Vicon-C, Disophal. Decongestants. Antiflatulents. Placebos," he said. "Candy."

And then he handed me the medical report.

There's a final desolation where the soul can see what it suffers only in the consummation of that fire that blackens all it burns, though bright itself and of the richest color, discoloring all it touches and feeds upon. All that had been inexplicably mysterious to me, all that had been explicably familiar—reciprocally matching—now coincided in one incapacitating testimony.

Farol never had the disease. I had long known that whatever had gone wrong with her—she'd often told me so—occurred during a period of doubt with her husband. A second marriage had been failing for both of them. She confessed she had refused to support and encourage him, though he'd asked her to, and began secretly planning to leave him before he left her. What she willed, however, her weakness called back in subconscious repulsion of an act even she herself couldn't completely perform. Apprehending the good, she was powerless to be it. Loyalty was impossible for her. She envied what she couldn't become and hated what she was. There is a specific neurosis where certain people, caught in a dilemma of unassimilable escape, experience illness rather than guilt. Conscience may make criminals of us, but it also makes us victims. Whatever's done in secret divulges to us exactly what we'd hide. It wasn't true that nobody was watching—*she herself* was. And as a consequence of all she'd do but didn't dare she became incapacitated for a time. Her legs stiffened, her gait became unsteady.

Clearly, her own *body* became her conscience. She knew, or some mysterious part of her subconscious knew, that if she couldn't walk she couldn't leave her husband. She misexpressed anger by temporarily crippling herself, a physiological mechanism of evasion that was literally self-prevention and bound up in an almost procedural intimacy with her failures with men. It was as if by some exercise of the divided self she were physically put in coventry by the same scheming mind that, filled with insatiable doubt, tried to shirk the deceit it nevertheless conceived to live by. And live by it she did. You can't lie to your subconscious. But you can lie to people.

She claimed to have MS. She infinitely preferred between the two to seem physically rather than mentally ill, for there was too much opprobrium in the latter. It was easier to confess to a physical illness than admit to the psychological humiliation of what indeed many people suffer from who are either not getting attention from others, or not bestowing it, and what it was in fact she had: specific abulia—*hysterical paralysis*. And this she overcame after three months by nothing less than the regimented intensity of finally coming to accept herself less for what she was than what, after two feeble attempts at marriage to prove otherwise, she knew she could no longer deny. She was an unfaithful wife. It was her lies that became her recuperation, not renewed health. Choosing what seemed a lesser evil created an even greater one. The recognition that restored her bodily function also twisted her mind and condemned her to a life of almost inconceivable manipulation. And it was there in her deeply muddled misassertions that her imposture finally began.

She proceeded to invent herself. What she desperately wanted, but never was granted, was recognition for herself on her own merits. A deep cynicism preventing this, not from being given, but rather from being accepted made up the central paradox of her life. Her illness, in essence, was that despair, and it left her spiteful and maimed, sicker by far in not being ill than otherwise. She despaired of herself very early because she knew she'd been unfaithful to life and to being and could no longer trust anyone to countenance the infidelity she could only perpetrate by being what she was. It was this beyond all else she could never forgive. And so with one eye open she lay prostrate for a while, her mind computing and calculating, until out of the quagmire of disgust and impotence stored in some central fund she called a heart she at last found a way to distinguish herself. She realized she could convert her mysterious illness into *strength*. And it was at the precise moment of conceiving this that with knife-straight blond hair swinging, her eyes glittering like warfires, she rose to redress all those wrongs that for so long had rankled within.

A plot formed. The mundane and the advantageous she calmly identified. At last something could be done, and it became the perfect solution for her: I am not well, I am ill, *I have an incurable disease.*

She recovered quickly. But it wasn't enough. As her hideous self-image was inconsistent with the return of her physical health, she decided not only to have reality imitate art but in a cunning attempt at secondary gain render herself flawed for congruence. Setting aside one face, she put on another, a pasteboard mask from the mouthhole of which her malicious double quacked its notes of misery and death to anyone who'd listen. It was her way of saying understand me, help me, pity me. Before all else it was saying *believe me!* And who could not, for the gravity of the way she chose? Illness was almost synonymous with death and to suffer one was often to experience the proximity of the other. But hers was much more than routine deceit, for although by being "ill" she had rendered herself powerless to execute the violence of leaving her husband, she could begin at the same time to hold those around her in bondage. Her illness became in the most damning way her salvation.

It explained her failures. It prevented enemies. It also absolved faults, justified her ambition, and all the while prevented intrusion— what she didn't need, couldn't use, had no longer the taste for. It had more advantages as a device than advantage could devise. It permitted excess, it excused irresponsibility, and best of all it explained her lack of accomplishments.

Nothing couldn't be forgiven by anything it fooled. It was a curriculum that gave her privileges, attention, method, authority, courage, romance, and even a sense of renunciation. It allowed indefiniteness. It won her pity. It even served to save her from having the baby she either feared having or didn't want. It was more than anything picturesque—the beautiful woman ill!—extending her circle, inviting prodigious solicitude, fostering inquiry, and creating an incessant longing in people to minister to her necessities. And that was the final turn of the screw. A disease. A doctor. A disease. The doctor was proof, not that she had the disease, but that she didn't have it. And in an instant it all became clear.

A psychopath can show uncommon discretion. Subtle depravity has everything to hide. There appeared nothing whatsoever of the brute in Farol. She didn't seek to avoid contrary impulses, she *used* them. The mask of illness, until she didn't need it anymore, served her turn to the degree that it gave irony meaning, for the more she tried to hide, the braver she seemed, the less she revealed, only the more noble she appeared. It gave her not only dimension and ruth, but almost an intelligence, becoming her sensitivity and making her actually seem good in her own eyes, for she hoped to instill in others the misassumption she herself came to believe that if you're sick you're also human. It was a scheme tight as wallpaper, an insidious caprice that could continually incorporate, contemplate, transform, and combat the smallest charge made against it. It was perfect. Every imperfection suited every lie.

What was clear she made puzzling, what was obvious confused. She wove words about life and then made life conform to what she declared of it, not by cleverness, but with the kind of imbecile cunning that alone can focus on what it looks at only by what else it never considers. She was her own nightmare, and it was almost as if her skill as a hospital therapist had been acquired solely by the absorbed observation of her own symptoms. She saw others watch her own funeral while gloating over the fact that she was still alive. She shone solemnly, she crowed, she spouted water, she roused up her dogs. Her lack of discrimination was accompanied, all the while, by a tenacity that might have been a quality had she any character. But she was characterless, and utterly shallow.

But was this a hindrance? Not at all. Again the handicap became the crutch. It let her play any part, wear any mask, assume any role— fill anyone's shoes—and win the belief she belied. She'd been an exquisite picture of health every minute I'd known her. Not a hobble or a blink or the shadow of a shiver. I'd often read by her eyeglasses, she by mine, and yet focal problems were among the first symptoms of the dread disease she claimed she had! I realized that while I never saw what was there, she always presented what wasn't. She was a chronic failure who, making her way through life at top speed, at the same time seemed straight only by dodges and hid by being obvious. Skepticism was her faith. She wouldn't trust anything she couldn't tap, jiggle, bite, or take away from someone. She suspected everyone she knew and lived only to see it proved. It is true, there is a time for fools to come forth, when only bandits can be kings.

And yet her misery was she also mistrusted herself. It was inevitable. Success meant defeat, and by nothing more than keeping up this pretense was she snared in a trap of almost Jacobean reversal, for while emotionally prodigal she was also bound up in the tactic of deprivation itself. She was a romantic ghoul, and her embrace became the perfect disguise, hiding in the grip behind you those hands like pawls tightened to lose nothing of all she hoped to acquire. But her misshapen soul had also hatched in her heart the sin of envy. She had pretensions to art; the more insecure a person is, however, the closer she has to keep to her personality. No real artist however can take such confinement. If he learns to do so, his creations only suffer in kind. And the final retribution was that even someone as hammer-hearted as she could suffer depression and have to be treated for it. She was determined to survive, but she sought control, not communion, choosing what she couldn't imagine to test what she couldn't be, a transaction so demented that it was virtually impossible to determine at what point illusion and disillusion, so inextricably mixed, met in that neutral mind.

And that was the sickest of all. For in what was surely the frankest acknowledgment possible of complete moral insolvency, she tried to appropriate by lies in a final fervent misspelling and mispronouncing indecency what, in the possession that she might save face, she had to call love.

But she *couldn't* love—it reminded her precisely of what she couldn't give to get. She had to be loved to acknowledge all she was not and so, winning lovers, was able to dismiss them for showing her so: a self-contained revenge. Seeking her fortune rather than awaiting it, she had to take every possible chance. But when each opportunity arose, which everywhere she sought to engender, she lived to betray what she feared to love and opted to have what she hoped to own. You do what you are. And yet the very thing she was she at the very same time used this incurable illness to deny!

It almost defied adult definition. It was insupportable, the most high-piping accent of despair I could possibly conceive. Anything more deranged, anything more lunatic I'd never known in the long list of human contrivance, and yet it was a lunacy with which cold cunning had more than a passing acquaintance. It was viper-colored and detestable and punctilious. It cheated. It hoarded. It tortured and destroyed and blasphemed. It defied the very rules of life, and only in the dark glass of correspondence by which it *might* happen could the injustice of such a complacence be jarred.

But there, there, for in her sadism, in her instinctive craving to violate, in her casual and unapologetic cruelty, in her self-mutilation and eviscerating envy that very sentence by some ultimate and preposterous masterstroke or irony had already been meted out.

The woman was truly diseased.

25

My immediate thought was to kill her. I could forgive her hating me, but what I was unable to forgive was her making me hate her. And I hated her to the soul. She had hurt so many others I thought she should be stopped, terminated, put down like a rabid dog. I longed for the chance to see her one more time, to confront her in one exterminating moment after finding out all she was with everything she wasn't, and yet the oddest thing happened—I did neither. I'd always known she was void of those qualities which activate men to do good, but the final ironic truth was that she was equally void of those qualities which actuate men to do evil. She was a complete mediocrity.

I only wanted her out of my life. It left only those bat-black nights by the receiver to tell me how much, when neither priest nor penitent, but monitoring confessions as foul as the stealth in which I heard them, I rose out of bedlam to become her conscience.

There was one deliverance—it had to be irreversible—she could never return to me, not again, and this time I was going to guarantee it. There is a time in human suffering when exceeding sorrows are but like snow falling on an iceberg, and I figured if two wrongs didn't make a right, three did. I began listening to their telephone calls, every one of them, hour after hour, night after night. He would call her, she him. They were long calls, exposing everything. I didn't care that I'd lost the moral advantage. She told me everything. She told me his name—she called him Scooter—and told me when they met, and where, where they were going to meet and when. But more than anything, she told me what she was. And oh the exchanges of love!

She shunned topics, skimped some, and, while showing great hospitality to others, was open and available to everything, the damp idea, the potted phrase, the promises of faith and fidelity repeating like a decimal what I myself had heard from her a thousand times.

It was amazing to hear how tender she became with her own memory, thoroughly believing herself while lying outright and making herself uncommonly comfortable as she spoke of the tolerance and patience that characterized her life with faithless men. She had told so many stories for so many years, truth and fiction were so inextricably mixed, that to check a new falsehood by a poorly remembered old one made her feel that in some way truth must be involved somewhere. Desperate liars, in fact, will often refuse what proves to be the truth, but it's not a case of a double personality acting, rather of half a personality *failing* to. I realized such a woman was a kind of monster in whom of necessity there was nothing to love because there was nothing to take hold of. A female gymnast, an actress, a mountebank for wages, she didn't literally hang by her feet from a trapeze and swing a fat man in her teeth, but she made the same use of her tongue and eyes as her twirling counterpart made of leg and jaw.

She chopped, shaped, edited, and abridged almost everything she said. As she put it, she had no faults, merely too trusting a nature, and the men who'd taken advantage of her were legion. She took cues from him of what he wanted her to say, trying to represent me to him as she once did Ted to me and so having to make her husband a far larger presence in her life over the past three years than he'd ever been. On many nights she literally wept over the phone in her craven dependence on this doctor. "But there's no one else," she pleaded. "I've been waiting for you all my life."

I heard hour after hour of bald and obsequious flattery about how important he was—the medical profession always attracts calumniators—and listened as night after night she ran down her husband in the same way and with the same words she had done for me, which confirmed in me the belief that her long resistance to divorcing him was proof of her experience, not her virtue. And I began wondering what woman that John Colorado ever met now could ever believe he wasn't at fault? I thought of Farol not giving a damn and of the money she took from him and of her going through life all expenses paid.

It was farcical having to listen to one of the most startlingly unoriginal minds I'd ever known trying to come up with something new each time. She revised everything. What was pieced out she filled in with absurd stories repeated with the insistence of a skilled tactician who had no intention of shifting from favorable ground. But there was never anything different in what she repeated over and over. It was the same tardy, antiquated, internally discordant deceitful identity living in a high wind of exhibition and configuration and banking on the continuity of her impersonations to get by.

"You are my best friend," said Farol. Play the "Largo" to *Xerxes* and try to imagine what years of practice brought to softening her words. "I want to be with you now and twenty years from now. I don't doubt my feelings for you. I feel like begging you to ask me to be with you. Please let's not prolong the agony. I don't want to learn to live without you again."

And the more she said, the more involved he became. I heard assurances and advice he gave as his voice rolled up from somewhere around his gut, which had the overample sound of someone who'd been sitting at a desk too long. I had a living portrait of him merely by what I heard him say. He was tall, fat, hairy, loud, arrogant, and, while like most self-important people a big talker and consequently possessed of no real pride, obvious and impatient and unoriginal.

But he also had money and a practice and was functionally prepared at every moment to oblige her. They planned trips and talked about hospitals and patients and his colleagues and her family and his parents and where they'd live together. He told her he had acted in plays. They discussed taxes and his brother and children and boats and went over and over the problems of divorce, loneliness, isolation, and needing each other, exaggerating the romantic and leaving the obvious vague.

The air was blackened with lies. Virtually everything he found verifiable he would have found falsified. She gave such false reports, such misleading and mauled accounts of her personal life, such a spurious imitation of truth borrowed like her voice to tell all she'd suffered alone these past few years while lingering breathless between the retrospective eternity she could not recall and the prospective one she could not know, but waited to be shown, I actually thought someone else was speaking. "I love your face," she said, dredging. "I feel alive with you. I feel like myself when I'm with you. I want to always be with you. I'll never leave you. My life is entirely yours."

For her it was never too late to put the self together with parts of other people to become a piece of the world they possessed.

But the devil's in the details, and I saw how she predicted the future by inventing it. There is no category of women more recklessly optimistic than the woman about to be divorced. It would be a sensible guess to believe otherwise, but that guess would be completely wrong. Most divorcées not only remarry within one year of the date their divorces become final, but it's usually the women with the most failures behind them who are the first to try again. And Farol of course was a star among that number, someone who now had to plunge boldly ahead or sink forever into bitterness and recrimination.

She might have tried self-reliance. But that wasn't her way. She could only dominate by submitting. She was a true lackey. A passenger. She had to attach herself to someone like a barnacle and characteristically—literally—suck to survive.

I remember her coyly and repeatedly questioning him about the advisability of his intentions with her and of his wife and children and whether he might decide to go back to them. And when one night he declared with icy finality, "Don't be ridiculous," it brought me back to an office in a Boston orphanage where more than thirty years ago I sat in a dark corridor twisting a pencil and feeling very much alone.

It was not surprising to see that I had become virtually a nonperson. It was altogether as if I had never existed. Years were skipped over as she spoke of her loneliness and the extent to which all along she had to cope alone. She couldn't explain me, couldn't account for me, couldn't confess to the extent of her involvement with me of course without seeming a whore, and I hated her lax conscience. But it was in this context one night that suddenly came to me what I'd been trying to think of that day at the beach the summer before when I had been waiting with her and watching the waves. Water itself doesn't travel along with the waves. *Only the shape of the wave travels through the water.*

I was the *fact* of her faithlessness, a living reproach, the dark and vindictive conscience she had to get rid of. And it was in seeing this—in recognizing I was not only a fool but now had no existence—that I decided by correcting it to say good-bye. There's an old adage: choose your enemies well, it's them you most come to resemble. It was true. I not only listened to the calls, I now gathered together all the letters she'd ever written to me, photocopied every last one of them, and under the guise that they'd been stolen mailed them to her husband. The student was ready just as the teacher appeared, and I became marplot itself. What she didn't want known, I wanted to make known. What she tried to hide, I decided to disclose.

What I heard, and didn't hear, made me privy to her fears, and her fears told me what to do to confirm them. Whereas at first I was driven by some masochistic impulse to verify the facts, now I wanted revenge. *Success.* I sought to bewilder her as she had done me and now began sending her anonymous letters portending punishment and filled with dire warnings about the futility of trying to deceive someone else whose name I mentioned and whose number I threatened to call.

Things now began to go decidedly wrong for her, and Farol had no idea who was behind it all, nor did he, as adulterers never have, for the many they offend in what they do. I was diligence itself and kept at it, always staying one pace ahead of them.

I reflected pitilessly that I had become like Dr. Trinity in writing these letters—and even worse, like Farol. But I didn't care. She became all I hated in myself for having loved her, and I became her double in hateful symmetry. I thought in my madness of converse etching and how methods of reproduction interchange left and right, where inversion is equally and oppositely oriented. And yet because all points and all directions in space are equivalent, there is no intrinsic difference between left and right—and so translatory symmetry exists only where we represent what we imitate and counterfeit what we copy. It was in broken symmetry that we found our legacy, and I began to wonder for all my failures when the couple as a concept first begin? Who in what aboriginal mistake set this pattern of going two by two together to the altar? Who of the many among us ever really cared to know two was not a perfect number except in what it mimicked to mock of one? But jackdaw perched beside jackdaw, and I put on her likeness like recreation.

Madness, do I say? It wasn't madness. I was completely rational, as calm as I was cold and as cold as camphor. I intentionally kept as far away from her meanwhile as I kept from my conscience and stayed seemingly uninvolved. I remained outwardly civil to her friends, acting as if nothing had happened. I kept to myself, the better to feel my contempt. The worst thing about infidelity is not that it breaks your heart, but that it turns your heart to stone, insures you to bitterness and the lack of mercy. Iron entered into my soul. I didn't dispense my anger the better to sharpen it, preferring to do what was effective rather to say what felt good—I swallowed my fury the better to know it and waited the better to watch.

My ambition was to alienate her. I wanted to confuse her—to mix things up like a master adulterer—and teach her by what I learned of contrivance enough to confound complication itself. I decided to become the suspicious person she thought I was, her equal in bad manners. I wanted to say good-bye the way we'd met in farewell to the way we'd lived. It was easy. Farol had become an object of ghastly simplicity: she was a woman who blew men and they married her for it. I tried for a while convincing myself I had loved another person on another planet, not her, but it was a pathetic lie, for I knew her as well as I knew myself by what I'd become.

I knew her dreadfully empty mind—had it been filled by judgment, she'd long ago have sat in a judgment upon herself—and I became its memory. A terrible ghost walked abroad following her unseen, counting every step. I took delight in the fact that all of us were lying, Farol, the doctor, and me in my disguises. I was Rumpelstiltskin. My methods, which were gauged according to the demands of the situation in which I found myself, could hardly be called ethical. A new scenario emerged with each telephone call. And as everything I heard told me what I should do next, note followed notification. What she confided one night came back to haunt her the next. Every disclosure brought danger and every whisper a welt like blister upon heat. I won't expatiate, however full of interest and color it may be, except to say only that here in this triangle the deepest of tragedies and lightest of comedies clasped hands!

What retarded evolution, Farol suddenly began wondering, had she unwittingly precipitated? And who was doing this to her? Who *knew?* Me? His ex-wife? Her husband? His mistress? Her other husband? Her *mind?* What was happening? Who but an intimate could know all the names, but why would an intimate betray? I listened almost transported with joy and no small sense of justice as each call became the poor gray medium by which she stupidly, helplessly, laughably groped to solve the very problems she only compounded by letting me hear them. At first she was outraged, then terrified, and her fear of me made me hate her more. Initially she couldn't express her hunch that it was me without making reference to and giving elaborate explanations for a hundred matters she'd never before mentioned, but when she began fussing and screaming that someone had broken into her flat and stolen her papers—with the doctor having to spend hour upon exasperated hour questioning what she'd done to let someone get her number—never saw her more shop-soiled.

She began locking her door now—useless, I had had a key made weeks before—and kept a flashlight in her car. It was monkey in the middle. Dodge ball. "I hate who's doing this!" she screamed. "It's not fair!"

Suddenly she was implicated everywhere. I loved it, for it was only fair play if I could turn it about. The horror again finding failure seated all at its ease where she'd only dreamed of success glaringly showed her past for what it was and made her explain what she couldn't excuse and expose what she couldn't explore. "It's not fair! It's not fair!"

She now began bitterly to have to admit in every phone call what she'd formerly hidden. Retrack. Correct. Fill in spaces. Clarify. Explain again. And the labor of all this, together with the labor she had to expend of keeping the pitch of it down, forced them not only into the détente I wanted to be rid of her but as a wonderful part of the same legacy also left her impossibly attached to what she most wanted to relinquish, which making her lie the more—and squirm—gave me the last wonderful look I needed to let her go.

A wrong is arguably unredressed when retribution overtakes its redresser. It is equally unredressed when the avenger fails to make himself felt as such to her who has done the wrong.

It took her a dunce's age to catch on—her stupidity was even deeper than her guile—but by mid-March continuing coincidence nudged her intuition, and she finally sent an armed policeman to my door with threats of reprisal never to bother her again, or her husband, or her current lover.

The doctor's name was Dr. James Wiggly, a forty-three-year-old general surgeon with a small practice, a loud cocky voice with an edge in it of always being irked, and a hysterical squirrel of a wife who'd been married to him for fifteen miserable years before their divorce. I learned more about him than ever I cared to know—the facts on the phone finding an astonishingly exact corroboration in the comic graduation photo from the Harvard Medical School Derek later sent me of a man wearing a paisley bow tie whose balding bulbous head with its deep-laired eyes and Balkan eyebrows looked like the blunt instrument left at the scene of the crime.

But it's what we do rather than say or resemble that distinguishes truth from the values it mimics. And he was his own malpractice, for the only fact that mattered was enough. He had walked away from his three children.

I never contacted him. There was no need. It wasn't only that he wouldn't believe what I told him—who could?—he'd have to learn first-hand the full measure awaiting him of future delights with a woman whose typical day at one point actually involved sleeping with me, then driving to the hospital to fuck him, while all the time being legally married to another man whom she'd not only been betraying for three years but through some kind of synchronized magic cozening in the end for a divorce and the advantage of property settlement.

No wonder she had nightmares.

But it wasn't nymphomania. It was the opposite. That was her ruthlessness. She was totally unaltruistic. She had no understanding of principle, only tactics. She was in fact showing poor, homely, suddenly ex-married Dr. Wiggly how to be single. She had perfected all the single person's pursuits while being with someone and yet claiming to be faithful. I had to tell him nothing. The freedom she represented to him was the freedom he'd come to lose in having her, for beyond all else what most she couldn't keep after giving it to someone was her word. And that would be his comeuppance. It was assured by what she uttered and uttered to shape and shaped to gain in that set speech, cold as proof, I nightly heard through the transmitter echoing the same words, the same phrases, the same stories, the same responses, the same promises, the same vows, the same expressions, the same formulas, the same premeditated and compensating repentance which turned lies into fate by nothing more than the cunning that not only informed but indeed had given them birth.

I realized it could just as easily have been him she left for me. I was his twin, matched to him by the principle of transitivity just as her husband was to me. I could only despise him by taking the rule of myself. We had all been changed like shoes. But with Farol it was the same old matchless falsehood. And I saw a final truth in the phrase *the same returns not, save to bring the different.*

26

Farol wasn't there anymore.

I never saw her again. I didn't try. I didn't care. And I was less surprised that I was astonished than astonished that I'd cared so much. I had found in her at least one thing in my life I didn't want. Tribulation detaches us from the things that are really valueless because their attraction cannot stand up under it, and I was grateful in my sorrow to see destroyed the value of something of such insufficiency and fashioned so falsely to fulfill the dreams I'd lost. My strength, paradoxically, was stronger than myself.

And yet as I looked at all the effort, the gifts, the money, the time—the long years—wasted on her, I thought of all the work I'd never done. I had never done a single painting of her in all the time I knew her. I never *thought* of it. Never. The word fit everywhere, and everywhere applied. I'd never known her a day, an hour, a minute when she wasn't another man's wife. I had merely acquired her by the law of adverse possession by holding her openly, notoriously, and continuously for a certain length of time. We hadn't a friend in common of all the people we'd known. Her letters never said anything but repeat my words. She never cooked for me and never thought of it and never thought of *that*. There was not one photograph of us together. Never mind affection, love wasn't even the result of conquest. It was hopeless. She merely framed what I painted.

A vigil, nevertheless, had been kept of a kind. I loved her, not for what she was, but for what she should have been, and what was lost was the reward I got for watching. She wasn't the antidote, only the poison, and the love I'd felt had the effect of killing instead of curing me. But being rid of her was the health I once thought sickness, and the inference I'd once been led to draw, that beneath the illusion was some superior reality loyalty should serve, at last told me enough about myself to bear the truth, that color blindness extends to the complementary colors. I was blind. She never understood that what she thought concealed her from what she was. And what she was was what I deserved for wanting her.

I thought she was doomed to failure—people who use words so casually always miscalculate. Everything purchasable she needed in order to be who she was would no doubt soon be hers, a new address, a summer place, a membership in the country club, and an overweight surgeon with a pound of hair taped to his head who out of a sense of guilt and desertion would be grateful enough to do her bidding. I thought of her multiple marriages and could already hear people over the years saying poor thing, she's been through a lot. She would need and depend on that. Anyone can project a future. But to suppress the past and turn away and think you can go onward and upward is to make a serious mistake. Perhaps she would see this one day. I couldn't say.

I only knew time would take care of her. Time is wonderful. It rewards the good and punishes the careless and makes fools of the socially and sexually ambitious, and that in a sense was the best justice. It wasn't prophecy, only the simple presentiment of the selfishness of small people who in taking think they give. Many had suffered because of her, but that didn't make her large. We make people important by what we feel for them. Perhaps she didn't care. Perhaps she did care but found the whole thing so unbearable that she feared it would ruin her peace of mind. And yet those who are happy at someone else's expense always fail, for in the long run one's peace of mind depends on how much one cared about the people one hurt.

But I was also talking about myself. I found in that place where memory meets reflection that I'd chosen her as mistakenly as she had chosen her husbands. Any property belonging to zero belongs to all numbers. The irony of it all was that she was my *own* fault. I confronted her in her inadequacy with the very love I lost her by, but what I sought in her was missing in myself! The most ineffective thing one can do is tell someone unworthy that she is worthy when she herself knows it's not true. But a harder thing by far is to admit your own emptiness in confessing it and the people you've wounded in doing so. She wasn't only what was wrong with us. Everything she was was everything wrong with me. I understood that now. I could no longer deny the time I'd spent with her was part of my own debt to discharge, and it was a terrible thing to learn that what I'd been prepared to say I hadn't been prepared to hear. It was even more horrible to realize I had given birth to the murderer who slew me.

The adultery she was now committing with someone else was only a variation of the same adultery we had both been involved in all along. There is frequently more justice than injustice in irony, and I suddenly saw I was myself the proof of what elsewhere I sought to prove. I had before my eyes from the very first the very fault and misperceived it. And my failure came by way of my own egotism as a message of her love.

I had possessed the truth once but had forgotten it, and, sadly, sometimes the only thing a person can do to recover that truth is become aware it is lost.

It is a strange but fortunate alchemy of our emotions that changes a thing dreaded into a thing finally done when the hour arrives to do it. I was desperate to believe that for all the evil I at least had a small glimpse of the knowledge of good and determined on it left a letter of apology one afternoon on her car window, saying

> *I'm sorry that I hurt you. I hope you can find it in your heart to forgive me.*

She never answered it, and I was glad, for it reminded me in a final unequivocal way of all I ever knew her by to be able to forget her. I retrieved the bug and transmitter from her room the same day and never looked back. I remember being in that room that one last time and how empty and unfamiliar it seemed. What haunted me, however, wasn't her. It was something else. I was just about to leave when a sudden and desperate impulse, a longing to love something, anybody, anything not imbued with wickedness overcame me. I can still remember the almost overwhelming feeling I had to be in the presence of innocence.

It was as if suddenly something importunate called out of that emptiness, that terrible void, the only thing left on earth that would fill it. I remember being almost out the door, when turning around I went back to Farol's phone and dialed a number.

I called Marina.

But there was no one home.

27

Spring arrived with disabling cold. There were patches of snow, hard-frozen, that lingered at first, and then it began to rain. It never stopped. It rained almost continuously, not a warm misty rain but the relentlessly driving kind that, turning days to night, left the streets smoking in ruin like the dark gas and dust in the galactic outskirts. Teaching had become pointless, and it was all I could do to hang on. With the hint of warmth that following April I took heart in the restlessness that is just this side of hope and looked for what I might have again.

All this time Marina had never been out of my mind. I hadn't seen her for more than a year. I hadn't heard from her. Where she was, what she'd been doing, I didn't know. I only kept remembering the way she recited her poems, which were soft as moonbeams in a room at night, strangely pure in feeling. Weeks passed. I couldn't reach her by telephone, but never could. The question of contacting her during the growing unrest and especially in the last infamy almost defied handling. Through my sin, I felt I had put myself beyond the compass of what even her goodness could do. I was wrong. I couldn't ask for her love. I didn't deserve it. But I could ask for her forgiveness.

I decided to try seeing her at work. The effect of my decision almost immediately made me wonder why I'd waited so long and gave me the assurance I needed. I thought: *I'm going to live.* I remember it was a gray rainy afternoon the day I drove to the Boston City Hospital, and the closer I got the faster my heart beat. I only wanted to hold her, feel her springtime, tell her that she reassured everything that was fleeting and fragile and delicate in life. I wanted to tell her that just the spectacle of her alive and smiling was something as true and constant in my life as air, as love, as even the certainty and blessing of change.

When I got to the hospital I fairly ran through the wards and long corridors. I headed downstairs to the X-ray department, fully expecting to run into her at every turn of a corner. At first I couldn't find her. I pulled open doors to various darkrooms following the red safelight; strangers looked up bewildered. Other rooms in the pod were empty;

there was only a chair or two, counters filled with bottles of hypo, fixer, and developer, the empty cavelike sounds of processors gurgling, trickling water all day long. I tried to find anyone I could. I approached several girls carrying cassettes, film magazines, receivers. I questioned them, but somehow no one knew her. And suddenly she wasn't there.

I finally saw a nurse I'd known before, and stopped her. She remembered me. I asked where Marina was. Although the name made for common ground between us, the nurse balked. I asked, "She still works here, doesn't she?"

Suddenly I was afraid the nurse might not take me into her confidence. She stared at me with still concentration quite as if for some inscrutable reason she was considering what she should or shouldn't tell me. She took me aside—I was trying to think ahead so fast I found it difficult to focus on what I had to follow—and told me what she knew. Apparently in a moment of matchless folly the previous September, inexplicable to everybody, Marina had gone and married a perfect stranger, another worker at the hospital who, it turned out, already had a wife. The marriage had lasted literally no more than five days, when she awoke abject and alone in a New York hotel. She came home alone, and the warm days quickly turned to cold.

The nurse knew only a few details. Marina's mother, who in accepting the inevitable had bought her a sofa as a wedding present immediately charged her for it when she came home and called her an idiot and told her she was an embarrassment to the family. Jilted, humiliated, Marina became more silent than ever and, having to move back into the house, was now completely at her mother's mercy. I thought she might have been sick. I remembered: chronic nonspecific anxiety. And I mentioned it.

The nurse hesitated before she spoke again and mentioned an illness—I couldn't see the point—sometimes caught by people exposed to asbestos which gravely affected the lungs. Pipe coverings, furnace insulation, things to do with panels and wiring. I remembered Marina's father once worked in a shipyard, and began to have a glimpse of something stronger than any conceivable expression of it.

Something in her manner seemed trying to keep a distance from the recognition she'd but a few moment ago confessed to. "It can be transmitted to their children and spouses by dusty clothes even as they're being washed." My heart contracted. "Have you heard—of mesothelioma?"

It was as if I'd read the words from her lips before she spoke them.

The bottom fell out of my being. "Not Marina?" I tried to say, but no sound came.

I felt a sensation in that cold stillness of the whole world going away. My soul began to drain, and I could scarcely follow her words. I was told Marina hadn't been well all last fall, which perhaps explained some of her unpredictability. She hadn't been eating enough, lost weight, and became pale and withdrawn. Her hair, losing its luster, had become brittle. Someone had once seen her arms black and yellow from a doctor's injections. She had apparently never said anything in all that time, however, but continued working, taking in magazines, running film through the processor, stamping and dating it. And then one day she took one of these X rays and placed it on the viewing screen in the corridor. An intern who was passing by but didn't stop merely pointed to it on the run and said, "That person has six weeks to live." Marina was looking at her own X ray.

A month short of the time that the doctors named as the outside period she could hold on—it was only two days before Christmas—she was dead.

I walked out into the rain. Whatever else the nurse said to me I can't recall. I only remember asking where the cemetery was and hearing thunder when I left the hospital. There was no voice with which to name that noise, no light traveling over the water to the horizon, nor even any mind to apprehend its meaning. There was nothing I could feel. There was nothing in the air but rain.

I was lost. The sky was dark. The people I saw, the streets I crossed, the wet trees made a fable of my passing by. Time ceased to have meaning, space was illimitable. I waited in the traffic, staring past the crowds of shoppers, staring past the rain. And as I drove all the light seemed gone, leaving only stain and shadow on my empty heart where space like a moan seemed too finite to contain the mercy of all I asked from the depths of my frightened prayers.

A terrible storm broke with a crash when I got to the cemetery. It began raining stair rods, and the wind intensifying was soon blowing like all the trumpets of the morning. I thought of my father saying, *I lie awake and think about the past, I lie awake and think about the past*. I wandered among the gravestones and didn't know which way to turn. I had never felt so alone in my life.

But we are all alone, I thought. We meet and briefly touch yet in the end we are only alone. It seemed painful, even pointless, to share a tender experience, for the future becoming the past so quickly left us only where we were. Without this sharing, it may be asked, how live? But living means nothing if not being alone. Under an iron, godless sky man is utterly alone. Not even abandoned. And isn't that the way of the last circumstance? Martyrs go hand in hand into the arena, but are crucified alone. The priest goes unaccompanied to the inner temple, trembling before the sacrifice he makes alone. We are not persuaders of each other's design. We seek ourselves in one another's eyes but fail to solemnize each other in the final madness, for isn't every spirit by its nature doomed to suffer alone what in the last immediacy awaits it of purgation? Are we not ultimately left alone with our dark unutterable wounds and in the isolation of having to face ourselves brought finally to that place where we are fed by ravens and there are no hours and we can only eat smoke in the poverty of our own solitary convocation?

The empty space of the sky swallows up the stars, I thought, and the hollowness of the womb teaches what in order to live we first must learn to know. People die laid out in rooms and pass away in the style of obituaries. They die painted and die in print. But we mortal millions are always alone.

I realized there was justice meted out to me as I dealt it and that seemed the only mercy. I could make sense of nothing but ached only to know how in this dear union I'd broken and thrown away like waste the tragedy of my double destiny could ever be unfolded. I looked at the desolation around me. There is no death, I thought—there was. Time itself is unreason, and half the things we do in life we do with tears in our eyes.

And then I saw Marina's grave. Only the ghost of it came through the demented rain that burst upon it and burst again. I walked through the downpour where Marina was buried, but somehow couldn't identify her with the name before me. I suddenly began to cry. I looked at that small stone and wept, for I saw even as I stood there that I'd been coming to this moment all my life. And I knew even as I loved that that love just as that stone and that place would soon be long ago. I suddenly realized all that I'd forsaken was everything I missed. Whom alone I needed I'd relinquished. All I truly loved I had forgone.

I wanted to cry in my exile on her gentle hair and on the lap of her loveliness lay down my head. I wanted to take her in my arms and spirit her to rest somewhere beyond the blue arcade among angels robed in the folds of winds. I wanted to take nothing away, leave nothing behind, only by some power beyond fathoming ask my poor question one last time to try to understand again how the child's eye gives life to what it loves. I stood listening to the darkness. I waited half bent over, shivering from the cold bite of wind and rain against my back. Bitter rain! The bitter water of the fountains! Bitter love of God that suffers for this merciless perishability that the planting wind blows over and withers! Bitter April!

I waited there, hovering under that wet roar punctuated by the drumming thunder as sheets of rain swept horizontally into my body. And then in an overwhelming moment when inexplicably I couldn't move, I felt something that long in the dawning came to me headlong and abrupt, the only way anything did anymore for the blindness of my adulterer's heart. I was listening to that darkness, listening to that deep darkness, when a small grace, making it an infinite mystery no longer, consecrated what it now revealed of someone whose goodness was beyond description because she herself refused to be described, who was virtuous beyond the sight of men because her name did not identify her. I looked up and seeing Marina playing in the sad springtime air suddenly saw her for all she was.

I felt as I had so often before the gentle blue visitation in her of a sense of tragic unfulfillment, a doom of incompleteness in her dearness, never quite brought to perfect bloom, as though her lighted way had been crossed ever so delicately by a shadow of error. And as I watched her bearing a ribbon and flowers upon her brow and gently waving a magical wand, she suddenly stumbled and she could not rise and yet struggling to rise somehow hurt herself and limped into her dance that others might do the same.

And she began dancing round and round, weaving her blue ribbon in and out, pale and innocent and wistful in her torn dress that whirled along as she leapt, an aerial creature, stumbling a moment, catching the broken petal of her dress that seemed to be withering, stumbling yet touched with some graceful light, lame but skipping and singing softly in a visionary movement of unearthly beauty. I saw again her dancing eyes, her laughing face, and for a moment felt touched myself by the delicate heartbreak of an April that would pass and never come again until the world and all its flowers and grass had been burnt by the frosts of autumn and buried under winter, when her ribbons of paper would fade and her poppy dress shatter, and the cardboard crown molt its silver stars.

I remember a stillness then. The rain never stopped. But there was in that strange overpowering quietness something that suddenly, belonging to me, opened up the fullness of all that memory meant by

knowing what in all I had forgone I might now be able to face. It was
as if in that moment the silence let me see a tree nearby just coming into
flower, and it reminded me that often when a tree is dying it will often
put out an extra flower in a last desperate effort to live. I picked one of
those flowers, which let me remember I was given love by that memory
and life by that love, and I knew if I never had it again I could say I
had it once. I held Marina's flower and knew that like it she was herself
the miracle she didn't expect. It was in all she never asked for and
never assumed that made her all she was. Importance wasn't important.
The emptiness is the form.

And I knelt down. I touched the flower to her grave, pondering the
passing of all those mysteries, how they sink through the currents of the
years, their adornment dissolving like petals of paper and pasted stars
and settling at long last onto the foundation of unalterable truth. All of
a sudden I had a memory of that day on the Provincetown pier and
what Marina had told me of faith being above belief. It was not an acquisition of faculties, but a shedding of them, a surrender, where one
did not dispense with reason but employed it as an instrument to learn
something higher about oneself, the sense of self-abandonment by which
alone one can be happy.

I suddenly saw in the transformation of that simple soul that there
was a life that, moving without being seen, had not been understood
only for her having lingered in the expectancy of what she could give
not get. But that sacrifice at last became clear to me. It was alone what
between two people mattered to make them one. And it was wonderful,
for when I realized that I realized I wasn't alone. Tomorrow the sun
would be lovely with the beauty of day, and under one aspect or another I knew I'd always had it before me, for I had found in all I'd lost
the only remaining—perhaps the only bearable—truth, that there is another kind of justice than the justice of number, which can neither forgive nor be forgiven, another kind of mercy than the mercy of law,
which knows no absolution.

There is a justice that cannot be measured, a mercy without explanation which I knew in its final mystery was the meaning of love, for by
it I had been redeemed to see what by giving me she had to die for me
to know of true and total union. I placed the sprig of lilacs on her
grave. I don't remember how long I knelt there. And then I stood up
and left the cemetery in the rain.

Walking through the gates, I couldn't look back for all that was in
my heart. I may have lingered too long in the hope of seeing her again.

I haven't the memory of that, I have only the regret. But regret as well as memory has its visions, and I am reminded of both by what I knew, and know now, I will never relinquish, by having come to see that what's withdrawn as fast as it's revealed leaves nothing else to know.

We all end up living secret lives. We create what we are willing to admire and admiring what we shouldn't confess to the secret of our own sin, our own insufficiency, our own sadness. We all end up taking our secrets into the world and handing them over to strangers, only to realize it's often too late to claim them back. The very nature of time passing is sad beyond words. Memories mean that they're gone.

West Barnstable
1986

About the Author

Alexander Theroux is the author of essays, short stories, poetry, and plays, as well as the novels *Three Wogs* and *Darconville's Cat*. He lives in West Barnstable, Massachusetts.